DEATH & DESIRE

A Snarky Urban Fantasy Detective Series

DEBORAH WILDE

te da media
vancouver

Chapter 1

I never expected *Touched by an Angel* to stray into bad touch territory.

"Tall, white robes, white wings. Was there a celestial light? Did anyone see a halo?" The questions I asked in pursuit of the truth.

"It's an Angel of Death. It kills people." Husani Tannous, a late-twenty-something Egyptian, adjusted his baseball cap to hide his receding hairline. "It doesn't get a halo."

Ironclad logic from a man who'd paired his masculinity issues with the semi-automatic at his feet. Like fine wine with cheese. Or gasoline with a match.

This living room was as much a battlefield as any muddy trench. There was even a dead body upstairs, and if the animosity down here got out of hand, more casualties to come. The fluttering in my stomach did double duty as nerves and a coiled excitement.

"I'm not trying to be facetious," I said, steepling my fingers and leaning back in a fancily embroidered chair. "But I do need the facts."

"The facts are that it murdered my brother!" He shook his fist. "And I will avenge him!"

His cousin, Chione, slowly stroked a finger over the handgun in her lap, all the while sucking butter off her toast.

I leaned in, fascinated by her particular brand of multi-tasking.

"Big talker, Husani. How will you find this angel? Are you going to fly up into the sky?" Chione said in Arabic-accented English.

"Don't be ridiculous. Flying magic doesn't exist." Rachel Dershowitz, early fifties and mother of the bride-to-be Shannon, was as bitter as the gin and tonic she gulped down. The gaudy rock on her finger had fewer facets than the sneer she shot Chione.

Chione's hand twitched on her gun and I stepped between the two women. "Did Omar have any enemies? Any reason why anyone would come after him?"

"Omar is a good boy. No enemies. This is a hate crime. Those sons of dogs killed our firstborns before and they're doing it again!" Thank you, Masika Tannous, the grandmother and matriarch of the clan visiting from Cairo. While the little old lady was knitting a sweater like many a sweet grandma, she wielded her needles with a savage ferocity that scared me more than the Uzi of questionable origin propped against her side.

Between Masika, Husani, and Chione, this mercenary family packed more firepower than the Canadian Armed Forces, but like I'd always said, Mundanes didn't require magic to be dangerous.

The physical weapons from the Tannouses were countered by serpents made of light magic that writhed above the table, ready to pounce on their victim and squeeze the life out of them.

I wanted to smack sense into all of them, but it was hard

enough doing my job, never mind exuding enough badass vibes to keep these two families in line.

"You brought death into my home. Jews shouldn't mix with Egyptians," said Ivan Dershowitz. The fleshy homeowner on my left sat next to his wife and daughter on a high-backed chair with spindly legs that strained under his weight. His light magic bobbed like a cobra.

The two families hurled racist epithets back and forth, this season's bridal registry must-have.

The delicate-featured Shannon let out a hysterical wail that probably used up her caloric intake for the week. However, she was the only one acting appropriately in my opinion, given her groom-to-be had been murdered. The heavens agreed with my assessment as a shaft of sunlight cut through the clouds on this March morning to confer a kind of benediction upon her.

What can I say? When I was right, I was right.

I whistled sharply. "Assuming we take the story of Passover literally, Malach, that Angel of Death, killed *all* the firstborn sons to free the Jews from an oppressive slavery. While it is Passover this week, we have only the one death, though I'm monitoring that." I turned to Masika. "I'm deeply sorry about the loss of your grandson Omar, but one murder isn't exactly mass smiting, not to mention, the Jews are sitting right here in their own home." Low class, but hardly enslaved. "We need to keep an open mind. Perhaps it's an Angel of Death and perhaps someone is using a good story, preying on centuries of superstition and hatred to hide what's really at play."

You point out one hard truth and suddenly the place was all twitchy gun fingers, snaky beams of light, and a knitting needle jabbed at you like a curse.

My command to shut it down was ignored. Fantastic.

The person standing in the center of the room cleared

his throat, and everyone immediately fell back into their corners, muttering angrily.

In his forties, he had white hair and a white suit that veered sharply towards the 1970s. Between his wardrobe choices and the fact that he was the right hand man of the Queen of Hearts, my moniker of White Rabbit Man was hardly a stretch.

One day, I'd call him that out loud.

Given his overall vibe, he shouldn't have commanded any respect, but the motherfucker of a sword in his hand helped.

Big deal. I could decapitate a few dozen people and get that response, too.

"If someone could show me upstairs so I could examine the scene?" Collecting the shreds of my patience, I met the cold beady eyes of the showpiece of this ostentatious living room: a massive crystal chandelier in the shape of a bird with its wings outstretched, soaring overhead.

Even the decor wanted out.

"Mr. Dershowitz," I said.

"Rebbe," he corrected.

Yeah, right. Ivan had earned that nickname not for his religious leanings but because, during his high-profile incarceration for assault and battery, he'd beaten a fellow inmate into a coma with a copy of Genesis. Can I get a hallelujah?

I gritted my teeth. "Rebbe—"

Ignoring me, he sent his serpent slithering to the ground where it circled the room. The urge to pull my feet up was strong. "This marriage was a mistake," he said.

No, the real mistake was coming to this shitshow. Although it wasn't as though I'd had a choice to refuse this "request."

"We can stand here and argue the existence of angels," White Rabbit Man said, "or you can allow Ashira, the private investigator vouched for by the Queen, access to

Omar's room so she can determine precisely what happened."

After another couple minutes of mutually insulting each other's matriarchal lineage coupled with some anatomical suggestions that I never intended to Google, Rachel called for a maid. Husani and the help escorted White Rabbit Man and me through the mansion down a long hallway filled with bookshelves that contained zero books but an extensive and disturbing collection of china bird figurines.

Birds! They're just like us. They nest, they whistle, they rub their genitals against tufts of grass in a lusty manner.

"Was beheading too fast a way to torture me?" I muttered at White Rabbit Man.

The tiny quirk of his lips was the only thing on his impassive face that betrayed his amusement.

"We can take it from here," I said to the people following us, when we reached the stairs to the second floor.

My escorts didn't move.

"The Queen thanks you for your service. I'll be sure to mention to her how you allowed me to do the job that she so kindly recommended me for."

Still nothing.

"We'll call should we require your assistance," White Rabbit Man said.

Sure, that got them going.

I stomped up the stairs, stopping in the doorway of the guest bedroom to gather my first impressions.

I'd spent a summer during university working in the coroner's office, mostly filing and doing data entry, but I'd been given the opportunity to accompany the coroner to the morgue. That's when I'd seen my first dead body. Seeing that person so cold and alone and irrevocably gone had hit me hard. The coroner had shared the deceased's tragic history and how he had been revived from drug overdoses on numerous occasions before finally succumbing to this one.

Struggling to remain as professional as my boss, I'd asked how she dealt with this. Her advice? Learn to straddle the line between empathy and being pulled under, because these people needed you to swim, not sink.

I'd taken that advice to heart, so while I had no problem with death, the naked hairy ass currently assaulting my eyeballs was another matter entirely. That shit demanded danger pay. To be fair, those glutes were tight, but damn, they were practically obscured in a pelt of dark hair. And now all I could picture was Shannon threading her fingers through it during sex and holding on for the ride.

Yeehaw!

The bloated corpse lay on his side, facing away from the door. Omar's skin was mottled purple and black and he was clad in only a white undershirt and a single white trouser sock. The other sock lay near his elbow. Given the condition of the body, my first thought was death by drowning, though he was bone dry.

Gingerly, I skirted the edge of the room and checked the ensuite bathroom. No bathtub, and while Omar could have been drowned in a shower with a clogged or blocked drain and then dragged into the bedroom, the shower and bathmat were dry and the drain was unobstructed.

Strangulation? There weren't any obvious ligature marks.

Shards of glass from the shattered skylight in the high ceiling dotted Omar's skin and glinted amongst the fibers of the area rug with its dizzying white and gold vine pattern. If there were birds hidden in there, I didn't want to know.

Letting the possibilities percolate in my brain, I touched a fingertip to the window frame.

"No wards," I said. "What kind of special idiot doesn't ward the many, many giant panes of glass in their house, given the shady characters they associate with?" Wards sensed hostile intent and then held potential attackers, freezing them in place and neutralizing their magic if they had it. I dusted my hand off on my black jeans. "With oversights like that, I despair for the continued success of the criminal class."

"I dare you to comment on the Rebbe's intelligence," White Rabbit Man said. "To his face."

"Hard pass. I refuse to engage in any activity that causes you glee as it will be detrimental and deleterious to my well-being."

White Rabbit Man shrugged. "Regardless, you'll have to deal with him now."

"If I take this cockamamie case."

"You will. Your greedy little fingers are practically twitching in anticipation."

I humphed. True, murder was a huge—and exciting—jump from the cases I'd generally dealt with since starting my own private investigation firm, but this particular gig came with a number of ethical implications.

My phone buzzed in my back pocket. I slid it out.

Imperious 1: *Come to HQ immediately.*

Me: *Busy.*

"This is murder," I said. "How are you going to keep the cops out of it? Nefesh or Mundane?"

"That is your concern." White Rabbit Man didn't take his eagle-eyed gaze off the staircase to ensure we weren't disturbed. "Both families were most insistent about that."

I snorted. Shocker. The magic criminals and non-magic guns-for-hire wanted to keep the fuzz far away. I snapped photos of the space, leaving a closer examination of the body to the end. Surveillance work was better suited to a proper camera but, for quick and dirty documentation like this, my camera phone worked fine.

Another text.

Imperious 1: *This is more important.*

Me: *My cases > your random problems.*

Nothing in the luxuriously appointed room was out of

place. Omar's clothing lay unwrinkled on the plush mattress. Other than the broken skylight, all the furniture was intact and the freaky oil paintings of—wait for it—birds that looked like Edgar Allen Poe had dropped acid with Andy Warhol hung in perfect alignment.

Imperious 1: *I thought you'd be interested that we identified the deceased Jezebel. But your cases >…*

Me. *Wait. What?!*

Silence.

Me: *Levi!*

Imperious 1: *We'll talk when you're less busy.*

Me: *You fucknugget.*

Imperious 1: *You've the soul of a poet.*

White Rabbit Man raised an eyebrow. "I trust this murder isn't getting in the way of your social life? Perhaps making plans with your delightful roommate, Priya?"

"Yeah, yeah. You can get to me if I step out of line." My flip tone belied the lead knot in my gut at him going after my best friend. "Spare me the 'Bad Guy 101' speech."

"But they made me memorize it to get my certificate and everything."

"Hilarious. The world of stand-up awaits you. Getting back to the case at hand, what about the fact that, according to public record, I'm listed as Mundane?"

"Since the victim is Mundane," White Rabbit Man said, "you're being hired by the Tannous family. There will be no conflict should anyone look closely."

"Someone is going to miss Omar. You planning on telling everyone he's moved to an island in the South Pacific, or do you expect me to procure a phony death certificate stating he died of natural causes? Technically, I can investigate this, but I'm not committing outright fraud."

"No need. Your job is merely to find the murderer and hand them over to me. That way you won't be violating the conditions of your license trying to make an arrest." He spread his hands wide. "Your professional well-being is our foremost concern."

I brushed away a pretend tear. "I'm verklempt. Hand the murderer over to you and I'll be bypassing such pesky things as law and order or justice entirely."

"Oh, there'll be justice." White Rabbit Man gave me a cold smile that sent shivers up my spine. "The Queen guaranteed your discretion. She assured the families that you would investigate this case without putting it on the radar of the police or House Pacifica. She's most insistent that your magic be kept under wraps for the duration of this job."

This was the second time in less than two weeks that I'd been hired with that specific qualification. The first time was by Levi Montefiore and now it was the Queen, ruler of Hedon. I was beginning to feel typecast.

"Now," he said, "are you satisfied, or do you wish to voice any other issues with your perceived moral dubiousness of this case?"

With White Rabbit Man and the Queen involved, the murderer was a dead person walking. Omar and his grieving family deserved answers and closure on this tragic chapter. Even if I wasn't already delighted by the prospect of my first murder case, I was the only P.I. with the skillset to pull it off. In this instance, I'd concede that it came in handy being Mundane on the record but actually Nefesh.

"The Queen doesn't want to get too involved if you're bringing me in to investigate instead of her own people. Why not?" I snapped a photo of the bed.

"The attack didn't happen in Hedon, therefore, the Queen has no jurisdiction to be a part of this."

I snapped off several more photos from carefully staged angles, zooming in on what I was missing. "I'm her way of staying involved without looking like she's involved."

"You're the only one we trust to handle this. If you refuse to investigate, neither family will go to the police for obvious reasons. It will remain unsolved, tensions between those people downstairs will spill into who knows what kind of bloodshed and retribution and—"

"Geez. I'll take the case." I pulled off the top blanket and covered Omar's dangly bits. Whatever had happened to Omar, he deserved a little dignity in death. "However, the status of my magic is Levi's call," I said. "He's House Head and if he pushes my registration through, it'll be public record. There's not much I can do about it."

Besides which, I had zero desire to keep my abilities secret. I had a world of Nefesh mysteries to tackle.

White Rabbit Man smiled thinly. "I'm sure you can persuade Mr. Montefiore otherwise."

Ignoring his implication, I noted that his shoulders were tense and his words clipped. He, or rather the Queen, wanted me specifically for some reason beyond the stated one. Normally, I'd have walked out the door at the very real possibility I was being used, but her knowledge of my blood magic hung over me like an executioner's sword.

I cut a sideways glance at White Rabbit Man's razor-sharp blade. Death wasn't the worst fate. A betrayal that left you bleeding out on the sidewalk and never fully healed was far worse. Until I'd removed the Queen's ability to blackmail or out me in a way not of my choosing, I was caught in this game.

I crouched down by the body.

A little knowledge was a dangerous thing. Especially in the hands of Her Highness. But everyone had secrets. She had mine, I'd get hers.

Meantime, I had a murder to solve.

Were Omar's features not frozen in an expression of agony, he would have been a handsome man. He was probably around my age of twenty-eight, with deep, soulful brown eyes, dark curly hair, and aristocratic features—other than the bloated tongue lolling out of his mouth.

"What's in this for the Queen?" I said.

"The wedding was supposed to occur in Hedon."

"In the matchmaking business, is she?" A closer inspection revealed no gunshots or stab wounds.

"She *is* the Queen of Hearts." White Rabbit Man stepped into the bedroom, his sword now magically gone, and smoothed out an edge of the area rug that had flipped up.

I examined Omar's hands. His skin wasn't scratched and his fingernails weren't broken, both of which would have indicated he'd fought off his attacker. Either he couldn't fight back or it was over too quickly for him to defend himself. "Could this be a veiled attack against the Queen? Why not strike in Hedon?"

White Rabbit Man laughed, then saw my puzzled expression. "Oh. You're serious. No one wishes to run afoul of the Black Heart Rule."

"Is that what you call the Queen's guards?"

"No. The guards police Hedon as a whole, but the Black Heart Rule is specific to the Queen or anyone she has placed under her personal protection. Any attack on those individuals results in swift and dire consequences. It's a very effective deterrent. While this attack wasn't directed against Her Majesty, she wishes to maintain the good relationships that she's developed with these people, and if there isn't going to be a wedding, then it's imperative to her to give the poor bride and groom's families closure."

I snicked a hand across my throat. "That kind of closure?"

White Rabbit Man remained poker-faced.

"Plausible deniability. Got it." I checked for bloodstains but found none. "If you want me to prevent Levi from alerting authorities, Nefesh or Mundane, that's a separate fee."

"Keeping the police away is part of the job you've been hired by the Tannous family to do," White Rabbit Man said.

It wasn't his completely reasonable tone that made me nod in agreement so much as the dark flash of anger he couldn't quite hide.

"Can't blame a person for trying," I muttered, and took a few more photos of the body from various angles.

From downstairs, Husani demanded to know what we'd found.

"Ah, the dulcet tones of the belligerent male," White Rabbit Man said.

"Hope your pay grade makes it worth it." I stuffed my phone in my back pocket.

"Not everything is about money, Ashira. Excuse me a moment while I parlay with Mr. Tannous."

"You do that. Me and Omar will hang out here." I shooed him away.

White Rabbit Man stepped into the corridor and shut the bedroom door behind him.

I moved around to the opposite side of the room to consider the crime scene from a different angle.

The two families had been staying together to get better acquainted in the run-up to the big day. Sometime around 4AM this morning, the crash of the skylight woke everyone up and they'd come running, guns and magic blazing. The angel, with robes and wings as white as a Hollywood cliché, had startled and flown the coop. I shook my head. If we were dealing with a real Angel of Death, everyone should have been obliterated.

Not that angels existed.

Our world ran on power. Mundanes hungered to wield it over Nefesh and Nefesh over each other. We lived in a reality where magic was out in the open, and if there were supernatural beings of the undead, shifting, or celestial variety, then at some point in the past few hundred years, they would have boldly stepped forward and declared themselves top of the food chain. As none had, I took it as pretty concrete fucking evidence that there weren't any.

However, I was a professional. Sherlock Holmes was a man of many theories, but he started each case with a blank mind. I had a room full of witnesses claiming to see an Angel of Death. Therefore, I would methodically pursue that line until I could, without any hesitation, cross it off.

Think an angel would respond to a pair of wings projected like the Bat-Signal? I snickered and eyed the body. "Okay, buddy, give me something to work with."

Having ruled out the other obvious means of death, poison was the most likely culprit. Gently, I turned Omar's neck, looking for any needle prick indicating an administered toxin or a point of origin if it was magic-based.

His neck was stiff and his skin cold. There was no pulse, not that I'd expected there to be.

When I turned his neck the other way, the motion caused his tongue to shift, revealing a white tip at the back of his throat.

"What have we here?" I murmured, worming my fingers into the gap between his locked upper and lower jaws. The item was slippery and the angle wasn't ideal. I tugged on it, but the damn thing was jammed fast down the poor guy's throat.

The scent of a hot sandstorm teased my senses, a delicate sensation of arid nights and dread. One more firm pull and I found myself holding a white feather that was a good eight inches—in ruler length, not man measurements. An ancient magic raised the hairs on the back of my neck. No, that couldn't be right. This feather felt like it had existed for millennia, like it was older than time. But magic, the kind of magic that we knew of at least, was barely four hundred years old, having been unleashed on the world in the 1600s.

These were facts. The feather was old. Magic itself was

not. And yet, here I was, holding a giant fluffy contradiction, still pristine even though it had been jammed down Omar's esophageal tract.

I forced my shoulders down from my ears and, setting the feather on the ground, moved Omar's head to see if there was anything else in his mouth.

That's when his eyes blinked open and a perfectly nice murder got a lot more complicated.

Chapter 2

I jerked back. "Fuck balls!"

Omar's eyes bore into me with a terrified pleading look.

The feather had paralyzed him, entombed him in a death-like state, but with it out of his body, its hold had loosened enough to feel the magic that wrapped around and through him like a spiderweb on a fly. It rolled off him in waves and I didn't have to get close to know that, left like this, that magic would slowly and painfully kill him.

My one-of-a-kind blood powers allowed me to strip away magic and destroy it. I could save Omar.

I could also stick my hand in a dark hole and hope it didn't get bitten off. If this feather was a weapon, engaging with its magic might make me the next victim, and who would come to my aid? I wouldn't even be the second Jew known for a resurrection. I'd just be—I looked down at Omar—that.

He'd upgraded from Mostly Dead to only Somewhat Dead, given the ongoing bloating, mottling, and corpse-like paralysis, and while this was an improvement, it would still put a major crimp in the wedding photos. Even if I took action, the jury was out on whether he'd make it back fully to the land of the living. His breathing was shallow and slow. He didn't stand a chance without me, but saving him could cost me my life.

I was very fond of my life, such as it was.

Omar's blinks might as well have been Morse code tapping out "help me."

I put my hands on my hips and shook my head at the utter disaster before me. That's it. I was changing my business name from Cohen Investigations to Clusterfucks 'R' Us.

"You'll be pleased to know I've secured your crime scene," White Rabbit Man said, striding into the room, "and the families downstairs agreed not to disturb—"

Omar made a strangled noise.

"Okhuyet!" White Rabbit Man swore, his sword now in hand.

I silently repeated the word a couple of times to commit it to memory, intending to find out what it meant and where it originated. That might give me a clue as to White Rabbit Man's background, since nothing had shown up. People tended to show their linguistic origins under stress, large quantities of drugs or alcohol, or anesthetic. I'd use anything to get intel on the Queen.

"This thing—" I pointed at the feather, "has mad magic, so unless you want me to shove it back where I found it and finish Omar off for good, you'll agree to my terms. Give me the vials."

A recent case had involved finding out who was creating smudgy shadows killing members of the Nefesh community. The shadows were actually magic that had been ripped from their hosts—that I'd nicknamed third-party smudges—and, now dying, were desperately looking for a new body to stay alive. I'd destroyed the two rampaging through Vancouver, but had discovered a lab with fourteen other vials containing smudges intended for sale to the highest bidder.

Selling stopped-up promises of magic was a hell of a con. There was no acquiring powers. They might skip a generation or two but you were either born with them or you weren't.

Unless you were me.

Unfortunately, the Queen had taken possession of the vials and while she swore she wasn't interested in selling them, those things had to be destroyed for good.

Part of me hoped White Rabbit Man would say that the smudges had already bit it.

The skin around his eyes pinched tight. "Agreed. As your fee for solving the case *and* healing Omar."

My bank account wouldn't benefit from this job but the world would. Ah, well. There might be a way to leverage this into a payout.

"Fail and your payment will take a very different form," he added, tapping the flat of his blade.

"I respect your clarity and intensity." I wasn't in beheading range—yet—and I'd prefer White Rabbit Man not get twitchy and change that. "This is a delicate operation so could you leave or lose Excalibur's sharper cousin there?"

He planted himself in the doorway with a stance that dynamite couldn't shift.

Fuck it. I excelled under pressure.

Since I wasn't trying to get at Omar's inherent magic, as he was a Mundane and didn't have any, I didn't require his blood. I did, however, require mine. My magic stemmed from and was fueled by it.

I gripped Omar's bare forearms. My powers swam to the surface of my palms in a silky red ribbon which I sent in through his skin.

Previously, when I'd come into contact with third-party smudges, there had been this horrible maggoty sensation that made my skin crawl because that magic was dying. This power was just as invasive but it was incredibly alive. It was

17

like plunging my hands into stardust: the whole history of humankind written in a dancing supernova, a galaxy bursting in a rainbow of color that beckoned me in.

My body tingled and my eyes rolled back into my head. I exhaled, lost to the greatest exhilaration, a rush that packed the punch of a rocket blast. I glutted myself, the taste of the cosmos on my lips.

I couldn't stop myself. I didn't want to.

Deeper and deeper, I fell into that magic, until I threatened to be lost to it entirely. What had been intoxicating became terrifying. Helpless against its onslaught, buffeted by the hot scent and gritty sensation of a sandstorm, I fought back hard, managing to tease the magic out of Omar.

It flowed out in a stream of golden motes and even as I battled it for my life, I craved another taste.

My blood powers morphed into a kaleidoscope of forked red branches, but they didn't anchor this magic in place so that I could destroy it like I always did.

They snapped like the thinnest of twigs.

My mind screamed that I couldn't do this, that I needed to get out of this now or else risk losing everything that I was to that all-consuming sandstorm. Giving in would be so easy. Except discord and danger peeked out from under that crooning lullaby, and my soul iced over.

I was a fighter. A survivor. I'd survive this, too.

Gritting my teeth and ignoring its lure, I redoubled my efforts, finding the shape of the magic strangling Omar. I gathered it close until I had trapped all that unimaginable power in my red magic branches. Thousands of white clusters bloomed along my thicket and ate the invasive magic up.

If I subscribed to the theory that magic was like a disease, then I was the ultimate white blood cell, fighting off these foreign invaders. It wasn't even a stretch: these white clusters that ate up the magic moved like white blood cells did in all the science videos I'd seen.

It gave "blood magic" new meaning.

I blinked the world back into focus, spent, sweat-drenched, and half-sprawled over Omar, who had mercifully fainted but at least had a steady pulse. His skin was light brown now, with no sign of the purple and black mottling.

Happy as I was that he was all right, the other ninety-nine percent of my brain was obsessed with getting another hit of that feather's magic. Even knowing down to my bones that this was a bad idea, my heart still sank when White Rabbit Man held it up to the light out of my reach.

"Gimme," I croaked.

He snicked his deadly blade through the air, stopping barely shy of my throat. "It's mine now."

Huh? He couldn't taste magic and holding the feather didn't do squat.

I broke into a full-body spiky blood armor, tore his sword from his grip with my enhanced strength, and jumped him.

White Rabbit Man hit the ground on his back, the sword magically back in his hand. He stabbed at me, but it didn't penetrate my armor.

I tossed the sword away and wrestled him for the feather. That got me nowhere so I kicked him in the balls. He twisted at the last second, mitigating most of the damage, and knocked me back into the dresser with a blast of electricity, his actual magic power.

The edge of the furniture smashed into the small of my back, but I barely registered the blow. This armor rocked. "Ha! What else you got, Bunny Boy?"

Balls of electricity shot forward like a baseball pitching machine set to high. My body armor crackled and sparked as I threw myself sideways.

Strikes peppered the wall above my head, leaving scorch

marks. Cracked plaster drifted into my eyes and one of the creepy bird paintings hit the ground, tearing as it knocked free of the frame.

Rachel was going to kill us.

The damn sword once more appeared in his hand, the perfect accoutrement to the manic glint in his eyes.

Grabbing the closest thing at hand, I chucked a small bedside table at him, winging him in the shoulder.

White Rabbit Man dropped the feather.

We both dove for it. I dogpiled him and, employing some recently learned fighting tips, aligned my first two knuckles to be the point of impact, taking care with my follow-through. There was a satisfying crunch of nose cartilage and the sword clattered to the floor.

Tears leaked down his face, courtesy of the nose being connected to the eyes via tear ducts, and inflicted a momentary loss of vision.

Taking advantage of his temporary disorientation, I hooked my magic into his. It tasted like that metallic bite in cool air before a rainstorm, but even though it was a watered-down snack compared to the juicy richness of the ancient magic, I ached for it.

That was a bad idea for many reasons, including that ripping his magic away would break him and I refused to let my dark nature out unless it was a matter of life and death. Even then.

"Stand down or lose your powers." I tugged gently on his magic. Gawd, it would slide free like butter and—No.

Luckily, White Rabbit Man took me at my word. He nodded and I rolled off him, the feather mine at last. As I scooped it up, I glimpsed myself in the mirror above the dresser, huddled over my prize. I wore the same desperate look as White Rabbit Man. Add in a "my precious" and I'd officially hit Gollum rock bottom.

If it meant tasting that feather's magic directly from the

source, pure and at full strength instead of the diluted version I'd sampled in Omar, I didn't care how I looked. And that was enough to shock a sliver of sanity back into me. I pried my fingers off it, shrugged out of my leather jacket, and wrapped the artifact up, but it required all my willpower not to suck the feather's magic out of it like marrow from a bone.

Ever since I'd first tasted magic a couple weeks ago, the desire for more had lodged in my brain like a splinter. I could no longer deny the constant longing, a song stuck in my brain tuned to low.

Levi believed there was a way to stave off the cravings, as otherwise rumors of people taking magic would have surfaced over the years. I hoped he was right. If this hum grew to a deafening roar, I'd no longer be able to curb my desire through willpower and self-disgust.

Denied my fix now, I wanted to curl up into the fetal position until the muscle spasms and stomach cramps subsided. That wasn't in the cards because White Rabbit Man was a predator; he'd sense weakness like a shark with blood in the water.

Speaking of blood… Chest heaving, I grabbed a sheet off the bed and tossed it over to White Rabbit Man so that he could stem the downpour from his nose.

He pressed the fabric to his face with a hiss.

I sat upright against the bed, legs hugged tight to my chest and waves of sharp agony rolling through me.

"Twenty minutes ago, I would have presumed that someone in this house had attacked Omar," White Rabbit Man said. "But they couldn't have withstood the feather's lure enough to leave it behind. Angels." He swore softly. "Just what we need."

"I'm not exactly enamored of the idea either but every possibility, no matter how slim, must be investigated." I wiped the sweat off the back of my neck with my sleeve. "It's not even that it's a white feather so much as its ancient magic being the strongest point in favor of an Angel of Death."

"Are you proposing that magic existed before humans laid hands on it?"

"Possibly," I said. "Conceivably, angels are older than humans and certainly older than our magic is." I frowned. "Unless part of its power is making us *believe* the magic is ancient. To fool people who might determine otherwise."

"Like a Typecaster," he said.

"Exactly." I was listing forward toward the feather so I straightened up. "It's too early to rule anything out, but using the feather as the murder weapon makes no sense."

He tsked. "Oh, of course. Kill a man with an object that drives everyone mad who tries to rescue him. How preposterous."

"I'm serious. Think about it. When a snake bites or a scorpion stings, they just do it. Predators don't mutilate themselves to get at their prey. If there was an Angel of Death in biblical times, it wasn't going around plucking off its wing feathers like a mangy turkey and shoving them down the throats of the firstborn sons, hoping it would eventually kill them. The murder method and suspect don't work as a cohesive whole."

"Perhaps. That leaves us with one last unanswered question." White Rabbit Man dabbed at his nose. "Why in heaven's name did you call me 'Bunny Boy?'"

Whoops. Aw, fuck it. "If you're going to dress like that and work for the Queen of Hearts, then you're inviting the comparison right in. And if you don't like it, you could provide your name so I could address you like a normal human being, White Rabbit Man."

Boom, I did it. Never doubt I'd make good on my threats and/or promises.

His eyes narrowed. Yes, I had some measure of self-preservation and didn't want to make an enemy of him, but I was tapped out and he'd started it.

A hand clamped weakly onto my wrist. My pulse spiked and I tore free, but it wasn't White Rabbit Man. It was Omar, who miraculously hadn't been injured in the melee.

"Feather," he whispered. Other than the look of blank shock on his face, he looked much better.

"Absolutely not." I shook a finger at him like a pissed off Mary Poppins. "You don't have magic, much less can taste it. This feather shouldn't affect you." The fact that it did meant its influence wasn't limited to Nefesh, but Mundanes as well, giving it the potential to do nuclear levels of damage. I glowered at White Rabbit Man. "You can't taste it either, so why did you want it so badly?"

White Rabbit Man pushed to his feet. He picked up his sword, did a cursory examination of it, and then made it disappear. "It tempted me with my heart's desire."

"Care to elaborate?" I said.

His fingers twitched. "For one shining moment, I believed I could have it all…"

He drifted off. The ellipsis on that statement turned into a period and then an awkward "are you still standing there waiting for me to say something more?"

I placed my fingers on Omar's temples and sent my magic inside his skull. The feather magic that had been strangling him was gone. "Odd. There's no trace of any other magic, like a compulsion." I swatted Omar's hand away again. Were compulsions even evident? I hadn't sensed anything inside White Rabbit Man other than his own inherent magic, either. Interesting.

"How close were you when this happened?" I said to White Rabbit Man. "Did the feather affect you when you first came in the room?"

"No, and I didn't touch it. I moved it out of your way with my sword."

"About three feet from you then?"

"Approximately." He stood further back from the feather than that, so he was in the clear.

"Do you still feel the compulsion now?" I said.

He shook his head. "It's faded."

"Then it's not widely broadcasting a compulsion and its hold fades quickly with brief exposure." Omar no longer had the feather magic in him, but he was still under its thrall, as if the compulsion that the magic exuded had seeped into his very bones. "We need to contain it," I said. "Do you have anything to do the trick?"

"Wait here," White Rabbit Man said, and vanished. He couldn't teleport, but he had a magic token on a chain around his neck that allowed him to access Hedon from anywhere. Given the black market had been stitched together from pockets of reality but existed outside of it, it was a handy little tool to have.

"Omar, what happened?" I said. "Who attacked you?"

"Feather," he whispered again.

I growled. "Considering it almost killed you, asking for it is a very poor life decision which I cannot condone. What's it promising you?"

He had nothing coherent to share.

White Rabbit Man returned with a thin metal pouch, etched with obscure symbols. He tossed it over and I sealed the feather up with a sigh of relief.

"Can I get one of those all-access passes?" I said.

"Hedon isn't some backstage groupie paradise."

"Obviously. Why get hot rock stars, sexual escapades, and a possible STI memento, when I could have nausea, hostility, and danger?" I waved the pouch. "Hedon has resources I suspect I'll require in order to solve this case. What do you say?"

White Rabbit Man dug into his suit jacket pocket and dumped a handful of bronze tokens into my upturned palm.

"Each of these will allow one shift in or out of Hedon. From anywhere. Think about where you wish to go and it will take you there."

No need to find an entrance. How VIP. "And the cost of so-doing?"

White Rabbit Man grinned slyly.

I ran a finger over one of the tokens. It looked so harmless. "Can't I have a gold one like yours and spare myself the pain?"

"Under no circumstances."

Whelp, at least I'd confirmed that his method of traveling was consequence-free. Every bit of intel around Hedon helped.

"Great. Guess I'll find out when I find out."

Omar remained a whimpering mess. White Rabbit Man, while he was keeping it together much better than Omar, still was pretty banged up, and I had no room to talk.

"I'd like to say this has been fun, but I try to lie as little as possible." I stood up on shaky legs and pointed at White Rabbit Man. "Are we copasetic?"

He gave me a measured look. "Moran."

"Is that slang? Like 'we're Gucci,' but more Irish? Have you been hitting up Urban Dictionary to stay relevant?"

"Are you quite finished?"

I shrugged. "I mean, I probably have one or two more gibes in me, but let's go with sure. What's Moran?"

"What you may call me. A name that, if you are as much of a Sherlockian as you seem, means something to you."

My breath hitched. Colonel Sebastian Moran was a skilled assassin who worked for Moriarty in the Sherlock Holmes books. Knowing I lived with Priya was one thing, but knowing about my love of Holmes? Was there anything about me that he and the Queen hadn't unearthed? Even more frightening was the danger this message implied. The

25

Queen had expressed interest in me; Moriarty had been interested in Holmes, too. I swallowed.

"Moran, it is." I managed to keep my voice steady. "I'm going to stash the feather someplace safe."

"Where would that be?"

I raised an eyebrow.

"I'm not asking because I intend to steal it," he said. "But you weren't exempt from its thrall. Is anywhere 'safe?'"

"Your experience was completely different to mine. The feather itself didn't tempt or compel me, touching it didn't do squat, and in fact, I hadn't cared about it at all until I engaged with the magic it released inside Omar."

My fingers tightened on the pouch. Why was it different for me? Combine this with the fact that there was no record, official or anecdotal, of blood magic, and the universe could take this special snowflake status it was hellbent on conferring on me and shove it up its ass.

"The cravings are even subsiding," I lied, my gut cramping up. "I'm not going to do anything to jeopardize this case and right now, this feather is integral to it. Trust me, okay?"

Moran searched my face for a long moment. "Very well."

A surge of relief blew through me.

In my mitzvah for the day, I reunited Omar with the Capulets and Montagues downstairs. It was kind of sweet when Shannon fainted in an old-school movie swoon and Omar roused himself enough to catch her, hugging her tightly and burying his face in her neck. Since he was still mumbling about the feather, Masika almost impaled me with a knitting needle, convinced I'd done some kind of voodoo on Omar to turn him into a zombie. She didn't buy my explanation that removing the feather had saved him from a magic that had been slowly strangling him from the inside, making it appear he was dead.

After that, an excitable Husani shot out a window with a

whoop, Rachel started laughing hysterically and drinking directly from the bottle, and the good times ended.

This was what came of thinking of others. The scene was bedlam; any more interrogations would have to wait a day.

I patted Omar's head. "Rest up, because I'll be back."

I left them in the sinisterly capable hands of Moran and headed out. I had a fucked-up feather to throw light on and an Angel of Death—real or otherwise—to find. Even with the vials thrown in, I wasn't being paid enough for this gig.

Chapter 3

I hurried out to my car, Moriarty, my shoulder blades prickling like I was being watched. I turned in a slow circle, but no one had followed me out of the house and the long driveway up from the front gates was clear. I stepped onto the grass, manifested a blood dagger, and carefully picked my way between the topiaries of giant robins.

These people needed to cool it with the birds. There was a difference between a design aesthetic and a Hitchcock film. Regardless, the bushy buggers only inspired a mild sense of unease and not the "Welcome to Stalkersville" energy someone or something was throwing my way.

A circuit of the yard didn't produce any skulking intruders, so I collapsed into Moriarty's driver's seat, and blinked against the bluish-white glow bathing my face. Outside the car window was a rough slab that was approximately five feet at its base. The tip of its triangular top stood taller than I did. Instead of the nubby texture of stone, this piece seemed carved from a block of the sky. It was pure light contained in a static form. One of Shannon's pieces. She'd forgone the family business to make a name for herself as a visual artist using her light magic.

I rubbed my right thigh, which ached from the rods holding my femur together. With the advent of my magic, the pain that had troubled me for years was mostly gone, but I'd over-taxed myself. I fumbled for the Costco-sized bottle of Tylenol in my glove compartment and dry-swallowed a couple of pills.

Sadly, that did nothing for the continued cravings that left me slumped over the steering wheel taking slow inhales and exhales and categorizing everything around me alphabetically: air vent, brakes, console… A self-soothing technique from years back.

I resolutely did not open my trunk where the feather was stashed. Even though I could taste, smell, and destroy magic, I couldn't actually identify what type it was from engaging with it. The best thing would be to nuke all the magic on that damned thing so it couldn't tempt anyone else, but until I knew what I was dealing with, I was reluctant to do that.

That was absolutely the only reason.

I locked the doors.

My magic followed certain patterns. Why I was the Cookie Monster of magic was a big "who the hell knows?" but I'd clung to what little clarity I'd had about my powers, and while the *fact* of my cravings was nothing new, the intensity of them this time scared me.

In all other instances, I got a high from engaging with living magic (versus with the dying third-party smudges). Usually, my psychological urges only turned to physical withdrawal symptoms if I aborted the process of destroying magic. Otherwise, I was bumped gently down from my high, temporarily satiated.

This feather magic was definitely alive, and while the rush had been greater than any before, I continued to want it even after I'd nuked it inside Omar. Equally as puzzling, he continued to be under its spell. Did I need to destroy the feather itself for our longings to go away?

While I was a puzzle wrapped in an enigma, I was also a woman with pressing questions in need of answers. Failure was not an option.

I glowered at my car's dashboard. "I'm having a shit day, so start on me or I'll scrap metal your ass."

Moriarty gave a single sputter in protest then purred to life. A gray, older Toyota Camry, he wasn't flashy, but he had the most important quality for my line of work: he was common enough to blend into almost any neighborhood. In theory, this model should have been easy to back out and turn, handle well, and have good gas mileage and power. In reality, he was okay on all that, but where he really excelled was fucking with me when it was time to start and making sure I never got too complacent.

I cranked the now-fixed heater, reveling in the warmth. My last paycheck had been enough to get on top of my bills with cash left over for this much-needed repair, but this sweet, warm idyll was only temporary. Soon the stereo volume would mysteriously get stuck on loud or a weird burning smell would come through the vents and our little dance would begin anew.

But for now, the drive to my next destination was nice and toasty.

Blondie's was my favorite dive pub, despite its surly staff and sticky surfaces, because it had the world's most perfect french fries and a karaoke list that was second-to-none. The low lights weren't mood setting; they were camouflage for the scuffed wooden flooring, splotchy upholstery, and bottom shelf drinks at top shelf pricing.

I generally avoided it like the plague during the day, since its already questionable food was not made better by the sickly rays of sunlight that made it through the greasy windows, but my quarry had a Norwalk virus-resistant stomach lining and enjoyed breakfast here on the regular.

"Buy you a drink, sugarbaby?" The sixty-something man leered from his barstool.

Leftover drunks: the other reason to avoid Blondie's in the AM.

Slightly bleary gaze, wedding ring, bulging wallet in his back pocket: he was making bad decisions in an incapacitated mindset, and yet, not my problem.

Shaking my head, I walked past him.

"Come on, sweetheart, smile. You're a pretty girl."

I stopped. A lecture, ignoring him, punching him in the throat—all were good options, but if I could keep another woman from being impinged on this way, then I should handle it.

I spun around, hooked an ankle under his stool rung and yanked it out from under him.

He toppled over onto his ass, sputtering.

I crouched down. "I hurt your pride. Someone else could inflict a lot more damage with the wad of cash in your wallet and the fact you're two drinks past rational thinking. Go home."

He mumbled protests of his innocence and how I didn't have to be this way. Then he really let me have it with "bitch."

I bent his wrist back. "I owe you shit and my facial expressions are my own. You want a smile? Put one on your wife's face." I exerted more pressure on his wrist, approaching the fine line between painful and broken. "Leave before I rethink my charitable public service and demonstrate how bad this bitch can be. Your call."

"I'll go home."

"Wise choice." I patted his head. "And smile. You're a pretty boy, sugarbaby."

Autumn Kelly, the redhead wearing her weight in flowy

31

scarves, barely lifted her gaze from her full English breakfast as I sat down on the barstool next to hers.

"What was that all about?" she said.

"My milkshake brings all the boys to the yard." The bacon on her plate made my stomach growl, but I knew from past unfortunate experiences with said breakfast meat at Blondie's that looks were deceiving. "Talk to me about angels."

Autumn slurped the toxic sludge that passed for coffee in this joint. I was almost tempted to order one since Moran had woken me obscenely early this morning to put me on the Omar case, but common sense prevailed.

"Last time I did that," Autumn said, "you called me a New Age flake with crystals for brains."

"It was a term of endearment."

"Fuck off, Ash."

I motioned to the bartender and ordered an orange juice and a side order of toast. Yes, it was Passover. Yes, I was a bad Jew. I was also a starving cranky Jew with a deep love of yeasty baked goods, and toast was the safest thing on the breakfast menu. "Name your price. How about a new deck of tarot cards?"

She toyed with her crystal bracelet. "Those things you described as wastes of tree bark that would be put to better use wiping your butt?"

I winced. Yeah, that sounded like me. "That might have been a bit harsh, but I wouldn't have said anything if you hadn't started us down this road."

"How?"

The bartender placed the toast and orange juice in front of me.

I took a sip and smacked my lips. Mmm. Straight from concentrate. "You said Sherlock Holmes was ridiculously unbelievable."

"He is." Autumn mopped up the last of her baked beans.

"He's also fictional. You getting your panties in a twist over a make-believe character doesn't give you leave to insult my beliefs."

"Sherlock stands for reason, intelligence, deduction, all things that you as a psychiatrist should stand for. How can you align that with the New Age movement?"

Dr. Autumn Kelly polished off the grilled tomatoes stacked in a pile to one side of her eggs. "You know there are Catholic clergymen who are also scientists and have made great contributions, right? It's about seeking answers. I'm simply taking a two-pronged approach to it. Science and spirituality are compatible."

Right and wrong had always been very black-and-white. It was like math: you either got the correct answer or you didn't. But the more I studied crime and motives, the more opaque the truth proved to be. Maybe Autumn had a point. I'd hold out for more evidence on the spirituality front, but I could at least respect where she was coming from.

"I apologize. I was an asshole, and I'm genuinely sorry for being snarky about something important to you. Also, I need your help."

Autumn wiped her mouth with her paper napkin. "Do a one-card reading."

"A what now?" The toast was both burned and cold, dotted with knobs of butter. I muscled the culinary marvel down anyway.

She set her bulky cloth purse on the bar top and pulled out a silk-wrapped deck of cards. "Think of a question and then select a card to receive guidance."

"May I say, in the most respectful way possible, that I don't believe in any of this, and this reading would be wasted on me?" The toast reformed into a congealed lump in my stomach. Carbs had never been so challenging to digest.

"Well, if you don't want to broaden your horizons, I

have places to be." Autumn reached for her purse, but I stopped her.

"I'll do it."

"Excellent." She unwrapped the deck and shuffled it. "If you want to be all sciencey about it—"

"Eight years of med school and you get 'sciencey?'" I chugged back some of my drink, but only got halfway through the glass. Juice wasn't supposed to burn like cheap booze.

"Jung believed that tarot cards were doorways to the unconscious. That, among other benefits, by using these psychological symbols, a person could find a path through their unconscious mind into the meaning of a situation." She fanned the cards out on their silk wrapping. "Pick a card," she said, once they were all laid out.

"Any card." I reached out but she stopped me with her hand over mine.

"Wait. First fix the question in your head. Then use your left hand to select the card. It's more connected to your unconscious mind."

Is there an Angel of Death? was the first question that came to mind, but she said this was about guidance so I came up with something more personal.

What lies ahead as a Jezebel?

I selected a card and flipped it over. "My answer is a stylized tree painting?"

"In this deck, trees embody the mythic ideas of the tarot. More interestingly, this is a Major Arcana card." She narrowed her eyes. "This question of yours has great importance in your life, doesn't it?"

I swirled the juice in my glass, searching for non-existent pulp like it was the Fountain of Youth. "It's a casual curiosity."

"You chose the almond tree, which symbolizes the Magician or Magus. You know what a Magus is?"

"A wizard?"

"The word originated in Persia around 520 BCE. Magi were men, predominantly alchemists and astronomers, who transformed chaos into order. Back then, that involved creating maps by tracking stars and planets and using the sun and moon to tell time."

"I'm transforming chaos into order?"

"Aren't you a detective?" She smiled wryly. "It's definitely about transformation and manifestation. Change isn't easy, but you have resources. Both your own intuition and possibly someone who helps bring it about."

I could live with my own intuition, what bothered me was this sounded too much like a destiny I had to fulfill. A random magical fate wasn't my calling: private investigator was.

"I'm not sure if this broadened my horizons or narrowed them," I said dryly.

Autumn wrapped the cards back up and replaced them in her purse. "Fair is fair. What did you want to know about angels?"

"You believe they exist, right?"

"Yes and no. I don't think beings with white wings and halos are floating around out there. They're not physical; they're spiritual. A higher life force that we can connect to in order to lift us up and guide us."

Too bad. That would have narrowed down the suspect list.

"Do you think the conventional type of angel could exist?" I said.

She motioned for the bill. "I think that people seek spiritual connections and might believe they've seen an angel, but if they existed in physical form, as beings of pure good, they should have given our world some damn miracles lately."

I paid for both of us, in exchange for the information

and repairing the breach where I'd tactlessly brushed off her beliefs. "It's the least I can do."

Autumn thanked me and slung her purse over her shoulder. "Why the sudden interest?"

I'd have loved to see Autumn's face if I told her about the feather, but professional discretion forbade sharing my client's details. "Curious if an Angel of Death really exists and would come after someone."

"If he did, you'd have to ask what the poor schmuck did to piss off God. According to a number of religions, angels are His tool."

"What about mass hallucinations? Like lots of people seeing UFOs?"

"There's no scientific basis for the idea. There's mass hysteria, but that applies to people having an overwrought or deluded belief, like they have a disease. To take the UFO example, those reports are from a few people across a large sample of the population. No reports of group sightings that couldn't be explained by lights or weather phenomena."

"But group sightings could be explained by Houdini magic." Nefesh with illusion powers.

"Sure." Autumn slid off the stool. "See you and Priya at karaoke next week?"

"I think so. Thanks, Autumn. And sorry again for being a dick."

"Yeah, well, sorry I insulted the love of your life." With a wink, she left.

I could do worse than Sherlock Holmes.

Surprisingly, Autumn had helped because I could strike off mass hallucination. That still left me with an actual Angel of Death (doubtful) or a person pretending to be one or fabricating one, and either way, it all came down to motive.

And that feather.

Back at Moriarty, I logged in to the House Pacifica database on my phone, using my professional 100% legitimate account (which His Lordship had made me pay for), and ran a search on all Nefesh with illusion magic located in the Greater Vancouver area. Nefesh magic was ranked on a scale from one to five. While any Houdini with lower level powers could make themselves or another person look like an angel, having that angel fly up into the sky and then having multiple people buy it took more control and finesse of their abilities, so I limited my search to those with level four or five powers.

There was exactly one person who fit the criteria: Levi Montefiore, Head of House Pacifica, one of only three Houses in Canada, whose rule extended from the west coast all the way to the Ontario border.

The well-being of his Nefesh would always come first with him, no matter who he had to run roughshod over. That attitude made him a great leader—as long as you were one of the people he was determined to protect.

I logged out of the database. How far would Levi go to protect his House and his Nefesh community, if Omar had crossed him? The more I thought about it, the more it felt like poking a toothache with my tongue—a dull aching pain that grew worse each time I revisited it. I had to remain objective about this and, until this was resolved, recuse myself from the sexual component of our relationship. Levi was potentially involved in this case and as such would be treated the same as any other suspect.

I opened my phone to change his contact name from Imperious 1 to simply Levi Montefiore, but couldn't bring myself to do it. Levi required special handling and—I wrenched my mind away from that totally inappropriate rabbit hole. Fine. The snarky nickname could stay, but naked time was off the table. I took a moment to thoroughly objectify him in my mind's eye, then moved on.

A point towards Levi's innocence was that since Omar was from Egypt, his attacker might be as well. Though Levi did a fair bit of traveling, meeting with other House Heads across the globe. For all I knew, he had a favorite hotel in Cairo and a bartender with whom he was on a first name basis in some bar down a back alley souk.

A reminder chimed on my phone to call my mother, derailing my thoughts about Levi. Talia had been avoiding me, worried that I'd try to force my "delusion" of having magic on her once again. She'd even instructed the concierge at her high priced condo to tell me she was out, no matter what time I dropped by. I wasn't encouraged to stay and wait.

She no longer phoned to corral me into all the Untainted Party fundraisers or to check in on me and harp on my life choices. I didn't like that part of our relationship, but now I kind of missed it.

Well, too bad. My one remaining family member did not get to ghost me.

The call I placed went to voicemail. Again.

"We need to talk," I said. "Don't shut me out. Please."

One return call. One text. I just needed an opening. I'd handled things poorly the first time, but I'd still been reeling from the shock of having magic. Expecting her to believe me without proof had been a grave mistake. Talia was very rational, not to mention the Senior Policy Advisor to an anti-Nefesh party. Of course she doubted my story when I hadn't been born with magic.

However, once I demonstrated my enhanced strength, honestly the least traumatizing of my powers, she'd have to admit I had magic. Seeing was believing, after all. If she was mad at me for dropping this bombshell on her, I'd remind her that our rule since my car accident and Dad's disappearance—the rule she'd insisted on—was "No Lies. No Games." If anything had come out of our therapy after the crash, it was the importance of honesty in our relationship.

I'd prepared myself for a very difficult conversation and

for things between us to be dicey for a bit, but getting through hard shit was kind of our jam. All would work out in the end. She might not leave her position in the Untainted Party, but she'd stop the dangerous direction of its messaging.

Wouldn't she?

She had to. I was her flesh and blood, and that had to matter more than this prejudice.

Since the ball was in her court, I drove across town to a pawn shop on the Downtown Eastside, not far from my office in Gastown. The locations, however, were worlds apart. Gastown, one of Vancouver's oldest neighborhoods that had been heavily gentrified over the past twenty years, boasted cobblestone streets, heritage buildings from the end of the nineteenth century, and a fuckton of tourists buying everything from Indigenous art and Canada-themed clothing to maple syrup-infused food and tiny soapstone sculptures of bears.

These tourist traps nestled amongst hipster BBQ joints and cafés, designer boutiques, high-end furniture stores, and my favorite, the flagship Fluevog Shoes store. But they were only blocks away from some of the roughest poverty in Canada on Vancouver's Downtown Eastside.

Freddo's Buy & Sell sat in the middle of a war zone. The area was the heart of the fentanyl overdose crisis, the inhabitants of these few square blocks living in rundown single occupancy hotels and on the streets, their belongings piled high in shopping carts. Old books, T-shirts, DVDs—goods were laid out all over the garbage-strewn sidewalks, hawked by people desperate to make a buck.

So many people were addicted to drugs and alcohol down here that the city had lowered the speed limit so drivers had a chance to stop in time, what with all the people who weren't entirely lucid jaywalking across this busy thoroughfare.

I pulled open the pawn shop door and sneezed at the years of must that hit me from all the glass cases stuffed full of personal items. It was a familiar sight but even my cold dead heart twisted at how often prized possessions were measured not in terms of sentimentality, but survival.

I rapped on a case to get the attention of some grizzled man watching screaming people on a tiny TV set.

"Yeah?" He didn't bother to turn around, crinkling his bag of corn nuts as he reached for another handful.

"Freddo in?"

"Nah." He crunched his nuts. I was tempted to do the same.

"Yo, Employee of the Year, I'm sure this baby daddy drama is scintillating, but I need to see Freddo and get an artifact checked out. When will he be back?"

He faced me with an aggrieved sigh, his fingers coated in BBQ dust. "Try back tomorrow."

"Morning? Afternoon?" Nothing. He'd been sucked back into the idiot box. "Thanks for going above and beyond, dude."

Back at Moriarty, I leaned against my car, debating my next move. The pouch was in a locked box that was bolted down inside my trunk, because Vancouver was notorious for vehicular B&Es, especially in Gastown. The locked box was a handy addition I'd made to secure evidence about a year ago. I planned to transfer the feather over to my office safe, but it was perfectly fine for a while longer.

I could check on it. I'd fit the key into the trunk lock before I'd completed the thought. Kicking Moriarty's tires didn't silence the damn song in my head nudging me to take one little lick of the feather's magic, but I got my ass into the driver's seat without giving in.

My day had been short on concrete facts, but hopefully I could strike one suspect off my list. Time for Imperious 1 to pony up.

Chapter 4

I called Levi, but the call went straight to voicemail. Despite Priya's crazy tech skills, we'd never managed to get tracking software on him.

I'd have to make a House call.

Stuck at a red light by the plaza at the Vancouver Art Gallery, a common gathering space for protests, I drummed my fingers as a crowd chanted in favor of the dissolution of all Houses in Canada.

From day one, the Untainted Party had hit the ground running, stirring up anti-magic sentiment. They'd moved to next level antics by attempting to disassemble House Pacifica, the only one in their province, and put those Nefesh firmly under the thumbs of Mundanes. Even though Nefesh paid taxes for House resources and protection, had to register in a database, and follow all our nation's laws, certain Mundanes hated that Houses controlled the policing and education of their own people, among other things. Houses were also politically powerful enough to mitigate the extent to which Mundanes could spread slanderous disinformation about them.

Had you asked me a month ago, I would have shrugged

and said that the system worked. We registered cars, we registered guns, it made sense to register magic. I prided myself on being inclusive when it came to gender and racial equality and LGBTQ rights, and yet, it never occurred to me how being constantly identified as Other put Nefesh, who only made up about ten percent of the world's population, in a state of constant marginalization despite their powers.

Kind of ironic when my own Jewish history was littered with the devastating consequences of being "Other." But like I'd said, our world ran on power, and growing up Mundane, it was easy to feel like we were the second-class citizens. Inferior somehow. That Nefesh were the special ones, the ones with the literal power. I didn't condone the actions of the Untainted Party and their supporters, but I could empathize with their position.

The groundswell to do away with Houses was only at the provincial level thus far, though if the spark caught, it could easily go federal, turning Canada into a draconian police state for anyone unlucky enough to possess magic. This wasn't paranoia; it was the pattern in countries that oppressed Nefesh.

My mother was doing a bang-up job drafting the legislation behind the bill they intended to bring forward.

A long metal winged serpent hazed the crowd and screams erupted.

Four guys standing on the corner yelled back at the anti-Nefesh protesters. The tallest one, in a dusty top hat with one of those stupid under-the-chin beards with beads threaded through it, waved his arms, controlling the swooping serpent. An Animator.

Once they'd herded the crowd into a tight circle, another member of their group flicked his fingers to the sky, then pulled sharply downward. An extremely localized rain storm drenched the Mundanes.

Police wearing both Mundane and Nefesh uniforms rushed onto the plaza as the light turned green.

The Untainted Party needed some remedial Kindergarten-level lessons in inclusivity, but the need for power, for control, was a powerful, primal urge.

I was betting on Talia's love for me to outweigh that.

The confrontation grew smaller in my rearview mirror, until I turned into the House Pacifica underground garage and it was lost to view.

House HQ was located in the middle of downtown on some of Vancouver's priciest real estate. Shaped like an "S" laying on its side, the seven-story glass building had an enigmatic quality to it—much like the man who ran it. The glass caught and reflected the light in a way that made the color of the building ever-changing.

Today it was the same deep blue as Levi's eyes. I snickered. Maybe the building was a giant mood ring, keyed to Levi's state of mind. Could I turn it "head-exploding red?" "Broke him permanently black?" How fun it would be to test.

Parking Moriarty on the level designated for guests, I debated changing out of my burned clothing, but decided against it. I liked the jaunty "tangled with danger and won" look that it conferred upon me.

After a quick stop at a kiosk outside, I headed up.

The first two levels of HQ held the central Nefesh police department, with cells that I was all too familiar with located in the basement. The next four floors were devoted to various House affairs.

The seventh floor, my destination, was home to the executive staff and His Lordship's office, which was guarded by Veronica, Levi's pet dragon. Or Executive Assistant, if you wanted to be technical about it.

I strode over richly polished wooden floor planks, taking a moment to enjoy the panoramic view out the floor-to-ceiling windows that showcased the Vancouver skyline to the water and North Shore Mountains. I may have grown up here, but I hoped I never became blasé to my city's beauty.

Levi's personal art collection, incorporating artists as diverse as Escher and Dali, graced pale gold walls. The unifying theme of these paintings and photographs was illusions, but unless you knew what the pattern was, it was hard to spot.

Veronica's face puckered at my approach.

Heh.

She stood up, physically prepared to get between me and Levi's door, if that's what it took. Her ferocious glower wasn't half as impressive as her air of effortless chic. She'd paired black cigarette pants with a crisp, white tailored shirt with nary a hint of a wrinkle, a linen blazer, and a scarf in rich red blooms knotted loosely around her neck. Her blonde hair was tied back in one of those messy buns at the nape of the neck that on her was fetching and on me looked like the bad hair day it was.

I'd noticed latte cups on her desk before, with the letters marking her preference for non-fat, double shots. Sure enough, there was already a takeout cup in the otherwise empty trash can by her desk.

I presented her with a still-steaming latte, hoping if she was caffeinated to the tits that it would boost her mood from her normal bristling hostility to a general dislike masked by an air of professionalism. We were going to cross paths a lot in the future, and I'd catch more flies with honey.

She took off the lid and, eyes narrowed, sniffed the drink.

Please. If I intended to poison her, I'd never be that obvious. I'd start with small ongoing dosages to get her progressively sicker, then stop, baffling everyone, but making her relieved that her mysterious illness was over.

Then I'd finish her off.

However, today was about playing nice, so I gave Veronica the smile that Priya had signed off on as being my most charming. "Is Levi in?"

"There's powdered sugar on your chin."

I wiped off the remnants of the hastily eaten donut when I'd bought her coffee. "Whoops. I hate wasting cocaine."

Her eyes jumped all over my clothing, unable to land on any one fashion violation. "Are those blood flecks on your shirt?"

I checked the white T-shirt under my leather jacket. Huh. Must have gotten a little parting gift when I'd punched Moran. "Yeah."

"It's eleven o'clock in the morning." Her voice vibrated with indignation.

"Not to brag, but you should see what I can achieve if I've had my second coffee." I jerked a thumb at the office. "So? Fearless Leader?"

"He's not here right now."

I considered threatening her with another disembodied golem's hand, because the look on her face that time had been priceless, but reminded myself the word of the day was "honey."

"Actually not here," I said, "or are you falling back on your stock answer where I'm concerned? Because you know I'll check. So how about we pretend we've already done this little dance and you tell me where he is?"

A little voice in my head that sounded remarkably like Pri's tsked at my distinct lack of honey. Oh, whatever. It was the thought that counted.

"Contrary to what you believe," Veronica said, leaning over the counter for emphasis, "Levi isn't a lackey at your beck and call. He's not only trusted with governing his Nefesh community, but overseeing multiple corporate interests and matters of public justice."

"Yeah, and he shits rainbows. I get it. He's important. However, he contacted me with a matter of some urgency."

"Then you should have responded in a timely manner." She sat down and pulled her monitor screen closer, her dismissal clear.

Golem hand next time it was. Could I order one online?

"Tell Levi I called."

"I will."

"As soon as he gets in."

"I'll tell him you called," she said, huffily.

Right, and I'd hold my breath in anticipation.

I headed in the general direction of the elevators, then checking that Veronica wasn't watching me, detoured into the restrooms. Had I had more time, Priya could have hacked into Veronica's computer, but this was pressing, and besides, my techie secret weapon was in a meeting.

I placed a call to the main switchboard of House HQ. "Uh, hi. There's a car alarm going off down here in the parkade. Window's smashed, too. I think it's Mr. Montefiore's assistant's car."

I lingered another couple minutes in the restroom, half-heartedly scrubbing out the blood flecks. When I emerged, Veronica wasn't at her desk and she'd taken her purse, so she wasn't in the photocopy room.

The latte I'd given her was nowhere to be seen either.

"You're welcome." I sat down in her chair and studied the password-protected screen. Neither "admin," "password1," or "1234" worked. Nor did any combination of Levi's birthday. I was tempted to try "IheartLevi" but refrained. I'd already hit six attempts out of my allotted ten before I'd be locked out for thirty minutes.

My estimation of her rose. Slightly. As Levi's Executive Assistant, she'd constantly have to leave her computer to deal with problems and general administrative tasks. She was smart enough to make sure no one got to the sensitive material on her computer since her desk was out in the open.

What else could it be? It might be randomly generated, in which case I was shit out of luck, but if she'd gone with something meaningful to her? What clues did her workspace yield?

I dismissed the postcard propped on her desk from some tropical location. Other than that, she had a taped-up photo of her and some guy at a Canucks game, both wearing the blue, white, and green jerseys of our Vancouver hockey team, and her pens were stashed in a Canucks beer mug. Neither of these items were visible from the other side of the reception desk, so they weren't things she was interested in showing off. No, her self-identification as a Canucks fan was something she drew comfort and energy from.

Three more tries were a bust. I cracked my knuckles. Last attempt. "WeAreAllCanucks1" was the winner. The combination of their slogan plus the most commonly used number tacked on to passwords to make them more "secure." Priya would have pissed herself laughing.

From there it was quick work to get into Levi's personal calendar and find out where he was. I left Veronica's desk as I found it and was back at the elevator bank when she stepped out.

"Why are you still here?" Her suspicion had a gleeful edge like she could rid herself of me once and for all. Sister, I wasn't that easy to shake.

I held out my damp, but mostly spotless T-shirt. "I didn't notice the blood until you pointed it out, and honestly, who wants to walk around with that on their shirt?"

Her eyes narrowed, but she didn't challenge me. Throwing her a breezy salute, I left to track down my quarry.

City Hall was an art deco building on Cambie Street in what was essentially midtown. Snagging a parking spot at the edge of the lot, I swapped my leather jacket for the short belted trench coat I kept in a duffel bag in the trunk. It was my selection of clothes and props should I need to get into character on a case. Buttoned up and with the collar popped, the coat hid most of the damage I'd sustained at Moran's hands, including the burn on my neck. Securing my dark wavy hair in a smooth ponytail, I grabbed a file folder of blank papers and slid on a pair of non-prescription glasses.

I exhaled sharply a bunch of times to get my color up, then ran inside, flustered and jabbering at the woman manning the information desk that I'd totally forgotten this file and did she know where Mr. Montefiore was because if I didn't get it to him, I was screwed?

The quiver in my voice was a nice touch.

The lovely gullible lady took pity on me and directed me up to the City Planning department, where I skulked in the hallway until Levi emerged chatting with a woman in a conservative blue dress.

"I appreciate you factoring in the unique needs of Nefesh in the overall livability plan proposed for Mount Pleasant," he said. "Having a preschool and community center that would allow these young kids freedom to master their magic without fear of hurting Mundanes would be an asset in this neighborhood."

I hadn't seen him in just over a week. As usual he was in an expensive suit that accentuated his leanly muscled frame, though he'd forgone a tie in favor of a shirt with the first button undone, exposing a very lickable collarbone. His raven-black hair, cut slightly longer on top than on the sides, was swept away from his face and slicked into submission, while his sharp jawline and cheekbones were softened by lush lips that had burned their way down my body.

I clutched my dummy file folder tighter. That was the

past. The present had to be different. I couldn't let emotion get in the way of the investigation.

I just wished it didn't make me feel like I was losing something important.

They shook hands and the woman retreated back into her department.

"Do you urban plan here, too?" I moved into his line of sight. "What a small world!"

Was I doomed to always smell the oaky amber scotch and chocolate scent of his magic? I only scented magic once a Nefesh used their powers, but Levi's was always there whenever he got all up in my personal space. It was, like many things about him, infuriating.

Levi let out an aggrieved sigh. "Is it stalker o'clock already?"

I fell into step with him. "Have you or the House had any dealings with Tannous Security?"

"Not that I know of."

"Where were you last night?"

Levi pulled up short for a second, but resumed his even stride. "Am I a suspect in something?"

"Answer the question."

"I was at home."

Did he have staff who could verify his alibi? "Alone?"

He paused before answering. "No."

Oh. Well, we'd never claimed to be exclusive frenemies with benefits. I wasn't an amateur and I didn't let my feelings get the best of me. Still, I hated the knot in my stomach when I asked, "Would she confirm that?"

And I hated it when he didn't contradict me to say it hadn't been a woman that he'd had over, and instead looked at the floor and said, "It's complicated."

Because of course we didn't matter to each other like that. For all the things that were exceptional about us, we were still just two people who had gotten caught up in an intense bonding situation that was now over. We were adults. It happened. The more important thing was the truth, and that meant the very real possibility that Levi was guilty and lying about his alibi.

"Ask anyway. It's important." Questioning his mystery lay was only slightly more appealing than a Brazilian wax, but it would be worse if he'd lied. However, if Levi wasn't involved, and the attacker was human, then either there was another illusionist from elsewhere, or what? There was no Nefesh flying magic, and everyone had agreed on the angel's winged departure.

"Was there anything else?" His voice dripped acid.

Our trust had been kicked into the gutter, but he didn't have to speak to me like he wanted to leave me there as well. I had a job to do, and Levi, of all people, should have appreciated me taking my work seriously. "Dropping the Jezebel's identity without follow-up was a dick move."

The sooner I got the information from him and cut him loose on that front, the better.

He shrugged, wrinkling the line of his blue pinstriped shirt. "You were the one who blew me off."

I swallowed hard against the memory of his weight on me, his skin hot against mine. "I. Was. Working. The world doesn't revolve around you."

"Mostly it does." Levi pulled the folder from my arms, noted the blank contents, and shoved it back. I smiled sunnily at him. "You tend to be the one irritating exception."

"You love it, Leviticus." Old habits died hard; I'd used my adolescent nickname for him that he despised, instead of the professionalism our situation demanded. "I mean, Levi." He shot me a weird look, which I ignored. "Since everyone else, and I quote, 'wants to kiss your ass or knock it down a peg.'"

"I rue the day I told you that." He bypassed the elevator for the stairs at the end of the long hallway. Fitness freak.

"Tough. No takebacks." I scurried after him. "Who's the Jezebel?"

All magic types had names. Metalheads could wrangle metal, Sirens had sexual attraction magic. I, apparently, was a Jezebel, capable of destroying the magic unleashed on the world back in the 1600s by a group of ten Jewish men representing the Ten Lost Tribes of Israel.

As devout practitioners of Kabbalah, they'd wanted to become one with the divine, or, in their terms, achieve the fifth and highest plane of the soul, Yechida. They just didn't want the years of studying it took. Like many a con, it fucked up big-time. Instead of them achieving full union with their god, Yahweh, the magic that they bestowed on about ten percent of the global population was rooted in the first level of the soul, Nefesh.

They failed their specific goal, but they still got powers, and blood magic was the one thing that could strip theirs away. Undermine it, the way that Jezebel in the Old Testament undermined the Jewish patriarchy with her continued insistence on the worship of the goddess Asherah—Yahweh's bride and the person I'd been named after.

Was my blood magic defensive? Offensive? Was I a pawn or a warrior? Did I get a choice either way? Those questions had plagued me since my abilities had activated.

I'd found one other Jezebel, that poor woman, chained up and forced to strip magic from innocent victims to create smudges. I'd rescued her, but the abuse she'd suffered had been too severe to make it out alive. Before she died, she said, "We looked for you," and that "we" had to stop Chariot. Occam's Razor and all. We equaled team.

Having the Jezebel's name was my first lead in tracking them down.

Once I found the others, I'd place my investigative abilities at their disposal on a part-time basis. Having it all, for me, meant a lifelong career as a Nefesh P.I. solving epic puzzles. I was willing to concede that outwitting Chariot did pose an interesting challenge, but the world was full of mysteries to unravel and I wasn't about to be pigeonholed into a single gig.

Who didn't love having a destiny dumped on them that in no way fit into one's five-year plan?

I poked Levi in the back. "The Jezebel?"

"Her name is Gavriella Behar." Levi pushed through the ground floor stairwell door into the lobby.

"And?" I winced as the door clipped me on the shoulder.

"She moved here fifteen years ago, right around the time your magic showed up. I guess we're going to see how deep this rabbit hole you've unearthed goes."

"We? This has nothing do with you."

Levi's eyes hardened to two blue crystals, his casual arrogance turning to an unquestioned power. "She lived in *my* territory all that time without registering and who the fuck knows what ramifications for *my* House are going to come to light. So, yeah. 'We.'"

This was not the "we" I'd had in mind.

I followed him to the limo waiting in a reserved parking spot, biting back my retort that he'd only been House Head for five of those fifteen years so maybe tone the drama down a notch.

I switched tactics. "You're not trained as an investigator. Let me root through her life and I'll share my findings with you."

"All your findings or just the ones you decide are relevant to me?"

I'd never withhold information that could actively hurt Levi or the House, but getting answers about Jezebels meant learning things about my magic. About me. Why did my life have to be an open book? His certainly wasn't.

Nor did I want it to be. Boundaries were a good thing. Especially with the power Levi held over me. As House Head. Or the power I held while investigating him. What a mess.

"I'll drown you in intel," I said sweetly.

"No need. I'll swim through the mass of information alongside you. Though the angelic smile was a nice touch."

I twigged on the word. Was this truly about consequences for his House or was he angling for a way to spend time with me to suss out my progress on Omar's case?

"Yay, a partner. Guess we're going together. I have my car."

"My apologies," Levi said.

I shot him the finger. "If you have Gavriella's address, I can follow you to her house to check it out, right after we make a pit stop. I need to lock up a dangerous magic artifact."

"Where's it now?"

"In my car." I deliberately didn't add that it was safely contained.

A muscle in his jaw ticked as he opened the back limo door. Heh. "Any other menial tasks I can assist you with?" he said.

"Not at the moment, but I'll keep you posted. You open your own limo door?"

He glanced at the driver's window and lowered his voice. "I let Simon do it at formal events but it's weird having someone else open it all the time. I have perfectly fine working hands." He grinned a pirate's grin, his white teeth flashing against his olive skin, looking utterly edible.

I clenched my jaw and silently chanted "suspect" three times. "Let's lock up the artifact and then you may chauffeur me."

"How generous. However, this'll have to wait until later," he said. "I'm busy."

I grabbed the top of the limo door. "You expect me to wait around until you slot me in?"

"Evidently." He got into the limo.

"I suppose giving me the address for a quick drive-by is out of the question?"

He shut the door on me.

How emblematic was that? Levi may have been a good ally at times and even the man who lit me up like no other, but when all was said and done, we understood each other too well. We saw ourselves in the other, both in how we breathed suspicion like oxygen and how we walked the thin line between monster and magic-user.

Much as I wished to deny it.

Even without the fact that I was investigating Levi, I didn't trust him. We'd worked together before, but there would always be walls between us. I'd been hurt enough by people who said that they trusted me and then couldn't follow through. I was done.

I shrugged off the hollowness in my chest and got in my car alone. Business as usual.

Chapter 5

Moriarty remained on his best behavior and started immediately, so I braced myself for my tire belt to break or something. Calling Priya on speakerphone, I rested my phone in the cup holder, then headed for my office.

"Hey, Adler," I said. A computer genius, I'd nicknamed my BFF "Adler" after both Irene Adler, the woman who'd bested Sherlock Holmes, and the brilliant hacker Raven Adler.

"Hey, Holmes," she replied. "Good timing. I just got out of the meeting."

"How'd it go?"

"Hang on." She ordered a warmed-up cinnamon bun and a large chai, before checking in with the employee about how his daughter was enjoying camp with her school this week.

I bemoaned people; Priya befriended them.

"Are you at Higher Ground?" I peered through the windshield at the dark cloud that had suddenly obscured the sun.

"I am."

"A treat, not a consolation, I hope?" I braked hard and hit my horn, flipping off the asshole who'd cut me off.

"Big time treat."

For the past several months, Priya had been working freelance building a complicated database for a high-end restaurant group. Not only had they worked her overtime and then some with all their dithering and changes, they'd had the gall to mansplain coding to her.

"I kept my happy face on while those douchenozzles did their debrief," she said, "and now I am free!"

The entire sky was darkening.

"Are we having a solar eclipse?" I said.

"No, dumbass. I really made it out of there without biting anyone's head off. You may now heap upon me glorious praise."

I bit my lip. Priya thought I was joking, and the other drivers and pedestrians didn't seem perturbed by the rapidly failing sun. I probed my head for any injury from my fight with Moran, but didn't find anything. "Mazel tov on being a free agent once more. Did you get any dirt on the Tannouses or Dershowitzes?"

Priya was also my part-time employee and I'd left her a note this morning to look into them before I'd set out, without going into specifics of the case.

"Piece of cake. Ooh. I should have cake, too."

"You totally should. Bring me home a piece."

Part of West Georgia was shut down for a film shoot, so I zigzagged through the downtown streets until I could turn onto East Hastings and immediately came to a standstill in construction. I rolled down my window but other than the deepening night, everything sounded, looked, and smelled completely normal.

"Eh," she said. "What have you done to deserve cake?"

"Grounded your naturally upbeat and open nature with my wary regard of the world since we were fifteen and kept

56

you from being pulled into a serial killer's sex van with promises of puppies and candy." How was no one else seeing the world had gone dark?

"But is that cake-worthy?" Priya snickered, sounding like an asthmatic braying donkey, which made me laugh, all too clearly picturing the stares that my gorgeous five-foot-ten friend was drawing with that horrific noise emanating from her.

I flicked my headlights on high because it was as dark as midnight now, but the beams merely cast a sickly weak circle. People carried on normally around me and Priya gave no sign of witnessing unusual activity. If I wasn't concussed, was I losing my grip on reality? This was not a good time to take a break from sanity, what with not wanting to commit vehicular manslaughter and the Queen expecting results.

"I met Grandmother Tannous, the brother, and a cousin, but no parents of the vic." I kept all traces of panic out of my voice, looking for a break in the orange traffic cones to pull over.

"They were killed in a car accident a few years back. Drunk driver." Priya swallowed her bite of cinnamon bun. "Tannous Security has a sterling reputation. They are very equal opportunity mercenaries. Sorry, high risk security specialists. They've done jobs for corporations, private citizens, and shady dictators." She spoke around a second mouthful of cinnamon bun. "Talk on the dark net is that this was an arranged marriage. The good Rebbe stands to get a much-needed infusion of cash. He's been living on serious credit. Jacob the Shark, not Bank of Canada."

"I gotta get myself a good nickname." I took a hard right, cutting across a newly repaired patch of asphalt to bump against the curb. "So it was this marriage or broken legs."

It was imperative that I hang on to this conversation, to

this normality, because I didn't trust what would happen when I ended it.

"Pretty much."

"If Ivan is that desperate?" I put the car in park, scanning for any other changes. "He wouldn't sabotage the wedding. What's in it for the Tannous family? They're Mundanes. Legally, they can't provide security for Nefesh clients, and if they're doing it illegally already, what do they need Ivan for?"

"Expansion and long-term planning," Priya said. "Ivan opens up North America for them. Husani is engaged to a Nefesh woman, and Chione will probably follow."

"They're thinking legacy, next generation. Get some Nefesh kids and that part of the business no longer has to operate in the shadows."

"They get a better class of clientele and can charge more," Priya said.

One of the roadside workers approached my vehicle, yelling at me to move.

I held up a finger. "If Husani and Chione are willing to marry Nefesh partners, then they're onboard with the plan. They wouldn't want Omar killed and their expansion put at risk. Even if someone in the Tannous family had a grudge against Omar as the heir, none of them have magic."

"They could have contracted out."

"Possibly, but that's risky. These guys deal in security. They're going to be extremely paranoid and cautious."

The worker rapped on my window. Behind him, a dense fog rolled in, obscuring everything. I couldn't be losing my mind and still be thinking lucidly about this case. Something else was afoot.

"Good times," Priya said. "I'll keep digging. Anything else?"

I pointed at my phone and motioned that I was wrapping it up. The worker stomped off.

"Make a list of all references in the Old Testament to the Angel of Death and what the reasons for his appearance were," I said. "And check for any connections between the families and House Pacifica or Levi personally." He would never have hired them in his business dealings but that didn't mean someone else hadn't pointed them Levi's way to screw him over somehow. He wouldn't take kindly to that.

"Not what I expected, but okay. I'm going to glut myself on sugar now, so I'll see you at home. Laters, Holmes."

"Pri, wait!" But she'd disconnected.

The world around me vanished, lost to the fog.

I squeezed my eyes tight, then opened them wide, but the familiar Vancouver streets failed to reappear.

Sit here like a chump or get out of the car like a chump? Both such appealing choices.

I opened my car door and stood up, one hand braced on the top in case I had to jump back inside. The air was cooler with a damp mulchy smell, and the only sound was the wind rustling leaves.

Hang on. Leaves?

Arms outstretched, I lurched forward like a zombie. In seconds, Moriarty was obscured by the mists that enveloped me. The ground was spongy beneath my feet. I knelt down and came away with dirt on my fingertips.

Creeping slowly onwards, I brushed something rough and screamed, my brain taking a second to process the texture under my fingertips. Bark.

"Listen up, jackass that brought me here. If you were hoping to make me question my sanity, you fucked up because I am a city chick and trees would never figure prominently in any hallucination. Show yourself and let's get on with your nefarious agenda."

The wind picked up, whipping my hair around my eyes, but it also dissipated the fog.

I stood in a grove that was totally devoid of the Douglas

firs, cedars, and pines found in my corner of the world. Leafy pomegranate trees hung heavy with fruit, feathery palms bore clusters of dates, and in the center of it all, a massive, sprawling tree covered in pink blossoms emitted this intoxicating buttery, honey scent.

I backed up against the pink blossom tree, its sturdy trunk a comfort at my back. "Come out, come out, whoever you are."

The air chilled and I tightened the belt on my trench coat, wishing for my leather jacket.

A table appeared in front of me with three bowls. One had cut diamonds the size of candy rings, one had gold coins, and the third… I squinted. Almonds? Seriously?

"You want me to choose." I sighed. "This is a no-brainer. Myth and legend dictate that you pick the most unassuming one." I picked up the almond bowl and tossed a handful of nuts into my mouth. "Needs salt," I said to the heavens. "Now what?"

Three blurry shadows burst out of nowhere to fly toward me.

I dropped the bowl, scattering almonds at my feet. What the fuck? Smudges? How were they floating free?

Magic danced under my skin.

The smudges blew up to enormous proportions and rushed me with a moaning sound that rattled my bones. For ghostly blobs, they did a great job of smothering me. I blindly fired my blood magic into them like gunshot, their darkness blinding me.

There was no maggoty sensation. If anything, they tasted dusty. Also, they didn't stink of death and feces like the other ones I'd encountered. Again, just dust.

I anchored them in place enough to pull myself free of their embrace, staggering back against the force of them thrashing against my red forked branches. It wasn't three times the effort, it was to the power of three, and I'd already fought the feather magic and Moran.

Black spots peppered my vision and the branches shook. The world narrowed down to a long tunnel with me at one end and the smudges at the other. On the verge of passing out, my head lolled back then snapped up.

One of the smudges reached a tentacle out. I skittered backward because no way was that thing making me its new host, but it didn't try to invade me. It wrapped its tentacle around my throat and squeezed.

Choking: an equally suck-ass option to possession, and yet more disturbing because it didn't follow known behavior.

I couldn't tear free, so I let the white clusters bloom, hoping I'd trapped the shadows enough to destroy them.

Two of the smudges, including the choke-happy one, were eaten up by the clusters, but one remained.

I collapsed onto my knees, one hand pressed to my side. It hurt to breathe and the outside of my throat burned.

The smudge broke free and zoomed toward me.

Hands over my head, I enclosed myself in a thicket of my red branches, their points sticking up. The smudge flew into it and snagged.

Clusters exploded on the branches, nuking the final smudge.

I stayed on my knees, my head bent and sweat running down my neck. Why the new variety of smudge, and how were they stable enough to exist without a host? They hadn't tried to set up shop inside me; they wanted me dead.

Was the amped-up attack because I was the only one who could see them? In coming to this grove, had I somehow torn the magic from some innocent Nefesh?

I clapped my hands over my ears against the memory of the tortured cries from the last person I'd taken magic from. Did every passing second that I moved through the world in ignorance of what being a Jezebel truly meant, make me the greatest threat out there?

My fingers flexed in the dirt. The only sound in the grove was my ragged breaths until a sharp snap echoed off the trees.

A man stood a few feet away, hands planted on his hips, but he flickered in and out of view like a hazy outline. I only got impressions of color: his short brown hair, a red bow tie, a blurry red-and-black argyle pattern on his chest.

If this shitshow hadn't been accidentally orchestrated by yours truly, that left three possibilities as to his identity: 1) he was a member of Team Jezebel, 2) the smudges were an illusion, making him a Houdini, or 3) he had nothing to do with the smudges, angels did exist, and someone had pulled me into a heavenly grove because he wanted his ancient feather back.

I was going to be so pissed if it was door number three.

"Ashira Cohen. Small-time private investigator with big-time aspirations." The man's image wavered and his British-accented voice went staticky. "You're no Jezebel. Stick with what you're good at."

I made a choking noise and pushed to my feet. Hell no. This across-the-pond dork did not get to insult my abilities. Even the ones I didn't want. "Think you've got me pegged?"

He shrugged. "Daddy issues. Anger issues. How's the leg?"

A fourth, more chilling explanation of who he was slithered into my brain.

Chariot. They'd had one Jezebel under their control, who's to say they didn't have more, forced to produce these smudges?

I flicked a sweaty lock out of my eyes. "What do you want?"

"For you to live a long and happy life running your detective agency. Full stop."

"I really hate being told what to do." I cracked my knuckles. "I defeated your smudges and you're a lot less imposing than they are."

"Yes, you obviously have the goods, interesting though your technique was." He didn't sound pleased about my powers.

"What are you? My own personal Statler and Waldorf? Listen, you want to throw down, I'm game if—" The rest of my words came out in a staticky screech that had me clamping my hands over my ears.

"You'd have to find me to take me on." He stepped toward me but I held my ground. "You're a Seeker—"

"Actually, I'm a Scorpio," I said.

"Wisecracks won't win you the day. You're out of your league. Give up before you find yourself broken and tortured like—" His remaining words were more static noise, but I got the gist. "If you can get out, that is."

He disappeared.

Evil. Wanker.

I took stock of my surroundings, tugging on branches and pressing knots on trunks. No convenient portal opened and I didn't sense any magic in the trees themselves. I stamped on the dirt a couple of times but the ground was firm under my feet, and above me, the treetops were obscured by more fog.

I sat on the table. The bowls were gone so I couldn't even use one of the diamonds to try and carve or dig my way out, and if there were any kindly magical woodland creatures, I had no gold to trade them for passage.

Get a grip, Ash. This isn't a fairy tale.

I stilled. But it was a test. Three of them, to be precise. The bowls, the smudges, and getting out of here. Evil Wanker hadn't expected me to defeat the smudges and now he hoped I'd be stranded.

Fuck that. I was the Girl Who Lived, not the Girl Who

Languished in Some Shitty Alternate Reality Until She Tried to Gnaw Her Own Arm off from Hunger and Subsequently Died.

Unfortunately, physically leaving the grove proved impossible. After a certain distance, I simply bounced back to the center under the big tree. A magic ward. I smiled. Now we were in my wheelhouse.

I walked toward the ward slowly, counting out my steps. At number sixty-five, I was bounced back. I retraced them, stopping at sixty-four. Squatting down, I inched my hands forward in the dirt.

There it was. Magic sang to me. When magic was activated, alive or dying, it had a taste and a smell, other than the smudges here in the grove which was a puzzle for later. In the same way that a stinky person couldn't smell themselves, I couldn't discern the taste and smell of my own magic, but what pulsed up now was the copper tang of old pennies.

Or blood.

Evil Wanker apparently did have a Jezebel doing his bidding. This magic club I'd found myself a member of had a disturbingly high capture rate.

One of the pink blossoms drifted lazily by on the breeze.

Oh. Autumn's reading. A person who would help me with my transformation and an almond tree. I hadn't recognized the scenario playing out here because the painting of the tree on the card only bore the vaguest resemblance to the actual thing and I'd assumed that the person would be a mentor figure, but evil enemy worked, too.

Autumn was going to be insufferable if she learned what had come to pass. Well, that wouldn't happen unless I got out of here.

I hooked my magic into the ward, making short work of it, and immediately wished for it back. An endless void stretched out in front of me, the grove a tiny island in its midst.

"Tests, leaps of faith, we are having a strongly worded discussion about your love of myth and legend when I find you, asshole."

I edged forward, my toes peeking off the dirt into empty space. My poor damaged throat grew tight and I struggled to drag in air. I liked answers. Certainty. Not massive fucking chasms. Was this another test? One where I was supposed to throw myself bodily into the void and believe?

I tried to shuffle forward but I was locked in place, my heart hammering in my ears. I wiped my damp palms on my jeans.

Fine. I'd do this, but I'd do it on my terms. Blind faith was for chumps and fanatics. Freeing myself involved belief and ability. I had that. I was capable.

A lonely howl echoed out in the distance.

Much as love was not enough to make a marriage work, given the roughly 30% divorce rate, my capabilities felt puny compared to the vast darkness yawning out before me. I had no trouble believing in myself, but this was the next move in an ongoing game and I'd only stumbled onto the board as a pawn.

I straightened up, my head held high. Even a pawn could be crowned queen.

"I am not a mark!" I hollered and threw myself into the brink.

Wind rushed past my face.

Falling … Falling …

It lasted mere seconds and a whole eternity.

HOOOOOONNNNK!

A car pinned me in its headlights, impact imminent.

I threw my hands over my head, bracing for death, with no angel in sight. At least I'd been right about that.

Chapter 6

A firm body rushed me, knocking me to the concrete and I blinked into the stormy blue of Levi's unamused gaze.

"You didn't happen to try and kill me with your illusion magic?" I said. "Say in a grove in an indeterminate reality?"

His body blanketed mine. I was safe. His hands felt so right curled up against my sides, holding me like I was something precious, and cars passed as I was caught between a road and a deliciously hard place.

My breathing kicked up when Levi turned his head to whisper in my ear, "The day you push me to a non-negotiable act of homicide, I promise you'll see my face."

It sounded like that day might come sooner rather than later.

I shoved him off me. "Really? I always figured you for a knife in the dark kind of guy."

It was evening and I was back at my car. Judging from the fallen traffic cone, I'd exited the almond tree reality and come back to this one right in the middle of the street. If Levi hadn't been there, hadn't knocked me into the construction area—my whole body shuddered at the crushing memory of those headlights.

Levi seized me by the collar. "What the fuck, Ash?"

"Leave her alone. Can't you see she's shaking?" Priya knocked Levi's hands off me, but from the tight grim line of her lips, it was only because she planned to kill me herself. Her green eyes flashed as she draped a blanket over my shoulders. "You've been missing for hours. Your phone was in your jacket so I tracked Moriarty, but you were gone."

I grabbed her arm. "Did you open the evidence box?"

"No." She tugged free, flashing her pink-and-black lotus tattoo on the inside of her right wrist. It matched the pink tunic and leggings that she wore with a black swing coat. Gold rings with rosy tints glinted on her fingers.

"Good. There's a dangerous magic artifact in there."

"It's still not locked up?" A vein pulsed in Levi's throat.

"Shoot me, I was kind of busy." I stomped over to my car and popped the trunk. "There. Happy? The lock is keyed to my thumbprint and the box is bolted to the trunk. Plus the artifact is sealed inside a special container. It's not a danger to anyone right now." I tossed my filthy trench coat in the trunk, but my remaining clothes weren't much better.

The ground felt precariously like quicksand under my feet. I clutched the edge of the trunk, letting the sharp corner bite into my flesh. Once more, I was unsettled by a feeling of being watched, but the sidewalks were empty. I was getting paranoid.

"What is it?" Levi said.

I tsked him. "Client-P.I. confidentiality, you should know that by now, dude."

And you're still on the suspect list.

"I meant what's wrong?" he said. "What happened? Where did you come from?"

My legs gave way and I crashed on my ass onto the bumper. "Tests, leaps into the void, mysterious Evil Wankers." I eyed him. "That part isn't new."

67

"I've upgraded to mysterious? Be still my beating heart," Levi said dryly.

Priya elbowed him aside to check my eyes.

"I don't have a concussion," I said.

"You're babbling. You should get checked out."

"No!" I calmed my voice. "I mean, no thank you. You know hospitals are a last resort. I just need time to process that bit at the end."

"Talking about it will help." Levi peered into the trunk like he could X-ray vision the lock box. "Start with the artifact."

"That has nothing to do with any of this." I slammed the trunk closed.

"Start with it anyway."

"Quit running roughshod over my life. Are you poking into all the other Nefesh investigators' cases or am I the only one with that privilege?"

And does it have anything to do with the fact that I'm the only one who suspects you of attempted murder?

Priya stood at my shoulder, a warrior in all-pink. "Good question."

I grinned at her. Best friends ruled.

Levi wiped a smear of dirt off his suit, the same kind that was on my hands and must have come from the grove. He'd ruined a suit to protect me. "I'll do whatever I have to in order to keep my community safe."

That's what I was afraid of. Especially if Omar's attack was precipitated by a perceived threat to Levi's Nefesh.

"Would there be any length you wouldn't go to?" I growled. "Because I really don't want a constant, very-high-profile shadow."

Levi shrugged. "If you don't like it, tough."

I dug in my jeans pocket for my keys, which luckily were still there. "You keep saying that, but I don't think that's the entire story."

"What else would there be?" he said.

With Omar, possibly something far more sinister. However, when it came to him making himself part of my inquiries on all things Jezebel, the answer was simple. "You're bored and want to play Scooby Doo in my life because it's way more fun than being House Head."

He looked visibly discombobulated for a hot ten seconds. It was the life goal I never knew I'd had. "You're casting me as a dog in this delusion of yours?" he said.

"Naw." I opened my door. "You're Shaggy."

Priya wrestled me for the keys, insisting that I was in no condition to drive.

I pulled them away. "Priya, please. I'm hurt, but I'm not concussed. I'm cogent and it's going to make me feel worse if I'm not in control."

She sighed and took the passenger seat. "Which of Scooby's friends are you?"

"I'm not in this cartoon. That's Levi's schtick." I gave Moriarty my superstitious double pat and whispered, "Who's a good boy?"

The car started, but before I could pull away, Levi clambered into the back seat.

"Did all you people take transit?" I checked the side and rearview mirrors, then signaled. "Why are you here?"

"Priya called me," he said.

"Gee, you didn't invite my mother to complete the welcoming party?" I said to Pri.

"Talia didn't have security people who could look for you," she said.

My turn signal ticked twice before I came up with a response.

"You did that?" I glanced quickly over my shoulder, addressing Levi.

"The sooner you were found, the less trouble you could get into. I like things peaceful."

I snorted. "Even so, I appreciate that. Both of you." The roadside workers had gone home, so I steered myself back into traffic. "But Levi, if you aren't going to respect my boundaries, Priya is going to make your life a living hell."

Boundaries were important, especially while I was investigating him for attempted murder. Did he know that Omar was alive?

I studied him in the rearview mirror. Levi appeared wrung-out and a bit annoyed, but not especially concerned about anything. Despite our history, at his core, I believed him a good man, but good men could be pushed to evil action.

Priya had removed a tube of pink lip gloss out of her purse and pulled down the visor to reveal the mirror. "Why do I have to do the heavy lifting? Make his life hell yourself."

"Work with me here."

She tucked a strand of her jet black bob behind her ear and applied the gloss. "Isn't threatening the dude foreplay between you two?"

"Jesus, Pri," I hissed, inadvertently glancing in the rearview mirror for Levi's reaction. Not that I discussed details of my sex life with Priya, but guys thought we did.

He pinched the bridge of his nose, his eyes rolled so far back they were practically all-white.

"Less attitude from the peanut gallery, Mr. Montefiore. No one lured you into the car." I drove through light traffic to my office. "I'm starting to rethink your open door invitation as well," I said to Priya.

"I'm just saying. You are not without resources, Ms. Jezebel," she said, rubbing her lips together to even the color out, which popped against her brown skin.

"You want me to take his magic? That's cold, even for—"

"Enough already. I beg you," Levi said.

Priya twisted around in the passenger seat. "That's a mild pleading at best. Put some effort into it."

I snickered.

Levi draped his arms over the backrest. "You win. Your cases are off-limits unless you share, but you asked if I tried to kill you with illusion magic, so perhaps I have some useful insights on whatever happened to you?"

"Pri? What do you think?"

She twisted the cap back on the gloss. "Three brains are better than one."

"Two and change," I said, still mad at Levi, even if he had a point.

"Drive, Ash," he said. So, I did.

Cohen Investigations was part of a shared work space on the second floor of a five-story walk-up with exposed brick, original oak floors, and cool steel cross-bracings that ran through the building, allowing it to sway in an earthquake should the Big One hit. It also had a view of an alley and cockroaches that I was on a first name basis with, but I didn't care. The second I saw the gold stenciling on my office door, my heart got a jolt of happiness.

The feather's hold on me had finally faded, so it was no problem—but still much relief—that I locked up the pouch in my safe, an obnoxious iron box about knee-height in the corner that weighed close to three hundred pounds. I'd inherited it from the previous tenant.

The longing for that feather magic had amped the regular song of desire playing endlessly in my brain from a three to an eight, so it was nice to have the volume tuned down again. My love of Sherlock stopped short of being an addict in homage.

My office was pretty basic: two desks, a couple of chairs for clients, and two filing cabinets. The only personal items were a framed photo of Priya and me graduating university on my desk that faced my chair, the dartboard hanging on the wall, and a mug reading "Baker Street Boys" that was crammed with pens—half of which didn't work, but I had yet to throw out. It had started as laziness but then turned into some weird dead pen collection that I just kept unconsciously adding to.

Levi and Priya had gone to pick up sushi from a small restaurant down the block, which was good because today had been so insane, I hadn't had a chance to go food shopping or grab something to eat. I did a quick sponge-down in the restroom and changed into one of my undercover outfits. By the time I returned to my office, the food was spread out over our two desks, and Levi and Priya had already tucked in.

"Not one word." I clomped over to my chair in my motorcycle boots and eased into my chair, adjusting my weight to compensate for the one wonky wheel that was Crazy Glued on.

Levi's grin was pure unholy glee. "Did my invitation to your wedding at the cult compound get lost in the mail? You and your sister-wives must have made such fetching brides for the charismatic leader."

"Ha. Ha." I snapped my wooden chopsticks in two. "My options were limited." To a white dress with a fitted bodice, puffy sleeves, and a ruffled hem that hit at the most unflattering point of my mid-calf.

"Limited because you don't do laundry and it was the only thing left in your costume bag," Priya said.

"This dress conveys sweet and innocent. I'll have you know it served its purpose admirably when I had to get some information out of a very nice grandmother at a senior's home."

"What kind?" Levi draped his suit jacket over the moss green wingback chair that was set out for clients. "How to churn butter and build a log cabin?"

"You can't have it both ways." I shoveled in my first piece of salmon sashimi. "Am I a cult escapee or Laura Ingalls Wilder?"

"Hard to say. They both have merit."

I wolfed down the rest of the sashimi order, the protein kicking in enough to relay the story of the grove and my suspicions about dealing with Chariot.

To say that Levi wasn't happy about any of it was an understatement. He stirred wasabi into his soy sauce with enough force that he was in constant danger of spattering my desk. "We need to figure out who that man was and verify any connection to Chariot. Perhaps that will give us some insights into their overall agenda."

"Start by determining if the grove was real or an illusion." My hands shook, phantom wind rushing past my face, but I covered it by stuffing them under my butt. If it was an illusion, it had felt absolutely real, but I guess that would defeat the point otherwise. "If we can establish his magic type, it could help track him down."

I wasn't ready to share my tarot experience about a stranger helping me manifest my life's purpose. If I even believed in that stuff, I'd have hoped for a mentor figure, not a fresh nemesis like Evil Wanker, but oh well. Tarot cards weren't proof of squat, so I'd work this angle like any other case, putting the puzzle together piece by piece.

"He called you a Seeker." Priya reached for a dynamite roll with an elegance of motion missing in my frantic eating and Levi's anger. "It's a weird way to describe you, especially from an enemy, but it's similar to being a P.I."

"He had the cheat sheet to my life." I opened a browser on my battered laptop, searching out any relevant symbolism of diamonds, gold, and almonds. "Levi, could the grove have been Houdini magic? The smudges didn't smell or behave like they normally do."

"It's possible it was illusion magic." He hated the colloquial term for his type of power. "Whoever cast it might have been misinformed about smudges' behavior."

"Like when you totally abused your privileges and

tricked me into thinking I was fighting one during our training session?"

Levi speared a piece of spicy scallop roll. "I was trying to help jolt you out of a defeatist mindset. What's the motivation here?"

"Testing to see if I'm really a Jezebel before they capture and kill me? Could the guy have been the caster?"

"Again, sure." Levi ate his piece of sushi, licking an errant drop of soy sauce off his lips.

Priya kicked me under the table and I tore my eyes away to untangle the ginger in the plastic takeout container.

"His image might have wavered because he'd overtaxed himself with the smudge illusion," Levi said. "But that's only part of the puzzle."

I heaped white slivers of ginger on to another piece of sashimi, scanning the current page loaded on my screen. "How so?"

As someone who'd lived her entire life as a Mundane, I only had a cursory knowledge about different abilities. Learning more about Houdini magic was fascinating to me. I made a note to get some reading from Elke, the librarian at House Pacifica, because if I was going to be pursuing Nefesh cases, then having a broader understanding of magic would be useful.

"When I cast the illusion that I was fighting Rick at Robson Square, everyone saw it," Levi said.

He'd hidden the fact that I was destroying a smudge in front of a captive audience. To keep my magic a secret, Levi had convinced everyone, including the news cameras, that it was him. Most of the hoopla over Levi's amazingness had died down, but his actions still merited the occasional mention on the news.

"Illusionists can direct their magic to a single person," Levi said, "but you were in a moving vehicle. Unless he was in the car with you, he couldn't target you that specifically.

The illusion would have been broadcast more widely and other people would have seen it or at least seen the dark sky and fog when it was first conjured. However, there were no odd reports of anything while you were gone. Miles was monitoring things from that end. Then you reappeared out of nowhere."

Miles Berenbaum was Levi's best friend and in charge of House security.

"Ash was taken somewhere," Priya said.

"A teleporter partnered up with an illusionist?" he said.

My stomach lurched. A member of Chariot had gotten into a jail cell at House Pacifica via teleporting and killed a man.

Levi dropped his chopsticks on his plate, his expression grim. "The grove itself could have been an illusion, even if you were transported."

I clicked through some more search results, then chuckled. "Get this. Dreaming of almonds can symbolize something precious. Usually related to sex. Maybe I just had a very vivid and unfulfilling sex dream."

"At least you got a snack," Priya propped her chin in her hands. "Sometimes, I'd trade the sex for a really satisfying nosh."

"TMI. And get a better partner," Levi said.

I steered us back onto the topic at hand. My enemy Levi, who I was in a weird thing with, already fit too easily into my life. Having Priya and him get cozy like besties was a no-go. "The almond tree was in a position of prominence in the grove. To what end?"

I searched "almonds and Jezebel" but didn't find anything useful. "Hmm. The almond tree is mentioned in the Old Testament in relation to menorahs." I scanned the page, then sat up sharply.

"What?" Priya leaned forward.

"The menorah is a symbol of the Tree of Life. Guess

who's connected to the Tree as well? Asherah." I'd done some research on both her and Jezebel lately. "Of course. Her temples were often groves."

I slumped back in my seat, wishing the connection to Chariot wasn't falling into place so easily.

"That's not the only thing the Tree of Life is connected to. Don't you guys remember your magic unit?" Priya said.

"From grade eight? I'm going with no," Levi said.

"Kabbalah." She whipped open her pink laptop and quickly typed, nodding to herself. "Yeah. This. Sephirot. They're the ten attributes God created and are visually represented as nodes on a tree. The Kabbalistic Tree of Life."

I drummed my fingers on my keyboard. "The original ten who unleashed magic were practitioners of Kabbalah, and when Yitzak first warded my magic, he used a Star of David tattoo."

"They also put a Star of David necklace on the sketch of Lillian and Santino circulated to the press," Levi said. They had been our undercover personas on the smudge case.

"Yeah." I stuffed a piece of spicy scallop roll down. "I'd asked Yitzak if it was a code. He didn't confirm or deny, but he spouted passages about Jezebel from the Old Testament, as did Mr. Sharp."

"Sharp worked for whoever was selling the smudges, right?" Priya said.

Levi nodded. "The same people who likely ordered and carried out Yitzak's murder. It had to be Chariot."

"The probability of this being a religious organization was already high, but what if specifically it's Kabbalah?" Priya spun her screen to us. "The first search result for Kabbalah and Chariot."

"Merkavah, derived from the Hebrew word for chariot, is the description the prophet Ezekiel gave to God's moving throne." I read on. "A school of early Jewish mysticism, named after the visions in the Book of Ezekiel. It's Kabbalah.

Blah blah blah. What were these visions? Glad you asked. Trippy creatures with four faces, flying wheels, then he does a virtual tour of a temple and witnesses some cult sex… I mean, if you're going to name your organization after an unreliable narrator, this is absolutely the dude you want."

"The connection to Chariot feels pretty solid," Priya said. "What now?"

"We visit Gavriella's apartment and find something to connect me with the rest of my tribe."

Levi pulled on his suit jacket. "Later tonight. I promised Miriam I'd stop by the opening of Le Rêve and I have to change."

"Wait. You mean *Chef* Miriam's new restaurant?" Priya tossed a chopstick at me. "How come you don't have friends like that?"

"Sure, she does," Levi said. "Miriam is a Camp Ruach alum." Camp Ruach was the Jewish summer camp I'd attended with Levi and Miles from ages thirteen to eighteen. Miriam had gone too.

"You guys were tight," I said. "We just bunked together."

"What's she like?" Priya said. "Was she a mean girl?"

I shook my head. "More very focused on things that interested her and no real attention for anything else." Like when she'd dated Miles for a year in their early twenties.

"That settles it," Levi said. "I'll meet you there, say at nine? Then we'll head over to Gavriella's apartment."

Why wait? Also, Levi was either way over-confident in my abilities to score hot opening night tickets via a years-past acquaintanceship, or, more likely, had forgotten that not everyone lived in his rarified world where all he had to do was snap his fingers and even the cliqueyest of circles happily admitted him.

How long would I be stuck hanging around until he'd made the rounds of his many admirers? And of course, any news outlets would want to grab him and spotlight the

House Head out on the town. Was this a "plus one" situation? Would his female companion be there with him?

I pushed my plate of sushi away. I'd text him from outside.

We walked him out to the common reception area and said our goodbyes.

Eleanor, the flaky graphic designer who ran one of the three businesses in our shared work space, along with Bryan, an insurance agent, strolled out of the kitchen with a tea cup.

Usually, I'd have given her a chin nod, but she'd been away traveling and I was trying my best to engage more so that Priya didn't bear the brunt of my human interactions.

"Hey," I said. "Good trip in Southeast Asia?"

Eleanor blew on the steaming tea, looking faintly surprised. "Yeah. It was amazing."

She took a deep breath like she was about to launch into details.

I cut her off with a "Great. Gotta debrief."

Priya patted my shoulder. "Baby steps."

Chapter 7

"You can't get us in to Le Rêve, can you?" Priya pouted as we sorted takeout detritus between the kitchen garbage can and recycling bins. She'd enthusiastically asked Eleanor detailed questions based on the itinerary that Pri had seen exactly one time, until I'd dragged her away to help me clean up.

"Nope. Sorry. Who needs a trendy loud restaurant anyway? We have our own celebration right here." I opened the fridge and pulled out a bottle. "To your being free of the douchenozzles."

Priya fluttered her hands around her face. "Your 'touch this and die' Prosecco that you've had sitting in the fridge for a year? I'm all verklempt."

I ripped the yellow Post-It note, with precisely that warning written in felt pen, off of the bottle and grabbed a corkscrew and two Red Solo cups. "You're worth it, baby."

"Plus you'll never actually sell Moriarty and toast his departure." Priya popped the cork and poured the Prosecco.

"True. But you're still worth it."

We clinked glasses. "L'chaim!"

Taking the bottle, we headed back into our office.

I slid off my motorcycle boots, wiggling my toes with a sigh, and swung my feet on the desk. "Look into White Rabbit Man as a Russian citizen. Also, we're calling him Moran now. Don't ask."

After a bunch of attempts to figure out the spelling, I'd Googled the word "okhuyet" and learned it was a Russian expression of shock or surprise. "Also check if there's anything tying either the Dershowitz or Tannous families to the Queen. But be careful. Don't send up any red flags that you're looking into them."

"That's insulting," she said, already typing. "Updates with the murder case?"

"It's downgraded to attempted murder."

"How does one go from murder to attempted murder? Forgetting to check the pulse? Zombies? Vampires? Some other new and exciting fantastic creature?"

"Nope. A feather that makes people crazy and a fake Angel of Death."

"Ah yes, the Old Testament references. I emailed them to you. How do you know it's fake? A couple weeks ago you didn't think golems existed either," Priya said.

"True, but those are man-made and I think people are capable of most anything." I pulled up the website for Tannous Security on my phone. "If there was an Angel of Death, there should have been an actual death, don't you think? I expect celestial assassins to meet minimum standards."

"Point taken."

I snickered. "To borrow from Sherlock, we have the Curious Incident of the Angel of Death."

"Except there is no Angel of Death."

"That's what makes it curious." The Tannous business website announced that they specialized in high risk security and provided a contact email. That was it. "The Tannous site is pretty sparse."

"They don't keep electronic records either. Or none that are connected to the Net."

"What about House Pacifica? Did you find a connection? Or anything in Levi's personal affairs?" I opened the email she'd sent about Angel of Death references.

"The House has a lot of vendors. Going through all of them would take ages, but there's nothing for Tannous Security in the past couple months."

"And Levi?"

Priya took a much longer swig than necessary. "No."

"You found something, though." I glazed over reading the first few references in the email. Death to the non-believers, yadda yadda yadda.

"I widened the search to his dad. Isaac Montefiore owns Lockdown Cybersecurity, a large data security firm, specializing in crypto and cybersecurity including data mining. There's no sign of specific dealings with the Tannous family, but check out this photo from last year's Technology and Cybersecurity Conference in London."

"Masika and Isaac." Admittedly, they were in a group of people and not even standing next to each other, but at the very least they had a passing acquaintance. "There's no love lost between Levi and his father. If Isaac hired Tannous Security and Omar was sent to sabotage Levi in some way, could it have triggered Levi into this bizarre ritualized killing?"

"You know him better than I do."

He considered himself a monster. Could a monster become an Angel of Death? I scrolled through the rest of the references she'd emailed. "Malach was the Messenger of Death. The Destroyer. Destroy your enemies."

Priya pushed her laptop away and rolled her shoulders out. "I'm running a script I wrote, searching for matches to the info you've given me already on Moran. Meantime, what's the deal with the feather?"

"It has compulsion magic, but it affected me differently from others. It tempts Nefesh and Mundanes with their heart's desire, at least it did with Omar and Moran, though it didn't have that effect on me. I had to hook into its magic and even then, it wasn't about temptation, I just wanted to devour the magic. It was freaky."

"Because you're a very freaky girl."

We simultaneously broke into the chorus of "Super Freak."

I'd been branded a freak after my accident. It had steeled my resolve to live on my terms, but I feared this strange magic might break me.

The last words of the chorus died on my lips.

"Whoever attacked Omar didn't take the feather," I said. "They used it to try and kill him."

"If they left it behind, then they weren't affected by its temptation magic," Priya said.

"If Levi happened to have the artifact on hand, and if he was the attacker, he *couldn't* have left it behind. It rules him out, but that's a lot of 'ifs.'" My head was going to explode. "That aside, it's an odd choice for a murder weapon, given how slowly the magic was strangling Omar."

"Why?" Priya kicked off her shoes.

"If you want someone dead, use a fast-acting method. Or, if you want to make a point and the feather was relevant in some way, you kidnap the target and keep them in a controlled environment to be sure it did the job. Also, do your research. Our suspect went after his target in a house armed to the teeth. Either because they're invincible and a real Angel of Death, in which case they should've done their damn job and killed Omar properly, or it's a case of human sloppiness." I tossed my phone down and reached for my Prosecco. "I need someone to verify exactly what this magic is and whether it was placed on some ordinary bird's feather or it's something else entirely."

"Like an angel's feather?"

"I would rather that not be the case. No Angel of Death should equate to no angels period."

"Your formal logic is flawed."

"What else did you learn about these fine people?" The sip I took sent fizzy bubbles tickling my nose.

"A whole lot of nothing," Priya said. "Omar doesn't exist on social media at all. I cross-checked with some family that I found who are employees of the business, but they don't have profiles anywhere either. To be fair, they're mercenaries and they're involved in a lot of dangerous scenarios. It's harder to use anything personal against them if they don't have a digital presence. As for the Dershowitzes, Shannon's social media is all about her art, Ivan has some ranty Twitter posts, and Rachel has an Instagram account filled with evidence of her many philanthropic endeavors."

"Curated by some lowly assistant. Rachel couldn't hold a camera steady enough to take a selfie." I drained my cup. "Enough about this case. What do you want to do for your next gig? I'd hire you full-time, but I don't have enough work or cash."

Priya laughed. "I'd kill you if you were my boss."

"I'm your boss now."

She reached across her employee-issued desk for the Prosecco. "Sure you are, Holmes."

"See if I write you a reference letter. Seriously, though. Any thoughts?"

She poured herself more bubbly. "I want a challenge. House Pacifica could do with a cybersecurity overhaul. I'd know. I've hacked them enough times."

"You can't work for them. That would be cavorting with the enemy."

Pri daintily sipped her alcohol. "Says the woman who had Levi's dick in her."

"That wasn't cavorting. That was hate-sex."

She snorted. "Then says the woman who just finished working for them."

"That also was not cavorting. It was freelance and I was in charge. And don't bring up Levi and the Jezebel thing because I have no choice in partnering up with him on that matter." I pouted. "You can't desert me. I need you."

"Aw, kitten. I'm not going back into nine-to-five servitude. I want a consultancy contract. Strictly freelance. Now, if your fears have been put to rest, can you get me a meeting with Miles?"

Not only was Miles Head of House Security, he was also the man who had met Priya exactly one time and, as I'd recently learned, bestowed the nickname Pink Menace on her. Ever since her engagement had blown up horribly a few years ago, she'd been holding herself back in relationships. Or what passed for them.

I didn't want Priya to settle for safe. She deserved all the passion in the world and while I had no idea if Miles was "the one" for her, I had a feeling that if these two met properly, sparks would fly.

Hmm. Perhaps I was being narrow-minded. It wouldn't hurt to have a mole in Levi's camp.

"You bet I can," I said cheerfully.

Priya narrowed her eyes. "What are you up to?"

"Nothing." I tapped a finger against my lip. "The best way to go about this would be to run into Miles socially. Then you can ease into the idea. He'll get all uptight and suspicious if we go the direct route. Maybe there's a way to get us into Le Rêve, after all. Give me your phone."

She slid it across the desk to me. "Why can't you use yours?"

"If Talia sees your number she'll assume something bad happened and pick up." If she didn't, there was no hope for us. I dialed my mother on speakerphone.

"Priya?" Talia said. "Is everything okay?"

I let out the breath I'd been holding. "Hello, Talia."

"Ash." Her voice turned wary. "What did you need?"

I'd told my mother that I had magic and at best she thought me deluded, at worst unhinged. From her perspective, the last time I'd gone off the rails this badly, it had ended in that devastating car crash, therapy, and rehab. Apparently, she didn't have the emotional bandwidth to go there with me. Again.

Except this time, I wasn't some angry, out-of-control kid. I had maturity, experience, and oh yeah, actual magic. I was on a wild ride, but I could steer myself through this. In all probability I was going to have to steer *us* through this, because I was most definitely going to have to take the lead.

"A daughter can just phone her mother to say hello." I made a face at the phone and Priya smothered a laugh.

"Of course she can, darling. Now if that's all, I'm very busy so—"

"What would it take for you to call Evie Kaufman and get two people onto the guest list of her daughter's restaurant opening tonight?"

There was a long pause. I mimed shooting myself.

"Evie is in France and I'm not sure I can reach her."

Funny, because when she was there last year, you two Skyped constantly. The smile I'd plastered on at the start of the call grew tight. I rarely asked my mother for much, so she understood that if I was reaching out, this request was important. However, if she wouldn't do this for me, I'd go to my fallback position.

There were two known entities that my mother approved of: schmoozing and Priya. Hopefully, Pri's well-being still counted for something in my mother's eyes. "It's a networking opportunity for Priya."

Pri batted her eyelashes.

"Very well," Talia said. "There's a cocktail party tomorrow evening. Senior staff, ardent Party members. We're drumming up support for our bill to restore governance of Nefesh to the Canadian people and eradicate House powers. My colleagues' families will be there and I require your presence."

I should have jumped at the chance to get in her orbit and been thrilled that here we were negotiating events just like our old dynamic, but I wasn't. It had taken playing the Priya card to get here, not me saying I needed help. Rage slipped through my veins like fire. It would be too easy to give in, let go, and fall back into being the angry, out-of-control teen who Talia still pegged me for. Cold, hard logic. That was always the answer.

And logic was saying that Talia didn't want me there, she only needed me there.

"You want me to choose sides," I said.

"You have no reason to support Levi, do you?"

No, but I had every reason to support the Nefesh community. "You can't honestly expect me to get behind something that fascist. What's next? Detention centers?"

"You're being melodramatic."

"You're being hateful!"

Priya raised her eyebrows at my heated tone.

"You can disagree with my politics," Talia said, "but the Party expects a show of solidarity from family members."

"I'm well aware." A scathing retort formed on my tongue, but reason prevailed. "I'll come."

"No lies, no games, Ash." I was counting on it. "8PM sharp. No standing me up, either."

"I won't," I said. "You have my word."

"That's not my sole stipulation. Be my supportive daughter. Make small talk. Do not cause a scene or make the day about you in any way. That's my price for calling Evie," Talia said. "Yes or no?"

Priya shook her head, emphatically no.

"I'll see you tomorrow," I said and hung up.

"Ash," Priya said. "Don't do this. I can find Miles a million other ways."

"No, this is good. First of all, it doesn't hurt to know who in the Mundane community is onboard with this stupid proposal. Talia's clever. She got what she wanted on two fronts: my presence and ensuring I wouldn't bring up the dreaded 'M' word, but I got what I wanted as well."

"Being on the guest list?"

"Contact. As soon as she announced the venue, I knew our talk wouldn't take place there. So, I'll go, be on my best behavior, and leverage this into another meeting where *I* set the agenda. Whether she wants to hear it or not, I owe it to her to demonstrate my magic personally before it becomes public knowledge." I rubbed my chest with the heel of my palm, hoping the sharp pang was heartburn. "Talia's reaction is going to be brutal, but I can't hide from her. I won't. She's my mother."

Priya ran her finger around the rim of her Solo cup. "What if she refuses to accept that part of you?"

"After all we've weathered together, I honestly believe that she'll come around, but even if the worst comes to pass and she doesn't? I was denied my magic for fifteen years. I don't want to live in the shadows just because it furthers other people's agendas or they won't approve. I value truth and that's how I want to live my life." I tossed my Solo cup in the trash. "If I'd stayed Mundane, and the only female P.I. in Vancouver on top of it all, how many more years of bottom feeder cases like spying on kids because their parents thought they were on drugs would I have faced? The difference in jobs in the couple of weeks since the ward was broken and my magic was restored is night and day."

"You're a puzzle junkie."

"I've been called worse." I smiled sadly.

Priya hugged me. "It'll all be okay."

I accepted the comfort. And the lie.

Then I went home for a necessary wardrobe change because I was two braids and a bonnet away from marrying a hard-working man called Pa. Damn it! I hated when Levi was right.

Chapter 8

Le Rêve was a large—and packed—space in Yaletown, the original Western Terminus for the Canadian Pacific Railway and a warehouse district until its transformation to a trendy neighborhood after Vancouver hosted Expo '86.

Talia had come through; our names were on the guest list.

Priya and I checked our coats and headed for the bar to take stock of our surroundings. My bestie wore a pale pink slip dress that made her skin glow and her green eyes luminous. Her bare legs looked a mile long in her strappy silver heels and her normally sleek flapper bob was a riot of crazy moussed-up curls.

She was gorgeous and getting her fair share of attention, but she wouldn't notice. She rarely did anymore, preferring to commit to one boring guy after another.

A DJ spun jazz remixes in one corner, a couple of tattooed chefs worked feverishly in the open concept kitchen, and the bartender mixed up an impressive array of martinis. The French-Asian fusion of the menu was reflected in the blue and coral vintage wallpaper with its delicate blossoms and paper lanterns mixed with rustic wood tables.

All of Vancouver's glittering socialites rubbed elbows, while camera crews caught up with local celebs.

And hello, Levi.

His Lordship stood in the center of the room, in the brightest spotlight, with his arm around Chef Miriam, saying something to make her laugh and shake her head. He pushed a lock of midnight black hair out of his eyes.

I'd made those eyes go wide and dreamy blue with the drugged out fog of lust. Did he catch himself smiling at odd moments, remembering our time together? Or was I just one of many lovers, as easily chosen as the fedora sitting at a jaunty angle on his head, and as easily discarded?

Priya pressed a highball glass into my hands. "Here. Drink this because you're licking your lips and staring and it's embarrassing."

"Am not," I muttered, flushing, and sipped the Jack Daniels she'd procured. Two fingers worth of Gentleman Jack with three ice cubes and a splash of water, just the way I liked it.

I peeked over the rim to where the interview was wrapping up.

Levi's lithe torso was emphasized by the fitted trousers and shirt with a cool Rat Pack vibe to its blocky design. He one-arm hugged Miriam, who swatted at him with her chef's apron and then hurried back to the kitchen.

Why couldn't there be some irrefutable body language of the guilty? Levi was an illusionist, he knew how to conceal his secrets.

"There's Miles," Priya said, pointing in the opposite direction.

"Let's do this." We kind of sidled up sideways to Miles' general vicinity, but I stopped short of approaching him, stopping in front of a server with a tray of tiny daikon radish boxes that were stuffed with shrimp salad.

We each helped ourselves to one.

"Wait for him to come over," I said, regretting that I hadn't taken a second daikon box. Fresh, crunchy, and creamy with a tang of lemon, these puppies were delish.

"How do you know he'll—"

"Are you stalking Levi?" Miles' deep baritone had a distinctly annoyed edge. At six-foot-four, he was a mountain of a man, with serious brown eyes and buzz cut blond hair. He wore a monochrome navy suit, exquisitely tailored to fit him. "How did you even get on the guest list?"

"Charmed to see you as well," I said. "Miles, this is Priya. Priya, Miles. You've met before I believe."

"Nice to see you again." She beamed up at him and Miles blinked.

Unlike my absentee father, whose charm was magically induced, Priya made everyone around her fall under her spell completely naturally. She was this ray of light and you couldn't help but be entranced.

I crossed my fingers and waited. Three… two… one…

"Hack my House again," Miles said, "and I'll nail your ass to the wall."

Priya bristled up at him. "If, theoretically, I had hacked it, you would never know."

There it was. Sparks. My smirk wasn't super huge, but just the same, I got very interested in the mini Korean BBQ sliders on buttery brioche passing by. I nabbed three.

"Exactly. I got very curious when this one"—Miles jerked a thumb at me—"admitted her involvement with the Scott girl. But when I checked the database, there was no sign of Ash verifying whether that family was Nefesh or not. She absolutely would have checked, and if there wasn't a record of that then someone erased it and didn't leave a trace." He crossed his arms, sending a ripple along his biceps.

"Whoops," I said, not at all chagrined.

Priya glared, since I'd asked her to delete all traces of my search, then jutted out her chin at Miles. "Maybe your database is deleting itself in humiliation for the sloppy coding and cheap patch jobs. Where'd you find your programmers? Craigslist?"

As the two broke out in a squabble, I strode away, satisfied with a job well done.

A hand clamped down on my shoulder. "Causing trouble?"

I spun to face Levi. "There you go. Thinking the worst of me again."

"You make it so easy."

"Well, I model myself after you." Motioning to Priya that I was leaving, I retrieved my leather jacket from the coat check.

Levi eyed my outfit of black leather pants and scoop neck crop top. "Your wardrobe points to a severe personality disorder."

"While yours would suggest that ninety-nine percent of the time you're repressed beyond all hope." This one percent exception was charged with a potent sexuality. The suits were safer. For me. "Let's go. You've made me wait long enough."

I followed Levi in silence down the block.

"Speak, Ash. You scare me when you get quiet and you're walking behind me."

"Don't worry," I said. "When you push me to a non-negotiable act of homicide, I promise you'll see my face."

"That I don't doubt. But seriously. Share the contents of your ever-whirring brain."

Ever since that night the two of us had attended the auction in Tofino, I'd shared thoughts with Levi that I hadn't even voiced to Priya. I wanted to tell him about my problems with Talia, but I didn't dare expose any vulnerable part of myself until I could safely vouch for him again. And since my weird feelings about him were definitely not a topic of conversation, that left only one way to answer him.

"I'm wondering how much Evil Wanker knows about Jezebels. It's like I'm on a teeter-totter and I've momentarily achieved this precarious balance, because I'm keeping my magic destruction usage to a minimum. What happens if my Jezebel responsibilities include taking magic on the regular? Will my cravings exponentially worsen? Will I have any control over them? What will that do to my moral compass? I'm bracing myself for one side or the other of this seesaw to come crashing down."

"Aren't you all about getting answers?"

"I am. Doesn't mean they're easy to hear."

"Fair enough." He beeped a car fob.

My mouth fell open and I scrambled around the side to get into the passenger seat. "A Tesla?"

He patted his steering wheel. "Did you think I'd have some gas guzzling muscle car to prove how big my dick is?"

"No." I snapped the seat belt in. "I figured you'd recline on a palanquin, carried aloft by your half-dozen minions."

"That's my weekend ride." He pulled onto Cordova Street—no, launched us into traffic, laughing at my streak of curses. Then he put his hands behind his head and got comfortable as the car merged into the lane.

I screamed and tried to grab the wheel, but he swatted me away.

"Autopilot, baby." He clucked his tongue. "Look at all those suckers with their clunky monstrosities."

My breathing was raspy and I clutched my seat belt in a death grip, bracing myself for impact.

"Ash? Oh, fuck." Levi took manual control of the steering and pulled over to the curb, cutting the engine. "I'm sorry. I forgot. I…" His expression tight with anxiety, he went to stroke my shoulder, then pulled back.

I only dimly registered all this, silently alphabetizing items in his car to calm myself down.

At some point, the vise constricting my ribcage disappeared and I let go of the seat belt, only to find I'd worn harsh red grooves in my skin.

"Ashira?" Levi said softly.

I nodded shakily. "I'm all right. What's a little PTSD now and then?"

"I'm so sorry. I didn't realize autopilot would upset you."

"I didn't either since Moriarty isn't the Batmobile, but that whole endless void bungy jump back in the grove doesn't seem scary anymore, so that's a win. Don't worry about it." I patted his thigh, his muscle flexing under my touch.

"Feeling me up, are you?"

"Yes, I was going for a worse trauma to override the PTSD." I settled back against my seat. "Carry on."

We drove through East Vancouver, Levi driving the car himself, swinging past older apartment buildings and low slung warehouses.

"I learned some other interesting facts about Gavriella, if you'd care to know them," Levi said.

"Not yet. I want to see her space unhampered by any bias or prior knowledge. By the way," I said, "we ought to come to an agreement on my fee for the case I'm working on."

"The one I didn't hire you for? Let's go with pro bono."

"Let me rephrase. You're not paying me for this case. You're paying me to destroy the fourteen vials with the smudges that I'm getting as payment for this case. A girl cannot live on smudges alone. Plus, it's a humanitarian act benefiting all Nefesh and as House Head, you can't say no. Wow, this car is really quiet inside. Super smooth."

"You're working for the Queen?" Levi smacked the wheel. "Ma vaffanculo. Are you insane?"

"I'm not working for her, she merely recommended me for the job. I then used my stellar negotiation skills for the vials. You're welcome. Also, officially, as Levi Montefiore,

Head of House Pacifica, you don't know any of this. You only know about it as my—"

I cut off, suddenly unsure how to finish that sentence. "Archnemesis" sounded a little grand especially now that Chariot was in the picture. "Hate-sex buddy," while accurate, didn't fit anymore. Boss? Hard pass. Friend? Something in me rankled. If I was truly friends with someone, I wouldn't be able to make them a suspect in a case. I'd know them well enough to say whether or not they did it.

"—Levi." I finished, limply.

"Know about any of what?" he growled.

"Exactly, that's perfect."

Levi beat his head against his seat, a gesture which cheered me up considerably. He drove through the light traffic at tortoise miles per hour, so overtly cautious in his overcompensation for earlier that he made half-blind grannies seem like NASCAR drivers.

I didn't have the heart to bug him about it.

"Anything else you'd like to dump on me?" he finally said.

"Since you asked so nicely? Yes. Once I've finished this job, I want you to push my registration through and get my enhanced strength verified to change the status of my P.I. license and openly take Nefesh cases."

My strength part was actually fairly low on the magic scale, maybe a two out of five, not like people with Tough Guy powers. I wasn't chucking cars around, but I was strong enough to do serious damage with my punches and I could pin a man down. Useful close contact fighting skills in order to then use my blood magic on a person.

Levi opened his mouth but I held up a hand.

"Hear me out. Both my birth records and medical records from the time of the crash when I was thirteen have me documented in like thirty different places as Mundane.

Every inch of me was examined. It'll quash any idea that I've been Rogue all this time."

Unlike everyone else who was born with magic, my best guess was that my powers had been passed down as a recessive gene from my Nefesh father Adam and activated after the trauma of my car crash when I was thirteen. I hadn't known any of this until very recently, when a blow to my skull had revealed a hidden Star of David tattoo that turned out to be a ward suppressing my magic. It had been scarred when I hit my head, and thus broken, allowing my magic to manifest.

"We'll simply fudge the truth a bit and say the recessive gene turned on when I bashed my skull last week. Between the documentation and your natural arrogance, no one will question you."

"Grazie." He paused. "Talia will freak."

No lies. No games. "We'll weather this storm. I can't live a lie."

Levi snorted. "Just a half of one. You want me to hide your Jezebel magic and only put your strength on the books."

"D'uh. I'd rather not have a target on my back with every whackjob and criminal trying to use me. It's better this way. At least until we understand why I have it."

"There's another solution." He pulled up in front of an older apartment building off Clark Drive with stone sconce flourishes that had gone grimy over time. After turning off the engine, he faced me, his teeth worrying his bottom lip. "Come work for me, off the books. Permanently."

Why? To control what I do and don't learn about you?

"Never," I said. "I worked my ass off building up my business. It's not much—yet—but it's mine."

Levi was quiet as he got out of the car, his strides long and his hands jammed in his pockets.

I peered up at him, moonlight etched across his features,

over his rugged cheekbones and those full lips that were currently tugged downward. "You mad that I don't want to be part of your fiefdom?"

Levi stopped and ran a finger along my jaw. The touch sent goosebumps cascading along my skin, and I wrapped my jacket more snugly around me. "There are benefits to having you under me," he said.

"Absolutely. It's that much easier to knife you between the ribs, you cocky bastard." I waved a hand around my face. "And you'd see my beautiful visage as I did so. As promised."

Levi gave me a snarky smile, unlocked the front door, and we entered the lobby.

Chapter 9

The faded red carpet was printed with either swirls or body outlines and the stairwell reeked of onions.

Levi fiddled on his key ring for the one to Gavriella's apartment while I checked for wards. Sure enough her magic, similar to mine, thrummed under my fingertips.

"Let's not test whether it finds us hostile or not." Since the ward was created with Gavriella's blood, I was able to hook into it, tease it out of the doorframe that anchored it, and destroy it. I experienced a mild high, a triple espresso shot level which dissipated, bringing me gently back down once I completed the process and finished the magic off. Momentarily satiated, the ever-present hum of longing in my head dialed down to a barely noticeable presence.

I motioned Levi inside. "Age before beauty."

"I'm only three months older than you."

"The statement stands."

Gavriella Behar's apartment, while small, was surprisingly bright, cheerily decorated with vivid pops of color, and smelled like lavender. I did a cursory walkthrough to see if anything jumped out at me. In the bedroom was a framed print of the Sagrada Familia, the church in Barcelona, and in the hallway was a painting of a flamenco dancer, her red dress spinning as she snapped a fan with maximum attitude. On Gavriella's kitchen counter sat a wide, shallow stainless steel paella pan, which I only recognized from an old Anthony Bourdain episode in Spain that Priya had watched. Food travel shows were her preferred binge-watch.

When I'd met Gavriella, she'd been battered and broken, unable to do more than whisper. I hadn't noticed any accent if she had one.

I checked her medicine cabinet for any medication or a handy patch that would quell the magic cravings, but the most potent drug was Midol.

"Gavriella was Jewish." I returned to Levi in the living room. "Got quite the stash of Manischewitz coconut maca-roons in her cupboard. I approve, because those things are delish to even us most secular of Jews, but it's Passover food. Not something non-Jews are gonna have on hand."

Levi snooped through the drawer of the large cherry wood sideboard in the dining area of the open concept space, his hands in the thin gloves I'd provided us both to prevent fingerprints. I'd assigned him the task of looking for an address book, phone, or laptop. "Perhaps all Jezebels are," he said.

"Might all be women, too." I wandered over to the bookshelf, because books were a fountain of insight into a person. "All female Jezebels fit with the mythology of worshipping the Bride of Yahweh and the Jezebel label. Something to consider."

Most of the books were Spanish paperbacks across a variety of genres, but there were English bestsellers mixed in there as well.

"Gavriella was Sephardic," Levi said. Those Jews had their roots in the Mediterranean and Middle East versus the Ashkenazi ones, like both sides of my family, who were predominantly of Eastern European heritage.

"You're Sephardic, too." Levi had been born in Rome. His accent only came out when cursing in Italian. Or sometimes during sex. I reshelved an Isabelle Allende novel.

"I think Behar is a Ladino last name," he said.

"A what?"

"Ladino. It's a Judeo-Spanish language dating back before the sixteenth century that's still spoken today by a small number of older Jews," he said.

"How did you even identify Gavriella? Did you check House databases across the globe and get a hit on one of the Spanish ones?"

"Arkady coaxed the information from one of the two men taken alive on the smudge case." Levi shoved the drawer closed and crouched down to check the cupboards.

"Such flowery language. 'Coaxed.'" I chided Levi.

Arkady Choi had moved in next door to me right after the ward was broken and my magic restored. He also happened to work for Levi on a covert ops team. They both swore it was a coincidence that he was my neighbor, but I didn't buy it and still half-believed that Levi had placed Arkady there to keep an eye on me.

Mistrust upon mistrust.

"When Arkady was done sharing his stone fists with the man's face," I said, "had he learned anything else about Gavriella or Chariot?"

"No. But I did." Levi's lips twisted. "Gavriella was a Rogue."

I did a double take. "A Rogue here in Canada."

That's why Levi was so pissed off about her presence in his territory. She should have registered with House Pacifica when she moved here.

"Nope." He popped the "p." "A Rogue. Period. She isn't registered anywhere." He scratched his chin. "Here you want me to throw you a coming out party."

"Only a half-coming out party, seeing as I'm bi-magical."

The lower bookshelves held a poetry collection in their original Spanish, mostly written by Pablo Neruda and Federico García Lorca. I straightened up, cracking my back. "And for the record, Mr. Man-Who-Hates-Rogues, you were the one who showed up with my registration papers, so delaying said registration is somewhat hypocritical, don't you think?"

"As House Head, it's my duty to bring all Rogues into the fold. If I only register your low level enhanced strength, then I'm complicit in giving your blood magic Rogue status. If I register all your abilities, like I should, then I'm handing the Untainted Party valuable ammunition about a dangerous Nefesh on the loose. Your Mundane status was documented enough that people might swallow the explanation about your powers turning on when you bumped your head the other week, but that anomaly combined with magic that shouldn't exist? Your situation complicates mine immensely."

"Amazing how you're making this all about you."

"It is about me, damn it. If I thought for a second that there was someone more qualified to lead House Pacifica, I'd step aside in a heartbeat, but there isn't and so I won't."

I'd have bet my business on Levi's entire identity being tied to House Head. If he entertained thoughts about stepping aside, what else had I misjudged him about?

He exhaled slowly, the corners of his eyes tight, and a deep weariness etched in the slump of his shoulders. Then he shook it off, fastening his top shirt button for extra fortification. "Until I get some answers and some clarity, you're stuck with me on this."

Part of me sympathized with him.

The rest devised how best to push him off a cliff.

"Maybe Gavriella Behar isn't her real name and she's not a Rogue," I said.

"It is," Levi said. "There's a birth certificate for her. Born in Barcelona, forty-eight years ago. Supposedly Mundane."

"Any family? Next of kin?"

"No. Gavriella was raised by her grandmother who died a few years ago. She bounced around the University of Barcelona but didn't graduate because she got married. Stayed at home until her divorce, then moved to Vancouver, probably to get a fresh start, and picked up a lot of shift work in the hospitality industry. She worked at some Mundane club before she was abducted and forced to create smudges."

"Got to have flexible hours for fighting evil." I swept a hand over her dining room table, scattering a pile of clean laundry.

"Why is that a problem?" Levi's brow furrowed.

"Because she dumped this 'tag, you're it' bullshit on me and then died without telling me what I was supposed to do."

"How thoughtless."

Sighing, I picked up the fallen items. "I am precariously low on concrete facts where Chariot is concerned."

"This team of yours should have answers once you find them."

"I'm not inclined to think highly of them at the moment. They didn't save Gavriella, and I'm on my own with Evil Wanker. Either we're all expendable or they're incompetent."

"Which makes what you bring to the table even more valuable." He said it matter-of-factly, like it was scientifically quantifiable, without looking up from rifling through a drawer.

I tried to reconcile this person with the one who could choke Omar with a feather and leave him to a slow, horrible death. It wasn't easy, but given how Levi had broken a man with the illusion of smothering him in ants, it wasn't impossible, either.

"I'm assuming all Jezebels have the same abilities," I said. "If some of them are happy to play caped crusader on a regular basis, more power to them. I want to be challenged and engaged in a variety of ways."

"You want to be Sherlock. What if Chariot is your Moriarty?"

"Even Sherlock didn't spend all his time chasing only Moriarty," I said.

"Sure, not at the start, but eventually he had to."

"Ugh. Did you Wiki him or something? Back off, Levi."

He held up his hands like he was placating a feral animal. "Those smudges were dangerous. Jezebel magic was the only thing that could stop them."

"It's the thing that created them in the first place. Is it an acceptable risk if Jezebels pose an equally bad threat to humanity? What if in stopping Chariot, we're expected to be okay with collateral damage?" I picked up a fallen pillowcase and set it on the pile. "I promised Gavriella that I'd stop Chariot, but I won't do it at the expense of my dream or my values. I won't manipulate innocent people and I won't be a mindless magic-destroying weapon. I have to be able to face myself in the mirror every day."

"You'll figure it out."

I shrugged and returned a couple of shirts to the pile. "Did you find anything?"

Levi stripped off the gloves. "No electronics or address books anywhere in the living room or bathroom, but I did find this in the hall closet." He held up a green Duo-Tang. "Photocopies. Gavriella's birth certificate, driver's license, marriage license, divorce papers, and her passport."

"An entire paper trail of a life laid out in one handy spot."

"Almost like she wanted it to be found." He tucked it under his arm. "I'm taking this."

"It fits the portrait of the person Gavriella presented to the world: a staggeringly normal middle-aged divorcée who liked to cook, was proud of her heritage, and had a slightly romantic streak. I'm surprised she doesn't have a cat. So, what didn't she want us to see?" I scanned the room for anywhere we might have missed. "I'm going to check her closet."

Certain spaces in people's lives were curated, designed to present a specific impression. They were public spaces like offices or living rooms. Bedrooms were more private, and closets? Like garbage cans, they were uncurated spaces and therefore brilliant places to find cracks in a person's public identity. For example, a nutritional zealot with chip bags stuffed deep in her trash.

I flung open the closet door, blinked twice, and burst into laughter.

Levi strode into the room. "What?"

"If this is Jezebel-issued garb, I may have to adjust my training regimen." I held up one of the skimpy outfits crowding her closet. Damn, I loved when people surprised me. "What was the name of the club where she worked?"

"Star Lounge."

"That's a strip club. Though Gavriella would be too old to strip." It was a tough profession and very few lasted after their mid-thirties.

"She could hostess or bartend or serve."

"Thank you for those very prompt answers," I said. "It's almost like you have first-hand knowledge of such places. Do you remember any of the other places she worked? Were they strip clubs as well?"

"She did some seasonal mail delivery for Canada Post and there were a few cafés. I'd have to check the specifics."

I pulled out an outfit consisting of six spangly strips of stretchy fabric and snapped one of the pieces. "That's either too many or too few."

Levi perched on the edge of Gavriella's bed and studied the clothing. He took off his fedora, briskly rubbed his hair, then repositioned the hat. "Too many."

"Kudos on your consistent predictability. You've really mastered that skill."

"I master every skill."

I hung the outfit up, and searched the pockets of the everyday clothing in the other half of the closet. "We should work on your confidence levels. Do some positivity training, maybe some visualizations. You'd have so much to offer the world if only you believed in yourself."

Levi gave an aggrieved sigh. "It's hard dimming my bright light so I don't blind you lesser mortals."

"We little people are ever so grateful. Be useful and check the bedside table."

"Ew. No. You know what people keep in there?"

"Sex things. Also, possibly address books and those electronics you didn't find in the rest of the apartment."

He put his gloves back on and did as he was told. Biddable Levi had his uses. *Biddable Levi on a bed. Oh, the possibilities*, my treacherous brain whispered. I shut it down. S-U-S-P-E-C-T—I sang in my head in my fiercest Aretha Franklin.

"Arkady's cover entails being part of the Nefesh Mixed Martial Arts League which keeps up his fighting skills and works in harmony with his secret job," I said. "Why would Gavriella work at a strip joint?"

"Money?"

"There are lots of ways to make money. People undercover tend to choose jobs that will further their goals somehow. Why do you think Clark Kent worked at the paper?"

"Lois Lane," Levi said, fanning himself.

I walked over and kicked his leg, before returning to the closet. "Oops."

He laughed, rubbing his shin.

"It put him at the pulse for finding out where trouble was. Maybe the club was ground zero for something in Gavriella's world."

There was a twenty in a lightweight coat, but she'd never get the small joy of finding spare cash ever again. Was her untimely death worth whatever she'd accomplished? I stuffed the bill back in the pocket.

Levi nudged the bedside table drawer shut with his hips. "Some T-shirts and a purple silicone dick. Happy?"

"Overjoyed. Any uniforms from a magic league of evil-fighters?"

"Unfortunately not. Looking to expand your fashion choices?"

"You can never have enough catsuits in your life."

Levi turned an interested gleam on me. "Really?"

"Not even a little bit. I wanted all this magic shit to be random, you know? Like I happened to have this recessive gene and it got activated, and suddenly my professional dreams were deeper and richer than I'd dared believe possible. Then I found out I was different from all the other magic little boys and girls and my powers have a purpose." I pulled a couple of old ticket stubs from the back pocket of a pair of trousers. "I don't want that. I want a choice."

"Control freak."

"As if you aren't. I refuse to be at anyone's mercy. I mean, like, the universe's."

He snorted.

"Yes, Levi. I have daddy issues. Catch up. Now I have to find some team who's going to have expectations around my participation on top of everything."

"Probably expect you to be social, too."

"Don't even get me started on that bullshit. They could have done me a solid and found *me*, because I have enough to deal with, but all I get are magic encounters with the bad guy and a distinct lack of anything resembling Gavriella's contacts." I stilled. "What if they did find me already, but have left me to deal with Evil Wanker on my own as some kind of test? Those are very popular these days." I searched her last pocket, coming away with a melted Hershey's Kiss. Grimacing, I pulled off my gloves and rolled them into a ball. "Trashcan?"

"There's probably one in the kitchen."

"Yeah, but I don't want to dump these in there. It's empty," I said. "I checked."

"That's convenient."

"Meaning?" I said.

"She was abducted after she took out the trash but before she had time to even throw out a tissue?"

We exchanged looks.

"Someone got here before us," I said. "Shit. Earn your seat in the Mystery Machine, Shaggy, and get your people to dust for fingerprints. Find out if it was friend or foe. And if it was a hostile how did that person get past the wards?"

"How about a 'please?' Ever heard the saying 'you catch more flies with honey?'"

"I tried it. Not my thing." I nudged him off the bed and lifted the mattress. Nothing hidden there, nor was there anything taped behind her bureau.

"What are you looking for?"

"Maybe a love of hidey holes is another thing Jezebels have in common." I lowered myself onto all fours and crawled into her closet.

"Nice ass," Levi said in the same tone of voice as he'd comment on the weather.

"It's the best thing you'll see all day."

"We need to work on your confidence levels."

Please don't let Levi be Omar's attacker. Our interactions were a lot of things, but never dull. I didn't want to give that up.

I knocked a bunch of spots on the wall. One emitted a hollow sound and I pushed on it until a panel popped off. "Et voilà."

Inside was a metal box that was latched but not locked. I flipped open the lid. "Feel free to tell me how good I am."

"Nah. Your neck couldn't support the weight if your head got more swollen."

I shook two pieces of paper out of an envelope. "Another birth certificate and a death certificate. Both for a Gracie Green. There's an American passport here, too. Expired." I did a double take at the photo. "It's Gavriella. Levi, hand me her birth certificate." I compared the two. "Gracie was born the same day as Gavriella but she died—" My breath left me in a sharp exhale.

"What?"

"Gracie Green died right before my magic activated in the hospital fifteen years ago." I checked the envelope, but there was nothing further inside. "Is that her real identity? The best lies contain a grain of truth." I had my father to thank for that pearl of wisdom. "It's not uncommon for false identities to share a birthdate, but they often share the same initials to help the person remember their cover name. Why go from American Gracie Green to Spanish Gavriella Behar?"

"I'll run Gracie's name and date of birth," Levi said. "See what comes up."

"Why kill off her true identity when she came to Vancouver? Was she in hiding?"

"Or she really died." Levi knelt down beside me to examine the documents.

"No way. They're the same person."

"What if Gracie flatlined for a few seconds?" he said. "I've never bought your theory about the recessive gene turning on after the crash. What if death is the trigger for a new Jezebel to be awakened?"

"That's why she was looking for me? She knew there had to be someone else, except that damned Star of David tattoo fucked it all up. Could there be another Jezebel triggered by Gracie's actual death?"

Would I be off the hook for any full-time Chariot duties if there were someone else to replace her on the team? I'd never know unless I found them, and meantime, Evil Wanker was on my trail.

"Let's call her Gavriella so we're accustomed to using that name when we talk to people." I placed the documents back in their envelope, tucking the box under my arm. "We'll have to check out the Star Lounge. Maybe she had friends or co-workers who saw people visit her there or she let something slip that would be of use to us."

After one more walkthrough, we let ourselves out.

"Is this what my life is going to look like if I fail and the next Jezebel-in-waiting finds my apartment? Travel goals I never accomplish, too-clean trash cans, and not even a pet? Does everything that makes me who I am get erased?" I swallowed. "And do my Sherlock dreams get sidelined for something this empty?"

Levi placed a hand on my slumping shoulder. "We'll get to the bottom of this."

You bet we would. Gavriella's ending was not my ending. Hell, I was just getting started. "The game is on and the best woman is going to win."

Chapter 10

After living the world's longest day, I dragged my butt to bed, collapsing face down on my pillow fully dressed. I managed to toe off one boot before sleep claimed me hard, enjoying the luxury of waking up on Tuesday morning after the March sun had risen.

I took a quick shower, threw on my only pair of clean jeans and a black hoodie, and went foraging for breakfast. Damnation, it was still my turn to do the shopping. I erased Priya's apology off the small whiteboard stuck to our fridge —I'd vacuumed for her—and asked her to get groceries. One or the other of us was always falling behind but we cobbled it together.

Frying up the last of the eggs and toast, I peered into the coffee tin, my soul shriveling at its mocking emptiness, and took my breakfast into the living room to eat.

The modern sofas, coffee table, and bookcases in our living room were hand-me-downs from my mother's last redecoration, but our personalities shone through with throw cushions made of vivid sari fabric that Priya had brought back from India and all of our books spilling off the bookcases. Old university textbooks kept company with her sci-fi novels and my Sherlock Holmes collection that was gifted by my dad shortly before he took off.

Photographic prints of a red phone booth on a London street, sunset over the Colosseum, and dazzling white homes with blue doors in Santorini hung on our walls.

Cozy as it sounded, Priya's shit exploded everywhere: a pair and a half of shoes abandoned on the floor, a slug trail of video cards, a canister of compressed air, and various tiny tools leading to her extra laptop under a chair.

I pushed aside two discarded sweaters, sat down and ate my breakfast, relishing the quiet. Priya was asleep and the hum of the fridge was soothing. Yesterday had been non-stop personal interactions and while Priya got off on them, they drained me. Throw in the fighting and the not-so-veiled threats and I'd gladly have spent today locked in my bedroom under the covers.

I took my time with my food, steeling myself to retrieve the pouch from my office safe. The melody of my magic addiction was not louder, but rather more insistent in the face of the upcoming proximity to the feather and I shivered in antici… pation. At least I amused myself past these urges.

I savored that precious half hour on my own, but Omar's case wouldn't solve itself. Minutes later, my dishes were in the sink, and I was stomping down my apartment building's stairs in my motorcycle boots and leather jacket.

"What ho, pickle?" Arkady passed me holding a steaming coffee cup and a bakery bag from Muffin Top, owned by two earth elementals with insane baking abilities.

"Do you get any discount as a fellow earthy Nefesh?" I said. "Special line-cutting privileges?"

"No, but I am totally proposing that the next time I go in there." He brushed some crumbs off his "Let Me Be Perfectly Queer" T-shirt. Of Korean-Canadian heritage and supermodel good looks, his chin-length black hair was loose today, his dark brown eyes half-lidded and sleepy. His jeans and leather jacket added to his badass vibe.

Mine looked like I was hiding stains.

I made goo-goo eyes at the coffee, but he pulled it out of reach. Whatever. I could adult my ass to one of the gazillion cafés here on the Drive.

"Hypothetically," I said, "if Levi had people dusting for prints somewhere, would you be one of those people?"

"Nope. But I know who would be."

"Great. Could you pass me the information first?"

"Betray Levi?" Arkady's full lips fell into a perfect "O."

Arkady would be devastated if his idol was behind Omar's attack. If Levi had done it, then I'd be right to expose him and bring him to justice. Not the Queen's version of justice, mind you. But it would still feel wrong sending a teenhood acquaintance to the slammer.

Even with all my suspicions swirling around him, I wanted to believe in the man I thought Levi to be. The Watson moral center of this crazy world. That pokey toothache feeling throbbed harder.

"I'm not asking you to stab him in the back," I said. "Just give me a couple hours head start with the information."

"Pickle, that's unseemly."

Spare me from His Lordship's admirers. "Will you at least tell me when he gets the results so I can harass him for them?"

"No." He brushed past me and continued up the stairs.

"Blind loyalty is not an admirable quality," I yelled.

"Nail your next training session and I might care about your opinion," he retorted and shut his door.

I swung by the Dershowitz estate but no one was there. When I leaned on—i.e., bribed—the maid who'd led me to the crime scene on my last visit, I was informed that the families had gone to Hedon to tell the Queen that the wedding was postponed.

That was either going to be a very short or extremely long discussion. Either way, I'd be better off gathering intel on the feather so I had something concrete to present when I interviewed everyone.

After a quick stop to slam back a double shot macchiato and a slightly longer one to retrieve the metal pouch from my office safe, I eased Moriarty into a spot out front of Freddo's Buy & Sell.

The boarded up storefront next door was plastered in posters inviting people to a town hall to discuss the Nefesh menace. They'd been heavily defaced with obscenities and taunts against the "Mundane pussies."

Whatever happened to live and let live?

I entered Freddo's Buy & Sell to find the man himself behind the counter. Short with Popeye-like biceps, Freddo looked almost exactly like he had when my dad used to bring me here years ago. The only thing that had changed was that Freddo's combover had gone from brown to silver.

"Help ya?" He blew canned air into a keyboard, his customary toothpick lodged firmly in the corner of his mouth.

"Remember me? Ash? Adam's daughter?"

Freddo set down the canister. "Little Ash. Go figure. How's that charming bastard? Haven't seen him in years."

I shrugged. "Me neither."

Freddo shook his head. "Nah. Don't believe it. You were your dad's whole world. Come on, between you and me. He's laying low, right? A con gone wrong?"

"I haven't seen him since I was twelve."

"Shame." He sucked on the toothpick. "What can I do for you?"

"I'd like to continue the business relationship between our families."

"Go on."

"I need to find out what type of magic is on an artifact, but it's a bit of a tricky situation because it has an adverse effect on people who get too close. Can you do it?"

Freddo was a Typecaster, with the ability to identify magic. Houses kept them on staff to verify magic types and strengths, but any good fence hoping to trade in magic artifacts honed that ability as well. I could have asked Levi to borrow his, but he wasn't in the clear yet, so I was forced to analyze the feather the more expensive way. Why couldn't he have given me some ironclad alibi and been done with it?

Freddo scratched his stubbled chin. "Five hundred."

I winced. That was more than I'd anticipated and I hadn't discussed expenses with the Tannous family. "Three hundred. Friends and family discount."

"Three hundred," he agreed. "Plus another two for danger pay. A read like that'll knock me out of commission for a couple days. Man's gotta make a living."

"Half up front," I said. "Half once you deliver the magic type."

"Deal."

I hit up a bank machine for his deposit. Upon my return, I startled Freddo, who was typing intently on his phone. "Got the cash," I said.

"Then here's to a long and fruitful business relationship." He locked the front door and flipped the sign to "Closed."

After replacing his toothpick with a fresh one, he led me into his storage room where metal racks held pawned items under the glare of a bare bulb. He pulled a large cardboard box off a shelf and set it on a battered metal table.

I placed the pouch next to the box. "Brace yourself. The compulsion is strong. It seems to work in a three-foot range and tempts you with your heart's desire."

"Got it. Ah. Here we go." Freddo pulled a blindfold, a lead apron, and a tin foil hat out of the box.

"Is this a joke?"

He propped the hat on his head, smoothing his combover, because a man had to look his best no matter what the occasion. "Nope. Family tried for almost a hundred years to find a better way, but tin foil does the trick. See, compulsion artifacts work in one of two ways. Sometimes both. Head and heart. Foil negates the effect on the brain."

"And the lead apron? It's for X-rays, not magic."

"Doctored. Protects the heart." He put on the apron, laughing at my skeptical expression. "Relax. Used this combo for generations with zero problems." He put a finger to his lips. "Family secret, no sharing. There's a brisk business in compulsions."

"I'm family?"

"Adam was a good friend."

"In that case, I wouldn't dream of it."

He held out his hand. "You got the cash?"

So much for family. I gave him two hundred and fifty dollars which he tucked into his shirt pocket.

Freddo tied the blindfold around his eyes, twisting his head to make sure he couldn't see. "Works best if I do this unprejudiced by sight. Ready when you are."

I opened the pouch and let the feather flutter into his outstretched hands. The call of its magic knocked me back a few steps and I dabbed at the sweat on my brow.

"The force is strong in this one." He stroked it, he licked it, and he smelled it. He even prodded it with the toothpick.

"What's it telling you?"

"Need more power," he grunted. He pulled out a switchblade and cut the tip of his finger, dropping blood on the feather.

His magic smelled like a summer Sunday afternoon, part grass and part sunshine with a hint of smoke. Swallowing, I gripped the table, trying not to focus on the smear of blood on his skin. There was too much magic in this room on offer. I skittered back even further, my hands in tight fists behind my back.

Freddo examined the feather in a brusque, business-like manner, then grunted. "I can't get a read on its type."

"Give me something." I kept a wary eye on Freddo, but his cockamamie anti-compulsion get-up continued to do its thing.

"It feels like it came from the beginning of time."

I feigned surprise since he believed me to be Mundane and I wouldn't know this fact otherwise. "That's impossible. Magic isn't that old."

"That's right and this can't be either. It's part of its trickery."

"Is it Nefesh magic?"

He popped the toothpick back in his mouth. "All magic is Nefesh magic. What kind of question is that?"

"Could it come from some creature we haven't realized exists? Like a vampire... or an angel? Uh, can you take off the blindfold? It's weird talking like this."

He whipped the blindfold off and slung the strip of black cloth over his shoulder. "Magic takes different forms, so it all feels different, but there's still an underlying similarity to it. A foundation that marks it as Nefesh. You follow?"

I nodded.

"This has that same foundation. If other creatures existed, they'd have their own foundation."

And buh-bye, Angel of Death. Though I was still totally keeping "The Curious Incident of the Angel of Death" as the name of this case because it sounded way cooler than "The Asshole Who Shoved a Feather Down Someone's Throat."

Since this was Nefesh magic, our attacker was human, and while Nefesh couldn't fly, they could make you think they did. Fuuuuuck. "Anything else odd about the feather?"

He gave a long pull on the toothpick like it was a

cigarette. "Artifact magic, no matter how potent, feels like a diluted version of ours. Same foundation, mind you. Makes sense because someone had to imbue the artifact with their magic. But this?" He tapped the feather. "More concentrated. Way more concentrated."

"Best guess as to its type?"

"No clue. Too strong. All I read is magic in screaming capital letters with no details. It's all big picture. Can try one more thing." He mumbled something.

The feather's magic flared: stardust and a hot sandstorm.

Spiky blood armor flickered in and out over my body. Desire warred with survival instinct, because if I wore the armor, I couldn't use my powers to ride that magic. I struggled to lock the armor in place because I couldn't go there again. I'd lose myself.

Freddo said something else under his breath and the blood he'd dripped on the feather sent up a column of smoke. He startled and jostled into me.

His hat was knocked askew.

A strange light slithered through his eyes and he let out a breathy sigh, gazing at the feather in adoration.

Oh shit.

Feather in hand, Freddo tore off the lead apron and sprinted for the open door.

I ran after him, grabbed him by the collar, and tossed him across the room. My blood armor was still going haywire, so I used the edge of my jacket and every drop of willpower to pick up the feather and seal it in the pouch.

Someone grabbed my right hand and my fingertips turned to ice.

No, not ice. Stone. My hand grew heavy as veins of black rock snaked through my palm, numbing my sense of touch and turning my flesh into dead weight. My armor flickered out entirely.

The pouch fell from my grip and clattered to the ground next to Freddo, who groggily rubbed his head.

Think, Ash. This is invasive magic. I destroyed it in other people with the third-party smudges, I could do the same for myself. I tried to hook into it but couldn't. My magic merely chipped off flakes of the obsidian mass spreading like a pernicious weed through my body.

A man in a balaclava brushed past me. "Hand over the feather, old man." His low gruff voice was totally exaggerated to disguise his real one.

"BBQ," I said. My arm hung limply at my side, half of my forearm turning to stone thanks to Medusa magic.

The thief frowned. "Huh?"

Freddo, you betraying little douche baguette.

"Corn nuts, meathead." I grabbed for him, but the dead weight of my arm threw me off balance and he sidestepped me.

The employee blinked at the corn nuts residue on his fingers. "Shit, man. She's made us." He grabbed the pouch, then extended a hand to Freddo.

The shock on the employee's face when Freddo pulled out his own switchblade and stabbed his accomplice in the leg was an expression I'd cherish for years to come. Provided I was still alive.

My entire right arm was now stone, causing me to list sideways under the weight, and the blackness was spreading down my hip and into my leg. I dragged myself forward to get to Freddo, but I was too slow.

Ignoring both me and the crumpled howling employee bleeding out on his floor, Freddo grabbed the pouch and made his getaway.

"Freddo," I croaked. I could barely hear myself over my heartbeat thumping in my ears. The stone magic continued to spread. If it got to my heart or my throat, I was toast.

Freddo turned.

"Help me. For Adam's sake."

His gaze flicked from the pouch to me.

My right side had gone dead. Unless I got this magic out of my system, I would be, too. "You kept a stash of Dad's favorite lemon candies, but you'd never share them with him. You saved them for me. Remember?"

I held out my left hand to him. "Don't let me die."

He hesitated and I swayed on my feet. Not totally an act. I was trapped in my own body, being buried alive and suffocating. Tears leaked out of my eyes. "Please."

Freddo bit his lip, then he came close enough to lay a hand on my cheek. "The magic is too fast-acting. You won't suffer long."

Relax, you'll be dead soon. That's what you had for me?

I snaked my hand out and grabbed his wrist, pulling it up to eye level. Blinking blearily, I sent my magic into his still-open cut and rode his blood.

We swayed together like waltz partners. Drunk waltz partners, though that might have been the blissful high from his magic. A dreamy cast engulfed the world, and the grassy taste of his magic tickled my throat, but it slid down smoothly.

As with Omar, there was no trace of compulsion magic inside him.

Freddo thrashed against me and I stroked a hand over his head, murmuring soothing words. The boost allowed me to penetrate the stone magic, cracking it enough for my red forked branches to snag it, but I didn't have enough power to call forth the white clusters to finish off the Medusa magic. I required more juice than Freddo had in him.

I turned my sights on the employee, who sagged against the wall, trying to staunch the bleeding in his thigh with blood-soaked hands.

Perfect. He was already primed.

I gasped. What was I doing? I wasn't a third-party

smudge, harming innocents for my own gain. There had to be another way.

Body shaking, I shut down our connection. Freddo's magic snapped into him, still intact. My red branches trembled, barely holding strong and keeping the stone magic from spreading.

"What are you?" Freddo recoiled from me and hurt flared in my chest as one of the final connections to my father fractured.

"No one you want to fuck with. Give me the pouch." I couldn't have fought Freddo if he resisted because while my right half was still stone, my left half was wracked with vicious spasms from abruptly stopping the sweet, sweet process of draining his magic.

Luckily, his exposure to the feather had been fleeting, and the compulsion had faded. That or his terror of me overrode it. Given his wide eyes and the way he tried not to touch any part of me, from this day forth, I'd be a monster to him. He'd never know what it cost me to withhold my full monstrosity and let him walk out of here whole.

He shoved the thin pouch under my left arm. Freddo would be fine. Physically fine.

My mirror-facing abilities had taken a hit.

I pulled out my phone. "Call me a healer."

Freddo knocked my cell out of my hand and fled. The cell flew sideways and I landed on my half-stony ass in a puddle of the employee's blood with a loud thunk. Magic tingled up through my fingertips.

I licked my finger and raked a considering glance over the employee.

His eyes widened. "Don't touch me!" He stretched out his hands to give me another infusion of Medusa magic but was too far out of reach, so the idiot yanked the knife out of his thigh to attack, and immediately fainted.

I had to tourniquet his leg or he'd bleed out.

The blindfold lay nearby. I rocked on my ass until I got enough lift-off to thump over to it. By the time I'd bandaged him, those branches of mine only had the most precarious hold on the obsidian blackness. Splaying my hands into the spilled blood, I Hoovered every bit of magic out of it with no harm to the employee. Sucking his power out this way was akin to magic dumpster diving, but beggars couldn't be choosers.

His magic had weakened outside his body, but it was alive and potent enough to allow me to draw out the stone magic. Those glorious white clusters bloomed and ate the nasty shit up.

I was myself once more, flesh and bone with not a trace of rock. After placing an anonymous call to 911, I stood up and my right leg buckled.

Pain was a funny thing. In short bursts, like a headache, it was front and center. It sucked, but knowing there would be an end made it bearable. Unfortunately, my leg pain since the car crash and my surgery had been a fifteen-year slow grind wearing me down. I hadn't lived at my fullest in happy Technicolor; life was blurred at the edges.

My newfound magic had pretty much done away with my pain unless I was severely overtaxed, and it had thrown my world back into sharp focus. Had the stone magic weakened me again?

I refused to return to that reality.

Sirens grew louder. I scrambled out a back exit, ahead of the Nefesh First Responders. Satisfied that the employee would be taken care of, I hit up a nearby corner store for Gatorade and some beef jerky to top up my electrolytes and get some fuel in my body. Sitting in a tiny deserted park, I wolfed it all down so fast that I was queasy. Better than dead.

All the while, I remained hyperaware of the feather, secured in the pouch and tucked into my waistband at the small of my back. I hadn't been ready—or able—to let it out of my sight and stash it in the lockbox in my trunk.

A quick call to the Dershowitz house confirmed that they were still in Hedon. Might as well catch them there and conduct my interviews.

Before I could palm one of the bronze tokens that Moran had given me, my shoulder blades prickled for a third time. This wasn't an overactive imagination. Someone was definitely spying.

A shadow fell over me and a figure, about six-feet-tall, with a lean build and white wings, flew down onto the grass. He wore a floor-length white robe with a mask obscuring most of his face and hair and heavy gloves on his hands. Worried I might recognize him? Regardless, I doubted this was standard Heaven-issue wear.

"I am Malach, Angel of Death," he said in a low distorted voice.

Cowering wasn't in my wheelhouse, but I wasn't yet energized enough to menace. Door number three it was.

"I am Ashira, Private Investigator." I held out a dried beef stick. "Jerky?"

Chapter 11

Malach's eyes glittered fervently. They were black, not blue, and the hair peeking out from the edge of the mask was a dark blond. The incongruities were dismissible because if this was an illusion, everything was adjustable, including the build, which was similar to Levi's but a couple inches shorter.

"Return that which is mine," he said, "and I shall allow you to live."

"You'll have to be more specific." I bit into the jerky.

"The feather." His lips compressed into a flat line.

If I needed a final nail in the coffin against Malach being a real angel, I had it. The feather was so chock-full of power that it rolled off in waves, therefore, his magic should have overwhelmed me, but I didn't even get a blip.

I didn't have any radar to verify if someone was Nefesh unless they used their magic and I smelled it. Levi's stupid magic excepted.

Wait. Malach *had* used his magic to fly here. I moved closer and inhaled. No oaky amber scotch and chocolate, instead, the peculiar combination of lilies and dust assaulted me.

Hope surged hot and bright in my chest.

After one last bite, which I took my time chewing and swallowing, I twisted the top of the jerky packaging and put the stick in my pocket. "Nah. Finders keepers."

"Then you shall die!"

I manifested my spiky blood armor. "While I'm aflutter with anticipation, I don't think you can do squat. Solid effort for the cover story, though. The Angel of Death did kill all the Egyptian firstborns in Moses' time, and yeah, Omar is an Egyptian firstborn, and it's Passover, which is a nice touch. But making him deep throat your feather is hardly murder of biblical proportions. Either you're slipping or you're a fake."

Malach backhanded me. I crashed into a tree trunk and bounced onto the grass, silently blessing my armor. Fuck me. Did he have brass knuckles sewn into his gloves?

Despite the pain radiating in my jaw, I bounced on my toes in glee. Levi wouldn't physically hurt me.

Come on. Get mad. Get sloppy.

I waved the pouch. "Tell you what. I'll consider handing the feather over if you tell me why you're wearing a mask. Aren't angels all 'behold the glory of my being because I'm so pretty?'"

He rushed me. I suspect being hit by a train packed a similar punch. And that was with my magic armor. The breath was knocked from my lungs and I fell onto my back.

Either he was built like a brick shithouse or he wore some kind of fortification under those robes. The pouch slid free and bounced on the grass.

I grabbed it before Malach could and stuffed it under my body. He kicked me in the ribs with steel-toed boots. Was he in construction?

My armor was literally a lifesaver, but the pummeling still took it out of me, and my tank was perilously low.

Rolling out of the way, I made the armor disappear, since I couldn't ride magic otherwise, and jumped to my feet.

Malach expected me to run, but instead, I skirted in nice and close and hit him with a swift upper cut. He staggered back.

I manifested a blood dagger and slashed the side of his throat. Since I had to mainline into his blood to hook my magic to his, I pressed my thumb to the cut.

"Why did you come back for the murder weapon?" I said.

He roared, jerking sideways before I could get an answer —or a lock on his magic.

Malach extended his wings and with a flap that sent dirt and grass up in tiny whirlwinds, flew away. Or he made me think he did.

One way to test that.

I hurled the dagger, striking him in his side. A gun would have taken him down for sure, but there were too many moving parts to ensure I wouldn't mangle its creation and blow my hand off. I stuck to creating simple weapons.

Despite Malach's cry of pain, he continued across the sky until he ducked behind a building and was lost from view.

If I'd stabbed an illusion, would he have made a noise? No, because the caster would be down here hidden in the park somewhere.

I collapsed on the grass, limp with exhaustion and relief. It wasn't Levi. I didn't have to take him down or keep the Queen from beheading him. He had a very nice head.

A glint of white fluttered, caught on a stalk of grass. I picked up a lone white feather with caution, ran a finger over it, and frowned. That couldn't be right. I slid my fingernail into its tip, making a tiny slit. The tip was plastic. This feather was a fake. Part of a costume.

Of course it was. It's not like a real angel suffered from wing-based bald spots and used fake feathers to pad out his wings. I snickered, imagining the angel version of a Rogaine commercial. Hair Club for Angels.

Nor did an illusionist need a costume. If it wasn't Houdini magic, then what? This second feather didn't possess any of that ancient magic, but that didn't negate this Malach having something. If this wasn't an illusion, then he had some kind of magic allowing him to fly.

Except flight magic didn't exist. Yeah, sure, neither did blood magic, supposedly, but that didn't help me. Damn it. If I hadn't burned Freddo, he could have gotten a read on this second feather.

Despite still having more questions than answers, I was elated. I'd crossed both Levi and a real Angel of Death definitively off my list. Levi was good. I was right. A dozen champagne bubbles, light and airy, rose through my chest and I told myself my dizzying euphoria was at the latter conclusion, not the former.

Plus, with this second feather, I had my first solid lead. I debated sealing the second feather up with the first in the pouch for safekeeping but opted against it. Should I find another Typecaster, I didn't want the second feather magically contaminated in any way, so I tucked it in my back pocket.

I took a quick breather to recover after all that, and then canvassed costume and theatrical supply shops in Vancouver. Aside from a store who'd sold a bunch of angel wings to a Catholic school for an Easter play, and another where the clerk remembered selling some for a bachelorette party, tracking the attacker via the costume wings didn't pan out.

Time to lean on the families and see who was hiding things. Clutching a bronze token in my hand, I mentally ordered it to take me to the Queen.

Oddly, the world didn't shift like it usually did when I went to Hedon. Instead, from one step to the next, I fell deep into a memory.

It was a week before my thirteenth birthday, and Dad was supposed to pick me up from elementary school and drive me to swimming lessons. I'd sat there on the edge of the soccer field until darkness fell and the playground was a nest of shadows, then I shivered all through the walk home, because I hadn't worn a warm enough jacket. My swim gear weighed down my backpack almost as much as the heavy feeling in my gut that deepened with every step.

Talia was cooking dinner. I don't remember what the meal was but I'll never forget the way her smile at seeing me turned to a puzzled frown at my lips that were blue with cold. How she asked me where Dad was and I couldn't answer. The hours that stretched into forever that night when she called everyone she knew with a forced cheerfulness to ask if they'd seen Adam, or the desperation when all that was left were hospitals and police stations.

I came out of my reverie in a formal parlor with tears glistening on my cheeks and the feeling I'd woken from a vivid dream. Except it wasn't a dream: it was the cost of using the bronze token, just like Moran had cautioned. My body crumpled in on itself, and I brushed the tears away with the back of my hand. There was the soft click of heels behind me. "Got what you wanted?" I said.

"Knowledge is power, blanquita. You of all people know that. And you can't say you weren't warned." The Queen of Hearts stood in the doorway. Her dark red hair was twisted in a chignon and her violet eyes betrayed no hint of emotion. Dressed in her signature red, today's outfit was silk men's pajamas that hugged her curves, her feet stuffed into fur-trimmed slippers with kitten heels.

Plus-size women didn't have it easy, but the biggest hater would think twice before tangling with the Queen. Even in leisurewear, intelligence and power radiated off her, from the shrewd cunning in her eyes to the total ease with which she lounged, as if it was on the world to earn its place around her.

Stiff red curtains blocked the windows, but the rest of the room was white and airy. A crystal chandelier twinkled softly above us, while the floor was covered with a Persian rug in rich jewel tones around which lushly upholstered furniture in red and white brocades were grouped.

"Can any rando show up at your door or did the token give me access?" I said.

"*I* gave you access. The tokens are another way to keep tabs on who is coming and going." Her Spanish accent flavored her words. She sat down on a white loveseat and patted the cushion beside her.

I lowered myself onto it, ignoring the twinge in my right thigh. A tête-à-tête with a self-declared monarch with a fondness for beheadings—just the pick-me-up my day required. "I need to interview the families."

"In a moment. This Angel of Death is causing me problems."

I threw my hands up. "Please tell me you don't actually think there's an honest-to-goodness Angel of Death running around?"

She raised a sculpted eyebrow and I swallowed, modifying my tone.

"If the attacker was truly the Angel of Death," I said, "he should have radiated the same magic that came off the feather that I pulled from Omar's throat. I recently tangled with him and he didn't. Then, there's this." I showed her the second feather. "It fell off his wing. See the plastic tip? It's a fake. Omar's attacker was a human with a grudge and an Old Testament fetish."

Her gaze sharpened. "Do you have the other feather on you?"

I could have said no, but she could see into the deepest recesses of my heart. I had no desire to test whether she could spot a lie. I handed her the pouch. "Don't open it."

"I was advised not to. What is this magic?" She flipped the pouch over, tracing a finger along the etchings.

"I'm working on it." I held out my hand. Seeing it in her grasp, even sealed, made me twitchy. "Can I have it back? It's central to the Tannous investigation."

There was no way the Queen should have handed over something this powerful and dangerous and yet she did. This wedding had to be important to her. Why else would she have involved herself to begin with? Why these two families in particular mattered remained a mystery, but I didn't care so long as I got my payment for services rendered.

I tucked the pouch in my waistband against the small of my back.

She watched me like I'd been put on a set of scales and she was waiting to see if they balanced. Creepy.

I pushed to my feet, pleasantly surprised when my thigh didn't ache. Fingers crossed I'd merely overtaxed myself. "I should question the families. Pin down the attacker's motive."

"¡Claro!" She smiled beatifically and I backed up a step. She threaded her arm through mine. "Walk with me."

Our footsteps echoed over white marble tile in a brightly lit corridor. It was filled with paintings of beautiful land-scapes, from rolling hills to still lakes, all depicted in full sun. To the casual eye, the Queen was a warm, engaging host, her fifty-something years giving her an almost grand-motherly feel as she escorted her guest on the grand tour. From my close-up perspective, her light grip was more inescapable than a dungeon. Great. Bet she had those, too.

"I persuaded the families that Omar would be safest here in Hedon," she said.

Made them an offer they couldn't refuse. "Because of the Black Heart Rule. You've put him under your protection."

"Precisely. Attacking him would be foolish, and since they all decided to accompany Omar, I am hosting everyone."

"They couldn't bear to have him out of their sight after his miraculous escape from the jaws of death?"

"Something like that." Her full lips pursed. "They wanted to postpone the wedding."

We strolled through a large sunken living room, decorated in all-white but with a red accent wall and red cushions on the furniture. Billowing white curtains framed a set of sliding doors leading out to a large terrace.

"They'd had a shock but I insisted that it was no reason to put off their beautiful day," she said, leaning into me like we were confidantes. "They agreed with my assessment."

What a mitzvah. "Mazel tov."

"By the time Shannon walks down the aisle, you will have found the attacker and handed him over to me. I assured them that five days was plenty of time for you to achieve this, no? The young couple wishes to feel safe moving forward with their new life."

I'd already pulled one miracle out of my ass and saved Omar. Now I had to find his attacker by Sunday so the Queen could have this ceremony? "There was no agreed-upon deadline."

The Queen waved her hand like this was of no consequence. "Now there is."

I stopped and tugged my arm free. "No disrespect, but the deal was I solve this and in return you give me the vials. I didn't have a due date and the wedding isn't my problem."

"If you have not wrapped things up for the wedding to happen as scheduled, you will not get your vials."

"Are you reneging on the terms of our agreement?"

"I merely want Omar and Shannon to start their new lives together free from worry." Her kitten heels clacked ominously along the tiles. "Get me the attacker in time and those vials will be yours. Fail and I'll begin negotiations with potential buyers."

I went cold. "You said you weren't interested in that kind of chaos."

The Queen unfurled a Cheshire Cat smile. "My interests change over time."

"Five days it is. Do any of them know about my magic?"

"No. Moran—" The Queen smirked as if it amused her to call him that. "He assured them that Omar was choking on the feather and that all you did was pull it out. That is the extent of your involvement in his recovery." She motioned me out on to the terrace. "The families are down by the gazebo. I'll leave you to it."

Yeah, right. More like you'll watch my every move.

"I will endeavor to live up to your confidence in me," I said.

She inclined her head. Not in acknowledgment of my efforts. More in "yes, of course you will or I'll crush you."

I stepped outside.

Hedon was a never-ending humid summer's night, the air sticky and velvety against my skin. At first, its magic had nauseated me, now it merely set my teeth on edge. It was a cacophony that I had to force to a dim roar each time. Its magic smell of axle grease and vanilla ice cream had subtly shifted, the ice cream now soured.

Gagging, I crossed the flagstones to the low stone wall with stairs leading down to the extensive gardens.

Lights twinkled through the park grounds. In the distance, above the trees, was a wash of neon floating above the stalls and shacks in the "business district" that I'd encountered on my first visit here. The electric blue ramen bowl was orange tonight, joined by a steaming coffee cup, and a pair of flashing blood-red pickaxes.

The garden was filled with night-blooming plants and the scent of jasmine. There were no walls enclosing it and people made free use of the space. A person of indeterminate gender and glowing gold eyes cycled past on one of those wacky high-wheeled bicycles from a bygone era. Another couple practiced their water magic on a fountain.

Picking out the slanted roof of the gazebo over to my left, I descended the stairs and ran into Moran coming up from the bottom. We did that side-to-side dance for a moment until I laughed and put up my fists. "Fight ya for passage."

He smiled indulgently at me. "It would be your last."

"I almost took you out when we fought earlier, buddy. Don't knock my skills."

"Ah, but we're in Hedon now."

"So?"

"The Queen puts those of importance to her under the Black Heart Rule. I am her right hand man. Draw the appropriate conclusion."

"What is that anyway? Does it involve dungeons and unspeakable torture?"

He gave me an enigmatic smile and tilted his head to the garden. "I'll leave you to solve this case. The clock is ticking."

"Uh, okay. Later, dude." I swept past him down the rest of the stairs.

The occasional guard in black tactical gear with mesh obscuring their face blended into the shadows. The Queen's logo of a heart with a crown and scepter was stitched on their upper arm.

Statues were dotted throughout the grounds, and I veered off the winding path to get a better look at a couple of random ones. The first depicted a young man wielding a machete, the other was a woman gathering up her skirts, ready to flee. The angle of the blade as it cut downward, the wind ruffling the woman's hem, the details were exquisite. Even their faces were personalized. The man had a gash across his forehead, the woman sported a birthmark on one cheek.

Their eyes were a little too wide. A little too aware.

I clapped a hand over my mouth, then tentatively reached out and touched a shoulder of the woman statue. "Hello?" I said softly.

The statue didn't reply, not that I expected it to, but there was someone in there. I pressed a hand against my belly, the wind knocked from my lungs.

The Black Heart Rule.

Omar was under the Queen's protection. If I failed to solve this case or failed to keep him safe, then this was what awaited me.

I curled my hands into fists and picked up the pace. Time was running out.

Chapter 12

I approached the wrought-iron gazebo, where seething resentment blanketed an otherwise charming space.

A table had been wheeled into the center with the two families in formation on either side. A military campaign was but a humble endeavor next to the seating chart being fought over by everyone except the bride and groom.

Omar was propped in a lounge chair at the back of the gazebo, while Shannon coaxed him to drink mint tea out of a small jewel-colored glass.

"Habibi," he said tenderly. He looked a bit wan, but otherwise in good health. "You drink it. The mint will help relieve some of your stress and there is sweetness for my sweet."

Shannon blushed and took a sip, while I steered clear of the Zone of Mushiness, lest it contaminate me.

"Greetings, Wedding Party." My stomach rumbled.

"Feather?" Omar asked me hopefully.

"He keeps asking about it," Shannon said.

"Someone has cursed him." Grandmother Masika gave me the evil eye. Better than trying to stab me.

"I only pulled the feather out. Any lingering effects are

not on my head." I approached the second table set up to the side, which was arrayed with an assortment of different cake slices. "May I?"

I took being ignored as consent and helped myself to some strawberry shortcake. The cake was light and fluffy, the strawberries sweet with a hint of tart that blended beautifully with the full fat of the whipping cream. If my P.I. dreams didn't pan out, I could happily hire myself out to all calorie-conscious brides and grooms as their cake consultant.

A nervous wedding coordinator in a pink so pale it was basically an embarrassed white, stood next to the center table, gripping a marker and a fistful of seating cards, her eyes darting back and forth between Ivan and Masika. "If we could get back to the chart?"

"We are paying the larger share. Our family will be Table One." Masika's knitting needles clacked with a menacing edge.

"I am Rebbe Dershowitz and I demand the respect of sitting at Table One." Ivan slammed his fist down, making the carefully placed seating cards jump.

I peered at my already empty plate hoping more cake would magically manifest. Rachel stepped sideways, blocking me from the dessert table, so I did not help myself to a second piece. I deposited my empty plate on the ground and sized up the group for whom to speak to first.

Such stellar choices: Ivan and his meaty fists, Masika and her knitting needles, Husani and Chione tossing the red color-coded ones assigned to the Dershowitz guests off the table, or Rachel, who "accidentally" sloshed half the contents of her martini glass on Husani, after another card hit the ground.

In the face of all this childish passive-aggression, I kind of missed their open violence.

"The Queen said you have to complete this today," the wedding coordinator stammered.

Chione smiled slowly and ran a finger over her holstered pistol. "Are we not?"

Again with the fingering.

The wedding coordinator looked like she might puke, so I edged in between them. "We are all playing nicely and no one is going to do anything stupid which they would live to regret. Capisce?"

Chione rolled her eyes and folded a seating card into a tiny paper airplane.

"Now, I have updates, which I will share with each of you as we chat. Shannon." I snapped my fingers. "With me."

I led Shannon to a bench on the lawn. Setting my phone in between us, I activated my voice recorder app. "Tuesday, March twenty-fifth. Interview with Shannon Dershowitz."

She darted glances back at Omar every few seconds.

"He's not going anywhere," I said. Unless… "Excited for your big day?"

"Of course." She bobbed her birdlike neck.

"You've got no opinions about the seating chart? Don't brides love doing all that wedding stuff?"

"That part is to make my father happy. I only care about being legally wed. Everything will be fine then." She smiled, but her fingernails were bitten down to stubs and her ring hung loosely on her finger.

"Did you and Omar fight about something?" I said. "Maybe something to do with why he was attacked?"

"He's suffering some lingering effects right now, but overall Omar is the perfect fiancé." She twisted her hands in her lap.

"Shannon. If you are being forced in any way to do something against your will, I can get you somewhere safe."

Her surprise wasn't feigned; neither was her firm refusal. "Oh, it's nothing like that. It's just, Omar is usually loving and attentive but ever since he got to Vancouver he's been secretive. Spending time locked away in his room." Her eyes pooled with tears. "I think he's having an affair and the Angel is a jealous husband."

Kind of a convoluted logic and it didn't account for the feather, but I cut her some slack.

"The angel is human, you're right about that." I searched for a tissue, but the best I could do was a wadded-up napkin I found in my pocket. "It's clean."

She took it and dabbed at her eyes.

"Did you check Omar's phone for texts that could confirm an infidelity?"

"I'd never—" She wilted under my flat stare. "I don't know his password."

"Where was he before he came to Vancouver? Back home in Cairo?" That would be the most likely place for him to carry on an affair.

"No, he was on a job. I don't know what. The family doesn't discuss them."

"When was the last time you saw him before this? That you'd say he was behaving normally?"

"About a month ago." She darted another look over at Omar, sitting apart from the families looking distracted. He sensed Shannon's gaze on him and mustered up a smile.

"Go." I flapped a hand at her and she bolted like I had when released from detention in my misspent youth. "Send Masika over," I called out.

I got Masika and Chione. A twofer. As I entered the date and the participants present into my voice recorder, Masika positioned herself in the best spot to stab me in the jugular should the conversation take a turn not to her liking.

"I've been able to confirm that the Angel of Death is human," I said.

"How did he fly?" Chione said.

"Not sure yet. He's magic, but we aren't working with divine retribution. Or an illusion. The attacker had assembled a costume. That involved planning and that tells me a couple of things. One, that the choice to use the Angel of Death was deliberate and tied to motive. Which brings me to number two: this was personal. Money, sex, revenge, power." With that kind of powerful magic, the feather could fall into any one of those four areas. "What was Omar's last job?"

"Our work is confidential," Chione said, re-rolling the ball of multicolored yarn that Masika was using to knit the sweater.

"As is this case that you've hired me to solve."

They sat there, two generations of stubborn in all-black, Masika in widow's weeds and Chione probably because it hid blood better.

"If this wedding doesn't happen, you don't get those Nefesh grandbabies you want to expand your business," I said.

Masika's poker face didn't even flicker, her needles clacking away, but Chione's fingers tightened on the ball of yarn.

I frowned as though the most outlandish idea had just hit me. "Unless of course, you've already started expanding. Shannon and Omar might be a love match now, but it started as an arranged marriage and you didn't meet the Dershowitzes because you travel in the same social circles. You'd done business with them, and having gotten a taste of the money to be made in Nefeshland, you wanted more." I wagged a finger at them. "You know that's illegal, right? Mundanes aren't allowed to provide security for Nefesh clients."

"It's a stupid law," Chione said. "If that's what we were even doing."

"I agree, but as one bound to uphold it as per the conditions of my Mundane private investigator license, I'd have to inform House Al Qahirah in Cairo of your actions."

Chione stroked her gun again. "If you could get out of here before I shot you."

"First off, get a vibrator."

Masika barked a laugh, making Chione split her glower between the two of us.

"Second of all, I'm under the Queen's protection," I lied. "You know what happens to people who break that?" I pointed at the statue.

"They get art commemorating their audacity?"

"No, they get to be the art."

Chione did a double take and Masika leaned forward with an interested expression like she was calculating how to incorporate that into the family business.

"You may be mercenaries," I said, "and you may be in the same league as Ivan and his cronies, but don't for a second think you can take on the Queen."

"Ah, but you won't always be in Hedon under mommy's protection," Chione said.

I smiled at her. My favorite smile with too many teeth that I never got to roll out as often as I liked. "You won't either. Don't underestimate me, Chione. The Queen hand-picked me to help you because I have very unique abilities. Pray you don't find out what."

Bluffing like a boss. The Tannouses were Mundane. They had no magic to destroy and even if I roughed them up some, they could pump me full of lead. "Now, either you tell me about Omar's last job or I walk away, untouched, and get House Al Qahirah to pay very close attention to you."

Masika and Chione had a brief and heated discussion in Arabic.

"It was a nothing job on an archeological dig in the Sinai Peninsula." Chione ran a hand over the ball of yarn, smoothing it out.

"Who were the clients?"

"Cairo University." She sneered. "Respectable enough for you?"

"Why hire you?"

She puffed out her chest. "Because we're the best. They had to transport some of the antiquities back to Cairo and were worried about looting, due to unstable conditions in the region."

"Could Omar have helped himself? Angered some powerful people?"

"Our reputation is everything. I'd expect you to understand that."

"Noted. Were their finds valuable? Could someone have targeted Omar because he prevented them from getting their hands on them?"

"Only valuable to history." Masika took the yarn and rolled it up with the sweater, threading the needles through everything to hold the stash together. "Wooden bowls, coins." She asked Chione a question in Arabic.

"Metalwork," Chione said. "The pieces were evidence of a nomadic culture in the region."

Masika nodded. "Aywah. There's a Bedouin legend about the existence of gold in a hillside cave in the high mountains of the Sinai. No gold found but the legend lives on. That's why fear of looting."

Nothing valuable and it was a university archeological dig. There was nothing on the surface to prompt an attack.

"Did Omar ever have a job go sideways? Get into a dangerous situation and offend the wrong people? Any competitors who would go after him?"

"We've successfully completed every job we've been hired for. As for competitors?" Chione laughed. "Our industry isn't known for its moral compass. There are many jealous business rivals but were they to attack, it would be more direct."

"Last question. Was Omar cheating on Shannon?"

"No." Chione's answer was a little too prompt and insistent.

"Omar loves her. He puts her welfare first." Masika sounded totally grumpy about the fact, which lent it credibility, because they were stuck with the Dershowitzes as in-laws.

Chione snickered. "Your precious grandson doesn't love you the most anymore."

Masika shot her a quelling look. "We are indebted to the Queen for her generosity in hosting this wedding."

"I'm sure she knows how appreciative you are. Thanks. That's—"

There was a muffled boom and the ground rumbled and pitched. We all clutched the bench. Hedon had earthquakes? How? It was stitched together from pockets of our reality. There weren't tectonic plates. Unless the seams themselves were fault lines. That wasn't terrifying or anything.

It lasted for the longest twenty seconds of my life. I was braced for Hedon to fall apart and all of us to pitch into some endless void, but the world remained intact. There were no aftershocks, other than my stuttering pulse.

The Queen's security force resumed their patrol of the grounds, which I took as a sign that all was normal once more.

Chione helped Masika to her feet.

"Could you give me a few minutes and then ask Omar to come see me?"

They nodded and left.

If the attempted murder was because of a woman, where did that get me? Start with the Passover story. The death of the firstborn was the final, most terrible threat inflicted on the Egyptians to convince the Pharaoh to let the Jews go. If that was the case here, then the feather down the throat was the final threat to force Omar to do something. However, it would have eventually killed him, so how could he then do anything?

I tried a different tack. Why did the attacker want the feather back? If he was compelled, he wouldn't have left it behind in Omar's throat to begin with. Not based on Moran and Omar's reactions to it. If he wasn't—and that was its own mystery—then why use it as a murder weapon only to retrieve it? Did he plan on using it again?

With a grunt, Ivan dropped on to the bench. "I'm here to be interviewed."

Interesting, since I hadn't asked.

I pulled out my voice recorder. "Tuesday, March twenty-fifth. Interview with Rebbe Dershowitz."

He slung an arm along the back of the bench, watching me with a small smirk, as if he was doing me a favor.

"Tell me about Omar."

Ivan made a dismissive sound. "Not the man I'd have chosen for my Shannon."

"But you did, thanks to your dealings with Jacob the Shark."

"Huh. I pegged you for nothing more than the Queen's patsy, but you dug that up pretty damn quick." He glanced over at his daughter. "I'd been backed into a corner and this was a way out. Better a loveless marriage than any harm coming to her."

He'd still been willing to sacrifice her happiness to save his own skin. At least she really loved Omar.

"Why do you think someone tried to kill Omar? To be clear," I said, "I've verified it was a human attacker."

"Good. Who wants angels around anyway? Malach was the ultimate expression of God's displeasure against his enemies, passing judgment on us. Waste of time. Humans manage to go to the darkest places on their own, regardless of where that lands them in the end."

"That was a very thorough summary. Got a vested interest in angels?"

Ivan laughed. "Had a lot of time to read in the joint. Lots of copies of the Old Testament around."

"Does Omar love Shannon? In your opinion?"

"Yes. He scoured the Egyptian market for this rare type of glass Shannon mentioned offhandedly that she'd always wanted to incorporate into one of her light sculptures. Took the idiot three weeks and he spent way more for it than he should, but he got it." Ivan stroked a hand over his fleshy jowls. "He leaves her sappy voicemails. As love letters. Name me one millennial who does that."

I honestly couldn't.

Ivan nodded. "But he's a weak man."

"He's a mercenary."

"Weapons give him power," he corrected, "but he's not strong. He's kind to Shannon though and he understands her in a way that her mother and I were never able to. He's her heart's desire."

"You're a wise man, Rebbe. I pegged you wrong, too."

"Being underestimated has its uses." He raked a shrewd glance over me. "I suspect you know that."

"I do, indeed. Any other wisdom you'd care to dispense?"

"No, that's enough for you. I locked down Table One while you had Masika and Chione over here. Consider my insights your thanks. Now to get my way on the booze." With a wink, he stood up. "I'll send Omar over." Hands in pockets, he sauntered back to the others.

Omar shuffled toward me like he was going to the guillotine. He sat down, hunched over. "I need the feather. Please."

"Ride it out, buddy. Your attacker was a person, not an angel. Thoughts on why he came after you?"

He shook his head, the picture of misery.

"Did you cheat on Shannon?"

He turned startled eyes to me. "What? No! I'd never do that to her."

I counted off the seconds in my head. Omar cracked before I'd reached forty-three. Ivan was right. He was weak.

"One time," he mumbled.

"When?"

"About three weeks ago."

"So much for 'you'd never do that to Shannon.'"

"It was someone I'd gone to school with and I'd always had a crush on her. We got drunk and... I was a fool. I hated myself afterward and I'll never do anything like that again. Please don't tell Shannon. I love her and want to spend the rest of my life with her."

"Was this woman married?"

"No." The tension in his posture was gone. He'd already confessed to the worst of it. He spoke the truth.

"What's her name?"

"Edrice Abadi. She's the site supervisor on an archeological dig I provided security for."

I'd follow up with her.

He cleared his throat. "I'd like the feather. To remind me how close I came to dying."

"Bullshit. What did it tempt you with?" I'd hoped its compulsion would have worn off by now. Moran almost took my head off for it and he'd only been exposed for a few minutes. How far would Omar go to get it back?

He worried at a hole in his jeans. "Tempt? No idea what you're talking about."

"Quit fucking around. The feather compels people. It tempts them with their heart's desire. What was yours? Aren't you putting your family in danger while you're under its thrall? Putting Shannon in danger?"

His lip curled. "I can handle it."

Of course. Strength.

"Did it promise you invincibility?" I pulled out the metal pouch. "The feather is right here."

His fingers twitched and his eyes gleamed.

"Your whole family is watching. Shannon is watching. If you want to be strong, prove that you can be to yourself first."

He tapped his head. "I can't get away…"

"From the song?"

He nodded.

"Trust me, I know what that's like, and how hard it is. But even if the craving is eating you up inside, walk away. It will wear off at some point. Meantime, take the first step to becoming the man you want to be."

He reached for the pouch. Stopped. White-knuckled the edge of the bench.

"You can do this. Go back to Shannon and live-happily-ever-after."

Omar bit his lip, then with a long look at his fiancée, he stood up and walked away. The price of turning his back on the pouch was etched into the twist of his shoulders, his bowed head, and his painfully slow gait, but he kept going.

Good for you, dude. The feather might have given you some initial burst of confidence, but you'd spend the rest of your life chasing that first high.

My fingers tightened on the pouch and I tucked it back in my waistband with movements as slow as Omar's.

I turned off my phone app, and switched over to my notes program, jotting down my thoughts. Judgment and temptation. I fit the pieces together until they fell into a shape I could work with.

What if the attacker's heart's desire was this Edrice and then he saw her with Omar? I'd assumed that like me, the attacker wasn't affected by the feather's ability to compel, the reason being that he'd shoved it down Omar's throat and walked away.

Except he'd come after me to get it back.

Flip it and examine that angle. What if the attacker was still under its thrall? That was why he was driven to this extreme method of murder. He didn't just want to kill Omar, he meant to pass the ultimate judgment on him, so he took on Malach's persona—the Destroyer. He used the feather to send a deadly message, but as the attacker was still compelled by the feather, he now needed it back.

Omar was still alive, and the attacker might be hoping to finish the job properly, provided he got the feather. Who knew what effect that thing was still exerting on his mindset? Evil artifacts were not known for their soothing and rational influences.

This was a working theory but it was simple and straightforward and it made sense. Love, revenge, and magic, all twisted into one ugly knot.

I had motive and I had Edrice, a focal point for my search, but there was one other thing I had to do.

The feather had to be destroyed because it was too dangerous to exist. I ghosted my fingers over the metal pouch. What if the cost of my success was being forever lost to the cravings for that magic? This wasn't the residual feather magic that I'd destroyed inside Omar—and that had been bad enough. This was a concentrated magic that even Freddo couldn't explain.

I could do it, but did I dare?

Chapter 13

I updated the Queen about Omar's condition and that she should keep guards on him until the compulsion had worn off.

In order to make a decision about the feather, I required facts. Namely, what kind of magic would I be engaging with? Were there ramifications to destroying it?

Freddo was a level four Typecaster, as was the one who worked for the House. I needed to level up and Hedon was my best bet. It was the black market. There had to be need of that skill.

The exit I took out of the Queen's park didn't lead to the section of Hedon with its crooked cobblestone streets and the electric ramen bowl sign that I was familiar with. I was alone in unfamiliar and probably hostile territory. It would be easy enough to turn back and get directions to that other neighborhood, but as the Queen had said, knowledge was power. In gaining access to my memory of the night that Dad had left, she'd achieved both where I was concerned, whereas I knew virtually nothing about her.

When I walked the streets of my hometown, I didn't merely get a picture of a particular city, I got a sense of how it was governed and what those in charge valued. In Vancouver's case, it showed a place where diversity was celebrated—unless you were one of the many Indigenous people who lived in poverty. A city that thrived on entrepreneurial spirit, but where the middle class couldn't afford housing and little was being done to actually address that. Somewhere that wanted to be on the world's stage, but had a definite streak of conservatism.

What might exploring Hedon tell me about the Queen?

I kept walking.

A narrow railway track stretched out in either direction as far as the eye could see, disappearing into the night.

There was no station. Instead, two identical squat brick buildings bordered one section of the track. A set of dice magically tumbled above one building, rolling double sixes over and over again. Above the other, the silhouettes of chorus girls bedecked in feather headdresses did the can-can.

The oddest little market had sprung up in front of the casino and dance hall. There was barely twenty feet between the track and each building to begin with, so these stalls crowded the rails.

At the stall nearest to me, a man in thick leather gloves held a pair of large metal tongs and an ice pick, systematically breaking pieces off a huge block of ice and chucking them into a blue cooler. He hacked into the ice with a grunt and pulled a jagged piece free. "Ain't seen you around before."

"There are other parts of Hedon to keep a person busy."

He jerked his chin at the other stalls. "Pick your payment. Same as everyone."

Payment for what? Nodding as if I had a clue, I jumped the track. I passed by a man with a dusty bowler hat and neat goatee snoozing in a battered dentist's chair, a woman with crazy curved nails that had scorpions embedded in resin in them who had a rough mani-pedi set up in her stall, and another lady, wearing her scissors and razors crisscrossed on her chest in a bandolier ammo vest, standing next to a hairdresser's chair, texting. Across from her was a small but well-stocked bar tended by androgynous twins with identical shoulder-length dark bobs, polishing shot glasses.

I stopped in front of a stall wreathed in incense smoke with a wooden wheel mounted on a base. The wheel was painted in a black-and-white swirl, but nothing was written on it.

The old woman manning the booth was plump with brassy red teased hair. "Welcome."

"What part of Hedon is this?" I said.

"The Dream Market."

"You sell dreams?" Not that I'd doubt anything in Hedon. I motioned between the two buildings. "Are the dance hall and gaming parlor to loosen you up before you buy your dream and go to sleep?"

"Not those kinds of dreams." She pointed to the dance hall. "Love. Or sex." Then she motioned at the gambling parlor. "Money. Them thing's dreams for many. Twas prudent to give easy access."

Were dreams currency for the Queen as well?

"Do the people who purchase dreams have to say them aloud?"

"Och, no. Dreams are private."

"So, no one else knows what they're buying?"

"That's right," the redheaded old woman said. "Except the Queen, of course. Seeing as she founded this market."

Did she now? "What if I wanted to trade in a dream? What does it buy me in these parts?"

The redhead smiled indulgently. "You can't buy someone's dream, dearie."

Sure you could. People did it all the time. The social justice lawyer who sold their dream of saving the world for a juicy partnership in a corporate firm. The spouse who sold their dream of a grand passion for an okay marriage because it was better than nothing.

It was interesting though. The Queen didn't care about dreams that had been given up on. Those had no worth.

"And these stalls?" I twirled a finger around the market.

"Same as the wheel. Attaining your dream costs, don't it?"

Ice in a cooler, a dentist's chair, hair, nails, and the memory of my father coming back from Hedon minus a rib. If the man who saw everything as a con had traded a piece of himself for some dream, how desperate must he have been to achieve it?

How far would I go to achieve mine?

I swallowed to get some moisture into my suddenly dry throat.

"I'm in the wrong place." I backed away but she grabbed my arm in an unbreakable grip, even with my enhanced strength.

"You sure, dearie?"

"I want to hire a Typecaster. I'm not looking for a dream."

The redhead released my arm with a sympathetic pat. "You say that, but you wouldn't have landed here otherwise."

"I can achieve my own dreams, thanks."

"Sure you can. You look like a smart girl. Since you're here anyway, it would be a shame to waste this opportunity. How about this? We play a simple game of three questions."

"What do I get out of it?" I said.

"You'll be given the correct path to attain your dream. Some are willing to pay outright for them. Others simply want a wee bit of direction to achieve their heart's desire."

My attention snagged on those words. A feather and a market, both promising the same thing. I wasn't a mark, but in my gut, I couldn't discount that out of everywhere in

Hedon, I'd ended up here. Something else tied to heart's desires.

"What does it cost? Do I have to give up body parts?" I said.

"No, dearie. Just answers."

"Three questions in exchange for the correct path. That's it?" I said. "No hidden costs? No strings?"

"Not at all."

Three questions meant three more opportunities for the Queen to learn about me. On the other hand, she'd always kept her word. If she founded this market, then the deal was valid. I weighed all the risks and made my decision. Giving her more knowledge about me was worth being set on the right path to my Nefesh P.I. dreams, because I wasn't sure how to steer a course through being a Jezebel with Chariot on my tail and Levi's hesitancy to register me.

Seems I was like my father after all, willing to trade away a piece of myself. Thing is, my hunches had been good lately and they were saying to follow this through. Ever since my subconscious had led me to draw the Magician card represented by an almond tree, my life had taken on a fairy tale edge that I'd be unwise to ignore, especially as I kept running into this pattern of tests of three.

A dream market reminded me of tales of faerie. So, I'd follow the same rules. Don't eat or drink anything offered to me, beware magic beings bargaining for things I didn't want to part with like my heart or soul, and no assumptions about anyone because the weakest child might be a powerful witch.

Long before my dad had turned me on to Sherlock, Talia had spent hours reading me fairy tales and myths at bedtime. Once upon a time, I'd had a mother who'd loved magic.

"Before I do this, tell me where to hire a Typecaster."

"What's the information worth to you?" the dentist said in a sleepy French accent.

I offered him my Taser but he sneered at it. Weirdly, he perked up at the power bars that I'd filched from Priya's stash, deciding that two was an acceptable trade.

"You'll be needing to see Vespa," he said.

Like the bike? Some hipster identity? "How do I find him? Her?"

The redhead here at the wheel shrugged. "Just Vespa. You need to make an appointment first. Vespa doesn't like unexpected visitors." She held out her hand. "I'll take the peanut butter one."

I slapped the bar into her palm, my patience frayed and my stash depleted.

"How do I make the appointment?"

The hairdresser looked up from her phone. "I'll do it for that little Taser. Hand me your phone." I gave her the gadget and my phone and she sent a text. "Done. Vespa will contact you to let you know when."

"Question time." The redhead pulled a pair of thin reading glasses out of her poofy tangle of hair. "Spin for the first question."

I gripped the rough edge and yanked the wheel down. It clattered as it spun, the black-and-white pattern dizzying. Hypnotic.

It stopped abruptly and the redhead leaned in. "Ooh. Interesting. What's your most complicated relationship? Remember, you must tell the truth, otherwise…" She jerked her chin at the bar, where the twins had stopped polishing to watch us, their heads cocked to the right.

What? They'd deny me a stiff drink? "Are you making this up? The wheel doesn't even have words."

"I am its Lady. I'm in no need of words," she said. A Queen, a Lady, Hedon was a regular royal court. "Answer."

"My dream has nothing to do with relationships."

"Your dream may not be relationships, but relationships are inherent to your dream."

"Ooh, pithy. Fine. My relationship with my mother is my most complicated." Levi was a close second, and once Talia and I sorted out my Nefesh status, I had no doubt he'd rocket straight to first place.

The wheel gave loud rumble like a lion purring and I jumped back.

"What the fuck!"

"Truth," The redhead announced in a bored voice. "Well, that was an easy one for you, wasn't it? Spin."

Once more I spun. The swirl lifted off the wheel to twine around my ankles, like the lightest tickling of fur. I held absolutely still until the wheel slowed to a stop and the pattern settled back into place on the wood.

"What's your most heartbreaking relationship?"

My only romantic heartbreaks had been crushes that left me upset for a few days. Only one relationship had shattered my heart, had made me crawl under the blanket for days, emerging only to deface Vancouver bridges with my novice graffiti, some part of me still hoping he'd see my messages and come home.

"My father."

Another purr from the wheel and indifferent acknowledgment from the woman that I'd passed.

"Final question." She nodded at the wheel.

I grabbed the wheel and spun. Once more the swirling pattern lifted off the wheel, this time to settle on my head like a crown.

"It likes you," the woman said.

I tried to poke it. "Is it housetrained?"

The wheel clattered to a stop but the crown stayed on my head.

"What's your most satisfying relationship?"

"Easy. My best friend Pri—"

My erstwhile crown roared and leapt off me like it had been scalded.

An orb of gold light blinked on over the bar.

"The game is forfeit!" the redhead cried, her eyes gleaming greedily. "I told you not to lie."

"I didn't!"

She laughed. "Even better. You think you're telling the truth."

One of the twins crossed the track, holding a small filigreed silver tray. Upon it was a shot glass of red liquid.

A coiled anticipation fell over the market, the air of excitement tinged with a slyness that terrified me. I'd only checked the price to play, not the price of losing, being confident I'd win. After all, a woman who valued truth would never lie to herself.

I palmed one of my bronze tokens because enough was enough, but I didn't go anywhere.

The twin stopped in front of me.

"Drink up," the dentist said heartily.

"No thanks," I said, throwing every ounce of "get me out of here" vibes at the damn token. "It's rule number one and I'm a stickler for rules."

"The only way out is through," the dentist said. Cheerful sadist.

"Drink," the twin said in a voice that brooked no argument.

I squeezed my fist on the useless token. There was no escape.

Drink this and I might be dead, chopped up for parts in that cooler. Or worse. I didn't know what worse might be, but I was positive that Hedon had all kinds of creative definitions.

Nauseous, but determined to face my end with dignity, even if I'd just peed a little, I sent up a silent apology to my loved ones, even Talia, that they'd never know what happened to me, and shot the drink back.

It warmed my throat, leaving a clove aftertaste.

I half-closed my eyes, braced to start losing body parts or black out, but nothing happened. I just stood there, hands balled up at my sides, waiting for the ax to fall.

A stunned hush fell over the market. The hairdresser's phone clattered to the cement.

"She is not ours to take." The twin's voice was rusty.

The dentist cursed, denied a good show.

"Why not?" I planted my hands on my hips. "I mean, yay, no death, but why am I different?" Again with the special snowflake status. What made me different as a Jezebel?

"You have a destiny," the twin said, plucking the shot glass away. "It is not for us to interfere in that."

"Fucking hell." I stomped my foot. "This is the Dream Market and I have a perfectly fine dream. Not any stupid destiny."

The twin blinked impassively, then pivoted sharply and walked back to the bar.

A train whistle sounded in the distance. The ground rumbled as the train drew closer and closer with a terrifying speed, its headlamps growing blindly bright.

Very calmly, everyone moved the bits and pieces of their stalls inches back from the tracks. Chairs and the bar were rolled out of the way, the table with the wheel lifted to safety. They cleared the rail in minutes.

Closer and closer the train came, while I was frozen like a proverbial deer. The old woman nudged me back, a frown creasing her already wrinkled face.

The train blew through on a cloud of hot, stagnant heat, fanning my hair back from my face. If I leaned forward, I'd have touched the blacked out windows with my nose.

It gave a shrill blast, then was gone as quickly as it had come, disappearing around a bend.

"It didn't take you." The redhead nodded at the twin who'd served me. "They were right." She patted a few loose strands back into her hairdo. "Exciting night, dearie. You're free to go."

This time the bronze token worked without incident. I was back at Moriarty, no worse for wear, unless you counted my lack of direction, constant questioning of what was really in my control in my life, and a nice new desire to smash things.

I'd seen movies. When you refused the call of destiny, it punched you in the throat until you cried "uncle." The biggest irony here was that if I had a heart's desire, it was for free will in my Jezebel future.

I texted Arkady, asking if he was free to train right now. He replied that he was at House HQ working but could take an hour break and to meet at the gym on the seventh floor.

Me: *If you can assure me that both Levi and Veronica will be in attendance and throw in a colonoscopy without anesthetic, I'd be delighted to meet there.*

Arkady: *Entirely the wrong use of ass, pickle. See you soon.*

After swinging by the office to pick up my back-up Taser and lock the feather in the safe, I drove home to change into workout clothes and grab a snack and then went to meet Arkady.

I skulked through the hallway to the employee gym. Arkady waited outside the door, still wearing his "Let Me Be Perfectly Queer" T-shirt. I was impressed with how comfortable he was. He didn't hide his identity from anyone. That's how I wished to live. Free and true. How I would live as soon as my magic was on the books.

"Not to abandon you, but I have to make a call." He swiped his card in the scanner and the door clicked open. "Be back in five. Meantime, feel free to warm up. Make sure you stretch your hamstrings."

Voices drifted into the hall and, not wanting to interrupt any actual employees working out, I hid behind the door and peeked in.

Miles and Levi were sparring in the middle of the gym. Both were stripped down to loose board shorts, their chests gleaming with sweat, and their feet bare. Miles' technique involved a constant assessment and a steady and methodical assault on his opponent. With his bodybuilder frame, he outmatched Levi in power, and while he landed a fair number of kicks and punches, it was like watching a bear wrestle a plume of water.

Levi's punches didn't knock Miles back as hard and he failed to gain much ground in moving his very solid friend, but he was in constant motion, balanced on the balls of his feet with a lithe grace and deceptively lazy movements that turned whip fast in the blink of an eye.

So much about Levi was a calculated illusion, from his magic to his suits that presented a mask to the world. This was Levi unguarded, a man that very few of us got to see, and I suspected, that I'd been privy to in ways he'd *always* kept hidden. It wasn't just the scars he'd shown me, it was how he'd allowed me to literally wear his face during that smudge fight in front of the cameras and the crowds, knowing that he couldn't control me, that he had to trust me.

I leaned in, mouth slightly open.

"You're telegraphing with your left hip." Miles jumped the leg that Levi swung out and pushed on Levi's shoulder.

Levi hit the mat and winced, stretching out a hand for Miles to help him up.

Miles grabbed it, and Levi gripped his forearm with his other hand, pulling Miles into some kind of roll and straddling him.

"Tap out." Levi's hair hung forward over his eyes.

Miles flung him off. "You had a good week when we were twelve. Haven't pinned me since, but optimistic of you to keep trying and recapture that dream."

Levi laughed and jumped up, catching his shorts with

one hand as they slid, exposing the glistening olive skin along the ridge of his hipbone.

"Take a picture, it'll last longer."

I jumped at Arkady's voice. "I wasn't—" I stammered.

He wasn't even looking at me. "No seriously, take a picture. I left my phone back at my desk and that would break the Internet."

Miles stretched up to grab his T-shirt hanging off a set of bars mounted to the wall, causing his back muscles to ripple, while Levi bent over to pick up a towel and rub himself off.

"Perv time is over." Arkady brushed past me into the gym, catching the attention of the other two men.

Miles grimaced. "Gym privileges are restricted to full-time employees, not random freelancers."

Arkady chucked him under the chin. "Ah, Mimi, don't be that way. Ash is an asset to the House and we need to keep her in tip-top fighting shape."

"Mimi." I tested out my new favorite word.

"Call me that and I'll break you in half, Cohen." Miles snapped his T-shirt at Arkady, catching him in the ribs. "And you, quit running your mouth."

Arkady batted his lashes. "You love it when I run my mouth."

"Only situationally." Miles shrugged into his shirt.

Speaking of mouths, mine was hanging open because was Miles flirting with Arkady? What did this mean for my Priya plan? More importantly, what did this mean for my entertainment factor?

I spun around, like a handy tour guide to this bizarroland might be standing behind me, and instead collided with Levi's chest. I stepped back, rubbing my nose. "Geez, wear a bell."

All traces of the easy manner and laughter he'd shown with Miles were gone. Even in nothing but shorts with a towel draped over one shoulder, he oozed haughtiness.

I narrowed my eyes. I could break that iron control of his and not even need my magic. I wanted to be the only one allowed to see his secret self, to ruin him for others. The ferocity of that desire overwhelmed and terrified me. I didn't lose control. Not since I'd stolen my mother's car and paid a horrible price.

Wild, reckless energy bounced around inside me. I tracked a drop of sweat that snaked down the ridges of his chest, wanting to do something unpredictable to throw destiny a curveball.

What's your most satisfying relationship?

My eyes slammed to the ocean of wintry blue looking down on me. No, Levi satisfying me came in one flavor: sex.

He'd inserted himself every step of the way on this Jezebel journey. Bound himself up in this, yet another variable taking control away from me, and if he left me in registration limbo, I'd never work Nefesh jobs. My future was partially in the hands of a man I didn't trust, couldn't predict, and often failed to understand.

Time to punch things.

I brushed past Levi, but he placed a hand on my shoulder.

"Did you still want to speak to my alibi for the other night?" he said.

Right. The mystery woman.

"That's no longer necessary." I stepped sideways, the hot flush staining my cheeks incinerating all foolish thoughts of a moment ago.

"Give us a moment," he said to the other two.

Miles scowled, but heaven forbid he disobey His Lordship. He dragged Arkady to the exit.

"Wait, you can't leave her with him," Arkady said, twisting around to look over his shoulder. "He's holding her hostage."

"Save me from Stockholm Syndrome, Arkady! I might start thinking Levi's a reasonable human being."

"I didn't sign up for two of you." The slam of the door punctuated Miles' words.

"If you wish to speak to my alibi," Levi said, "I'll phone her right now."

"Like I said, no need. Really." Please do not push this point. "You're off the hook. And besides, this is training time. Not sleuthing time."

Levi narrowed his eyes and I tensed under his scrutiny, but he gave a nod and let the matter drop. "Arkady is training you?"

"Are we playing 'state the obvious?' Then, yes, because your attention span on that front lasted all of one session. Your turn."

"Why don't you need my alibi?" he said.

The topic was supposed to be closed, you big jerk. "You're off my suspect list."

Levi stepped closer to me. "What, exactly, was I suspected of?"

I jutted my chin up. "Attempted murder."

The gym around me wavered, then spun and spiraled in on me. The only stationary thing, starkly clear in this nauseous claustrophobic mess, was Levi, face pinched with anger and pain.

The illusion stopped, Levi once more in control.

"You used your magic on me?" I dropped the blood dagger that I'd manifested during that ordeal and took a deep breath. His scotch and chocolate scent filled my nostrils, but this time it wasn't intoxicating, it was cloying. "In case I wasn't clear the last time you pulled that stunt," I said icily, "don't ever do that again or I'll show you what I'm capable of."

He laughed, but there was no humor in it. "Trust me, I know."

Something about the way he said it made me think he wasn't referring to my magic. "What's that supposed to mean?"

"You always want to prove how smart you are, and yet after all this time, you know nothing where I'm concerned," he said. "You should have put your brilliant deduction skills to work and trusted my character."

"The way you trusted mine when you kept accusing me of being a Rogue?"

"That was different." Levi crossed the gym to a small duffel bag and pulled out a sweatshirt that he yanked over his head. "Based on all known understanding of magic, you'd hidden yours."

"Based on what I knew of this case, you were the only illusionist around powerful enough to pull off the attack. Multiple people claimed to see an Angel of Death descend from the heavens and attack a dude, and I only know one jerk with the kind of magic that can fool crowds and cameras. I'd have been a fool not to put you on the suspect list."

"What was my motive?"

I hedged my words. "There was a tentative connection with your father."

There were no terrifying illusions this time. No walls rushed in on me, gravity remained completely normal. Levi was utterly still, a beautiful statue carved from granite. And that would be all you'd see, unless you'd known him enough to know his tells, to pick up on, just for a second, his eyes flashing something not unlike hurt.

Levi picked up his bag and I spoke my next words to his back. "I'm sorry for thinking that you'd strike back at him in that manner."

"You thought this attempted murder was in retaliation for something Isaac had done to me?"

"That's what I said."

He prowled toward me. "No, Ash. You said there was a connection to him."

"Huh? Ew. No. I didn't think you were working on his behalf."

"Good to know I have standards. Low bar though, don't you think?"

"I was doing my job. How about you run along and do yours?"

He saluted me, the bag hefted on his shoulder, but as he passed he briefly caught my hand. "What took me off the list?" He ran his other hand over his jaw that showed a faint dusting of dark scruff, his eyes trained on me.

"A feather from a set of costume wings."

"Ah, yes. My views on the use of props while committing murder *are* rather well known." He snorted and dropped my hand.

"The attacker hit me, okay?" I stepped back. "You insult me, you annoy me, you push every single one of my buttons, and lose the smirk, Leviticus, I don't mean that in a good way. But you'd never physically hurt me. Or maybe I'm just good at my job and know that you'd never lose your precious control in that manner."

Levi went quiet. After a moment, he opened his mouth, then caught himself and shook his head. "There were no matches off the prints in the apartment."

Was that an apology? An olive branch? Or simply a statement of fact?

Arkady threw the door open. "Forty-five minutes left on my break. Pickle, start running laps. Levi, go away."

"It's my gym."

Arkady threw him a "so?" look. Levi huffed a laugh and left.

Damn Levi for fucking with my reality so easily. How could I even sift through our layers when the ground kept shifting beneath my feet?

"Bossy men are the worst," Arkady said.

"Agreed." I started with an easy jog. "Is Miles your boss or what? Don't you work for Levi directly on some covert team?"

"Levi uses people as needed."

"Doesn't he just?"

"Meaning…" Arkady gave me the stink eye at dissing his hero. "Miles as Chief of Security for all House matters is my boss, but he coordinates with Levi for operations that Levi directly wants to oversee. Which doesn't happen often. Now, enough chitchat. Run like the hounds of Hell are on your tail. And pick up your feet. You're not a zombie."

Bossy men were the worst. I ran.

Chapter 14

The training session was light on punching and kicking, but getting out of all of Arkady's holds drained the razor sharp curl off my reckless mood enough to keep a civil tongue when I showed up at the cocktail party that Talia had bargained me into. Part of me wanted to bail, but I was determined to connect with my mother, even if it meant associating with the Untainted Party in a way that I vehemently disagreed with.

The small hotel ballroom was beige and bland with appetizers to match. Though if bigotry was a spice, we'd have had a hell of a zesty party.

I plucked at the sleeve of my cream pantsuit with the brass buttons that was Talia-approved and relieved me of the stress of what to wear for all those yachting dates in my future. The fabric itched and I'd had to quickly abandon the drinking game I played with myself, where I took a sip of overly dry red wine for each insult hurled at Nefesh, or risk alcohol poisoning.

Talia supervised me for a while then cut me loose to continue working the room on my own as the dutiful daughter here to support her, while she stayed with some old dame in a satin turban spewing forth on how "the magics" were lowering her property values.

Other than the fact that my city had more magic-haters happy to legally have Nefesh under their thumbs than I'd realized, and were willing to throw a lot of money behind this, I failed to learn anything important or useful. The party's legislation was still in draft form, and this meet and greet was one of many to suss out public input.

I made small talk for a couple of hours about how proud I was of Talia, while perfecting my use of noncommittal noises about how vital this bill would be to the well-being of our society. I didn't even stab anyone.

When I'd reached my limit, I did a last tour of the room, battle weary and searching for Talia. My circuit took me past a couple of businessmen, whom I glanced at in passing. My jaw clenched, because despite the short hair and lighter eyes, one of them was Arkady.

Even if I hadn't been at the top of my game, I'd have known it was him because I'd just spent an hour escaping his holds.

He didn't betray a flicker of recognition, but it was him in a wig and contacts. My magic surged under the surface of my skin, my fingers tightening on the stem of my wine glass as I fought to keep from detonating in the middle of this Nefesh-hating crowd.

My suspicions that Levi used him to keep tabs on me deepened. Did he not trust me where Talia was concerned? Did he think I'd pick her over the safety of the Nefesh, especially as I was one?

He and I were in for a reckoning.

I got myself under control and, setting my glass on a table, found Talia in order to arrange another meeting between us where I'd demonstrate my magic.

She'd schmoozed her way to the back corner, a shark in a navy silk dress and seven-hundred-dollar pearl earrings.

"Sorry to intrude, Mother. I'm leaving." Never calling Talia by her first name in public—one of our endless negotiations.

"Ashira, isn't it?" a man said in a strong Italian accent. "I believe you went to camp with my son."

I turned a polite smile on the speaker, then almost swallowed my tongue, because the person before me was Levi in thirty years. A handsome man with a winning smile, he was the last person you'd suspect of physically harming his child, but I'd seen the scars. I'd seen how Levi carried himself to conceal them or illusioned them away, how he'd startled when I'd felt them under my fingertips the first time. How he'd honed his own power so he'd be able to make them disappear longer. Now here Isaac was openly throwing his support against the Nefesh community that his son led.

Levi was wrong. We weren't the monsters.

On the other side of the room, Arkady had perfected the art of surveilling without appearing to be watching. It was all in the angle of the body and the tilt of the head allowing for slightly more peripheral vision.

Talia subtly nudged me and I found my voice. "Yeah. Five summers at good old Camp Ruach."

My mother flashed a tight smile. She had no love for her Jewish upbringing, but after Dad had left and Mom had gone back to school, she'd been forced to turn to her Orthodox parents for financial help with my various rehab and therapy costs after the accident.

My father had been estranged from his family in Montreal, and I'd never met my grandparents on that side. My maternal grandparents had been incredibly generous, and we'd even become close during those nights when Mom's classes ran late and I had dinner at their house. My grandmother did nothing to advance the cause of Kosher cuisine, and their religion informed their rather rigid views on a lot of topics, but they weren't unkind, and we kept up our semiregular dinners until they'd passed away a few years ago. Talia maintained they'd mellowed by the time I came around. Since their only stipulation for all their support had been that I go to Jewish camp to give me a connection to my faith, I'd gone.

It hadn't been all bad. I'd actually enjoyed activities like archery and kayaking and I could hone my sullen teen vibe as easily around a bonfire as in a skate park. I'd even had a few outcast friends to hang with year after year.

"It's important to stay connected to our heritage," Isaac said.

"I couldn't agree more. I would hate to deny any part of myself." I unfurled my favorite toothy smile.

Talia looped her arm through mine. "If you'll excuse me, Isaac, I'll walk my daughter to the door."

Walk, strong-arm me, same same.

"That was uncalled for," she said.

"I agree. His son is Head of House Pacifica. He shouldn't be here." I tried to snag a bacon-wrapped fig, but Talia denied me even that simple pleasure, hustling me past the server before I could get my hands on one.

"Isaac is Mundane and if he shares our viewpoint, so be it. It's actually a coup to have his support. He's a leading businessman with a lot of important connections."

Some of them were even legal.

"Dad worked for him. Did you know that?"

"That was years ago."

"You disapprove of your baby father's magic, but having the shady boss he worked for on board is 'a coup?'"

Talia amped up her smile as we passed an older couple chatting with Jackson Wu, leader of the provincial Untainted Party, a genial man of Chinese heritage in a well-tailored suit.

I threw him a cheery wave as befitted my stature as Talia's sole progeny.

"This is neither the time nor the place to discuss your father or Mr. Montefiore's legitimacy as a businessman," she hissed.

"How about this then? Take off the Party hat firmly wedged on your head and look at this as a parent. This is the worst betrayal of Levi." I retrieved my jacket from the coat racks set up by the entrance.

"Yet you keep insisting he's nothing to you."

"His dad is publicly supporting legislation to impose legal strictures on his life because he has magic."

"Levi's an adult. He can take care of himself."

"That's not the point. Could you hurt me that way? Choose a belief system over what I am?"

The soft piano music, the hum of chatter, all of it fell away into a loaded bubble of silence as I waited for her to answer.

If she was wrestling with some moral dilemma, it didn't show in her hostess smile. "You're Mundane."

"Pretend I wasn't and answer the question."

My mother stared into her mostly empty glass like she was wishing for a top up. Or the bottle. "If you had magic," she said carefully, "it's not something you'd have to make public. No one would believe it. The hospital certainly didn't when that nurse made her ridiculous complaint."

I flinched. She knew about that? Of course she did. Talia was my mother. They'd have informed her. Which meant… She believed me that I now had magic.

I wrapped my arms around myself, suddenly uneasy at the truth laying bare between us. "I wouldn't hide nor would I live as a Rogue."

"Why do you have to make everything so hard for yourself? So hard for me?" Her voice broke.

"No lies. No games," I said.

She met my eyes. "Then I'd choose my beliefs. I have to be able to live with myself."

Like mother, like daughter had never been such a bitter pill.

I pressed my fist into my stomach. Some betrayals were the sharp devastation of a car crash that you never saw coming. Others were a tornado. You watched it approach from miles away, frozen in its path and unable to do anything about the havoc about to wreck your life.

"Ashira." She reached for me, but I shook my head, my hands up. "It's a moot question because I'll never have to choose," she said. "You'd never make me."

Tears filled my eyes. "I have to be able to live with myself."

All pretense of this being hypothetical was gone.

We stood, mere feet apart, but the endless void back in the grove hadn't been this vast.

I pulled myself together by the skin of my teeth. "I'll let you get back."

She nodded, her expression unreadable, but didn't stop me.

My drive home was a blur.

Priya was out with Kai, the human Cheez Whiz that she was dating, when I got home, so I flaked out in front of the television with food I'd scrounged up. Priya hadn't made it to the grocery store either, so I sat there with half a box of kinda stale Stoned Wheat Thins crackers, a container of hummus, apple slices, and my billionth rewatch of BBC's *Sherlock*, which I much preferred over the American *Elementary* version.

As white noise, it did little to quell the storm knocking around in my head. Talia believed me but it didn't matter. She hadn't chosen me. Her values were more important to her. There was probably some pithy self-truth the universe hoped I'd take away from that, but I couldn't get beyond a dull thudding in my head and a profound sorrow.

The first episode had barely kicked in when there was a

knock on my door. Arkady stood there with a bottle of wine and an unopened veggie platter. His chin-length black hair was pulled back with a pink scrunchie and he'd changed into sweatpants.

"Stay the hell out of my life." I slammed the door, but he shoved his foot in, conveniently turning it to stone so the door didn't even hurt him. Lucky for him, my door fared equally as well.

"It wasn't what you think," Arkady said. "Isaac—"

"Did Levi know I'd be there?"

Arkady hesitated. "He suspected. Let me in. Please. After a couple hours of all that hate, I want to be around a friend." His eyes narrowed and he raked a far too shrewd glance over me. "Methinks you need that, too."

He hadn't had the weary tightness at the corners of his eyes when we'd trained earlier, but I was too pissed off to feel compassion.

"Friends don't spy on friends."

Arkady pulled his now-normal foot back, but I didn't slam the door. "Levi could have sent someone who you wouldn't have recognized."

"Is that supposed to make it better?"

"No, but my guess is that he's struggling with this." He juggled the wine and the platter. "Could you talk to him directly and leave out the middle man, because this tray is heavy?"

I cracked the door wide enough to take in the contents of the platter. No peppers and it came with ranch dressing dip. Being alone would do shit for my mental well-being right now, because I'd only keep obsessing over what had gone down with my mother. This way I got food and maybe I could punch Arkady. I let him in, gesturing to the platter. "Are we at catered levels of friendship?"

"Levi had a meeting with the Heads of House Ontario and Maison de Champlain to discuss counter proposals to the legislation your mother is instrumental in drafting." He sighed. "Support for the idea is spreading across the country. Anyway, Veronica sent a 'hands off the catering' memo."

"You defied her for me?"

"See how much you mean to me, pickle?" He shoved the platter at me and flopped on my sofa. "I hate people. How do you stand those events?"

"Drinking helps." I got us a couple of wine glasses and some plates, because no need to be total barbarians about our feast, and collapsed next to him. Pouring myself a drink, I clinked it to his. "I hate people, too. Some more than others. Here's to misanthropy."

"Let's move to an island. Priya can come," he said.

"Obviously." I restarted the episode and shaky images of a battle filled the screen. "How about Miles?" After this afternoon, I'd find someone else to snap Pri out of her dating ways.

"How about Levi?" he retorted, stuffing a pillow made from pink sari fabric behind his back.

"Don't make me vote you off." Then I put aside all the emotional fuckery of the day and let myself be lulled by the brilliant mind of Sherlock Holmes.

PRIYA SPENT the night at Kai's so by the time we reconnected at the office on Wednesday morning, I was setting up a whiteboard with Omar's name at the top. Underneath him was written Edrice Abadi. From there we'd include anyone from her personal or professional life who harbored romantic feelings for her.

While we worked, I told Priya about my encounter with Talia. I'd have to see my mother again. My magic was going to become public sooner rather than later, and she owed me a heads up on how she was going to respond. And any idea on whether our relationship was salvageable or not. But as excited as I was to plunge into that new familial wound again, I couldn't see her yet because there were too many other things going on. That, and I'd hope she'd change her mind.

Priya hugged me, but this defied even her optimism that all would work out.

Throwing myself into work, I got Chione to call Edrice, saying she required a list of everyone employed by the archeological excavation because their insurance had questions about the security previous to the Tannous family's arrival. If they didn't get this settled, it could cost the dig more.

It wasn't watertight logic; it didn't need to be. Edrice got the request from someone she'd previously dealt with, and, thanks to the successful completion of the job that Tannous Security had been hired for, trusted. Throw in an insurance company and their endless inane requests, plus the opportunity to save some money when every cent of the dig would be stretched thin, and Edrice promptly emailed the info over.

Priya and I split the list, starting with the easiest way to eliminate anyone—by using the House Al Qahirah records in Cairo. Of the twenty people working on the site, thirteen were men, and eight of them were Mundane. Our attacker had magic, so we were down to five possibilities.

From there we narrowed the field further with social media. Two of them were gay and Edrice was likely not their heart's desire. That left us with three suspects, except none of them had left the site in the two months that they'd been employed. This was verified by their daily posts about life in the high mountains of the Sinai. It was still a desert ecosystem with a lot of volcanic rock in the area, but the excavation was situated on a relatively flat stretch with a lot of scrubby brush.

Sifting through this information was boring, detailed-oriented work and made up the bulk of the jobs I'd worked on. Smudges and Angels of Death—even phony ones—were way more fun.

Edrice's social media mostly featured her tiny dog Isis. Her other photos tended to be of coffee or group shots of her co-workers.

"Nothing jumps out." Priya threw her fork into her takeout salad container. One thing about Gastown, you couldn't go ten feet without hitting a restaurant or café.

Salad was not my first, second, or twelfth choice, but Priya had nixed my suggestion of sushi, since Kai always ate sushi after his squash games and hadn't wanted to upset his routine last night. Priya tried to talk him into something else, but Cheese Whiz had grown a spine on this issue. So when Priya growled that we were having salad today, I'd agreed.

I leaned back in my creaky chair, munching on a cherry tomato. "How do I play this when I contact Edrice? I can't cast any aspersions on the Tannous family and especially not on their professional reputation. If I say I work for the Dershowitzes, the whole 'other woman vibe' might keep Edrice from speaking to me."

"What about the HR angle? Say you got an anonymous report that Edrice was subjected to sexual harassment and you're checking it out. Even if she's employed by Cairo University, no one ever knows all the staff in HR."

"That would work, if I could speak Arabic. They wouldn't conduct the conversation in English."

The whiteboard remained frustratingly devoid of suspects.

Priya stood up and grabbed some darts out of the wall-mounted holder. "Darts to clear our heads?"

Times like this, we didn't play a proper game, but rather ran through a practice routine.

Priya positioned herself in front of the dartboard and

fired a dart into the double twenty. I took her spot and did the same. We pulled our darts out and moved on to double nineteen.

None of the ideas we tossed out had merit. Missing double fifteen, I started again from twenty.

Pri got down to double elevens before she missed. We still didn't have a viable reason to call Edrice and find out about any men in her personal life.

"Fuck it." I pulled out my phone, looking up the time difference between 12:30PM Vancouver time and the Sinai Peninsula. "It's 9:30 at night," I said. "Not too late."

"Hang on a sec." Priya leaned over her desk and double-clicked her trackpad. "When Malach kicked you, he was wearing steel-toed boots, right?"

"Right. Oh. That could narrow it down to someone in construction that she knows."

"No. They wear them on the sites." Priya turned her laptop around to show me a photo. It was one of the group shots and everyone in the front row wore dust-streaked work boots. "You can't tell if they're steel-toed or not, but a bunch of websites discussing equipment for digs mention them."

"We're back to the dig and out of suspects. Nothing to it but to do it." I phoned Edrice and introduced myself.

"You're from Canada? Why do you wish to speak to me?" she said.

"Your friend Omar was attacked right before his wedding."

She laughed. "I'm sorry. That's not funny, but Omar is hardly a friend."

"You had a relationship with him," I said.

"We slept together once and I'm in Egypt. I can hardly be a suspect."

"You're not, but we're investigating the possibility that someone saw you and was jealous."

"Doubtful. I haven't left the site in two and a half months."

"Perhaps they outsourced?"

"A hitman?" She laughed harder. "This is a joke, yes?"

"No. Could anyone there harbor romantic feelings for you?"

"With this bunch? Not likely."

"You're sure?" I tapped a dart against the desk.

"Positive. We're here day in and day out. Together all the time. I'd have noticed."

So much for that. "Did any of the items that you excavated contain magic?"

"No. Everything is catalogued in detail."

There was nothing further to learn.

"Back to square one?" Priya said.

"Back to square one. I still maintain the attacker was under the feather's compulsion when he assaulted Omar, but there's no motive and no identifiable suspect." I needed a win and phoned Levi. "Make yourself useful, Leviticus, and help me work out my frustrations," I demanded. My voice went low and sultry. "I need you bad."

Chapter 15

Levi choked on his end of the phone and Priya's eyebrows shot into her hairline. Even I wasn't sure where that had come from.

"I could spare fifteen minutes," he said.

"A glowing recommendation."

"And have five left over after I'd gotten you off."

"If I was that hard up," I said, "I'd visit the laundromat with the rattly dryer and do the job myself. Gavriella's workplace. Houdini me into looking like her so I can pay a visit and see what shakes out. Someone there might know Evil Wanker."

"That's a brilliant idea. While you're there, you can pick up a shift, make a couple bucks in tips," he said.

I drew a picture of a dick on the whiteboard and gave it blue eyes. "It's a lead and we're sparse on those. Besides, Gavriella might have left personal effects behind in a locker, given she didn't intend to be abducted."

"I'm sure the motorcycle gang owners of the place will be reasonable about returning them. Or not holding a grudge about being left in the lurch."

"I doubt these people expect two weeks' notice. I'll be at

the club in twenty minutes. Do what you want with that." Sliding my phone into my pocket, I grabbed my leather jacket off the back of my chair. "Did you get a hit on Moran or the Queen? Her interest in this wedding doesn't make sense. Ivan Dershowitz isn't a major league criminal, and she doesn't need to cultivate Mundane connections."

"You're thinking it's personal?" Priya said.

"Yeah."

"My script didn't come up with anything, but I'll adjust the filters and try again."

"Thanks, Pri. By the way, what happened with Miles?"

"We're meeting to discuss my proposal. A working relationship. That's all this is. I saw your stupid gleam when we met. This isn't a case of besties double-dating."

"Levi and I will never date."

Priya slapped twenty bucks on her desk and smirked. "Care to take that bet?"

"I think Miles may be interested in Arkady."

She sat up so fast, the twenty flew off the desk. "You sure?"

"Mostly." I laughed. "Now who's got the stupid gleam?"

"Me." She waved me away. "Go give lap dances. I have plans to make."

"My injured leg precludes twerking on some guy's dick."

"It's stronger now. Give it a whirl, you might like it."

I shrugged. "We could do with some new office furniture."

"That's the spirit."

I might not come back richer, but I was damned if I'd leave there empty handed.

THE ENTRANCE to the Star Lounge was marked by a dirt-streaked sign of a chesty woman with star-shaped pasties riding a crescent moon. It was the classiest business on the block.

A woman in a purple fleece jacket, her dark hair flecked with gray, and a sharply beaked nose stood on the stoop, stomping her feet to keep warm.

I charged forward and slammed her up against the wall, my fist bunched in her jacket. "Gimme Gavriella's face, Levi."

She spread her hands wide. Her "Fuck Me Red" polish was flaking off her nails. "Take it," she said in Levi's infuriatingly smug voice.

My gaze dropped to his lips. Her lips. Argh. What was wrong with me? "This was my idea. My plan. Or didn't you trust me to carry it out? Hey, I know. You could send Arkady to spy on me while I do it, since that seems to make you happy."

Levi's magic rose up around me and I stiffened. I could take it and teach him never to get in my way again—I pushed away, my hands balled into fists.

He dropped the illusion.

"Oh my god." I rolled my eyes. "You wore a suit to a strip club?"

"I was at work and unlike you, I don't have a duffel bag full of charming costumes. And what exactly was I supposed to do? Trust that your loyalty was to your newfound Nefesh identity and not your mother?"

"Yes." He was supposed to trust me absolutely, not situationally like he did with other people.

"You were at an event specifically designed to get support to crush my community. Real loyal."

"It was complicated."

"Everything with you is complicated," he said. "You're playing so many angles, I don't even think you know what the game is anymore."

"Fuck you."

A customer exited the lounge. Levi and I moved aside for him to pass, rain misting down over us.

"My life *is* complicated," I said. "All this shit has happened, but I'm moving forward the best I can and I'm not going to apologize for that. It's not a character flaw and it's not a betrayal. I'm not your father."

"That's another thing," Levi said. "Isaac is a master manipulator and if you don't think he'll try and find a way to use our acquaintanceship—"

"Good to know where we stand," I muttered.

"Fucking hell, Ash, he doesn't know we slept together. He's so twisted in his anti-magic beliefs that he'll do anything to stay in control. Damn the cost to his own son." The thread of bitter anger almost overpowered his quiet words.

Our world ran on power. Isaac hated not having magic and Talia's marriage had been upended by someone with it. Both of them were trying to stay in control of their lives.

Understanding it didn't make it hurt less.

"Talia knows about my magic." I raised a fist. "Go Untainted Party."

"Fuck," Levi said.

I shoved my hands in my pockets and rocked back on my heels uncertain of where Levi and I went from here. We weren't that different, both of us attempting to find the right path and so used to being on guard that we couldn't see that maybe our emotional fortress doors didn't have to be battened down against absolutely everyone.

He gestured at the club. "You still want to do this?"

I nodded and he locked his Gavriella illusion into place again.

"You've got to be kidding," I said.

"I'm not doing this to be an asshole. Not totally an asshole." Gavriella grinned, but when my stony expression didn't change, dropped the charm. "You sprung this plan on me and we didn't get a chance to discuss it. I have to stick close to you to keep up the illusion. Who am I supposed to be that would allow me to follow you anywhere in the club?"

"I don't know," I said stiffly.

She nodded. "And another thing. These are Mundanes. You can't punch them and you can't take their magic, but I can fuck them up. Let me be Gavriella and you go in as her daughter. It means one less person to illusion and less energy expended on my part. You've both got dark hair, and there's a big enough age difference that it's plausible. If we get split up, it doesn't matter and you can ask questions as her concerned kid."

I banged my head gently back against the brick wall. Levi had thought this through calmly and rationally and I'd been ready to charge in unprepared. My uncharacteristic lack of foresight galled, especially in front of him. Between the twin in Hedon with their destiny crap and my lack of answers on the Omar front, I'd spiraled into acting out of frustration.

"Must be nice always being right." I hadn't meant that bitter sound bite to slip out.

"It is," Gavriella continued in Levi's voice. "Too bad you're a total loser who's never on top of her game and certainly doesn't get to have an off-moment where she hasn't anticipated the next six moves. Should I continue, or do you want to get over yourself and take it from here?"

"No, your stirring pep talk did the trick. You should make House T-shirts reading 'get over yourself' on them. Add your snarky mug and they'd sell like hotcakes. The gospel according to His Lordship."

"My wisdom does verge on biblical proportions. I'll talk to my merch people."

"Do that. Meantime, ask around about Evil Wanker. See if he's come sniffing around this joint while Gavriella's been gone or if they remember anyone visiting her before."

"Friend or foe. Got it. Anything else?"

I compared his Gavriella disguise with my memory of her—minus the bruising. The illusion was flawless. Levi excelled at his magic and there was something incredibly sexy about someone that capable. I squirmed, uncomfortable, because my nipples were hardening while he wore the face of a dead woman and that was a shade too far of weird, even for me.

"Get into the dressing room and see if she left anything behind," I said in a brusque voice and stepped inside.

The front doors opened on a room with all the charm of a failing Las Vegas casino, tarted up in a thousand kinds of bling in the hopes that all that glittered must be gold.

Rows of bottles glinted behind the bar to the right, illuminated by pink and blue-green neon tubing and epilepsy-inducing starbursts from the not one, not two, but three disco balls. The white stage needed a good coat of paint, but the clientele appeared satisfied with the impressive display of core strength demonstrated by the dancer flipping around the pole to Britney Spears' "I'm a Slave 4 U."

We made our way to the bar and Gavriella rapped on the U-shaped bar top to get the bartender's attention. "Hey. I'm back." Her voice had a light Spanish accent.

It was a gamble that Levi's voice impersonation was correct, but people were so visual that they'd trust their eyes above everything else and find a way to justify anything that didn't add up.

The bartender, in a tube top and short shorts, did a double take, her hand stilling above the lemons on her cutting board. "Elektra. Where the hell have you been hiding?"

Gavriella shrugged. "Around."

"Who's this?" She cast a wary look at me.

"Her kid." I jerked a thumb at the door to the left of the stage. "Any chance Mom's stuff's still there?"

"More likely Brandi and Crystal split it." The bartender peeled a rind off one of the lemons in a single curly strip.

"Can I go check?" Gavriella said. That would give Levi access to the other dancers.

"Stevie wasn't happy about your cut and run." She jabbed the peeler at us. "I'd get outta here before—"

The front door slammed shut.

"You gotta a lot of nerve coming back," a man bellowed.

"Too late," the bartender murmured.

The dancer on stage was a consummate professional who didn't even stumble in her choreography at the outburst, though a few of the customers glanced our way.

Levi-as-Gavriella was crowded up against the bar by a guy who made Miles look slight. Every inch of him was covered in tattoos. He even had horns tattooed on his forehead. The knuckles on his hands read "your next."

"Got something to say for yourself, bitch?" Stevie said.

Gavriella's eyes darkened. Levi did not stand for bullying women.

I muscled in between them before he could do anything stupid. Gavriella wouldn't have stayed under the radar only to mouth off to her boss. I tapped Stevie's knuckles. "The 'you're' should be a contraction, not possessive."

"Huh?"

"See, you've got this great threat all lined up to smash into someone's face, except you used the wrong version of 'you're.' It undercuts the menace. Now if you'd written 'your turn' that would have been scary *and* grammatically correct. A win on all fronts."

Gavriella clamped her lips together. I surreptitiously pinched her hip so she wouldn't laugh.

Stevie went that red specific to cartoon people before their head blew off with a kettle whistle. "The fuck kind of mouth you got on you?" He waggled his tongue between his index and middle fingers. "Maybe I oughta show you a few other uses for it."

Gavriella-Levi grabbed his arm. "Please, Stevie. She's sorry. She doesn't know who you are." Her wide eyes, tilt of her head, and soft pleading voice seemed like overkill on the blow-smoke-up-Stevie's-ass front, but he ate it up, puffing his chest out.

I made a face out of Stevie's view, and Gavriella shifted to step on my foot.

"You ran out on me," Stevie said. "Left me without a bartender on a Saturday night. I oughta toss you out the door."

Gavriella's shoulders slumped and she dropped her gaze to the floor. "I get it. But, could I please say goodbye to the others?"

"Fine. Fuck." Stevie stomped behind the bar and poured himself a shot of whiskey.

"Back in a sec," Gavriella told me and went through the door to the left of the stage.

I slid onto a barstool, tamping down the urge to run after Levi and control the play. He could search backstage fine on his own. "Has any guy come around looking for Elektra? Brown hair, dresses kind of nerdy, British accent?"

"Nope." The bartender wiped her peeler off on a clean bar rag. "She in trouble?"

"Not sure. Elektra plays her cards close to her chest, you know? I don't even know how long she was working here."

"She started about six months ago." Then disappeared after three when Chariot took her.

"Do you know her well?" I helped myself to some pretzels in one of the tiny wooden bowls on the bar, then immediately wished I hadn't because they tasted like cardboard.

"Not really. We tended bar on different shifts." The bartender swept the rinds into a small metal bowl, then grabbed a small manual juicer and efficiently squeezed the lemons. "Elektra kept to herself. A lot of the girls are all drama, dragging in every detail of their personal life."

I swallowed a few times to clear my throat of pretzel dust. "She ever hang out with anyone in particular?"

"Dancers or dudes?"

"Either," I said.

The bartender poured the lemon juice into a shaker, her eyes sweeping the bar. They paused somewhere over my left shoulder for a moment, but I resisted turning to see who she was looking at. "Sorry. No idea."

"Thanks anyways. Is it okay if I go back and find her?"

"Go ahead."

I scanned the gloomy interior for whomever the bartender had lied about. A scruffy Asian guy watched the dancer who was now gyrating to "American Woman." He absently munched on pretzels.

He was between me and the stage door, so I was able to head in his direction without arousing suspicion.

Was he Gavriella's boyfriend? Her pimp? He didn't look as hardened as pimps I'd come across but you never knew.

One of the disco lights flitted over his face exposing his besotted expression as he enthusiastically applauded the dancer. She flashed him a sweet smile. Probably not a pimp, and if he was anyone's boyfriend, it wasn't Gavriella's. Why else would she have hung around him? Was he a dealer? He had a backpack with him, so that was a possibility.

Was Gavriella taking drugs? Was that why Chariot was able to grab her? This job suddenly made a lot more sense if she was addicted, since she'd have easy access to product, but it didn't fit with the profile I had of her. Unless something had happened to drive her to start using? The same thing that had her start working here six months ago?

One lead at a time.

The backstage area was brightly lit and surprisingly clean. Gavriella-Levi chatted with a blonde woman with a hard face in a skimpy sailor costume festooned with red and blue sequins. Their words were drowned out by the music from the stage that played even back here.

The blonde held out her hand and Gavriella gave her a wad of cash. The blonde counted it, then satisfied, dropped something into Gavriella's palm.

"Elektra?"

Both women looked up at the sound of my voice. The blonde nodded as she passed by to exit out into the bar.

I joined Gavriella. "What'd she give you?"

"A ring." Gavriella-Levi held up a dark wooden band burnished to a soft gleam. "She asked me if my shithead ex had caught up with me, then demanded her three hundred for keeping my dad's ring safe until I came back."

"I think Chariot grabbed her here at the club. If she sensed they were closing in and hid this from them, it has some value to her." Taking the band, I ran my thumb over the ring, then I sniffed it. There was a faint scent of a buttery, honey smell. "This ring smells like the almond tree in the magic grove. It's tied to Evil Wanker somehow, and while I don't see him being the shithead ex, is the father part true? Was she close to her dad? Could she have meant a father figure? Someone on her team?"

"My people are still digging into Gracie's background. We'll know more soon," Levi said. "How old was Evil Wanker?"

"Look at you getting all codenamey. You loooove this, Shaggy."

He got a mock affronted expression. "Pfft. I'm merely stooping to your level to humor you."

I patted his arm. "Keep telling yourself that. I couldn't see his face, but I got the impression he was around our age. If he was old enough to be her father he'd have been about seventy. He didn't have the voice or body language of someone that age from what I could tell." I tucked the ring into my pocket.

"No, please, you hang on to that."

Did Evil Wanker believe I already had the ring when he'd brought me to the grove and had wanted to eliminate me because of it?

"This ring's properties might be specific to Jezebels," I pointed out.

"They might not."

"Guess we'll find out. Now switch faces with me."

"Why?"

"Gavriella may have been on drugs and I want to chat with her potential dealer."

"Of course you do." Levi seamlessly switched illusions.

"Too weird looking at myself." I shuddered. "Let me talk to the guy alone."

We returned to the bar and I sat down across from the dealer. I didn't say anything, waiting until he noticed me and did a double take. "Elektra, babe. You don't write, you don't call."

"Life." I scratched my arm, twitchy. "Can you help a girl out?"

"Looks like you've helped yourself plenty elsewhere."

"No way. I only trust your product."

He snapped a junky pretzel in half with such force it shattered. "My 'product?' What am I? Some asshole corner pusher? Get the fuck out of here." He turned his attention back to the stage.

How'd I insult him? Not a street dealer. Was he higher up on the food chain? If that was the case, where was his security? None of the other few customers were keeping an eye on him. Nor did they look like bodyguards, and a drug lord wouldn't casually be hanging out in a titty bar unaccompanied.

What did that leave? His clothing was nondescript,

nothing flashy or any identifiable name brands to give me a clue to how he self-identified. Up close, he was younger than I'd originally guessed, with acne-studded scruff on his jaw.

He popped another pretzel in his mouth with fingers that were stained red. That twigged a half-buried memory. Something I'd learned at a seminar about the drug crisis in Vancouver.

Iodine was often used in the manufacturing of drugs. It stained fingers and clothing red or brown. There was a tattoo of a skull and crossbones on the inside of his wrist. He was either a pirate or the brains behind a drug that Gavriella had gotten herself into.

"I don't think you're some pusher," I said. "You're an artist."

He flicked his eyes to me.

"How you even come up with those chemical compounds is incredible. I don't know anyone else that smart." What drug had he given her?

He relaxed against the seat. "Youngest graduate of the Chem department ever." He patted the backpack, revealing a university logo. "They tried to boot me out for being too forward thinking, but fuck 'em. I got my paper."

"Academics wouldn't appreciate your talents. But I do."

"Everyone thinks smack's so great 'cause it lets people nod off, escape it all. My design blows that shit out of the water."

Great would not have been the word I used for heroin, but I nodded anyway, my brain whirring. Gavriella hadn't been taking a stimulant like cocaine. She'd gone for something to escape. From what?

"Can you help me?" I said.

The chemist drummed his fingers on the table. "Song's too loud."

I glanced up at the speakers. "Yeah, I guess."

"Not that." He tapped his head. "It's why you came back, right? Couldn't handle your demons."

Was this how she stopped the cravings? That ever-present humming? I threw a couple crappy pretzels into my mouth so I wouldn't grab him by the lapels and yell "gimme."

"Please. I have nowhere else to turn." The quiver in my voice wasn't faked.

He straightened up, clearly pleased with my appeal. The way to this man's drugs was through his ego. He rummaged around in his backpack and came up with a vial of clear liquid.

"I've been clean these past few months," I said. "How much do I start with again?"

"One drop under your tongue."

"It'll last for…"

"A day, give or take. Don't you remember?"

I shook my head. "I was hitting it pretty hard back then. Now I only want enough to get through the day and still function."

"Follow my instructions and you won't nod off or anything on Blank. You'll live your life, just in the quiet."

Blank. How apt.

"Thanks." I paid him and took the vial, heading straight out of the bar and trusting Levi to follow.

Levi dropped our illusions as soon as we stepped onto the street. "Trading alcoholism for drugs, are we?"

"Come with me." I jaywalked across the street to Moriarty.

"Remember the part where I was at work?" he said, pulling out his phone and swiping through the texts from Veronica.

"Please. I'd like someone there in case things go wrong."

"Here we go. Why ever would anything go wrong, Ashira?"

I held up the vial. If the chemist's cryptic comment

about the "song in Gavriella's head being too loud" did refer to her cravings, then this drug could be my salvation. And without her around to ask, there was only one way to find out. "Because I'm about to take an unknown drug and if I drop dead, you get the honor of dealing with my body. You in?"

Chapter 16

While Levi issued instructions to Veronica on speakerphone, I studied him covertly as I fiddled with the heater vent in my car. She was seriously displeased about him rescheduling his meeting with Accounting about next year's budget, especially since his only explanation was that something came up, but Levi insisted with a calm authority, and not a single snarky comment my way about how valuable his time was.

My *life* was pretty damn valuable, yet I kept trusting him to have my back. And he kept being there. All this time I'd emphatically stated that I didn't trust him, and look at me. My "trust as an absolute" ideology was malleable enough for me to trust Levi situationally, too. So where did that leave us? I turned up the radio once his call with Veronica was finished, not wanting to make small talk. Or worse, meaningful conversation.

Despite my protests, Levi directed me to his house since he had the backyard space to bury my body if need be.

I was quiet as I drove us over. Even in my wayward youth, I'd never done anything more than smoke pot a couple of times. I didn't like the loss of control. Despite what the clandestine chemist had promised, I had no hard proof that Blank would work on me as promised. Or if it did, how bad the ride would be.

Levi didn't push me to share, which I appreciated.

When we pulled up to his gate, he beeped a key fob to open it, and I drove up to his front door.

I shucked off my motorcycle boots inside his foyer and hung up my leather jacket in the closet which was located next to a gorgeous painting of a boy seeming to come directly out of the frame, as if it was a trapdoor. Levi and his illusions. "No biscotti this time, huh?"

"Convince me this is a wise idea and I'll make you some," he said.

Setting the vial on the coffee table, I sat down on his sofa, my eyes drifting out to the bluish-gray water of Burrard Inlet outside his floor-to-ceiling windows.

The leather cushions depressed as Levi sat beside me. He draped his suit jacket and tie over the back of a chair and rolled up his shirt sleeves, exposing olive skin over flexed muscle.

"I appreciate you watching over me," I said. "I couldn't ask Pri. She's got zero tolerance for drugs." Her ex-fiancé had gone through an addiction to amphetamines during his medical residency, and it had sent their relationship careening out of control.

"Why do you want to do this?"

I explained about my theory that this Blank was how Gavriella had quieted the cravings. "The urge to chase the high I get from snuffing out magic is like a song on repeat in my brain. How am I supposed to live with that?"

"It's only a hypothesis that this drug will work the way you hope," he said. "If you're wrong about this, it could cost you your life. People are dropping dead every day on the streets of Vancouver."

"From fentanyl. This guy was too invested in his art. Also, this is a liquid. I doubt he cut Blank with it." I bit my lip. "Best case scenario, I'm right and it works as advertised, I'm dependent on a street drug for the rest of my life."

"As opposed to the worst case scenario of being dead or addicted to a really awful drug?"

I fiddled with the vial's stopper.

"Are the cravings that bad?" he said.

"I can withstand them on my own, for now, but my magic exists to destroy other magic and certain interactions amp them up. I don't want to crave magic. I despised myself for what I did to Sharp."

Levi covered my hand with his. "Sharp was doomed whether you took his magic or not. You were trying to save those abducted kids."

"Good reason, right? What about when the line gets a bit blurrier? I had a run-in with a Medusa yesterday—"

"Of course you did," he muttered.

"My magic wasn't strong enough to counteract the effects. I needed a boost, so I worked my mojo on another person, but it still wasn't enough. The poor Medusa was bleeding out, but all I felt was satisfaction that he was already weakened and it would be easier to take his magic."

"Did you?" There was no judgment in his voice.

"No. I spared them both. That time." I scrubbed a hand over my face. "How long until my justifications get flimsier and flimsier and I'm out there hurting innocent people like some kind of magic-sucking vampire? Years? Months? I agree that there has to be a way to curb the urges otherwise we'd have heard about Jezebel powers." I rolled the vial between my thumb and forefinger. "What if it's this? Or some version of it? I know so little about being a Jezebel. Taking this isn't my first choice, but Gavriella used it for a reason, and this is as safe a circumstance as I can ingest it in."

"You could wait until you meet the rest of your team. Ask them."

Did I have the luxury of finding them, or would I buckle

the next time I interacted with the feather? I wasn't ready to share how bad those encounters were yet.

"What if this team *wants* me to have the cravings because it provides an edge in dealing with Chariot?" I said. "Some kind of bloodlust for taking them down? I idolized a man who, thanks to his Charmer magic, took from people without their consent, even if it was something as small as a smile. After I'd experienced firsthand what it meant to be a mark, to be the one burned and left picking up the pieces, I swore never to find myself in that position again, and certainly never to be the one causing it."

"You're not your father."

"I'm the one who has to face myself in the mirror."

He sighed. "Okay, Gargoyle Girl. Take it and I'll make sure of your continued existence."

I glared at him. "Gargoyle Girl?"

He grinned. "You were the one turning to stone."

"Call me that and I'll replace that Photoshopped bio pic on the House website with the photo I have of you after you stepped in poison ivy when you were fourteen."

He waved a hand around his face. "No need to Photoshop perfection. Also, that's insulting. I have illusion magic. What the hell do I need software for?"

"Ah. You do admit to enhancing yourself." I waggled my eyebrows at him.

"No, Ash. You've just never had a man of my caliber before."

I rolled my eyes, then uncorked the vial. "One drop under my tongue."

I couldn't make myself move. I closed my eyes, my stomach knotting up.

"Want me to do it for you?"

Eyes still closed, I handed him the vial, and opened my mouth.

A single tasteless drop hit under my tongue and I

opened my eyes. "I didn't ask how long it takes to kick in. Got any board games?"

Levi stilled my jittering leg and shot me a lascivious wink. "No, but I've got fifteen minutes. Excuse me, ten."

Priya had once talked me into taking a yoga class. I'd had to stand in one-legged mountain pose with my eyes closed, and I'd been certain the world was sliding sideways, because why else would it be so hard to stay connected to the earth? I had the same feeling now, except with my eyes wide open.

I wet my lips and forced a jovial note into my voice. "Sounds good. I'll flap around on you like a fish out of water. That's how you do the sex, right?"

"Something like that." We both laughed, but my stomach was knotted up because I wanted to make him forget his alibi woman and realize that I wasn't so easy to discard.

Our gazes snagged, the tension around the Blank turning to a lush promise of something else on offer.

Levi searched my face, until I nodded the go-ahead, then he cradled my face in his hands and kissed me.

It was broad daylight, but this kiss was moonlight edged with shadow. I fell into it, my breathing quickening and my hands tightening on his ribcage, pulling him closer. I curled my toes under, lust licking at them, swallowing my feet and rising like a flood.

His tongue tangled with mine and a shiver ricocheted up my spine.

"What are we doing?" I whispered.

He ran suggestive eyes over me, darkened to the mysterious blue of the ocean depths. "Distracting you. Is it working?"

All too well, but he was still firmly in control whereas the mere touch of his lips sent me into dizzy free fall. I didn't want flowery promises or commitment, but I did want to shred his precious control with a vengeance that was so physical that I flexed my fingers as if I could literally tear it apart.

His lips slid down my throat, his fingers unbuttoning my shirt, lowering my guard one button at a time. "Say the word and I stop. Any time."

My shirt fell open. "Levi."

He immediately stopped what he was doing.

I lay my hand on his cheek and he nuzzled into it. "Take off your shirt."

He undid the first couple of buttons and then pulled it over his head in a smooth motion that caused his rock-hard abs to ripple. Broad shoulders and sculpted pecs narrowed to a flat waist, faintly dusted with dark hair.

Straddling him, I inhaled the scent of his magic and ran my hands over his torso, slowing when I traced the slight ridges of the scars on his back. "You didn't illusion them away."

"I don't bother with fellow members of the monster support group."

"Yeah? How many members are in this club?" Did *she* qualify for membership?

"Two." He brushed his lips against mine. "I don't know what we're doing either, but can we continue until it doesn't work?"

The stripped-down need on his face sparked like static across my body, his hand cradled against the small of my back my sole anchor point tethering me to terra firma.

I draped my arms around his neck. "We can."

His hand slid into my hair and his mouth came down on mine in a rush.

I rocked against his hard cock and with a groan, he placed his hands on my hips, standing up and taking me with him. I wrapped my legs around his waist, not breaking the kiss as he stumbled backward out of the room and down a short hallway, Levi divesting me of my top. Laughing and making out like teenagers, we crashed through a door, where I was unceremoniously tossed on my ass on his bed.

"Suave," I said.

"Oops. Slipped." Levi dropped onto his side next to me.

"Rude. You should make it up to me." I claimed his mouth in a loose and sloppy kiss that crackled the air between us, blurring the lines of all that we were into something less jagged.

Levi rolled me under him, undoing my bra and pitching it into the corner. He palmed my breast, my flesh hot and heavy under his touch. I arched up and he sucked it into his mouth, one hand on my waist, pinning me down.

My hips rolled, the heavy ache to have him inside me pooling deep in my belly.

Unsnapping my jeans, I hooked my fingers into my belt loops and wriggled my pants down my hips, kicking free of them.

"You went commando," he said in a strangled voice.

Not doing laundry would do that, but why kill the mood?

"Didn't you?" I pressed the heel of my palm against his erection and he hissed. "I should check." I tugged his zipper down as Levi licked across my other nipple, rasping it with his teeth. Fumbling at his belt, I yanked his trousers and underwear off, taking his cock in my hand and luxuriating in the sleek satin of his skin.

His breath gusted out in a whoosh and he gave me a smile that was half-seductive and half-evil. "Hold that thought."

Levi slid down my body, trailing kisses that lit me up like a pinball machine. He nipped at my inner thigh, then ghosted his lips over the long, puckered scar on my right thigh.

I tensed and pulled my leg away.

"Did that hurt?" he said, eyes wide with concern.

"It's just not a part of my body I'm used to other people touching."

"Then they're idiots. I've got you naked in my bed and I want all of you. You good with that?"

"Only one way to find out." I stretched my leg out.

Levi licked my clit and I bucked off the mattress.

"Wait. What about my scar?"

"If you have some freaky scar fetish, keep it to yourself."

I huffed a laugh and pushed his head between my legs. "Stop talking smack and put that purdy mouth of yours to good use."

I propped myself up on my elbows to watch him, a head of tousled dark hair between my legs, his eyes focused on me with single-minded determination, and his tongue playing my clit like a virtuoso.

My head fell back, desire tightening deep in my core and lashing out like tongues of flame inside me, but I didn't want to come like this. I pulled him up until his body covered mine.

"Get a condom," I said, stroking him slowly.

"Keep touching yourself." He slid off me and I felt colder for the lack of contact.

I played with myself, my breathing growing raspy, watching him find a condom in his nightstand and put it on.

Levi lay me on my back. "Wrap your legs around me."

I did as commanded, so aroused that I balanced between pleasure and pain. My clit was throbbing and I bucked my hips to let that thin edge cut me more sharply, pushing me closer to the brink.

He pulled me to him, his hands feverishly roaming my body, and his lips devouring mine in exquisite torture, while he fucked me into the mattress.

Our motions grew to a frenzy, sweat beading our skin.

Levi trained a drugged-out gaze on me. The curve of his

mouth grew wider, his grin as filthy as the murmured words that fell from his devil lips about how I felt on his cock. His thickening Italian accent drove me higher and hotter, my nipples tightening, until my entire body clenched and I came so hard that I had to grip his shoulders for balance.

Levi sucked on my bottom lip, then shuddered. "Fuck, bella."

The endearment rolled over me, and I quivered in orgasmic aftershock, holding him tight.

Levi pulled out of me. I splayed out on his bed while he disposed of the condom. "Distraction achieved?" he said

"Gold star you," I said when he came back.

He laughed and waved his hand, sending a cascade of gold stars showering down on us. Smiling, I caught one in my hand, and blew it back at him like a kiss.

"This is good," he said softly.

Gold star levels of good in a casual relationship which was complicated by situational trust, conflicting loyalties, and Levi's mystery alibi woman.

"Yeah," I said, more wistfully than I'd intended.

"Bella—"

"How about that biscotti?" I said brightly, rolling in toward him to inhale the delicious scent of his scotch and chocolate magic. All I smelled was his lemongrass shampoo and a faint touch of sweat. I jackknifed up into a sitting position, icy tentacles spinning through my veins.

"What's wrong?"

"I can't smell your magic." I reached for my power but got nothing except a terrifying flatness.

Levi took my hands in his. "What do you mean?"

"The good news is the drug worked. My head is quiet and the cravings are gone." I swallowed. "But so's my magic."

We double and triple-checked. Levi had me try to manifest a coin and make my blood armor appear, but I couldn't do either, and even when I made a small incision, hoping the blood would call my magic to the surface, all I got for my effort was a Band-Aid.

Numb, I sat on the sofa, wearing one of Levi's sweat-shirts that fell mid-thigh, wrapped in a blanket that he'd draped around me with a mug of tea in my hands. Not my first choice, but he refused to mix alcohol with the Blank.

Levi wore jeans and a long-sleeved T-shirt, his arms cradling me. "The chemist said a day. It should wear off by morning."

"I'm not worried about losing my magic for a day." Though it was scary how quickly I'd accepted its presence in my life. How quickly I'd reframed my identity—and my dreams—around being Nefesh. Even so, it was better than the Mundane alternative. "If I take the drug, no one gets hurt."

"No going after Chariot or getting sucked into a destiny you don't want." Levi massaged the base of my skull in steady, soothing circles.

"Like Gavriella did? If she was on Blank, then she'd turned her back on being a Jezebel." I wrapped the blanket tighter around me to force some warmth into the empty hollowness in my chest. "Hell of a choice. No cravings or no dreams."

"You can still be a private investigator without your magic."

"You don't understand. In my Mundane career, it was as if I'd been going down this endless hallway and way at the far side, I could just make out a door with a gold star on it. If I could get through it, only then would I be rewarded with a wealth of fascinating cases. The problem was, not only was it a long, boring path, that door never got any closer. But when I became Nefesh, suddenly there were doors everywhere and each one had some exciting adventure behind it."

I pressed my fists into my eyes hard enough to see stars but they weren't the gold ones. They were dull and cold like the future unspooling in front of me.

"I don't want to go back to that endless trudging, but who am I to attain my dream at the cost of other people's magic? How do I live with that?" I laughed bitterly. "Damn my pesky morals."

Priya would have said that everything would work out. That there had to be another way and I'd have gone along with it, knowing the truth in my heart.

Levi didn't offer me false hope or empty comfort, but he held me until the afternoon sunshine weakened into lengthening shadows, while I wrestled with which version of myself I could live with.

Chapter 17

I was woken by a text from a blocked number that said Vespa would see me tomorrow.

Groggy, I rolled out of my bed and did some much-needed laundry. I'd wanted to sleep in my own space, so I'd bid Levi farewell late last night. Coffee and the half of an omelet that Priya had left—along with a note that she'd gone to meet Miles—kicked my sluggish brain into gear. Bless her for restocking our food supply.

The Blank still coursed through my system, my magic off-line. Much as I didn't want to use my powers on anyone, not having it left me jittery.

I kept Gavriella's ring on me, even though I wasn't about to test it without my magic.

Gathering the laundry, I dumped the clean clothes in a heap on the cream antique sofa with carved wood trim and tufted upholstery that I'd inherited from my grandparents. It had come with a large tapestry entitled *Paris in the Moonlight* that was made up of abstract geometric shapes suggesting the Eiffel Tower at night, which dominated the wall across from my bed. Neither fit my personal design aesthetic, but they reminded me of sitting on that sofa and watching my grandmother get dolled up for all the parties at the predominantly Jewish country club that my grandparents had been members of.

I rooted through the pile, picking out my favorite black jeans and a faded but very soft skater hoodie.

My first stop of the day was my office. Thursdays tended to be quiet around the shared workspace, because Eleanor worked from home, Bryan met with clients at their workplaces, and unless Priya was around, I was alone.

At the sight of the smashed glass in the door to the workspace, I stumbled over the final step to the second-floor landing of our building. Pulling out my spare mini Taser, I crept inside, careful to avoid broken glass. The common reception area was untouched and Eleanor's and Bryan's offices were undisturbed.

The frosted glass office door with my business name stenciled in gold, however, was shattered. I ran inside and cried out, doubling over like I'd been punched in the gut.

My office was destroyed. The filing cabinets were knocked over, though thankfully still locked, and furniture had been flung around the room, smashed into unrecognizability. My desk chair lay on its side, the wonky wheel broken off and rolled into the middle of debris like an undetonated bomb.

The dartboard lay on the ground surrounded by busted darts, a dirty smeared boot print covering the fibers. The photo of Priya and me graduating university was gone.

I dashed away tears and hurried to the safe, which had been dragged about a foot away from the wall. There was a gouge on the floor under the corner, like it had been dropped, but the door was locked and, when I opened it, the pouch lay safely inside. I grabbed it and hurled it against the wall, screaming at the top of my lungs.

My office wasn't fancy and I only had a part-time staff of one, but it was mine. I'd worked my ass off to get this far.

Coming through the door with my name stenciled on it lifted me out of any funk. My apartment was my home, but my office was my heart.

The Blank hadn't left my system yet and I was still without my powers, otherwise, I'd have nuked that feather's magic without a second thought. Even if I couldn't smell any lingering magic to confirm any residual lily and dust scent that proved Malach had been here, my gut said it was him.

Compulsion or not, he'd violated my sanctuary.

I swept my useless office furniture into a pile against one wall, but left the safe where it was since it was too heavy to move without my enhanced strength. Same with trying to right-side up the filing cabinets.

From the dents on my drywall, Malach had hurled my whiteboard against it repeatedly. The notes had been erased, but I remembered the names and magic types of the five men who worked with Edrice. Three of them were elementals with fire, water, and earth power respectively. There wasn't a trace of any of those powers here, so it wasn't them. One had invisibility magic which may have allowed him to get in undetected but he couldn't have done this type of damage without super strength.

The final employee on the archeology site had a rare type of ability: he could temporarily null magic, which was cool, but didn't help with either the attack on Omar or this vandalism. And there was still the matter that none of them had left the site.

I lay down on my floor, staring up at the ceiling. What hard facts did I have about Malach? He was about six feet tall and had some way to fly. He had a lean build, but didn't want his face seen, and he wanted that feather. I turned those facts over and over in my head, until shouting and raucous laughter from the street broke my concentration. I went to the window to yell at them to keep it down. A group of teens were sharing a bag of chips as they horsed around. The tallest kid had an androgynous look about him.

Why "him?" I had no idea what gender if any that teen identified as, but I'd been quick to make assumptions.

I phoned Edrice, keeping the pleasantries short. "What about a woman having a crush on you?"

"The only lesbian in our crew is happily married, and her wife is much more interesting than I am."

"Are any of the other women Nefesh?" I said, grasping at straws.

There was just one: Nadija Culianu, a Romanian archeologist, consulting on the dig.

Not only was Nadija tall, but she had Animator magic. That could explain how she'd flown; she'd animated the costume wings. They didn't need to be large enough to follow the laws of physics because this was magic. It also explained how she'd destroyed my office. She'd simply animated the objects and flung them around.

Best of all? Nadija had completed her job on the project five days ago and left the site.

My gut tightened with the excitement of closing in on my quarry. I still didn't have motive, but I'd get that out of her once I found her. Edrice gave me Nadija's cell number, so I tried it, hoping to set up some kind of meeting, but it was no longer in service.

I texted Priya what had happened and not to come here. Then I called a glass repair place and locksmith, using up my emergency credit card reserves to get them to my office right away. I spent the next couple of hours cold-calling every hotel and motel in Vancouver asking to be put through to Nadija's room.

By the time I found her at a budget motel in East Vancouver, the glass in both the workspace doors and my office were replaced. My poor door was naked without Cohen Investigations stenciled on it, but that would have to wait. I'd fixed the locks on both doors and left notes for Eleanor and Bryan to discuss going in on an alarm system. We'd had one when we originally rented the space, but the company that managed our workspace had changed a couple of months ago, and it was no longer part of our rent. The three of us meant to share a monitored system, we just hadn't gotten around to it yet. That was on us.

I left them new keys to my office, as we'd eventually entrusted each other with a spare set.

Checking the safe three times that the pouch and feather were secured until I took them to Vespa, I locked up and drove to the motel. The rooms were actually individual bungalows with the one Nadija had rented located at the far end of the property.

She didn't answer when I knocked and said, "House-keeping." Ensuring that no one was around, I picked the lock and slid inside.

The room stank of lilies and dust so badly that my eyes watered. That wasn't right. The Blank hadn't cleared my system and I shouldn't have been able to smell her magic.

Her angel robe and wings were packed in an open suit-case, along with gloves that were reinforced with some type of heavy metal bar in the knuckles and a weighted vest. I searched through her things but found no weapons. There were clothes, a minimal amount of toiletries—and the photo of Priya and me with a red X over my face.

Wonderful. My own creepy stalker. Well, rule number one: no face-to-face confrontations until my powers came back. What had been the most cautious way to determine if I could beat the cravings was now a major thorn in my side. Given the attack on my office, she was enraged, likely still compelled by the feather to act out in extreme ways, and she had magic while I didn't.

While I didn't plan on facing off with Nadija, I did have to find her, and I couldn't stake out this motel 24/7 on my own. Nor could I go to the police. Not the Mundane ones for obvious reasons that they legally couldn't apprehend a Nefesh suspect, and not the Nefesh cops since according to all records, I was still Mundane and shouldn't be working a case with a Nefesh suspect. The irony being that, at this moment, I really was Mundane.

Levi had the means and ability to put people on a stake-out, but Moran had been clear about not involving him or the police and I wasn't about to do anything that risked getting my hands on the smudges in the vials. That left the Queen, who had as much of a vested interest in resolving this as I did.

If she'd get involved.

I probed the idea for every way this request could blow back on me and explode, but it seemed like a fairly low risk. The Queen wanted Nadija caught and my magic kept on the down-low. This situation certainly fit both of those criteria. Unless I did something stupid and pissed her off—not in my plans—Her Majesty would have no reason to go after me.

Bracing myself for the price I'd have to pay this time, I used another precious bronze token to go back to her mansion.

July of my thirteenth year was a hot one. Even in the shade of the ferry terminal building, sunshine baked my skin, causing my heavily applied eyeliner to run down my cheeks. I dug in my day pack for a tissue and fixed it as best I could, watching the other kids being dropped off by their parents in Mercedes, BMWs, and Range Rovers.

Talia and I weren't poor, but we weren't rich, either. Not like these kids. I recognized some of them from the country club that my grandparents belonged to. The girls wheeled suitcases, their skin shiny and their hair straightened.

With the tip of the cane I'd been given in rehab, I pushed my scruffy backpack behind me, and tried to pull my shorts down over the long red gash on my right thigh. Talia had bought me a bunch of khaki pants to wear, but my declaration that it was my body and I'd wear whatever the hell I wanted to didn't seem so badass in the face of openly disgusted stares.

A Town Car pulled up and this gangly boy with black hair and the bluest eyes I'd ever seen got out of the front seat. He didn't say goodbye to his dad, who popped the trunk without a word to his son. The boy grabbed his suitcase and watched his father drive away with an unreadable expression.

Even Talia and I, both thrilled for time apart, had hugged when she dropped me off.

The boy caught me looking. "Got a problem, Frankenstein?"

That got everyone's attention. They closed in on me like a pack of wolves. Idiots. I was The Girl Who Lived. I'd survived worse than them.

I twirled the cane between my fingers. "Frankenstein was the doctor. If you're gonna insult me, at least be smart enough to do it properly."

One of the girls laughed, but dropped her eyes to the ground when her friend elbowed her.

The boy came closer, a smirk on his face. "How'd you get it, huh? Did you cut yourself in some Satanic ritual?"

"You're awfully interested in my scar," I said. "How come? You got some freaky fetish?"

He flinched. "Fuck you."

A stocky kid about half a head taller than everyone with a serious expression loped over to the boy and punched him in the shoulder. "Forget her. I heard they finally got a decent cook."

Everyone broke into chatter about how bad the food had been last year.

The blue-eyed boy gave me a look that this wasn't over. I

smiled grimly at him, picked up my backpack, and strode inside the terminal.

Momentarily dazed to find myself standing in the sticky night of Hedon and not that long ago summer, I crossed the flagstone terrace to join the Queen. She sat in a chair with a martini, looking out over the Tannous and Dershowitz families down in the grounds, who were marking out the dance floor with the wedding coordinator.

"What possible interest could you have in that memory?" I said.

"I don't choose what gets revealed." The Queen sipped her martini, the picture of cool in a red slip dress that revealed her impressive décolletage. This was a woman who luxuriated in her every curve, and why not? She was damn sexy. "You give me too much credit, chica."

"No, I give you exactly enough, Your Highness."

She laughed, a tinkly sound like ice against a glass.

"I found Omar's attacker."

The Queen looked around. "Where is he?"

"She." That didn't even rate a flicker of surprise. Then again, look who I was talking to. The Queen knew exactly how formidable women could be. "I found her motel and all her stuff, but I can't stake it out constantly. I need help please. Would you give me some of your guards?"

"Didn't Moran explain it to you? I cannot involve myself in matters that occur outside Hedon. No, Ashira, I brought you in to handle this, and I expect you to do so. Or those vials will not be yours."

"With all due respect, there has to be something you can do. At least let Levi help."

"Mr. Montefiore may be fond of you, but he will not turn a blind eye to formal channels of justice in this matter. I regret you're on your own."

"You're being unreasonable."

She raised an eyebrow.

I hurriedly dropped my gaze. "I'm sorry. I had no right to speak that way. I'm anxious to wrap this up, but I'll figure it out."

"Do you know why this woman went after Omar?"

"No. Her sole focus seems to be this feather so I don't even understand why she'd—"

A crazy thought hit me. I jumped to my feet, jogged down the stairs, and grabbed Omar by the shirtfront. "Did you swallow the feather, you stupid son-of-a-bitch?"

Shannon screamed and Husani tried to pull me off, but I stomped on his instep.

Someone calmly cleared their throat. Moran had appeared, sword in hand, looking pointedly between me and Omar.

"If I'd actually attacked him, he wouldn't be standing." I released Omar, smoothing out his clothing. He wasn't worth me turning to stone. Again.

"Your gentle demeanor reaffirms my faith in humanity," Moran said.

"Thank you for seeing that. It's hard dimming my bright light so I don't blind you lesser mortals."

"Play nice, Ash," he said and left.

I whirled on Omar, who shrank back. "You did swallow it, didn't you? You came across the feather on the site and stole it from her."

"Her? You got attacked by a woman?" Chione broke into belly guffaws. Masika swatted her, but that only made her laugh harder.

"Gonif! Thief!" Ivan said.

"Takes one to know one," Husani said.

"You're too stupid to marry my daughter," Ivan said.

"Daaaaaaddy," Shannon wailed.

"He is right," Masika said, and spat at her grandson's feet.

"Teta!" Omar gasped.

"Look at you in-laws coming together. I'm delighted I provided this bonding moment," I said. "Your entire history with that damn feather. Now." I glared at Omar until he answered.

"I didn't steal it." He sank into a chair. "Not exactly. I was supposed to accompany the trucks with the antiquities back to Cairo when I heard something break in one of the tents in the living quarters. A stranger came out, and figuring he was a looter, I approached. That's when he pulled a knife on me."

Shannon gasped. Husani and Chione nodded like this was business as usual.

I prodded Omar's shoulder. "Keep talking."

His expression turned distant. "I only meant to disarm him, but when he got close, I saw the feather and…"

"Did you bury the body?" Masika said.

Omar huffed. "Of course, Teta."

So much for plausible deniability. I could never go to Egypt.

"Is that where you kept disappearing to when you got to my house?" Shannon said. "You were spending time with a feather?" Her voice rose in a furious shriek.

Really? The murder wasn't the issue?

Omar flushed and Husani gave him the universal head shake of "not cool, dude."

Rachel handed her a drink which Shannon took a pretty good slug of without coughing.

Omar hung his head.

"Then this Angel of Death showed up," I said, "demanded it back, and you swallowed it."

"It was the only way to keep it," Omar said.

"You're sure you dug deep enough?" Masika jabbed Omar in the chest with a bony finger.

"Teta, yes. I put him in the grove."

I froze. "What grove? Wasn't the site in a flat scrubby area?"

"Yes," Chione said, "but there are a lot of orchards and natural pools."

"Orchard or grove?" I growled.

Omar frowned. "What's the difference?"

Asherah was the difference. "Orchards have rows of fruit trees."

He shrugged. "Grove."

"Did the man say anything to you? Did he have a German accent?"

Husani stepped in between me and his brother. "Calm down."

I shoved Husani aside. "Did he?"

"I don't know. He spoke Arabic but he was Jewish."

"Got some basis for your racial profiling?" I said.

"He wore a Star of David necklace."

I stilled. Chariot. This fucking feather had been unearthed on an archeological dig near where Asherah was worshiped and Chariot had come looking for it. I rubbed a hand over my jaw. Was Nadija part of Chariot and the man had tossed her tent because she'd been compelled and refused to hand the feather over? Had Evil Wanker brought me to the grove not because of the ring, which may well have belonged to Gavriella's father, but because he suspected I had the feather?

Chariot had first touched my life fifteen years ago when Yitzak tattooed the Star of David ward on me despite his loyalty to that organization. They were this spiderweb, their gossamer fine strands spinning through both the Nefesh and Mundane worlds. When they'd appeared nothing more than a criminal organization with a religious bent, I'd been mildly intrigued, but they kept crossing my path, to even this seemingly unrelated P.I. case.

Now they had my full attention, but I had to tread very carefully.

"I still say you're too stupid to marry my daughter," Ivan said.

Rachel glared at her husband and put an arm around Shannon. "Don't listen to him. He can't stop the wedding."

Omar squirmed like a worm on a hook. "I never—I didn't mean—I couldn't help it."

"You probably couldn't," I agreed. "But you could have said something after the attack. She didn't touch you, did she?"

He shook his head, abashed.

The Queen watched the entire proceeding from the terrace.

"You still want this woman brought to justice here in Hedon?" I called out. "All she did was come for what was hers by trying to scare Omar."

Nadija hadn't attacked Omar but she had trashed my office and she might belong to Chariot. She was mine to apprehend. I hoped.

The Queen looked beheading-level angry. But not at me, so I sat down to enjoy the fireworks.

Masika stepped in front of her grandson, her hands together in supplication. "Your Highness, I beg you. He is a foolish boy but he didn't mean to deceive."

Shannon's lip quivered. "Please let us get married. I love him."

Omar better have a magic dick, because otherwise, cut him loose, lady.

Chione was still snickering and I failed to give a damn one way or the other so long as I got Nadija and the vials. Everyone else did statue impersonations while they waited for the Queen's verdict.

"The wedding will proceed," the Queen said at last.

I raised my hand. "What about the woman?"

"Who was the German you're interested in, chica?"

"Different case," I said. "House business."

The Queen gave me a look like we'd return to this subject at a future date. "Then this Nadija is yours."

"How about our deal?" I stood up.

"Still in place. Same terms. This case must be wrapped up before the wedding."

"No loose ends." I stood up and boffed Omar across the head. He scrunched into himself, thoroughly miserable. "Way to go, dumbass."

On that high note, I used one of my few remaining tokens and vanished.

Chapter 18

"Hey Miles, you still meeting with Priya?" I tossed my cell, which was on speakerphone, onto Moriarty's passenger seat and started the engine.

"I can't understand you."

I swallowed the bulging mass of tiny Ritz crackers and cheese in my mouth. "Priya. Is she there?"

"Yeah, why? Did you want to speak to her?"

"No. Apologize to her for interrupting but I need your help. It's urgent." I explained about Nadija as succinctly as possible, starting with the attack on Omar that wasn't, moving on to the vandalism on my poor office, and finally my speculation that she was connected to Chariot.

The Queen had handed the woman over to me to deal with and I was bringing the House into it as the most expedient way to wrap this up, with the least collateral damage to any innocents.

Traffic and construction were fairly minimal between the office and my apartment, so I was almost home by the time I'd wrapped up.

"The attack and the vandalism make this a job for the police," Miles said.

"The same police who tipped off a member of Chariot, enabling him to assassinate a man in your jail cell? Do you know yet whether you have cops on Chariot's payroll?"

"No," he grudgingly admitted.

I backed Moriarty into one of the three parking stalls behind our building. "Can you swear you don't have any cops feeding intel to the Untainted Party either? Because Nadija is under the influence of a powerful artifact, and if they find out about its existence, it'll throw fuel on the fire."

There was a pause. "You're protecting Levi."

"I'm making sure our city stays riot-free. Consider Nadija possibly unhinged and therefore dangerous." I locked up and headed around the side of the building to the front door.

"She's an Animator?" he said. "Okay, we'll take proper precautions. My people will find her."

"Appreciate it. Let me know when she's apprehended."

"What about the artifact?"

"I'm dealing with it. Oh, and watch out for her wings."

"Fucking hell, Cohen." Miles hung up.

I inserted my key into the front door of my building and jerked back like I'd gotten a whopper of an electric shock. My magic had returned, bringing the cravings back with a vengeance, the song in my head blaring.

I tried to open the door, but my hands were shaking and I dropped my keys. I'd gotten them in the lock once more when a guy walked past with a young woman, lighting her cigarette with a tiny flame that he conjured up.

I salivated, smelling the charcoal of his magic, and fell into step behind them, my eyes narrowed on my prey.

"Ash?" Beatriz, the earth elemental who owned my favorite bakery Muffin Top, stood in front of me, frowning. Her baby, Miguel, was snug against her chest in a cloth carrier. "You don't look too good."

My prey rounded the corner and was lost to view.

I swallowed hard. Beatriz was a powerful Nefesh. The rush would be insane. The tiny sliver of rationality left in my brain screamed to get out of here, but I couldn't seem to make my feet move. All my energy was engaged in sizing her up like a prime cut of beef.

"Do you need help?" she said.

Miguel gurgled and batted a chubby fist at me. He had magic, too. It would taste as sweet and innocent as his smile.

I gently caught his fist. "Gotcha."

The baby laughed and tugged free, waving at me to grab him again.

My magic surged under my skin, the song tightening like a noose.

"Gotta get upstairs," I croaked and fled. I locked myself in my apartment, sliding down against the door to the floor, my head in my hands, until my lungs expanded enough to drag in a deep breath and the rushing in my ears faded.

How did Jezebels handle this?

I went into the bathroom and splashed cold water on my face with a renewed resolve to find my team and hope they had a way forward for me, because Blank was not the solution.

Starting tomorrow, because it had been a long day and I needed sleep.

Friday was bright and sunny, making it easier to haul my butt out of bed. Priya had texted about staying with Kai again so I foraged for breakfast in the quiet of my apartment.

Omar's case was wrapped up, more or less, and it wasn't time to go visit Vespa and learn more about the feather.

Knowledge was power, after all.

Right now, I required knowledge of a different sort. Dressed and sitting comfortably on the sofa, I held up the ring that Levi had gotten at the strip club. Was it something sinister, simply an item of sentimental value for

Gavriella, or a token that would transport me to Jezebel HQ?

I shot off a quick text to both Priya and Levi. If things went sideways with the ring, they'd have a starting point for figuring out what had happened. Plus, it was only right to give them a heads up, since being left in the dark when I'd been transported to the grove had shaken the two of them.

Crossing my fingers that the ring led me to my team and not directly into the clutches of Evil Wanker, I slid it on my middle finger…

… and found myself in a round windowless room.

Five square smooth pillars, each one about waist-height, occupied the center of the room. Three of them glowed softly while one was actively dark and the last one neutral.

They were smooth to the touch, but they didn't do anything.

One section of the curved wall was covered in custom-built shelving. The top shelves held a jumble of scrolls, the center section was lined with chunky leather books, and the lower ones contained more modern Moleskines and journals.

Stretching up on tiptoe, I pulled down a scroll and carefully unrolled it. The parchment was yellow and brittle, covered in tiny writing in some Cyrillic-based language.

I exchanged it for one of the leather-bound tomes. This one was in French, and while I could pick out some of the words, most of the verb tenses were incomprehensible. I finally found a book written in old English. The first few pages detailed the training regimen of a Jezebel called Catriona. The chronicler was exhaustive to the point of anal-retentive with such fascinating details as her preference for porridge with honey and salt.

I shelved the book and sat down to peruse the bottom shelf. Pulling out a Moleskine, I flipped it open to a middle page. The block printing was uniform and very neat.

Rachel, our newest Jezebel, is proving to be a quick student of Kabbalistic concepts. Today we discussed the concept of "the divine spark" in regards to Yechida. How Yechida is the level of the soul that in essence transcends all worlds, since it is never separated from G-d. It is a spark of the Creator within the created.

I flipped ahead, since I'd learned that in my grade eight magic studies unit. A drawing of a ghost-like blob stopped me.

Rachel questioned why Repha'im tasted different to the shades pulled from a person when destroying magic. In the Hebrew Bible, the living, both those with magic and those without, are referred to as Nefesh Hayyah, the living body or spirit, while the dead are Nefesh Met. Their spirits are Repha'im who've crossed over and inhabit Sheol, the underworld.

Jezebels can fight those Repha'im who once had magic, though they behave and taste differently to living magic—like dust—being deceased souls. But as a Jezebel has no power over a Mundane, so is she helpless against those Repha'im who never possessed powers.

Did those ten who brought magic into our world know that in creating Nefesh magic, they tore a hole between our world and Sheol, the place of darkness that houses the dead?

"How did you get in here?" Evil Wanker appeared, startling the crap out of me.

I hastily stuffed the book on the shelf and scrambled to my feet. Solid as the room was, he remained a flickering figure. There didn't seem to be a bow tie on today's agenda but I got the distinct impression his jacket had patches on the elbows.

I twirled a finger around the room. "I expected more dripping candles and a chandelier made of skulls for Chariot's evil lair."

His brows knitted together and then he barked a laugh. "You think I'm Chariot?"

"Your opening monologue was straight out of some grade B henchman playbook, you took me to a grove with an almond tree, both associated with Asherah, and you warned me off being a Jezebel."

"With good cause. This insanely misguided deduction of yours confirms that you need to spend more time learning to be a detective and much less time playing around with this magic. You're not fit to have it."

"Not fit" sounded suspiciously like he cared who *was* worthy. "Fuck balls, are you Team Jezebel?"

In answer, he rolled up his sleeve, revealing an ornate almond tree with pink blossoms tattooed on the inside of his forearm. It stood out in stark relief to the obscured details of the rest of him. "By George, I think she's got it."

The Evil Wanker moniker hardened into concrete form.

"I already have the magic, bub. Find me lacking all you want, there's not a whole hell of a lot you can do about it."

He dragged one of the two chairs away from the modern rectangular cherry wood table and sat down. The furnishings were a mishmash of periods: there was also an antique desk with a hole for an ink pot, and two vintage high back chairs with tufted sage green upholstery.

"Once again, I see you are woefully ignorant," Evil Wanker said. "Did you know that unless you meet my standards of being a Jezebel I can take your pretty little powers away? I do hope you ask me to prove that I'm serious. I've been waiting to be rid of you for a very long time."

I flinched. Lose my magic? It would destroy my dreams. Okay, calm down, Ash. Think this through. "You talk a big game about knowing more than I do, but somehow my finding this place still surprised you."

"Yes, and I'm still wondering how. It shouldn't be possible until you fix our connection, and as I still can't see you properly, you've obviously failed at that simple task."

Yup. Evil Wanker.

I gave him the finger. "Can you see this?"

"No need to be rude."

"I meant the ring." I tapped the band on my middle finger.

He grabbed my hand, but passed through my flesh like he himself was a ghost. "Bloody hell! Is it a wood band?"

"Yeah. Same scent as the almond tree in the grove."

He exhaled. "It was Father's. I did wonder what had happened to it after his passing."

"Gavriella had it."

"I searched—" He snapped his mouth shut.

"*Gracie's* apartment? Yeah, I know that too. The ring wasn't there. Guess you're not as good a Seeker as I am." Though that explained how he'd gotten past the wards. No hostile intent. "But nice of you to take out her trash. What more do you want from me? I passed your three tests in the grove, I found the ring, and I found you."

Evil Wanker sighed, and looked tired. "If you truly want this so badly, then convince me you'll bring something substantial to this fight."

Perfect. I just so happened to have a feathery ace up my sleeve. "I bet you didn't know that Chariot—" The rest of my sentence was a burst of static. I tried again—to equally dismal and eardrum-jarring results. "God damn it! What is that?"

"Another point against you. Nothing about your magic is acting as it should. It's never played out this way before."

"You smooth talker," I said.

"Aren't I just? If you have something pressing to tell me, you may find me and share it in person. If you can. Your faulty magic has complicated things for fifteen years, and I refuse to waste more time on a broken toy. I have a mission to see to, and if you're unwilling to step up, you are more than welcome to step aside." He vanished.

"Fuuuuck!" I pulled off the ring, finding myself on my sofa once more.

This jerk was serious. He could strip me of my magic and then I'd be back at square one. And as much as the cravings and the responsibilities threatened to sideline me from being the world's greatest Nefesh P.I., I'd take them any day over being powerless again. So he wanted to vet me before accepting me onto the team? Fine. I'd been a stellar detective for years with zero magic. I'd blow his pompous, doubting ass out of the water.

How would I find him? I had no name, no idea of his exact magic powers, and no clue if he was a Jezebel himself. I spun the ring between my fingers. He was British and there were only four Houses in the UK. Provided he wasn't a Rogue like Gavriella, hopefully he'd be registered in one of them. I could make a list of the types of magic he was most likely to possess and cross-check them against his guesstimated age and gender. It was a clunky idea, but it was a start.

All fired up, I put on my motorcycle boots, only to remember my trashed office. I had to put it to rights. The list of everything I'd have to replace was expensive and depressing. My credit history was shaky enough that no bank would qualify me for a loan, and even if they did, it would take time to jump through all the hoops.

I needed money and I needed it now. Priya didn't have that kind of spare cash laying around and there was no way I was going to Levi for a handout. We didn't need the extra complication of money. That left one person who could loan me the cash immediately.

I clutched my phone running through all the ways I could possibly pitch this. *Hey Talia, remember our conversation about me having magic that upset you so much? Could you forget it for the moment and lend me some money because I'm in a bit of a bind?* Ten minutes later, I'd come back around to my initial conclusion that there was no good way to make contact.

I texted her before I lost my nerve.

Me: *Can we meet sometime?*

The three little dots appeared and disappeared too many times for a simple yes or no answer, then vanished entirely with no incoming message popping up.

So this was what we were now, two contacts who couldn't figure out how to communicate anymore.

Me: *My office was broken into and I'd like to please discuss some financial help to put it to rights.*

Talia, Destroyer of Egos: *Jackson is speaking in the atrium of the Law Courts tomorrow. Meet me there mid-afternoon.*

Summoned to the belly of the beast. That was one way to assure I behaved, but I was in no position to argue. I texted back that I'd see her then.

Another text came in on the heels of that one.

Imperious 1: *You used the ring?! If you're not alive, I'm going to kill you. If you are, same offer.*

Me: *Love you, too.*

I caught myself before I sent that message and changed it to a thumbs up emoji.

The front door opened.

"Honey, I'm home," Priya called out. "Knock once if you're stuck in some alternate almond dimension."

"Would you come find me?"

She dropped her bag on the floor and collapsed into a chair. "No. If you were stupid enough to use the ring without a safety buddy and get yourself in trouble, then I'd leave you there. Though I'd miss you when the rent was due and eat a slice of cake in memory on your birthday."

"Nice. Say aren't those the same clothes as yesterday? The walk of shame really brings out the green in your eyes."

"Right?" She fluttered her lashes.

"All's well that ends well. Sort of. I'm still alive and Evil

Wanker is Jezebel-affiliated, not Chariot, though he's still an Evil Wanker."

"Eventful morning."

"You have no idea. Tell me about your meeting with Miles. You all House Pacifica now?"

"Yup. I'm getting the official T-shirt and everything. I'm going to be part of a group overhauling all of their cybersecurity. I met a couple of them and it'll be good to be working with like-minded people."

"World domination is on track. Mazel tov. Is Kai happy for you?"

"Kai's always happy." Yawning, Priya kicked off her ballet flats. "I negotiated that one day a week I'm all yours. Oh!" She sat up. "Someone broke into the office? Did they take anything?"

"They wanted the feather. They didn't get it but the place is trashed." I failed to keep my voice from wobbling.

"Aw, sweetie. I'm sorry. What are you going to do?"

I grimaced. "Ask Talia for a loan to replace everything."

"How do you know she won't lock you up first and listen to your proposal second?"

"We're meeting in public and I'd fight arrest?"

Priya's eyes narrowed. "Where?"

"Jackson Wu's speech at the Law Courts. It's the safest place when you think about it. Talia won't dare draw attention to herself by going ballistic on her kid for having magic with that crowd around." I bit my lip. "I'm kind of hoping the pity card might be a way forward for us."

Priya sighed. "You've spent a lot of years pushing her away. She might find being needed a nice enough change that she softens towards you."

"Or enough of a shock that carrying out my doom falls to a distant second place. This sucks, but on a happier note, her payback terms will be better than any bank. Might as well upgrade from second-hand furniture for all the high-falutin' clients I'll have."

"Did your laptop bite it?" she said hopefully.

"Would you believe it made it through without a scratch?"

"Sadly, yes. That's it. I'm making an executive decision. I'm getting you a new laptop. I'll wire you up on a faster internet connection, too."

"I can't accept that. You don't have the cash."

"I will soon, baby. This contract? Cha-ching." Her eyes narrowed on a water stain in the corner of the ceiling that we'd nicknamed Fred, the Demon God of Moisture. "This place is gonna be history."

I mustered up a smile. Everything always hit at once, didn't it? "I'll go apartment shopping with you."

A pillow hit me in the head.

"Idiot. You're moving with me. I am not one to live alone. We'll figure out who pays what. Worse comes to worse, you can live in a closet and I'll use the second bedroom for my fabulous new wardrobe. It's not happening any time soon anyway. We'll be here at Grotto Outrageous for a while longer." She yawned again and curled up in the chair, her cheek on her fist.

"Exhausted from riding Kai like a stallion?"

"Quit harping on him. He's nice."

Don't forget happy and fond of his routines. How tedious. Priya deserved challenging and exciting and—you know, nice had a lot to recommend it.

"Okay. No more Kai digs."

My phone binged a reminder that it was time to see Vespa. I massaged my temples, exhausted from all the balls that I had juggling in the air right now. How was I supposed to prioritize when everything was Code Red important?

I debated blowing this visit off because I had to find Evil Wanker or kiss my Nefesh P.I. dreams goodbye, but this feather was dangerous and this might be my one chance to get the low-down. Also, it probably wasn't smart to piss off anyone in Hedon, and after everything I'd gone through at that damn Dream Market to get the appointment, I sure as shit wasn't missing it.

I grabbed the fleece blanket from the small storage unit built into the cushioned bench by the window and draped it over Priya. "You done good with Miles. I'll be home later."

Priya caught my hand and squeezed it. "'Kay. Love ya, Holmes."

"Love you too, Adler."

Priya was right. I was not without resources, and her friendship was one of my strongest.

Chapter 19

Going into Hedon didn't require me reliving any memories.

This time.

Certain there was still some price to pay, I put my worries aside to deal with it when the time came, because right now I had worse problems. Worse even than my heightened awareness of the contents of the metal pouch I'd retrieved that was in the purse slung across my chest.

"How the fuck is there an ocean in Hedon?" Wet sand sucked at my boots. The inky night sky only had the faintest dusting of stars, seeming to stretch on forever before melting into the faraway horizon. Waves lapped at the shore in a muted roar.

I'd fixed my destination in my mind before I used the bronze token, same as always, but there was nothing and no one out here, so unless Vespa was some cosmic spirit, I was screwed. I didn't have any way to contact them either as their number was blocked.

In the distance was a plethora of lights in brilliant blues, greens and scarlets, with plumes of fire twirling and dancing like some kind of carnival. Since it was the only sign of life, I trudged towards it, but twenty minutes later, it remained as far off as ever.

"I hate this place." I sat down on the sand and unlaced my boot, dumping sand out of it.

The ground rumbled and rolled, knocking me sideways. I rode out the earthquake, the foundational magic of axle grease and sour vanilla ice cream turning my stomach. The usual stickiness of the air was more pronounced, like suction cups leeching onto my skin.

The final quake sent a wave crashing down that drenched my jeans from the hem up to mid-thigh. Sighing, I laced up my boot.

"Problem?"

I startled, my hand on my heart. "Geez. Yeah. You could say that."

A wizened little man, wearing purple-tinted sunglasses and a top hat sitting askew on his head, reclined in a lime green lounge chair that hadn't been there five minutes ago. He'd paired those accessories with striped pantaloons and a matching vest.

"I need to find Vespa," I said.

The man cackled. "Many try."

"I used one of those bronze tokens but it brought me here instead."

"What are you messing about with those barbarous devil-pawns for?"

"Moran gave them to me. The Queen's swordsman," I explained, in case Moran went by some other name.

"That dried bull's pickle." He spat on the sand. "May the pox take him."

Yeah, well, the pox could take a lot of people because this was going nowhere. I pulled out a token to go home, because my time was better spent finding the angry British dude than listening to vague riddles from the psychedelic

Mad Hatter here, but the man kicked it out of my hand. It sank into the sand and out of sight.

"You daft, girlie?"

I dropped to my knees digging at the spot, but the token was gone. "That was my last one, you batshit little gnome! How am I supposed to leave?"

"Where there's a will, there's a way."

"Spare me the platitudes." I stomped off, but he followed me.

"Those tokens bedevil the being and plague the personage," he said.

Was this guy for real? "You mean they fuck with people?"

"Such a turn of phrase, you have."

"Likewise, but at least I make up for it with my winning personality. I'm well aware that using them comes with a cost. Twice they've dredged up old memories, now I've landed in the middle of nowhere."

"Wherever you are, there you be."

"More sage greeting card wisdom to chart my life by. Where am I?"

"The Lost and Found."

I stopped and he crashed into my back. Regretting the question before I asked it, I said, "Am I lost or found?"

He poked me with a gnarled finger. "You're here to find what you lost. Or lose what you've found. Either way, you're here because of the token, and it likes to—"

"Fuck with people," I finished. "I remember. Can I go to Vespa after this?"

"I imagine so."

I pinched the bridge of my nose. Continue walking on that stupid beach indefinitely or go with this Willy Wonka guide? The tokens demanded payment and if they didn't want a memory, my fastest option was to get this over with. I had enhanced strength, blood armor, the ability to rip away magic, and my very sound instincts. I could handle this.

"Alright, take me into the beast."

He clapped his hands twice and the sand beneath my feet liquified.

I screamed, hurtling downward to land with a thump in a warehouse that was crammed to the rafters with every item you could imagine. Bicycles, umbrellas, stuffed animals, phones, styrofoam mannequin heads, baseballs, fishing rods, all of them dumped in no particular sorting order on metal shelving units that weren't even lined up with each other.

His eyes gleamed in wonder. "Amazing, isn't it?"

"It's something, all right."

A deafening chorus of barks, howls, and mewls rose up.

Wincing, I covered my ears. "Pet section?"

The man nodded as an elephant trumpeted somewhere in the bowels of the warehouse.

I didn't ask about lost children.

Finally, the noise died down enough that I didn't have to yell to be heard.

"How am I supposed to know what to look for?" I said.

"Start as you mean to go on." He hopped onto a counter and began flipping through a copy of *People* magazine that was so ancient the original *Charlie's Angels* actresses graced the cover.

"Thanks for nothing." I picked my way through the shelving units. Maybe I'd lost my mind and had been sent here to retrieve it. I certainly hadn't lost cars or furniture. The items got weirder and weirder the deeper I walked. I hadn't lost any prosthetic limbs or wait, was that a severed penis? Yes, yes it was.

A coffin, a crashed airplane, what I hoped was a dummy corpse in a pink bunny costume, nothing applied. Then things turned surreal with signs floating over empty shelving units: hopes, dreams, youth, virginity. That last one warranted a lookie-loo since the experience had been thoroughly underwhelming and I wouldn't have minded a do-over, but nothing showed up.

I laughed. What did I expect? My untouched hymen?

The lighting dimmed as I pulled up short before a sign reading "loved ones."

My father stood there, hip propped against a shelf and his legs crossed like we'd arranged to meet.

"Little jewel." Dad's chocolate brown eyes twinkled. His dark brown hair shot through with salt-and-pepper was cut short and he wore the brown and cream diamond-patterned cardigan that he'd called his Mr. Rogers sweater.

"Nope. Not buying it. We've done this illusion dance before, false Adam. Begone. I've already lost you and you're not what I'm here to find."

"Never take anything at face value. Come on, Ash, I taught you better."

"How's that relevant?"

He winked. "It's elementary." With that, he melted back into the shadow of shelving units.

Elementary. Basic. Simple and straightforward. Don't take him at face value. Not here to find my literal father. My symbolic father? What did he represent? My lost childhood? No, that would have been filed under lost youth.

Answers to unresolved questions.

A kernel of hope sparked in my chest. Would I finally learn what had happened to him?

I raced through the warehouse, following glimpses of him and the scent of his beloved lemon candies, but after many dead ends and much backtracking, I hadn't caught up to him.

The passage between the shelves grew narrow enough that I had to walk sideways, going as fast as I could and yelling for my father. I burst through a door, only to find myself back on the beach under the stars.

Alone.

Bewildered, I tugged on the door, using all my enhanced strength to wrench on the handle, but it didn't budge.

"Empty-handed, are you?" Talia stood beside me, the picture of cool in an ivory dress and matching heels that didn't sink into the sand.

"There's been a mistake," I said through gritted teeth, still whaling on the door handle, since I only had the mental capacity to deal with one parental head trip at a time.

She considered me for a moment, then shook her head. "No mistake."

"I saw Reasonable Facsimile Dad. He wanted me to find him."

"Did he? Or are you clinging to a childish dream when it's time to grow up?"

My shoulders slumped and with one last half-hearted tug, I let go. "Which childish dream: finding Adam, you and I having a semblance of a relationship, or being a Nefesh P.I.? That covers all the 'find what I've lost' and 'lose what I've found' bases, right?"

Talia adjusted one of her pearl earrings. "I haven't known what was going on in that head of yours since you were thirteen. Why would I be able to answer that question for you now? Honestly, Ashira." She turned and walked away, growing fainter until the breeze blew the last remnant of her image away.

I screamed and kicked the door.

The little man reappeared and held out a white bunny. "Thank you for visiting the Lost and Found. Please enjoy this parting gift."

"Absolutely not."

His face fell. "You sure? They poo everywhere and I get them faster than I can find homes for them. Ridiculous Easter gifts, if you ask me, but they're a lovely memento of your visit."

"You want to give me a memento, get me another bronze token."

"Stay away from those foul barnacles. Magic artifacts never lead anywhere good."

My hand went to the metal pouch. "No, they don't."

The little man brightened and pointed at the water. "You can get to Vespa now."

He made the bunny wave bye at me with its paw. The rabbit twitched its nose, thoroughly unimpressed, and let loose pellets of shit on my boot that I had to shake off.

Fucking Hedon.

A path of ice cut across the waves to the carnival lights that had somehow shifted position. I leaned one foot on it, testing my weight. When the path held, I started walking, a warm breeze blowing my hair about my face.

Hedon or the Queen or whatever had seen into my heart about my father more than once. Now it had added my mother to the mix. Maybe I should be grateful for small mercies. What would this place have done if I'd fed it memories of Priya and given it ammunition about what she meant to me? I shuddered to think.

My phone rang. "Miles. Did you find Nadija?"

"Not yet. Does the smell of lilies and dust mean anything to you? We checked out her motel room and it reeked."

The ice under my foot cracked and I jumped. Had Jesus spent each step peering nervously down at the water wondering when it was going to stop supporting his weight? Because the Bible didn't mention that part. "That's her magic, but you shouldn't be able to smell it. Have you ever smelled magic before?"

"No," he said. "It reminded me of my grandmother's hospital room when she was dying."

Dying magic. A tenuous idea took hold.

"Let me check something out." I got off the phone with

him and called House Pacifica, asking to be put through to Elke, the librarian.

I decided to deal with these reality-to-reality phone calls the same way that the coyote in the Bugs Bunny cartoons dealt with gravity: all would be well and I wouldn't come crashing down under the pull of crippling long distance charges so long as I didn't think about it.

The carnival lights grew closer, along with the faint sound of drums.

"Hi, Elke, this is Ashira Cohen. Remember me?"

"Sure. How can I help you?" she said.

I skidded along a particularly slick patch, one hand out for balance, the other on the pouch for safekeeping, with the phone welded between my chin and shoulder.

"The day I was at the library," I said, "you explained a theory postulating that magic was a disease that had invaded our bodies." It made sense, given my white clusters acted like white blood cells to kill magic.

"That's right."

As I closed in on the shore, small waves splashed over my feet making the already slippery path a death trap. I slowed down because the water on either side looked cold and deep.

"Is there anything that can kill magic?" Other than me.

"Not kill, but there are some rare instances where the body decides to fight off the magic. We don't know why it happens, but the power essentially atrophies. It's incredibly painful for the afflicted person."

"Can they be healed?"

"No. Their magic withers away, leaving them to live in excruciating pain for the rest of their lives. Most choose to end the pain sooner rather than later."

Lilies and dust. The magic inside her was dying. Nadija hadn't kept the feather because she was part of Chariot. It had tempted her with her heart's desire: a magic life free from pain. "What about drugs to help with the pain?"

"The amount of painkillers they'd need would preclude having any kind of normal life and comes with its own problems, like addiction and hitting a threshold where the drugs are no longer effective. It's not something that's talked about much and there hasn't been a lot of research done in the area. There just isn't the awareness to warrant funding."

At long last, I reached the shore and stepped onto the sidewalk near the fire dancers gracing the boardwalk. They twirled magic balls of flame while drummers beat out a hypnotic rhythm. A small knot of people cheered them on.

"Are there drugs that take away magic?" I said.

"Thankfully, research in that field is globally banned. Can you imagine a Pharma company who shares Untainted Party values pushing that? All Nefesh would be at risk. Who'd want to volunteer for those trials, anyway?"

A fire dancer split his ball into four, throwing them high into the air where they hung momentarily, suspended in primary colors.

After thanking her, I called Miles back and told him to call off the search. Nadija wasn't dangerous, she was sick and I was going to help her. It took some persuading, and Miles wasn't pleased that Nadija wouldn't pay for her crimes, however minor, but if no one would corroborate the charges —and I certainly wasn't pressing charges—he couldn't bring her in.

The drums picked up, the fire dancers weaving their flames around their bodies like silk ribbons.

"I hope you know what you're doing," Miles said. "You're handling the artifact, handling this Nadija woman, and if you play this wrong and things go sideways, it'll be Levi's ass on the line."

The drums beat faster and faster, the flames growing larger, their crackling a melodic counterpoint to the percussion, building to one final burst, and then darkness.

I shivered in that split second where all light seemed to

be sucked from the world. "Considering I've saved both your butt and the city, how about you have some faith in me?"

"Nah," Miles said and hung up.

One of the fire dancers pointed me in the direction of Vespa's shop. So far in Hedon, I'd visited the business district, the Queen's home and gardens, the Dream Market, the beach and Lost and Found, and now this boardwalk area. Hedon was much more than a black market. It was its own world.

The blur of lights I'd seen from far away turned out to be the glowing tops of carnival tents, each with a colorful hawker promising rare sights more captivating than the last. Sentient steampunk ponies did tricks, there was a tattooed lady whose animated ink told different stories to each viewer, and something called Pumpkin Joe and His Pokey that had a long line-up.

There were no families or children. This was the playground of the Nefesh underbelly. A man in a gas mask with metal horns bought fresh roasted chestnuts, while a Japanese woman with a thundercloud on a leash tethered around her wrist like a helium balloon slung pints of dark beer to a group of Italian mafioso whose skin gleamed with iridescent poisons that smelled of vinegar.

The road I'd been told to follow got quieter and quieter, the carnival sounds and crowds falling away until it was only me and my footsteps. There were no torches or stars to light my way here and the darkness pressed in on me like a shroud.

I was about to retrace my steps, sure that I'd been misdirected, when a structure in front of me lit up. Light shone through walls bearing a texture similar to coarse homemade paper. Translucent, it was shaped like an acorn laying on its side, with a large round opening set into the thin end.

"You're late." The words were a monotone buzz that emanated from the structure.

No, not structure. Hive.

Vespa. The Italian word for wasp.

Well, if I wasn't stung to death, this would make great dinner party conversation, should I ever like enough people to host one.

Chapter 20

Inside was a labyrinth of dense honeycomb-shaped chambers, all with that translucent glow. Each hexagonal room was a self-contained tiny treasure: one pinky-red, made of petals that smelled like roses, another emerald green with feathery grass stalks higher than my head, yet another a brilliant sky blue where you crossed on fluffy clouds.

My footsteps echoed off a fallen trunk that traversed a miniature forest rich with the scent of pine. Vespa had created a microcosm of nature within this hive.

I headed deeper and deeper inside. "Hello? A little guidance here?"

"Right, right, left," Vespa buzzed. Their voice both boomed through the space and drilled down from the crown of my head to my toes like a precisely wielded jackhammer.

I reached the center, finding myself in a room maybe five feet by six feet wide, all bathed in a golden light. The floor was hardened with a gleaming resin and honey dripped off the walls.

Vespa sat in a threadbare oversized armchair. My first impression was a huddle of multicolored rags more than any being. Their body was that of a human woman, but their face was out of a 1950s B movie—which would have been funny if it wasn't so unnerving. Large aviator sunglasses hid Vespa's eyes, but not the yellow-and-black mandible protruding from underneath. Two antennae twitched in my direction.

A low buzz emanated from them, skittering down my spine, but I stood firm.

"My apologies for being late," I said. "I used a bronze token to come here and it redirected me to the Lost and Found."

Vespa laughed, somewhere between a rusty gate hinge and a gong. "Magic artifacts are not to be trifled with." They ran a hand over their still-human body, the buzz growing agitated and setting my teeth on edge. "I'd know."

"The keeper of the Lost and Found took my last token. I don't have any way of getting back."

"I will return you once our business is concluded."

"Thank you." I appreciated a business owner who understood the value of those little extra touches like free parking, customer reward cards, or returning you to your home reality.

I held out the metal pouch and Vespa took it from me with a cool hand, the Typecaster's touch reminiscent of a dry papery husk. "Careful. It compels people through temptation."

"I am beyond compulsion now." Vespa opened the pouch and the honey-scent of the room was drowned out by that of a hot, gritty sandstorm.

My mouth watered and I stepped as far back as I could.

Even with those sunglasses on, Vespa's stare my way disconcerted me enough that I forced myself to relax and smile. Nothing to see here.

Vespa dumped the feather into their palm, then rose from the chair and burst into dozens of tiny wasps.

I screamed and ran.

"Come back," they buzzed. "I will not harm you. This is how I read magic."

I stopped three rooms over in a pocket desert. The sand rose in a small tornado, nudging me back toward Vespa.

"Don't get your wings in a twist. I'm coming." I skidded across the ground, propelled by the sand funnel.

By the time I returned to the room, the swarm hovered in a tight ball, presumably around the feather, though I no longer sensed that ancient magic. I dared not question my good luck.

"Can you tell me what type of magic it is?"

"Yes. I never fail. Do not disturb me further." All the wasps spoke in unison, a hundred buzzy sounds pricking me.

My skin broke out in chilly goosebumps.

Ten minutes, twenty minutes, half an hour passed. I sat on the floor, half-dozing, watching the play of shifting wasps.

Why was this taking so long? What about the feather's magic was confusing to Typecasters? Was it the added overlay of feeling ancient? Were there too many layers of magic on the feather to untangle them? I snorted. Maybe its magic had been warded and that had screwed everything up. But my magic wasn't screwed up and it had been warded.

Oh! Shit, it was. The connection with Evil Wanker. He'd been annoyed that this wasn't playing out as it should. My Star of David ward must have interfered with whatever magic process would generally connect a newly made Jezebel with the rest of the team.

Vespa was still engrossed in reading the feather's magic, so I pulled up my solitaire app to kill time until my ass was numb and I'd eaten the half roll of butterscotch Lifesavers that I'd found deep in my jacket pocket. This was going nowhere. Better to wrap it up and get back to confront

Nadija. "Could you give me anything you've got on the feather and send me home?"

The swarm rippled but didn't answer me.

"Maybe it's illusion magic of some sort?" I said, shifting on my butt cheeks to get blood back into that area. Bad idea. My vagina had fallen asleep and I winced through the pins and needles feeling that stabbed through my knish. Yiddish had the best slang for ladytown.

"No. It is Nefesh but more so." Vespa's buzz was weak.

"Concentrated. Yeah, that's what the other Typecaster said."

One of the wasps hit the ground, dead.

I dropped my phone.

The swarm moved in an agitated fashion, several wasps bonking into the walls, dazed. "Not concentrated. Pure. Do not disturb again."

"Stop." I waved my hands at the swarm. "It's hurting you."

"I never fail."

"It's not failure. It's me saying I have to leave. I'm the one aborting this, not you. Give me the feather and return me to my office."

Honey with a pungent bitter undertone glopped down from the ceiling, splashing over me and hardening into a conical prison dotted with tiny air holes. How considerate.

I punched it, but my enhanced strength barely cracked the surface. "Let me out!" My voice rose in a shriek as another couple of dead wasps dropped out of the swarm. I placed a hand on the resin, sending my magic inside to try and destroy it, but it wasn't magic. It was just stupidly well-fortified.

Plan B, then. I felt for my phone, but it wasn't in my pocket. That's right, I'd dropped it. I searched on either side of me in the narrow space between my body and the resin, but it wasn't there. My heart sank. The phone was about a foot away on the other side of the resin. Fuck balls. No calling in any cavalry.

"I see the edges," Vespa buzzed. More wasps hit the ground, dead.

"It's killing you! Stop!"

Nothing. Just the sound of wings and sand.

"Let me out, you suicide mission!" If they died, I could be trapped here forever. I bashed my fists against the resin, the panic swirling in my gut packing an extra punch. My legs were trapped too close to my body to kick effectively.

I took every hairline crack as a win. My fists were bruised, the skin split and blood coating my knuckles. Arkady hadn't prepped me for this particular scenario. Remiss mentor. I laughed, fear making me half-hysterical and lost to a haze of pain. The brief rests I took barely energized me enough to keep going. Finally, with a blow that made me whimper and stars appear in my vision, I punched the top off the cone. I fumbled for my phone, but it was just out of reach.

I grabbed the jagged edge of the hole and tore at it, ripping off most of my index fingernail with a shriek. Tears swam in my eyes and my fists were reduced to bloody hunks of meat, but I finally hit a weak spot, and with a crack, the resin split in half and fell away.

I blinked through sticky lashes, spitting a strand of resin-encrusted hair out of my mouth, and grabbed my phone, but my fingers were so pulpy and bloody that I couldn't get either the home button or my password to work.

"Vespa, get me out of here!" My pleas fell on deaf ears.

"Close now."

I covered my head as more of the swarm splatted to the ground. A bunch bounced off me on their descent, but I barely registered them. "You have to stop!"

My phone rang with Priya's number. I vigorously wiped

off one hand and stabbed at accept, catching the call before it went to voicemail. "Pri!"

"Guess again." The woman had a heavy Slavic accent.

"Nadija." I jumped to my feet and stepped free of my resin prison. My voice was steady, but the rest of me shook. "Where's Priya?"

"Keeping me company."

"Ash!" Priya screamed from the other end. There was the sound of flesh striking flesh and Priya whimpered.

A terror purer than any I had ever known pierced my core. "Nadija, this isn't you. You don't hurt people."

"I get what I want."

"The feather? Did it make you believe that it could heal you, let you keep your magic?" My pulse spiked when she gave a strangled roar at my question. Shit, shit, shit, I went too fast. Priya's life was on the line, which was exactly why I couldn't rush, even though all I wanted was to fast-forward to the part where my best friend was safe. "Don't hang up. Nadija, listen, the feather can't help you. But I can."

More wasps fell to the ground. I flinched, covering my head.

"You lie," Nadija said. "You can't fix this."

"You're right. I can't. I wish I could, because I know how important having magic can be. But I can end your pain."

"By killing me," she spat.

I rolled my eyes, even though she couldn't see it. "Lady, I have a long list of people I'd rather go to prison for killing. Get over yourself."

There was a shocked silence on her end. "Then how?"

I could use my blood powers, but the cost to her sanity wasn't worth it.

"There is a drug that would mute your magic and, I believe, your pain. I can't one hundred percent guarantee it would work, but it's worth a shot, isn't it? You have an amazing career that doesn't require powers. You could live a full and pain-free life. You just wouldn't be Nefesh any longer."

"I want my magic. The feather—"

"Is lying." I paced in a tight circle, one eye on the swarm.

Nadija was silent for a long time. "The feather gave me hope," she said, "when I found it on the dig. Then it was stolen and I was furious. He thought he was clever, covering his tracks, but I figured it out and followed him. Why should I work with you when you probably think I tried to kill him?"

"You didn't hurt Omar. That idiot did that to himself. You don't need to convince me that he swallowed the feather to keep it for himself and that you didn't want to cause him any harm. I already figured that part out on my own. You just wanted the feather back."

Nadija's pause lasted seven wasps falling down dead and a million years.

"How do I know that what you say is true?" she said. "That the feather can't help me?"

"Has it? Was your pain any less for possessing the feather? Did your magic return to full strength?"

"It takes time."

"The feather tempts people with their heart's desire. It played you and that's not your fault, but you deserve to be healthy and happy. Magic isn't the determining factor in that." What a hypocrite I was, spouting this bullshit when I refused to give up mine.

No one wants to admit their dreams are childish, something whispered in the back of my head.

"Think of your friends and family," I said. "They want you in their lives, Nadija." I used her name as much as possible to create a bond.

"If I come to you, you will arrest me?"

"I won't. I promise. No one will press charges for trespassing, and I give you my word I won't for the vandalism, either. There's still time for us to fix this, undo it completely. But all that changes if you hurt Priya."

"You don't care about me. This is about your friend."

"No—"

"Enough! I am the one calling the shots now. You want her so badly? Give me the feather."

"It won't help you."

"You say that because you want to keep it for yourself, but you are a liar and a thief and I am Malach, the Angel of Death. Give me the feather or your friend will die and you can live with the same kind of pain that I have."

She was totally unhinged. How was I supposed to reason with her? How could I not? Priya's safety was at stake. I switched the phone from one bloody hand to the other.

"Yes. Priya for the feather. Just like you want. Tell me where and when."

The remaining swarm vibrated like it was doing the wave. What fresh madness was this?

"You have two hours." Nadija's voice left no room for debate. "6:30PM."

"Where?"

"There is a park near your apartment. With a small school."

"McSpadden."

"It's wide open. Nowhere for you to hide or people to ambush me. We will meet in the middle and make our trade, but if I see a single sign that you are trying to trick me or bringing in other people, you will feel my wrath." She hung up.

A curious numbness fell over me and I turned dull eyes to the swarm. "Give me the feather, Vespa, and take me home. I'm begging you."

The swarm buzzed angrily, but I'd had enough. Priya's life was worth more than Vespa's pride in their track record.

I reached for the swarm, ready to plunge my hand in, grab the feather and find another way back, regardless of the consequences, when the swarm reformed back into Vespa's human form.

Sort of.

A chunk of their mandible was gone, they only had one antenna, and their torso was lopsided and kind of melted looking. All those dead wasps represented missing pieces.

"I did not fail." Vespa's buzzing was smug.

"Great. What magic is on the artifact?" I didn't even care anymore. I just wanted out.

"Not an artifact. This is an angel feather." Vespa's form rippled, their voice more a squeak than a buzz.

That brought me up short. "Impossible. It's Nefesh magic. It has the same signature."

"Nefesh magic is angel magic. We are the dilution."

A whistling noise filled my ears as I sank to my knees. My thoughts tumbled over themselves in light of this revelation, but the only thing I got out was, "I need the feather and then I'd like to go home."

Vespa sealed the feather in the metal pouch and handed it to me. Then their body stuttered like a projection out of frame and a low groan punched out of them.

"Vespa?"

They jerked violently, gasped, and with one last feeble buzz, toppled over.

Alarms wailed.

I knelt there holding an angel's feather with mangled hands, deafened by the sirens and stranded in a hostile world. Not because of my lack of a token, but because some invisible force had pinned me in place.

The Queen appeared in the doorway, dressed in head-to-toe red leather.

Moran stood behind her, sword in hand. He crossed to

Vespa's body, crouched down and checked for a pulse, then shook his head. He closed Vespa's eyes.

The Queen sighed. "Oh, blanquita."

"I didn't kill Vespa."

"The alarms dictate otherwise," Moran said. "The Black Heart Rule is woven into the fabric of Hedon itself."

"Vespa was under the Queen's protection?" I said, sluggishly.

The Queen stepped forward, her authority demanding such absolute obeyance that merely breathing in her presence was acquiescence.

"Ashira Cohen," she said, "you have broken the Black Heart Rule. By my power as Queen and ruler of Hedon, I hereby sentence you to eternal entombment."

I struggled to free myself and move. "No, please. You don't understand. Priya—"

"Enough, child." Her violet eyes filled with sorrow, but she shook it off and turned to Moran. "Take her."

Chapter 21

I broke into my spiky full-body blood armor before Moran could grab me. "Touch me and I'll finish what I started. I'm already damned. One more assault on my rap sheet won't matter."

"The sword won't penetrate her armor," Moran said matter-of-factly.

The Queen waved her hand and the alarms cut out with a chilling suddenness. "You can't escape your fate, Ashira."

The hold on me loosened and I stood up. "I brought Vespa the feather to determine what type of magic was on it. Vespa burst into this swarm and spent hours figuring it out. Then parts starting dropping off, dead." I pointed to the wasps on the floor. "I begged Vespa to stop, but their pride was at stake. They claimed that they never failed."

"Intentional or not," Moran said, "you gave Vespa the artifact that caused this."

"Because I was working a case for you! Does that make you and the Queen culpable? How about Omar, who is also under the Queen's protection? Does Vespa's protection trump his? And Omar's the one who stole the feather in the first place. How far back do we want to take this blame game?"

"¡Cállense!"

Moran and I fell silent.

The Queen crouched down and ran a hand over Vespa's wasp head. "Vaya con Dios, mi amiga."

"Let my people prepare Vespa for a proper burial, Highness," Moran said.

She remained with her friend for a moment longer before straightening, and allowing Moran to take her arm.

We switched locations: to a dank and gloomy dungeon. Called it.

Its thick stone walls held one tiny window open to the night and barricaded by thick bars. The door was heavy wood with a large brass lock. Moran and the Queen stood on the other side of it, visible through an open slot.

My predicament hit with staggering force. I was going to languish here until my blood armor ran out, at which point, I'd be turned to stone and Priya would die. I forced a breath into my lungs. "Your Highness—"

"Did Vespa succeed?" The Queen's voice held only the mildest curiosity, but her eyes sparkled and gleamed.

I'd wondered before what kind of chaos the Queen was interested in and now I had a partial answer: powerful artifacts fell squarely in that purview.

"Yes. But Vespa took that secret to the grave." The best lies contained a grain of truth. I'd never dared to be anything other than honest with the Queen before but I was already on the executioner's block and if I didn't get out of this ASAP, I'd condemn Priya to the same fate.

A rat ran over my foot. I flinched and kicked it against the wall. It slid to the ground, shook itself off, and disappeared into one of the shadowy corners.

"Give me the feather," she said. "And we can discuss your predicament."

"Discuss" left an awful lot of wiggle room and a shit-ton of scenarios that ended badly. I was playing to win, playing to *live*, so what did I have in my hand? I had the feather, but that alone wouldn't do it.

Alone. That was it. I was not without resources, after all.

I slapped the metal pouch against my armor and it vanished under the shield. "Bring Levi here. Nadija kidnapped my best friend. The trade is Priya's life for the feather. If you aren't going to release me, Levi has to Houdini himself to look like me and do the trade. You want the feather after that, have at it."

"You're hardly in a position to negotiate," Moran said.

"Priya now works for House Pacifica. Check if you don't believe me."

The Queen pursed her lips, smart enough to pick up on what I'd implied. Priya wasn't Nefesh, but Levi's sense of responsibility was legendary. I was already covered. If Priya died and I was missing, Levi would utilize every resource at his disposal to uncover the truth. Up to and including marching into the very heart of Hedon and turning it upside down.

"Were this a chess game, you'd have put me into check. Whether you contact him or not, Mr. Montefiore's involvement is an unwelcome complication," the Queen said.

"Is it?" I widened my eyes comically. "That didn't even occur to me. How about this, don't add me to your charming garden, let me do the trade, and we'll call it a day."

"The Black Heart Rule was triggered," Moran said. "The people will expect an unveiling."

"You can't seriously call it that. Do you serve tea and sandwiches, too?"

He bared his teeth. "I'm partial to the little cucumber ones."

My stomach growled. That sounded pretty good about now. The pain in my hands was achy and stabby and the dried blood itched, while the resin in my hair was giving my scalp a rash. It all paled in comparison to my fear for Priya.

The armor covering my feet flickered. I fought to hold onto my powers but I'd tipped too far into exhaustion and they were rapidly slipping away.

"Leave us," the Queen said.

Moran hesitated.

"If I could get out of here, I'd be long gone," I said. "Since I'm no threat to Her Majesty from inside my guest suite, could you arrange for turndown service while you're gone? A bed with bedding to turn down in the first place? No?"

He gave me a sour look. "I'll return shortly."

The Queen sat down on a bench outside the door, one leg crossed over the other. "You are becoming less interesting, blanquita, and more of a pain in my ass."

I dropped my armor and rested my head against the dungeon door. "I'm tired, Your Highness. I just want to live and keep Priya alive. I don't want to play games with you because I don't consider myself smart enough to outwit you, and I certainly don't want to make an enemy of you. If I've played check, then you sent Moran away because you're about to put me into checkmate. But you've always been fair, and I implore you to remember that the responsibility for Vespa's death doesn't stop with me. It's tangled up in this entire case."

"It's true. This is a unique situation." She tapped a finger against her red lips. "Perhaps we need to change it."

"To what?"

"A business proposition. What I'm about to tell you does not leave this cell." I nodded. "What was your first impression of Hedon's magic?"

How to delicately phrase that it was an abomination that made me want to vomit? "It had quite a strong flavor."

The Queen chuckled, but there was no warmth in it. "That's one way of putting it. Hedon is broken."

"That's why the magic smelled sour. Is that what's causing the earthquakes?"

"Sí. Most people aren't sensitive to the odor. Only you, me, and the Nefesh with Architect magic who built it before my time as ruler. Hedon is more than a black market, it's my home. The people who live and work here are my people. I must save it before it unravels."

"You're as bad as Levi."

She grimaced. "Never say so. But there is a problem. There is only one original Architect still alive and only he can put Hedon to rights."

"He doesn't want to?"

"No. He swore off magic twenty years ago when a design of his went awry and collapsed, killing his wife. Abraham Dershowitz."

I whistled. "Wow. You weren't moved to host the wedding because of Shannon and Omar's beautiful love? Frankly, that mercenary attitude from the Queen of Hearts saddens me."

"I hate to disillusion a pure romantic such as yourself."

"Abraham is what, Shannon's grandfather?"

"Correct. There's no one he loves more."

"You hold the wedding here, Abraham comes, and you make him fix Hedon. What do you want from me?"

"Abraham is a wily old man." She sounded full of admiration. "He's refusing to attend. You are going to convince him otherwise."

I dropped my shoulders, then hitched them back up again. She couldn't mean for me to take his powers if she required them to fix Hedon. "You want me to threaten his magic. Done."

"If he doesn't attend and agree to save my home, then you will take Shannon's magic. If he tries anything funny, you take her magic. If at any point in the future, anything happens to Hedon, you take her magic."

My throat went dry. Shannon was flighty and strange, not to mention she'd fallen for a complete doofus, but she didn't deserve that. "It'll break her. Her life is her art. She can't do that without magic. You want me to nix all that as insurance that this guy does what you want? She's innocent in all this."

"She's expendable." The Queen's expression iced over. "Is Priya? You want checkmate, blanquita? Levi or any House Head can only go after me if I leave Hedon. Should I wish it, I can destroy all entrances and seal us off permanently for whatever time we have left. It's your choice."

Some choice. Horrible or unimaginable. "How can you be sure Hedon won't break down again even if Abraham fixes it? What if it's beyond repair?"

"It's not. I am attuned to its magic." Apparently, but how? Now was not the time to ask. "Abraham can make it so that Hedon is stable and incapable of further expansion. Once he's completed his task, you will take away his powers seeing as he doesn't use them anyway."

"Tying up loose ends."

"Protecting what is mine," she said, placing her hand on her heart.

I kicked the door. "Was using me always your endgame? If this hadn't happened with Vespa, would I have ended up in your debt another way?"

She spread her hands wide.

I wove my anger around me as tightly as any armor. Sizzling hot armor underlaid with tempered steel. Right from the start, I'd suspected I was being played, but I was shocked into a headache at how badly I wished I'd been hired for different reasons.

This case wasn't a stepping stone on the path to fulfilling my dreams, handed to me because she'd recognized my abilities. It was a con. Was my future as a Nefesh detective going to be any different from that as a Mundane, or was I throwing away my relationship with Talia and forcing Levi into a difficult position for nothing more than pride and delusion?

For a dream only I believed.

And maybe that's what seeing my parents in the Lost and Found had meant. Dreams tempted and compelled far worse than any magic artifact, and yet we chased them anyway. There was nothing so powerful or dangerous as our heart.

I stood tall. "Well played, Your Majesty. Unfortunately, your citizens will be disappointed with the lack of a new unveiling, because I'll not die for Vespa's refusal to value their life over their pride. My freedom in exchange for Hedon's survival. And those vials are mine as soon as Abraham agrees, regardless of whether Nadija has been apprehended yet or not."

"Agreed. Hold up your end of the deal and you will not be part of the unveiling." There was still going to be one? Did she have spare bad guys on hand? Nope. Not asking.

The Queen stood up and the door between us swung open. "I am not your enemy, Ashira."

"Beg to differ." I swept a low mocking curtsy.

"Moran will text you Abraham's address in Vancouver. Be there 9AM Sunday. The wedding starts at eleven and I don't want to give him time to change his mind." With that, she waved her hand and I found myself in Moriarty, back in the driver's seat.

This time, I wasn't leaving it.

Sherlock Holmes once said that "the chief proof of man's real greatness lies in his perception of his own smallness."

My smallness had been driven home. Now to be great.

Chapter 22

McSpadden Park took up most of a city block. Houses bordered two sides of the green space, while a playground and elementary school anchored the top of a gently sloping hill. There was also a small community garden comprised of boxes of dirt in various stages of preparation for spring planting.

On this drizzling late March at dinner time, my only company was a man in a fleece jacket and toque throwing a ball for his dog at one end of the grassy expanse. I sat down on a bench in the middle of the park's lawn next to a sidewalk that curved through the space. Lampposts cast eerie cool circles of light, but the thin sliver of moon softened the many shadows in the park.

Foot jiggling, my eyes darted in every direction, but 6:30PM came and went with no sign of Nadija or Priya. They descended jerkily from the sky a few minutes later, Nadija in full Malach regalia but minus the mask.

"Oh, the Angel of Death is a person in my neighborhood," I sang. I had to be glib or else I wouldn't be able to hold my voice steady at seeing Priya so scared.

Nadija released Priya, but there was no visible weapon or

indication that she trained a hidden gun on my friend. After assuring myself that Priya looked frightened but unharmed, I studied Nadija's face for the first time.

It was easy to see why I'd mistaken her for a man. Not only was she taller than most women, but she had broader shoulders and a strong jawline. She'd be a handsome woman were it not for the constant grind of her teeth, the grooves worn into the tight corners of her eyes, and the slight twist to her torso like standing upright was beyond her capabilities. Her dark blonde hair had probably once been lustrous, but was now piled in a lank messy bun on her head.

I'd experienced that all-consuming, bone-deep level of pain after my accident, even years later when I'd pushed myself too hard. You were in flight or fight mode all the way, and as much as you wanted to stop running, you just couldn't escape it.

"Show me the feather," Nadija said.

The man with the dog was too far away to be affected.

"Let Priya sit on that bench so it doesn't compel her." I gestured to another bench about twenty feet away.

"If this is a trick…"

I held up the pouch. "It's not. I'm the only one who can be close to it without being compelled. You want to risk her stealing the feather like Omar did? Because I, for one, don't want to fish this sucker out of another person's throat."

Nadija thrust Priya away from her. "Go."

Face pinched tight, Priya hurried to the bench.

"Open the pouch." Nadija was breathing heavily, bent over with her hands braced on her thighs.

"Need a moment to catch your breath?" I said to Nadija. "Priya's heavy, huh?"

"I heard that," Priya called. She twisted her fingers tightly, but the fact she sounded mock-annoyed gave me hope for her being okay.

"Open it," Nadija growled.

It took me a couple tries with my still swollen and disfigured hands.

"What happened to you?" she said.

"Doesn't matter." I pulled the feather out and placed it in her hand, needing a second to relinquish my hold. I stepped back. "Satisfied?"

She clutched the feather to her chest like a newborn baby, murmuring to it.

"L'chaim." I held up an imaginary glass. "May you two be very happy together."

Moran appeared, sword in hand, wearing a stupid tin foil hat and lead apron to protect himself against the compulsion. So much for Freddo's family secret.

"It's not a party until the man with the large sword arrives, half-cocked and primed for action." I manifested my spiky blood armor.

"Fully cocked, if you please," he said. "You were the one who told the Queen to 'have at it' once the trade was enacted."

Nadija spun on us with wild eyes, hovering a foot off the ground with madly beating wings. "I am Malach, the Angel of Death. Touch this feather at your peril!"

"Those idiots bought this getup?" Moran shook his head.

"To be fair," I said, "she had a mask when she attacked Omar. It really tied the look together."

Moran swore—I'd swear in Russian—and broke into a run after Nadija, who'd flown off with the feather. Except she was zigzagging like a drunk chicken and couldn't seem to get more than five feet off the ground.

That's what you got for making a grand entrance. No juice left for the getaway.

I sprinted after them.

Priya jumped off the bench and out of compulsion range in the nick of time before we blew past her.

Moran overtook Nadija, nabbed her by the robe, and

slammed her down on the sidewalk. The feather floated up into the air, but before Moran's hand closed on it, I launched myself, spiky armor in place, and grabbed it first.

"Touchdown!" Priya yelled and shook imaginary pompoms.

I yanked off Moran's hat and flung it as far as I could. He didn't glaze over, as he was out of compulsion range, but he did brandish his sword, which was scary enough.

I rapped on my armor. "Can't touch this." Humming the MC Hammer song, I moonwalked—badly—away from Moran, who spun and sprinted to retrieve his hat.

The dog barked and ran for the shiny new toy while the man yelled at us that tin foil wasn't healthy for dogs.

Priya waved at him. "Sorry!"

I'd held myself in check as long as I could, but the feather magic swamped me and my mouth watered. The urge to taste it hooked into me with a dozen sharp spikes, flaying me raw with need, my lungs locked into breathlessness.

I made the armor vanish in order to ride the magic and destroy it once and for all. I ran the feather against my lips. Maybe there was a way for it to exist safely and—

"Ash!" Priya danced nervously away from Nadija, who was getting to her feet.

I shot my magic into the feather and fell into that cosmic sandstorm, swaying at the orgasmic high that punched through me. Zero to blast off in seconds flat.

Nadija recovered enough to knock me to the ground, assuring the feather that she'd protect it while she wrestled me for possession. I was too hooked into the magic to fight back. The best I could do was curl over top of it, Nadija's punches a distant irritant, and my spirit hovering above the chaos in serene bliss.

The world turned Technicolor sharp and clear, every

image broken into tiny distinct dots like reality was a Seurat painting. I tasted sand at the back of my throat.

Hat firmly back on his head, Moran cold-cocked Nadija with the flat side of his sword.

"Tiiiimber," Pri yelled.

Nadija's weight fell off me, replaced by the tip of the sword pressed into my side.

"The Queen requests the feather."

Nothing was getting between me and this magic.

I grabbed Moran's blade and yanked as hard as I could on it. Copper blended with the scent of hot sand and warm liquid dribbled down my arm, but I didn't feel it. I didn't feel anything besides the eternal wind over dunes and a deep clarity.

Moran didn't lose his grip, but he stumbled, grabbing the tin foil hat to remain safe. "Of all the stubborn…" He vanished for a second, and Priya shrieked, Moran now holding her around the waist, the blade against her throat. "In the name of the Queen, give me the feather."

My insides were glitter, the world a dreamy haze, and the mysteries of the universe mine to unravel.

"Ash," Priya squeaked.

Her anguish penetrated my euphoria. Slightly. "The feather. Yes."

I pried my fingers off it, but in the seconds it took Moran to release her and move close enough to take the feather, I pulled the magic out of it in a black smudge. Red forked branches pinned it and the white clusters bloomed.

Still caught in the grip of the high, I laughed hysterically.

Nadija, demonstrating an exceptional determination and impressive recovery time, screamed in rage and ran at me and then it was pandemonium as Miles' people poured out of a van.

The feather in my hand had gone from white, fluffy, and full of magic, to grey, limp, and impotent.

"All gone," I said to Moran. Seeing was believing, after all.

"Welcome to the gameboard." Moran inclined his head at me and disappeared before the security team reached him.

Priya gasped, rubbing her throat. "Is it over?"

A woman in a House Pacifica uniform wearing the same tin foil hat and lead apron, yanked the feather out of my grip and secured it in the metal pouch.

I grabbed her by the throat and fired my magic inside her, but was ripped forcefully away before I could hook into her powers. I pressed back against Levi's fleece jacket. "Hello, sailor." I inhaled deeply. "Mmmmm. I like your magic."

Levi let loose with a string of Italian curses. "Ash, you need to get this out of your system. Come on, bella, fight it."

I laughed at the silly boy as reality fractured into atoms and I sailed through the heart of the universe.

"Do something," Priya said, her voice tight with anxiety.

I tried to assure her that I was fine, but then a dog licked my cheek and the roughness of his tongue sent me spinning sideways through a black hole, and I left the world behind.

I WOKE up on my sofa. Moonlight streamed in through the open slit in the curtains and the house smelled like cookies, which was a weird brain glitch because my mouth tasted like sand and my cheeks were stained with tears.

Priya was curled up in a chair in a pair of pink pajamas, asleep, and even Levi had dozed off on the other side of the couch, wearing the same toque as he had in the park.

My brain processed that my feet were in his lap, but not

much more than that because I was dizzy and pain flared in my left side with each breath. "What happened?"

It came out "wharmmgigggappgged," along with a lot of drool from my overly thick lips.

Levi's eyes snapped open. "Welcome back. Don't try to talk. We gave you a powerful tranquilizer to combat the withdrawal effects of the magic."

My pulse spiked and my blood turned to ice. I'd been out for who knew how long and Evil Wanker did not exactly sound like the charitable type when it came to deadlines. Jolting upright, I grabbed the top of the couch as the world swung sideways and I fell. My hands were fat mittens under layers of gauze.

Levi caught me by the shoulders and set me upright. "Try not to damage yourself more than you already have. I had to pay the House medic overtime to fix you up."

Adrenaline cleared enough of the slur from my speech to be understood. Levi could have cost me everything. "You put me under like a dog and your big concern is going over budget? Take it out of what you'll owe me for the vials."

"So much for not talking," Levi said.

"He didn't mean it like that about paying the medic," Priya said.

"He meant it exactly like that. The only people Levi actually cares about are born Nefesh. Might as well get used to it as a Mundane working for him now."

"Priya is deserving of all my respect and care," he said.

The implication stung. So I hadn't gotten there as quickly as I wanted to. So I'd hurt my best friend by getting her wrapped up in this. I got it, okay? "You aren't authorized to make that kind of decision. Or was the thrill of breaking my will such a lure that little things like consent flew out the window?"

"Breaking your will?" Levi slapped his leg. "Oh, if only I

had that superpower." He stood up. "Fun as this has been—"

"Stay. Please." Priya put out a hand to stop him. "Lack of control makes her crazy. She's sorry." She kicked me. "Apologize."

I crossed my arms.

Priya crossed her arms right back and added a chin lift. "*I* made the call, okay? Not Levi. Your eyes had rolled back to the whites and you spasmed so violently that you fractured a rib."

I breathed out deeply through a knot of pain, and sure enough, under the loose pajamas that I'd been put in, my ribcage strained against a bandage that was wrapped around it. I rubbed my mitten-hand against my scalp, trying to soothe the itch from the dried crystals and wondering when I'd be able to shower.

"Anytime we talked to you, you either replied in gibberish or laughed like a deranged hyena, so yeah, I gave the go-ahead to knock you out." Priya clutched a pillow, her fingers making grooves in the fabric.

I gnawed on my bottom lip, weighing my right to feel violated against what I'd have done in that situation. Then a bit more of my brain fog lifted and I remembered I was a terrible friend because she'd been kidnapped thanks to me and I hadn't even checked in on her. "Did Nadija hurt you?"

"It wasn't pleasant, but I'm fine." Her cheerfulness had a back-off bite, her smile was brittle, and she'd bitten her thumbnails ragged. She hadn't been this low since her engagement had blown up but push her too fast and she'd shut me out. I'd learned that the hard way.

Guilt clogged my throat, turning my voice harsh. "How long was I out?"

"Ash!" Priya glared.

"I'm sorry for thinking the worst of you," I said stiffly to Levi. "Though it's not like you don't have a track record of that very behavior where I'm concerned. I can provide an itemized list starting with our first meeting, if you need help with your recall."

"Straight from the heart." He laughed bitterly, but he did sit back down.

"Pri, can you get me my phone?" Step one in getting Priya to talk honestly about her condition: lower her guard by playing helpless. Not entirely an act right now.

Priya picked my jacket off the ground and reached inside a pocket, coming out with the photo of us with the X over my face. Her lips flattened out into a thin line and she tossed it onto the coffee table.

Levi glanced at it with no discernible expression.

Pri found my cell and unlocked it. "Tell me what you need."

I had to find Evil Wanker, but there was still my outstanding debt to the Queen in order to get possession of the vials, and I was too groggy from the tranquilizer to think my way coherently through a search. I allowed myself a bit more time to clear the drug from my system. "Missed calls or texts."

"There's one from an unknown sender. An address with a crown and red heart emoji."

Abraham's. "Get me whatever you can dig up on Abraham Dershowitz and the accident that took his wife's life," I said. Step two: get her focused on other tasks, then sidle in sideways to the topic. "Why was the wife there when his design collapsed? Had they been fighting? Was she suicidal? Did she suffer from dementia? Fast as you can pull anything together, please."

"No problem." Priya nudged my leg with a pointed look between me and Levi.

Gnawing the inside of my cheek, I curled into the far corner of the sofa. My concerns regarding being knocked out were justified, but perhaps voiced poorly. I probably owed Levi another apology. "How long was I out?" I repeated.

"Ten hours," Priya said. "Levi and I stayed with you the entire time."

"I wanted to return to the office, but every time I tried to disentangle myself until the tranq kicked in, you shrieked like a banshee and sniffed me," Levi said.

I groaned and buried my face in my hands. The gauze scratched my face.

"Trust me, it was no picnic for me either," he said. "I had to bake to get over the horror."

"He made biscotti, which should be cool soon," Priya said.

"What flavor?" I lifted my head, the conversation finally taking a turn for the better.

"They're for Priya and me," Levi said.

"It was very nice of him to help me get you home and stay while I kept an eye on you in case anything went wrong." Priya's smile this time was genuine. That was good, even if Levi wasn't the same recipient of her guardedness as I was.

"In case it went more wrong," Levi said. "This is Ash we're talking about, after all."

"What do you have to say to him?" Priya's loaded stare was my cue to thank Levi, but I couldn't force those words past the barbs of guilt, anger, and shame clogging my throat. I was totally being a bitch, but I was incapable of acting otherwise.

"Where's the feather?" I said.

"You can't have it," Priya snapped.

"Is it secured in the pouch?" I clarified.

"Yes," Levi said. "Miles took it."

Priya relaxed. "You don't want the magic anymore?"

Levi must have filled Priya in on the fact that the magic on the feather was intact. Our ploy to make it seem like I'd destroyed it had worked—at least where Moran was concerned.

"No," I said, lying.

Levi didn't even pretend to look like he swallowed that whopper. Perversely, his open antagonism fueled me. *What's your most satisfying relationship?* Ugh.

Of course I wanted the magic, but the last part of trying to take it had been terrifying. I'd gone into a black hole and become empty. It was worse than I imagined death to be, because there was no end. The opposite, in fact. There was a void that hollowed me out one molecule at a time. My dissolution would take eternity. The scary part, however, was that I'd felt so good I didn't care.

Best I could through the stupid gauze gloves, I curled my fingers into my sides to assure myself that all of me was actually present. The reassurance combined with the tranquilizer's healing time had muted the siren song in my head to a two out of ten. Not gone, just not all-consuming. For now.

Priya stood up. "I'm making tea. Want some?"

Levi shook his head. "Bring the biscotti."

"Sure." I caught her hand as best I could. "Pri, maybe you should move out on your own." The offer, while genuine, made me die a little inside, but it was a way to check on her without directly alluding to her feelings. "It's my fault that Nadija came after you."

She yanked her hand away to plant it on her hip. "Are you gonna quit talking to me as well? Because that's the only way that anyone with half a brain wouldn't think I'm the most important person in your life."

"She has a point," Levi said.

"Shut up. I want you to be okay."

"Says the woman who looks like she went three rounds with a meat tenderizer. I'll be fine." Priya beamed at Levi. "Levi is going to hook me up with a counselor he knows."

"It's just House medical benefits," he said gruffly.

"Which technically, I wouldn't qualify for yet." She patted him on the arm and left.

She'd agreed to seek immediate help. That was huge. I didn't begrudge that the offer had come from Levi. Quite the opposite.

Levi stood up to stretch out his shoulder and caught me staring. "I take it back. Insult me, but don't look at me that way. It's unnerving."

"It's gratitude," I said. The tranq must have destroyed my generally infallible touchy-feely blocker, because the more I dwelled on how he'd helped both Priya and me, the more the warmth in my chest blossomed. "That's a thing. There are cards for it and everything."

"Expensive wastes of trees," he said. "Now, gratitude blow jobs, on the other hand."

"That sounds obligatory."

He stroked his chin. "Obligation blow jobs. Is that a thing? Can we make that a thing?"

I snapped my teeth at him. "You bet, baby."

Levi pulled off his toque, rubbing a hand over his flat hair, spiking it up. His movements were missing their usual elegance, his blinks slow. How many of those ten hours had he been awake for? He'd stress-baked. In my house, missing meetings, just to keep me safe. Once again, Levi had shown up for me and then stayed up to make sure I was okay.

I put on my big girl pants. "I'm sorry. Truly. I know you take care of people. Even me. You're a good man, Watson."

He scowled. "Moriarty."

"Still delusional about that, are you?"

"Rude. Who masterminded that illusion that you'd destroyed the magic on the feather to fool Nadija and the Queen's henchman?" He straightened the print on the wall of the red phone booth in London.

"You. In the name of good. See how you're missing a key

concept? Now you get another apology that I couldn't actually nuke it."

He shrugged, pulling an old psych textbook off the shelf and flipping through it. "Losing yourself to the magic was a possibility. That's why you called me with Plan B. Oh, and good call on the henchman showing up."

"Well, I'd kind of invited him. But you don't get it. Yes, I was caught up in the magic, but the second I hooked into it I knew I couldn't destroy it. The magic on that feather defied mine."

"How? That's what your power does. What the hell is on that feather?"

I bit my lip.

Levi gave me a tight smile. "Gonna play the P.I. confidentiality card? You called for help and I answered, no questions asked, but it would be nice if you had a little faith in me."

"It's angel magic," I blurted out.

His mouth fell open and I laughed, as much from the lightness in my chest in sharing this secret with him as from the look on his face.

"We're the only living people who know that." If that wasn't faith, then I didn't know what was.

"Ma vaffanculo!" He shoved the book back into place so hard that the one next to it popped out and fell to the floor.

"Pace yourself, Leviticus. We're not at the bottom of the rabbit hole yet. Magic has a signature, right? On an artifact, it should feel like a weaker version of Nefesh magic, and the feather's signature was definitely Nefesh, but more so. The Typecaster who determined it was angel magic also determined that Nefesh magic stems from angel magic. We're the dilution."

Levi was quiet for a long time. "How are we the only living people with this information if there was a Typecaster involved?"

"That's what you want to lead with?"

He sat down on the chair that Priya had vacated, directly across from me, and leaned forward. "If someone decides to profit from this info—"

"Impossible. The Typecaster is dead."

Levi narrowed his eyes. "How?"

"Reading the magic off the feather."

He went "head-exploding red" and I wondered what color House HQ was right now. If they were tied together like a mood ring, that is.

"If this is where you yell at me for trying to destroy the feather when it already had a body count, save your breath," I said. "Remember my power exists to destroy other magic. I considered all the risks. My death wasn't one of them. Though, to be fair, I didn't expect its magic to trump mine."

He rubbed his temples. "Where's the body?"

"The Queen took care of it. The Typecaster was a close personal friend of hers."

"You called the Queen to help instead of me?" His voice dropped to a dangerously low growl.

"It happened in Hedon."

"Lie. You'd be stone if that was the case."

I frowned. "How does everyone know about that?"

"You went into Hedon multiple times and didn't?" The growl became more of a strangled roar.

"Shoot." I snapped my fingers. "I was so busy enjoying the parades they threw for me every time that I forgot to read the helpful brochure in my welcome package with all the rules and dire consequences laid out. I'm not lying. The Queen and I came to an agreement."

"What agreement?"

Oh, one where I either take an innocent woman's magic or an old man's. No biggie.

"And here's tea." Priya sailed into the room with a tray holding a pot, two mugs, milk, honey, and a plate of golden brown biscotti covered in sliced almonds. "I made Earl Grey but I see I should have made 'Chill the Fuck Out.'"

"Ah yes, a fruity blend with notes of muted aggression and chamomile," I said.

Priya set the tray down on the coffee table, just shy of a slam.

"You're right. Let's change the subject." I reached for a biscotti, then stopped, stymied by my stupid mitten-hands.

Levi laughed.

"Could someone please get these off me?"

Priya took my hands and carefully worked the gauze off. My knuckles were still badly bruised, but the swelling had gone down and they were no longer hideously misshapen.

I squeezed her hands, barely wincing. "I'm here for you."

She squeezed mine back gently. "I know. Let me work through this."

It was as good as I'd get. I leaned over to snag a biscotti, but Levi stole it away from me and handed it to Priya.

"Could you be more immature?" I said.

"My biscotti. My rules."

Priya, the traitor, munched away, her eyes half-slitted in bliss.

"You realize that constitutes taking sides," I said. "I'm never sharing your mom's pity food again."

"I'm open to counter-persuasions," she said, spraying crumbs. "Like dinner." She patted her stomach. "We missed it and I'm starving. Levi, you hungry?"

"Wait a minute," I said. "If I'm bribing you to like me, why do I have to feed him as well?"

"I'm making it a condition."

"I'm not hungry, but I appreciate the offer, Priya." Levi took a biscotti and sat back in the chair with a smile. "Smart and kind. What a wonderful way to go through life."

"Almost as good as my delightful brand of misanthropy."

I poured myself tea, splashing some onto the tray. "Did Miles check in about Nadija? Did he give her the Blank?"

I'd left the vial at Levi's house and when I called to arrange the plan for him to be at the park for the hand-off, I'd instructed him to give it to Miles and why.

"He administered it and it seems to work for both the compulsion and the pain."

"It was confirmed that she had that disease?" I stirred milk and honey into my mug and then pointedly took another biscotti.

"It was. I'd never even heard of that condition before." He shook his head. "Hell of a thing."

Between her medical disorder and the compulsion, Nadija had been dealt a shitty hand. I'd forgiven her for trashing my office, because I understood all too well how far a person could go to relieve their pain, but she'd brought Priya into it. I'd never forgive her for that. This wasn't about petty revenge though. Other than murder and rape, kidnapping was one of the most serious charges under the Canadian Criminal Code and I wouldn't stand in the way of justice on that front.

"Her illness may mitigate her sentencing down the road," he said, "but she's been charged with kidnapping and unlawful confinement."

Priya's spoon clattered against her mug. "I'm okay," she assured us. "Just thinking about having to testify."

"I'll do everything to make it as painless as possible," Levi said. "But yes. We'll need your testimony and Ash's, as well."

"I figured. You'll need to speak to the Asian chemist from the Star Lounge and get more Blank. Nadija's pain is a lifelong condition. Even in prison, she needs to manage it."

"Already on it. We'd like him to deal exclusively with us."

"Get the magic-suppressing drug off the streets before

anyone realizes that Blank has that side effect on Nefesh," I said.

"That and it would be a useful tool in our arsenal."

"Made him an offer he couldn't refuse?"

Levi smiled enigmatically.

I sipped my tea. "There are a couple more loose ends to tie up, and then the Curious Incident of the Angel of Death will be a wrap."

"Where'd you get the dog?" Priya said. "He was a cutie."

"Jasper belongs to a friend of mine," Levi said.

The same friend he'd spent the night with when Omar was attacked? Not my business. "Thank him or her. He was a useful prop."

"I will."

While I'd still rather gouge my eye out with a rusty spoon than meet Levi's alibi woman, it would have been nice to have a Googleable name. Then again, curiosity killed the cat, and jealousy around Levi was an uncomfortable emotion. Best to let it lie.

I yawned, my mug listing perilously. "Order food and put it on my card. I want a shower." A nap would have rocked, but I had too much to do.

"I'm off, too." Levi grabbed a biscotti for the road and stood up. "Oh, one more thing. Gracie Green. Born in Miami, which is where she lived until she came to Vancouver. Never married, no father listed on her birth certificate. One interesting fact, though. Senior year of her college degree, she suddenly withdrew for medical reasons, but there are no records of anything wrong with her."

"Unless a sudden magic awakening was what was wrong." I gathered up the tea things and carried the tray into the kitchen, raising my voice to be heard. "If some Jezebel died and it activated Gracie."

"True," Levi said. "Like Gavriella, Gracie was a Rogue."

"Was she though?" Priya said. "She was born Mundane."

"She didn't register in either Florida or here in Vancouver when she did have magic," Levi said.

I joined them at the front door. The grogginess had dissipated enough to get back to work.

"There's nothing in place for someone whose magic switches on and who wants to comply," Priya countered. "She wouldn't have been believed and, therefore, she'd have been arrested for being Rogue her entire life, which she wasn't. It's not like Ash, who has medical records from her accident at a verified point where she was Mundane. What would you have these Jezebels do? There's so much fear and suspicion of Nefesh already. Why would anyone with this magic ability ever come forward? Especially if it's only women who have it? It literally would be a witch hunt."

"Tell that to your hardheaded roommate." Levi knelt down to put on his shoes. "She's insisting on getting registered. Even if it's just her low level enhanced strength, she's kicking a wasp's nest. I'm not one to support unregistered Nefesh but this is going to be a shitstorm. It's too unusual a registration. Word will get out."

I opened the door for him. "Don't worry, Levi. I'll protect you from my mother."

He gave me a hard look. "But who's going to protect you?"

Chapter 23

Priya was in her room with her share of the pizza we'd ordered, digging up info on Abraham's wife, while I took a very fast shower in preparation for going in to the office to track down Evil Wanker once and for all.

The hot water and citrus soap unwound my tense muscles, helping me work through the problem. Fact: the wooden ring was important enough to Gavriella for her to hide it away if she believed Chariot was closing in on her. Fact: it belonged to Evil Wanker's father. Conclusion: he was the father she'd referred to.

I stepped onto the bathroom mat, drying off with a fluffy Disney princess towel that neither Priya nor I would claim.

Why would Gavriella go from an American identity to a Spanish one, forced to become proficient enough in details about the culture to pass for native? Growing up in Miami, she could easily have been bilingual, though she'd have had to adjust her pronunciations to account for differences in pronunciation and word choice with Spanish spoken in Spain. Also, her exposure to Hispanic culture would have been mostly to a Cuban one.

The simplest answer was that Evil Wanker's father was Spanish and she'd taken on that persona to honor him. He must have been a mentor to her. Maybe he was even the team leader.

I shoved some pepperoni and artichoke pizza into my mouth as I got dressed. Since I had to meet Talia, today wasn't a jeans day, but I was petty enough not to want to go full business appropriate either. I settled for nice trousers and a green pullover sweater, styled my hair instead of throwing it into a ponytail, and took care with my makeup beyond eye shadow and lipstick. I slid my feet into my motorcycle boots, arranged with Pri to meet at the office later, grabbed a nice trench coat, and left to pursue this much more promising avenue of inquiry.

For my first stop, I hit up the lounge for a chat with the blonde dancer who'd hung on to the ring and was open to financial transactions.

Gavriella had never mentioned the ring owner's name to the dancer, but fifty bucks got me the name and number of a waitress that Gavriella had gone out for drinks with a few times. An extra twenty ensured that she didn't ask questions about why Gavriella's supposed kid was asking the name of her own grandfather.

The beauty of cold, hard cash.

I hit pay dirt with the waitress, identifying myself not as the daughter, but a private investigator trying to confirm Gavriella's relationship for an inheritance. People were more inclined to help when a payout was involved.

Gavriella's "dad's" name was Franco. The waitress was certain of that fact because her grandfather's name was Frank. Gavriella had mentioned he'd passed away shortly before she'd started working at the strip club.

Franco Behar. Now that I had his name, I could search all the databases, House and P.I. based, that I had access to and track his son, Evil Wanker, down that way.

I stopped by a hardware store to buy a folding chair and small table as temporary office furniture, until I could secure a loan from Talia, and with much trepidation at facing the devastation once more, dragged myself up the stairs to my office.

"Ash?" Eleanor strolled out of her office when I entered the common reception area. "I let the delivery people in to your office. I hope that was okay."

"What delivery people?" I dropped the folding chair and table with a clatter and ran to my office. Could the Queen and Moran have figured out my ruse and be springing a delightful and terrible trap for me? I stopped in confusion at seeing Cohen Investigations once more stenciled on the glass.

"Who ordered this?" I said.

"Didn't you?" She tucked the pen she held behind her ear. "I'm sorry. It all seemed legit."

I jammed my key into my lock, opened the door, and gasped. The room was transformed. Gone was the detritus of Nadija's attack; my shitty office furniture had been replaced with fancy ergonomic chairs for Priya and myself and desks in a glossy walnut. The filing cabinets had been set right-side up once more and the safe pushed back against the wall. Even the gouge in the floor had been covered with a smart area rug.

"If you didn't order all this, then who did?" she said.

"Priya? She got a new contract. You made the right call letting them in." I dropped into my chair, testing out all its levers until I had it set to maximum comfort. Then I bounced in it for a bit, because damn, that was deluxe.

I smiled at the photo of Priya and me, which had been reprinted and replaced in a new frame on my desk. A brand new top-of-the-line dartboard and darts holder once more occupied a place of prominence, though on the opposite wall from where they had been. I glanced to my left where they had originally hung and my hand flew up to cover my cry.

Fifteen to twenty framed prints of vintage Sherlock Holmes book covers hung on the wall, like a pantheon of my favorite cases.

I burst into tears, scaring Eleanor, who skittered away as fast as she could.

I had worked and fought hard to build up every tiny aspect of my business, even my crappy office furniture, and I didn't begrudge a second of that time. I'd had accolades: from grateful clients and from Priya who was my biggest cheerleader, but this act of unbridled generosity wrapped me up in its tenderness like a fleecy blanket. There was nothing behind this generosity other than an incredible kindness. No, it was more than that. Replacing the furniture was a gift of the highest order, but those items were functional. The addition of the Sherlock posters transformed the office into the specificity of *my* space, an act of deep thoughtfulness and intimacy that I hadn't experienced from anyone in my adult life.

Through my sobs, I called Muffin Top and asked Beatriz for a special order to go out in a rush delivery. She agreed, once I'd convinced her that no one had died and this was happy crying.

That done, I went to the bathroom, loudly blew my nose, and washed my face.

I made a makeshift coaster out of printer paper so as not to mark the pristine gloss of the desk with my coffee cup, opened my crappy laptop, and got to work. All the tedious digging through databases to find Franco Behar barely dented my euphoria. My ass didn't go numb and my properly postured back sang in sweet relief.

Slowly, I narrowed down possibilities, cross-referencing them until I'd found not only Franco, but his British boarding school educated son, Rafael. Oh, Evil Wanker, I had you.

I was about to start phoning hotels here in Vancouver like I'd done to find Nadija, when my cell rang. Glancing at the number, I smiled and answered.

"Cohen Investigations. Ashira speaking."

"Three dozen jelly donuts is kind of overkill, don't you think?" Levi's smooth baritone was lit with amusement.

"I'm not sure it's enough. Why did you do this? Not that I'm not grateful—"

"Which we talked about."

"This is above and beyond. You must have spent a fortune."

"It's just money." Said by me on no occasion ever. "It was no big deal to get you new furniture."

"And replace my photo and get me a new dartboard and… those book covers." My voice caught on a sob.

"Shit, don't cry. I'll have to quit tormenting you if I make you cry."

I gave a shaky laugh. "We can't have that."

"Exactly. Now go forth and solve a mystery."

"I shall and I am. Hopefully I'll have news about Evil Wanker for you soon."

"There you go." Levi paused. "I'm glad you like the prints."

"They're the best gift I've ever received. Thank you, from the bottom of my heart."

"You're welcome," he said softly. He cleared his throat. "Now quit being mushy. It's making me more diabetic than those donuts you sent. And thanks for sending office gossip into overdrive about who they were from and what they were for with that unsigned card of yours."

"Veronica totally read it."

"Of course she did. Your 'best day ever' was perfectly

vague and insinuating enough to drive her mad with curiosity."

"Achievement unlocked." I leaned back in my chair without fear of toppling over. "Does this mean we're friends?" I turned the word over, trying it on for size with regards to Levi.

"God, no," he said and hung up.

I held the phone a moment longer, as if that would prolong the warm sparky feeling in my chest. I was glad the two of us were back in our familiar Zone of Antagonism, but at the same time, it didn't quite fit as comfortably as it had.

There was a low whistle from the doorway. "How much of a devil's bargain did you have to make with Talia?"

I pointed at the stretched-out, tattered sweatpants with Dalhousie University Schulich School of Law embroidered on them that were a hand-me-down from Priya's brother and a sweater that looked like it had formerly done duty for a chimney sweep. "Why are you wearing the latest in Dickensian urchin-wear? Oh, geez. Don't tell me you broke up with Kai and you're actually upset about it."

"If I had, your empathy would have me back on my feet in no time," Pri said. "I wore it because I figured you'd want help cleaning up the mess. I see I was mistaken."

"So mistaken. Come imprint your fine ass on your new chair." I motioned her over.

She handed me a single sheet of paper, before sitting down and swiveling her seat from side-to-side. "Oh yeah, baby. Bond with mommy."

"Well, that made it weird." I read the details of the Dershowitz case that she'd unearthed. "This is useful information. Thank you."

"No prob."

I studied her covertly from behind my computer screen.

"Quit it," she said, not even glancing my way as she adjusted a few levers to reposition the height.

Best friends who knew you better than you knew yourself were annoying. "Sheesh, some people don't appreciate being smothered with concern."

That got me one of her donkey-braying laughs, though it was half-hearted. Baby steps.

"Even with money," Priya said, "how did you arrange for all of this so quickly?"

"I didn't. It was Levi."

Priya misadjusted, her seat dropping with a sharp jerk. "Was it now?"

"I may have been unfair to him last night."

"You *may* want to drop to your knees in gratitude. Literally." She rolled her chair back and forth. "If you don't, I will."

"Have at it," I said blithely. "I already thanked him in jelly-laden pastry."

"Ash, even you, my socially dense friend, must understand the significance of this gesture."

"Don't go putting conventional mores on whatever Levi and I are. He's loaded. The money didn't mean anything to him. It was a kind deed for a broke friend." I stumbled over that last word.

"Bullshit," she coughed. Her eyes narrowed on the vintage Sherlock book cover prints. "And I wasn't talking about the furniture."

I wheeled my chair over to her, because I could and it was fun, and pushed her out of her seat. "Lovely of you to drop by, but I have work to do and as you must have a crust of bread to beg for or a pocket to pick, run along."

She walked to the door, shooting me the finger. "We should go out tonight. Karaoke?"

"Noisy and crowded. You up for it?"

"I don't know, but it's our normal, and I could use that."

"Karaoke it is."

"Laters, Holmes."

"Laters, Adler." I refilled my coffee cup, set it carefully on my makeshift coaster, and dove in to phoning hotels.

It turned out that Rafael Behar was staying at the Pan Pacific, one of the priciest hotels in the city. If Jezebeling came with an expense account, I would spend the shit out of it.

I drove Moriarty down to the massive white hotel and convention center on the waterfront. Shaped like a boat, it was complete with ninety-foot-high sails and had become a Canadian architectural icon. It was the main cruise ship terminal here in town, and as such, bustling.

I sprinted inside, weaving through tourists like a quarterback going for the winning touchdown at the Super Bowl. Skidding up to the front desk, I grabbed the hotel phone and placed a call asking to be connected to Rafael Behar's room.

"Yes?" His voice was posh with the condescending edge of all upper crust British accents, much like highly polished cut glass.

"Rafael Behar, this is the Seeker," I said, pitching my voice low and gruff, and breathing like Darth Vader. "I have found you and now must decide whether I plan to keep you."

"It doesn't work that way," he said, with more than a touch of annoyance. "Wait at the Coal Harbour bar. I'll be down shortly."

"Wear that snazzy little bow tie so I recognize you."

"How will I recognize you?"

"I'll be the day drinker with the can-do attitude."

"I rue this meeting already," he said, and hung up.

Tucked in a corner of the soaring atrium, a burbling fountain wound through the bar out to a large patio area. It failed to boast the "gloomy, functioning alcoholic" ambiance that I preferred in my watering holes.

Two five-story cruise ships were docked alongside the hotel, blocking any view of the water or Stanley Park. It was too cold for anyone to be out on the rows of stateroom balconies, and the desolation gave the ships a forlorn air.

I ordered a Coke and grabbed a secluded table for two in the far corner with my back to the white behemoths. When Rafael entered, I waved him over.

Other than his black eyes behind round spectacles, I didn't see much to indicate a Spanish heritage. Rafael's short hair was medium brown with reddish highlights and he possessed the vampiric pallor of a librarian who'd been trapped in the stacks for a hundred years. His shirt actually had gold cuffs, his tree tattoo hidden under the long sleeves, and his outfit included a dove gray sweater vest and softly pleated trousers.

On first glance, you'd dismiss him as mild-mannered, which I suspected was his intention, but those bothering with a second, more detailed study were rewarded with a glimpse of the alpha under that Clark Kent exterior. For one thing, there was nothing soft about Rafael's body. Dude didn't have an ounce of fat, his shirt snug around his muscled biceps. For another, he moved with that same deceptive lithe elegance as both Levi and Arkady, and his eyes were suffused with intelligence and a piercing sharpness.

"I suppose I should congratulate you on finding me." Rafael sat down.

"I'd say it's a pleasure," I said, "but let's not kid ourselves."

"I do appreciate honesty." He sniffed my drink and grimaced. Motioning a waiter over, he ordered a glass of house red.

"Your libations all sorted?" I said. "May I impress you

with my dazzling Seeker skills now and convince you of my worthiness?"

"You may try." Rafael leaned back in his chair, his fingers steepled.

"Did you know that Chariot is after a magic feather that compels people with their heart's desire? It was found on an archeological site near a grove that may have been a site of Asherah worship."

The waiter placed his drink in front of Rafael and he murmured his thanks.

"That's interesting," he said once the waiter had left, "but hardly surprising. They excel at chaos." He took a sip.

"The feather is an angel's feather. You know, like how Nefesh magic is a dilution of angel magic?"

Rafael sputtered out his wine, then grabbed a linen napkin and dabbed at his mouth. "There's no way you could have learned about the angel connection on your own. Not that quickly. Who told you? Did Gavriella say something to you before she died?"

He knew I'd been at the lab? "No one told me. I'm damn good at what I do. Go ahead. Report back to the others that I'm keeping my magic and you can all shove your issues with me up your collective asses."

"What others?"

"The rest of the team."

"You're looking at it."

I gripped the table. "No. This can't be a partnership. I don't have time to fight Chariot fifty percent of the time."

"Why would you believe there's a team?" Rafael said.

"Gavriella implied more than one person had searched for me. That 'we' had to stop Chariot." I dropped my head into my hands, pulling on my hair. "It can't all be on us."

"It's not." I raised my head, hopeful, but he added: "It's all on you. I'm merely your support person."

The bottom dropped out of my world. "I have a career.

See, I've always dreamed of being a private investigator and I started my own business and—"

"You'll have to wrap that up, I'm afraid. Being a Jezebel takes priority. Shift work is best. Pays the bills, allows for flexibility and sudden moves if necessary."

"No. Go activate someone else."

"I think not. You've proven yourself." He nodded, satisfied. "You appear to have valuable skills needed for this fight, after all."

Hoisted by my own petard. I slammed my hand on the table. "Then I refuse. Seems like that's what Gavriella did."

"Gavriella never rejected it. Not consciously. She made a series of choices out of grief and anger leading to her abduction and torture at Chariot's hands to further their goals."

I didn't care. I wasn't taking on this fucking destiny as my full-time gig.

"What is Chariot's ultimate goal? Money? Power?" Stupid curiosity.

"That's part of it, certainly, but it's not their endgame," Rafael said.

"What is?"

"Immortality."

I choked on a piece of ice.

"Indeed."

"Hang on. So everything we were taught about the original ten men of the Lost Tribes attempting to achieve the fifth level of the soul, Yechida, wasn't about a metaphoric spark of the divine?"

"They were trying to become gods on Earth, and those behind Chariot have been attempting the same ever since. We are all that stands between them and their goal." He gave me a wry smile. "That is part of a larger conversation."

"That doesn't change my decision." Except I had to face myself in the mirror. "If I refuse, are they left unchecked?"

"There is a ritual, used in a handful of cases, that transfers the magic of the chosen Jezebel to the next most worthy potential, provided the woman has not yet said the words, 'I accept the Mantle of Jezebel.' Should you desire, this can all be over for you by this evening."

"Including my powers."

"Obviously. Think carefully, Ashira. Neither the world, nor I, desire a Jezebel who has to be dragged kicking and screaming into saving us."

I could walk away.

"I need a minute." I fled the bar and went outside, gripping the patio railing, a stiff breeze washing over me.

My original dreams had been founded on being a Mundane P.I., and yeah, sure the elixir of what I could now reach as Nefesh was a heady one. But while I was all kinds of selfish, I wasn't actually evil. This fight with Chariot deserved a Jezebel who was in it for all the right reasons. Who would give everything to it.

There were a lot of reasons to walk away: the world would be in good hands, my relationship with Talia would remain intact-ish, Rafael would get a do-over with someone whose magic hadn't been tampered with and was committed to the cause, and any potential problems for Levi because of me would disappear.

There was only one reason to stay: my revised Sherlock dreams, now fueled by magic.

Ah, but there was the irony. Keep the magic and my dream was dead. Give up the magic and my dream was alive, but lesser. I'd begin again at the bottom of the Mundane P.I. heap. Scrounging for scraps as I trudged to that far-off door.

The wind curled around me in frigid lashes, but the icy hands I pressed to my cheeks encountered flushed skin and the uncomfortable truth that I'd shiv anyone who tried to take these powers from me.

That in itself should have been reason enough to step aside gracefully: so the magic could choose someone truly worthy who would make the quest to take down Chariot their calling. Not me, a selfish cow already computing how much this Jezebel gig would get in the way of my actual pursuits and how far I could bend the parameters of being chosen without breaking them entirely.

Do this and I'd be running a con on being a hero. Adam would be proud.

I slammed the railing. Why'd the magic have to choose me anyway? In what universe had I been deemed the worthiest? A thirteen-year-old kid with anger issues and a bum leg? It had cost me the few precious illusions I had left about my dad and was making me feel like a shit-heel because I was too selfish to prioritize humanity's well-being, like an actual Chosen One should.

What could this magic have possibly seen in me to justify all that?

Much as my heart demanded I put my dreams first and keep the powers, my conscience had another counter-argument to chime in with. Staying Nefesh guaranteed that I'd end up taking more magic away from people, breaking their spirits and destroying their lives.

The fact that I'd only do that to bad people left a sour taste in my mouth and made me a liar, because look at me now. One threat to Priya's life and I'd agreed to ruin Shannon's or Abraham's.

Selfish.

Walk away and one hundred percent of my time would be devoted to my dream, but I'd have to live with the sorrow that it would never quite be all that it could have been.

Accept the Mantle and live with my dream always being an afterthought, because taking down Chariot came first.

The Queen had once said that life was a series of choices and, in the end, we hoped we came out ahead. That would never happen if I gave up my powers.

I needed a third choice: keep the magic *and* face myself in the mirror by doing good in the world.

If I was clever, I'd find a way to combine my dream with my destiny.

I smiled. I was very clever.

Teeth chattering, I walked back inside, sighing at the warmth easing through me.

Rafael sipped his wine like living in the moment and savoring this experience was of paramount importance. He made a disgruntled face at my reappearance, but wiped it away in favor of a polite expression of interest. "What's it to be? Mantle or no Mantle?"

"Mantle. With modifications."

"Absolutely not," Rafael said.

A bowl of peanuts had been delivered to the table.

"Peeled and everything. How quality." I tossed a couple of nuts in my mouth.

"It's an as-is deal," he said. "Take it or leave it."

"Hear me out, okay?" I explained my idea.

His skepticism lessened as I presented a valid counter-argument to each of his objections. "You're positive you can achieve this?"

"Yes." Ninety-nine percent positive. Solid mid-eighties for sure.

"Perhaps different times require different tactics," Rafael said. "God knows our progress over the past four hundred years has been less than admirable. Are you certain you want this?"

"I am."

His lips twisted wryly. "Let me rephrase. Ashira Cohen, do you wish to accept the Mantle of Jezebel with a full understanding of and commitment to those duties?"

"I do."

"All right. We'll use your idea. But should it not pan out,

it's back to the old way and you shut down Cohen Investigations. Agreed?"

"Agreed."

"Then say the words."

"I accept the Mantle of Jezebel." My blood warmed, the magic humming almost like a happy sigh, and the taste of cloves filling my mouth, reminiscent of the drink the twin had given me at the Dream Market.

You win, destiny. Just this once.

Chapter 24

"Are you my Giles?" I said.

"Let me make something perfectly clear." Rafael vigorously wiped off his hands with his linen napkin. "The first rule of making this relationship work is no pop culture references. Especially not that one. Our work is serious business with very real ramifications."

"Immortality. Gods on Earth. I get it. Okay, start by explaining—" I shook my head, sighing in frustration. "I know virtually nothing and have an endless list of questions."

"That's normal as a new Jezebel, but as that will require a much longer conversation, what do you wish to know at this moment?"

"What was supposed to happen when I got my magic? Jezebels one day wake up with powers, which would be terrifying, because we've always been Mundane. If there hadn't been extenuating circumstances at the time my magic manifested, I would have had no idea what was happening and on top of that, I was supposed to find some strange man? Dude, I was thirteen when my magic first activated."

"Gavriella was right." He stared blankly down at his wine, then shook off his stupor.

"Ever hear of stranger danger? I would never have gone looking for you. Not to mention, you would have been a kid, too. This system is screwed up."

"Your *magic* is screwed up."

What a peach. I calculated my chances if I slashed his throat with his wine glass. Better still, poison, applied in a remote location where my face would be the last thing he saw in his agonizing twisty death throes.

I crunched down on a piece of ice from my Coke, enjoying his flinch. "Death is the trigger, right?"

"You've surmised correctly," he said. "Normally, your Attendant, who back then would have been my father, would have sensed several magic hot spots, the cities with the strongest potentials, and instigated the magic test which would start with the worthiest candidate. The brightest spot. Yours."

We were totally coming back to this Attendant idea. Did he do laundry?

"I was never tested back then because my magic was warded-up until recently. Part of that longer conversation," I added, off his puzzled look.

"Ah. Well, Gavriella flatlined for several seconds during a mission, and while Father sensed the hot spots when he cast the test, it didn't go anywhere. Presumably because of this ward."

I nodded. "From that point forward from your perspective, there were no more Jezebels. Gavriella was the last of the line. Then she died for real a couple of weeks ago. Where's the second Jezebel?"

"There isn't one. I'd inherited the mantle of Attendant by that point and I did as required with the test. There were a number of hot spots, but yours, the one in Vancouver again, remained the brightest, despite it flickering in and out. The test didn't find you immediately, and I feared we were in the same predicament as fifteen years ago."

"If you knew I was in Vancouver but nothing more than that, how did you find out my name and what I did?"

"I found the lab." He fiddled with the stem of his glass, his expression unreadable. "Too late to save Gavriella, but I saw you and wondered. Then I overheard you exchange contact details with another woman and did some research, all while I kept attempting to cast the test. When it finally took hold, there you were. My hypothesis was correct."

I appreciated a man with a good hypothesis. "Were you and Gavriella close?"

"My father had been her Attendant for my entire life. She was an irritating older sibling who claimed the lion's share of his attention."

I was well acquainted with that blithe tone and the hurt it concealed. "Still, I'm sorry for your loss. Both your losses." I ate some more peanuts. "What happens if the potential fails?"

"They die during the test and it moves to the next person. I can only assume that as you didn't technically fail it, seeing as the magic never found you in the first place, that it went into a kind of limbo until it once more connected with you to test you properly."

"What was I tested for?"

"The first test with the three cups determines whether you choose and, by extension, protect the almond tree, symbolic of the goddess Asherah who created you all."

I sputtered out my Coke. "Made us? I'm not human?"

"Poor choice of words. Apologies. Bestowed this magic upon the first Jezebel."

"Are we all female?"

"Yes. It's a matriarchy, like Judaism. You're related to the first Jezebel through your mother."

I laughed so hard that I choked and had to thump my

chest, while Rafael stared like I was unhinged. My mother, a champion of curbing Nefesh rights, was the reason I had magic. I wiped my eyes. "Longer conversation."

"Second test, do you have the ability to defeat the Repha'im, which proves you can destroy magic, and finally are you smart enough to find the way out of the grove? Jezebels aren't merely warriors. Thwarting and ultimately defeating Chariot involves your Seeker capabilities."

"Repha'im. Those are the things I fought in the grove? They're from Hell?"

"Sheol isn't Hell," he said in his crisp British accent, "but yes."

"But ghost stories have been around longer than the 1600s when magic came into being."

"Not all ghosts are Repha'im, but all Repha'im are essentially ghosts."

"And they're floating around doing what? Are they dangerous?"

"Not generally. Not unless they're provoked. That's when you get your hauntings." He paused. "And such."

"Back up, buddy. What's with the loaded hesitation? Define 'and such?'"

"Longer conversation," he said.

"Fine. But you implemented a fourth test involving whether or not I could find you."

"Once you'd defeated the Repha'im and I arrived in the grove, we should have seen each other's faces, allowing our connection to click in like a phone line. At that point, you'd have known how to find me, and once we met in person, the bond would harden. So long as we were both alive, we'd always be able to find each other."

Ew. That sounded like the premise of a cheesy Hollywood romance.

"I don't feel any bond," I said. "Could that ward be the reason why we don't have this connection you spoke of?"

He stared into the depths of his wine, a thoughtful expression on his face. "I suspect it is. Regardless, we don't have it and that fact fueled my previous conviction that you shouldn't be a Jezebel."

That longer conversation needed to include a thorough inventory of what I should and should not be able to do.

I drained my Coke. "This complicates things, doesn't it?"

"Everything about you complicates things."

"You're not the first person to say that." Rafael and Levi could never meet. "Where was this location-sensing bond of yours when Gavriella was taken? Why didn't you rescue her?"

Rafael toyed with the stem of his glass. "Gavriella spiraled after my father's death. She numbed herself with drugs."

"The Blank."

His hand stilled. "You know about that?"

"Assume I am a phenomenal Seeker and save yourself constantly asking that question and boring me with repetition. Blank kills the cravings and the magic."

"It also killed our connection. Chariot captured her and forced her off the drug. Her magic returned, but they had her so heavily doped up that between the damage that the Blank had done to our connection and the powerful sedatives, I couldn't find her. Only sense her…" His eyes clouded over. "Distress." He shot me a brittle smile. "Quite wretched actually, to be that helpless when one's life work is to serve and protect. And yet, I find myself in the same situation with you."

"Trust me, Rafael, our situation is nothing like that one. You're not my house elf. Though if you do laundry…"

"I do not."

"Can't blame a chick for asking. This is going to be far more of an equal working relationship." I held out my fist and Rafael tapped his knuckles against mine with the look of someone who feared they'd made a pact with the devil. "Welcome to Team Jezebel."

～

GETTING me up to speed required clearing my schedule for a while, which couldn't happen until I'd discharged my duties to the Queen. Rafael planned to return home to London and pack up his things to move to Vancouver, at which point we'd meet in earnest and hammer out our next steps.

I was cautiously excited about this plan. I'd accepted the Mantle, so my P.I. dreams were riding on my ability to implement it.

My original reason for meeting with Talia, the loan, was no longer necessary. I could have cancelled, but I needed closure, even if the thought of not having her in my life gave me a stomach ache.

I dragged my feet up the stairs to the atrium at the Law Courts downtown.

The large open space with its polished concrete floor, generous amounts of greenery, and tons of light from the multistoried sloped glass roof that ran the length of the space, was packed with Mundane business leaders, there to hear Jackson Wu push his anti-Nefesh agenda.

An aide directed me to Talia, who stood at the back, nodding along with the party leader, as if mentally crossing off each talking point.

"It's almost over," she said.

Jackson's speech was cleverly written and he delivered it with conviction and gravitas. He didn't preach outright hate, but instead enumerated sound financial and social reasons for dissolving House Pacifica and bringing Nefesh under Mundane control. It was a persuasive argument that played to the crowd, and when he finished, he received loud and enthusiastic applause.

"Come." Talia caught me by the elbow. "There's a small chamber where we can have some privacy." She tugged me through the crowd.

Jackson was still up on the low makeshift stage, a line of business leaders waiting to speak with him. He conversed with a woman who, from her hand gestures, and the way she turned her body, was introducing him to the man beside her. As they shook hands, the man moved into profile and I stiffened.

It was a slender man dressed in an expensive business suit—the German who'd killed Yitzak.

All noise flattened out to static and my peripheral vision narrowed to pinpricks. I broke free of Talia's grasp, took a couple of steps and stopped.

My mother placed her hand on my forehead. "You're cold as ice."

"Who's the man talking to Jackson?"

"Your party leader gives a good speech." Leah Nichols, a reporter with shark-like instincts who I'd encountered while illusioned as Levi, stepped in front of Talia and thrust a microphone into her face. I edged out of camera range. "How far away would you say this legislation is from being put before Parliament?" she said.

I rose onto my tiptoes to keep the German in sight while Talia deflected from actually saying anything concrete and Leah pressed her for more.

Jackson said something that made the woman laugh and the German gave a tight-lipped smile.

The crowd shifted, blocking my view for a second, but by the time my line of sight was restored, the German and his companion were gone, and Jackson was speaking to a group of South Asian business leaders.

Leah moved on to other quarry and Talia returned her attention to me. "Which man?"

"He's gone. He was with some blonde woman in a black dress."

Talia spread her hands, indicating the many who fit that description. "If it's important, we could go over and ask Jackson."

My hands balled into fists. No, we couldn't, because even though I didn't think that Jackson was part of Chariot, I had no idea who in this room was. They lived in the shadows, and I'd have to as well. Whatever Chariot was involved in, I was the only one who could stop them and that meant acting like a fox, not a wrecking ball.

If Jezebels were the only Nefesh who weren't born with magic, but had it triggered, then registering even my enhanced strength with the explanation that it had turned on after the crash was too much of a risk. Should anyone involved in Chariot find out, they'd immediately be suspicious and Talia was too public a person for my Nefesh registration to fall quietly under the radar.

"Ashira? The loan?"

Mind reeling at this turn of events, I docilely followed her into a small chamber. When she shut the door, the silence was as stifling as being wrapped in cotton batting.

She clearly expected me to say something, but what? I couldn't tell her about being a Jezebel as I'd planned. I couldn't tell *anyone* and I certainly couldn't register as Nefesh. Had I fucked up by accepting the Mantle?

No, I didn't regret my choice, because there was still a way forward. It wasn't what I would have ever chosen for myself, and it involved trusting my dream to someone else, but I wanted to believe we could make it work.

I'd been wrong in thinking that since magic was out in the open, anyone who was top of the food chain would declare themselves. Chariot had brought magic into this

294

world and, in one way or another, had been attempting to control it ever since. That made them incredibly powerful, but they kept to the shadows. The only ones who could defeat them, Jezebels, had to keep to the shadows, too.

I could still be Sherlock, I just had to reconcile living a public persona that was a total fabrication while not unconsciously exposing myself through some tiny detail.

That challenge was kind of cool.

My mother's brow furrowed. "You needed a loan?"

"Right. I did, but not anymore. I was offered an ongoing contract with an insurance company," I improvised. "A Mundane company."

Talia lay her hand on my cheek. I yearned for the contact and the assurance that I would still have her in my life, as much as I grieved that she'd never accept the Nefesh part of me. "That sounds like a wise choice," she said. "What's the job?"

"They want someone to investigate fraudulent claims. It's a good pay bump and great benefits."

"What about Cohen Investigations?"

"I'll still have it, just with an exclusive client and a sure way of making rent every month. I'm tired of struggling. The fact that I had to ask you for help hammered home that my priorities have changed."

She gave me a genuine smile and hugged me. "I'm happy for you, darling." When she released me, she smoothed back a strand of my hair. "All grown-up. This will be an exciting new chapter of your life."

Thanks for the backhanded compliment, Mom. "I'm sure it will be."

"I'm glad you've…" Decided to live in the closet? "Shown such a mature and responsible attitude. How about we grab dinner? My treat."

Her enthusiasm for this fake decision was both buoying and depressing. Our relationship was better than ever, except for the part where it was built on us both being complicit in a total fucking lie.

No lies, no games. It was supposed to be what saved us.

"Rain check? I have a few loose ends to tie up before I take the other job."

"Of course." She kissed my cheek, laughing when I wiped her lipstick off.

"Okay, great. We'll talk soon. And Mom?"

She blinked at my use of that word since there was no one around to hear it.

"Be careful with this legislation."

"We have very good security and people monitoring all Nefesh activity."

"You can't be too vigilant," I said. "Watch for any unstable element, even with Mundanes. If someone doesn't feel right, then trust your gut."

I couldn't be more specific because this fight against Chariot necessitated keeping Talia in the dark. For her own safety.

Facing myself in the mirror wasn't as simple as it seemed.

"So suspicious," she said. "A benefit in your new job."

"Yeah." I kissed her cheek. "I'll call you soon."

With that, I walked away, leaving Talia to mingle with my enemies—both in the open and the shadows.

Once upon a time I'd had a mother who loved magic. She'd snuggled under the covers with me, told me all sorts of fantastic tales, and taught me to believe in the impossible. I'd lost a lot growing up and I'd stopped believing in happily-ever-after.

But my mother had stopped believing in me.

Chapter 25

Pulling down my visor mirror, I carefully finger-combed my hair and reapplied my lipstick, determined to look my best for my next stop.

"Failure is not an option," I said, and turned the key. Moriarty didn't start until the third try. Third time's the charm, right? Taking it as a positive omen and not a sign that my life was about to derail, I drove to House Pacifica.

Levi often worked Saturdays—him being there now wasn't a stretch.

Veronica watched me approach with furrowed brows, speaking to someone over a headset. When I got to her desk, standing there politely and waiting for her to finish, she kept craning around me, looking for something.

After the second time, I stopped checking for whomever she was waiting for.

Finally, she finished up the call and pulled the headset off her high ponytail without messing up a single hair. "He's not in."

I pushed down the hot rush of disappointment. "Would you please give him a message to contact me immediately? It's extremely important. And I'm sorry he makes you work weekends." I thanked her and headed back to the elevators, wondering how long Rafael would give me before declaring my plan a bust and making me close down Cohen Investigations.

I'd almost made it back to the elevators when Veronica called after me. "Am I being pranked?"

I stopped and turned. "No?"

She waved a hand at my outfit. "You show up here looking halfway professional, you behave politely. Are you sick?"

"No."

"He's obviously inside." She huffed in annoyance, picked up the receiver, and said something quietly into it.

Totally confused by her behavior, I'd barely made it back to the executive area when Levi's office door banged open.

He took in my outfit and frowned. "Are you sick?"

"I can dress nicely without it being indicative of disease. My professionalism is unparalleled."

Veronica and Levi exchanged a doubtful look.

I threw them both the finger—behind my back where they couldn't see—and walked into Levi's office, thinking calm thoughts.

Levi shut the door and sat down, turning his office chair away from its customary view of the window and towards me. "What's up?"

"I have a present for you."

He wheeled backwards, looking faintly queasy. "Is it more donuts?"

"No. Consider this your official notice that the vials will be in my possession tomorrow. No more smudges."

He chewed on his bottom lip for a moment. "I guess you want to discuss payment."

"About that." I rubbed the back of my neck. "I'm going to take you up on your offer."

"Of obligation blow jobs?" He grinned.

"Of the offer to work exclusively for you."

If I didn't have everything riding on this, it would have been comical how he half-rose out of his seat, before dropping heavily back into it. He picked up a pen and clicked it several times. "Why?"

"I don't want to cause you problems by registering my magic and with my unique abilities, I'll be an asset to the House. Protecting the Nefesh community is important, and I'd like to be a part of that." The speech I'd rehearsed on the way over came out perfectly.

"No." He spun around, his back to me, and moved his mouse to bring his monitor to life. "Thanks for the heads-up on the vials."

My mouth worked, but no sound came out and a red haze washed over my vision. I spun Levi back around and shoved his chair up against the desk hard enough to jolt him. "Why don't I get the job?"

"I wasn't aware I owed you an explanation."

"You offered me the gig and you know damn well I'd be amazing at it. I'd be your own secret weapon and don't tell me that doesn't get you all hard."

"I hope not. Pretty sure that falls under HR sexual harassment and I have more than enough paperwork to deal with already." He pried my hands off his lapels.

"You can't do this!"

"Why not?" His mild curiosity pushed me over the edge.

"Because I banked everything on you!" I thrust my hands into my hair. "There's no team. Taking down Chariot, protecting humanity from their evil, it's all on me. I was given a choice. My destiny at the expense of my dream or walk away from the magic and go back to being a nobody Mundane P.I." I paced his carpet. "You were my answer to having it all. Working for you keeps my status under wraps, which allows me as a Jezebel to pursue Chariot from the shadows and fulfill my Sherlock dreams."

Levi caught my hand as I passed him for the fourth time. His eyes had that same blown-out look he got post-orgasm. "You had me at 'I banked everything on you.'" He spoke the words in falsetto. "The job is yours."

I stumbled, and jerking free, punched him in the shoulder. "That's what this was about? You wanted to hear me beg and admit that I needed you in my professional life?"

Levi rubbed the tender spot. "That was a beautiful moment, but no. I wouldn't have offered the job to you if I didn't want you to take it. But I wanted *you* to take it, Ash, not some bullshit version of who you think I want you to be. You getting mad was the first honest thing you'd done since you showed up. Other than give Veronica and me the finger."

"I did not."

He stared at me flatly.

"Whatever. The job is mine?"

"I said it was." He scratched his head. "Though I don't see how that helps with your 'destiny at the expense of your dream.'" He did the quotes.

That was the other part of the very fine pitch I'd prepared. "Part of my duties here would be my Jezebel ones."

Levi drummed the pen on his thigh. "You want me to foot the bill to take down Chariot."

"Think about how much trouble those smudges they created caused and how dangerous it was to our magic community. If you think about it, this falls squarely under House obligation. Also—"

Levi groaned.

"You should give me a team. I already have Rafael—"

Levi crossed his arms. "Who the hell is Rafael?"

"Evil Wanker. My Attendant, silly. All Jezebels get one. He's very stuffy."

"Do I have to pay him as well?"

I sat down on his sofa, one leg over the other, swinging

300

my foot breezily, now that this was going much better. "I'm not exactly sure. He might have independent means, but maybe. Hmm. That would be four people budgeted under this operation."

"Four?!" Levi threw the pen at me.

"Yes. I want Arkady. He's being underutilized here and he loves excitement." Also, if Levi continued to use him to spy on me, I could control the flow of information. And possibly turn him. "Priya is only one day a week because the rest of the time she's already on your payroll as a separate line item. Also, if you want to come play Scooby Doo, which I know you totally do, you wouldn't need to pay yourself."

Sherlock had to gather a team to defeat Moriarty: Watson, Mycroft, Lestrade, even Scotland Yard and his Irregulars. Molly Hooper got added in the series. If Sherlock couldn't do it alone, I certainly couldn't. This lone wolf needed a pack.

Hopefully, I wouldn't gnaw my paw off in the process.

I clicked the pen, as another point occurred to me. "The rent on my office is a taxable deduction."

"I'm paying your rent?"

"No point having all that money you spent making it so lovely go to waste."

"You're gambling that my sense of duty is enough to compensate for the burden of taking all this on," he said, flippantly.

"It does. You're Watson." Click. Click.

His eyes narrowed. "You're not helping your case."

"You're a good man, Levi, and deep down, I'm sure you can see the benefits of this arrangement. You already offered me the job. I'm simply negotiating the terms and conditions. It's not like I'm demanding a month's paid holiday time to start." I shot him an innocent look. "I don't suppose—"

"Shut up. I beg of you."

I mimed zipping my lips.

Levi glared for three minutes, then he came over, his hand outstretched. "Deal."

I jumped to my feet and shook. "You won't regret this. Do you prefer I address you as His Lordship, Imperious One, or Fearless Leader?" I gave a celebratory click of the pen.

He stole it away, tucking it into his suit jacket pocket. "And so the regrets begin. Alright. I'd regret missing the opportunity to take Chariot down even more, though. Just, uh—for both our sakes you should know that, um." He glanced down, wet his lips, and his hand tightened on mine. "I'm betting the House on you," he said quietly.

His shirt was kind of crumpled from all the times I'd attacked him and grabbed it in this visit, and the circles under his eyes indicated that he hadn't quite caught up on sleep after monitoring me post-feather debacle. But his eyes were the ocean against a brilliant sunset, at once both scared and exhilarated, like he too had leapt into an abyss and someone had been there to catch him.

"I won't let you down." I slid my hand free. "I guess this makes us boss and employee now."

"Yeah." He gave me a rueful smile that echoed my own feelings that sleeping together from this point forward was a bad idea.

"Would you—okay, well, Priya and I are doing this thing tonight. You'll probably think it's stupid, but we love karaoke, and maybe you want to come with us? I could invite Arkady and if you wanted to bring Miles, that would be okay."

His expression was comically horrified.

"It's not like I'm asking you to handle dangerous reptiles."

"That might be preferable," he muttered. "Do I have to sing?"

"Noooo. Spectator status is good. I figure we could try being fr-friends, seeing as we'll be working together for the foreseeable future, but if you're busy or chicken?" I shrugged.

Maybe friends was where we'd needed to start all along.

Levi's expression was similar to that of Indiana Jones when he saw the pit full of snakes. "I'll come, but we'll see about the friends part."

"You're extremely vexing, Leviticus. See you at Blondie's at eight."

THE PURPLE GLITTERY tiara dangled from my fingertips. "I was going to celebrate my Jezebel official status with whiskey, not plastic aspirations of royalty, but okay."

"The two aren't mutually exclusive." Priya mushed my cheeks between her palms. "Who's a pretty Jezebel who kicks bad guy ass?"

"Oy vey." I slapped the plastic crown on my head. "Happy?"

"I can't believe you didn't get me one," Arkady sniffed, holding the door to Blondie's open.

"You're not a Jezebel," Priya pointed out.

The place was already pretty full with karaoke regulars. A hockey game on the TV mounted over the bar played on mute accompanied by Rolling Stones on the stereo, and the air was replete with cheap cologne and stale beer.

"I'm the one who's been reassigned to be at the beck and call of Queenie here," he said.

I pointed to a couple free tables near the back. "Yeah, those boy band moves you pulled out when you heard what you'd get to work on were infused with sorrow." I hurried over to push the tables together. After a bit of wrangling with the table next to ours, occupied by, ugh, newbies, I snagged a fifth seat for our group.

Arkady tossed his duffel coat over an empty chair and smoothed out his "Keep calm and kiss boys" T-shirt.

I shrugged out of my leather jacket, feeling much more myself in a tight black shirt shot through with silver thread and my leather pants. My favorite skinny metallic scarf was wound around my neck and not because I was hiding hickeys. Not that I'd be getting any to hide, what with our employer/employee status and all. Fuck that. I did not require His Lordship's assistance with my hickey acquisitions.

Priya poked my lip. "Quit scowling. This is a party."

She'd outdone herself on the pink front, even threading pink flowers in her hair. If she was that hellbent on enjoying herself this evening, I wouldn't kill her buzz.

I tapped my tiara. "Bring on the fun."

Jodie, the prehistoric server who was my gold standard of misanthropy, came over to take our order, half-engrossed in the text she was sending. "What's with the crown? If you're trying to get free birthday shots, pull another one."

I pressed my hands to my heart. "Ah, Jodie. Your radiant visage has lightened my soul and shrunk my hemorrhoids. A JD on the rocks with a splash of water, my good lady."

She grunted and flicked a finger at Arkady, who perused the chalkboard menu behind the bar.

"A Guinness and an order of ribs with…" He trailed off at Pri and my frantic head shakes. "A burger?" More head shakes.

"For Chrissakes, girls, tell him to order the fries and be done with it," Jodie said.

"He'll have the fries," Priya said. "As will I. And a Stella."

"Make it three," I said.

"Like I didn't know that," Jodie grumbled and wandered off.

"What just happened?" Arkady said. Jodie had sat down to continue texting. "Did she even take our order?"

"Oh, sure. Settle in for the long haul and all will show up eventually. Just don't ever eat anything except french fries here," Priya said.

"This place is a gem," he said.

"Consider yourself blessed that we—" I slapped a hand over my mouth, a snort escaping my lips.

Priya followed my gaze to the door and let out a soft "oh."

Arkady picked up the knife that had been left on our table and jabbed it at the newcomers. "Do not even *think* of sitting here."

Miles and Levi frowned at each other, twin pictures of innocence as they lumbered toward us in Metallica (Miles) and Def Leppard (Levi) shirts under jean jackets. But the pièce de résistance were the mullet wigs they'd unearthed.

Miles hooked a leg around the leg of the chair that Arkady was trying to drag away and sat down with a chin nod. "S'up."

Levi flicked the "party" part of his mullet off his shoulder, taking the seat between Priya and me. "Yo."

Jodie arrived, sloshing liquid as she deposited our drinks with zero care. "Anyone ever tell you you look like Nikki Sixx? Now there's a real man." She chucked Levi under the chin and sashayed off with so much hip sway that dislocation was a distinct possibility.

I fell back in my seat, helpless with laughter.

Priya wasn't doing much better. "She hit on you and still didn't take your order."

Levi grimaced and tried to pull the wig off, but I clamped a hand down over his, a fizzy spark hitting me at the contact.

"No way, Nikki. You made this bed. Now lie in it." I tilted my head to Jodie. "Bet she'd lie in it with you. Rawr."

"Only if she can borrow your tiara, princess." Levi grimaced. "That sounded better in my head."

"Whatcha drinking?" Miles asked Arkady.

Arkady crossed his arms. "I do not converse with hosers, Mimi. Some of us have an image to maintain."

"That's very intolerant of you," Miles said.

Arkady waved a hand around Miles' entire getup. "I can't even."

"Can't even? Like ohmigod, Becky, are we gonna have a smackdown?" Miles said in a girlish voice, motioning Jodie over.

Arkady went bright red, and Miles crossed his arms causing an avalanche of bicep and tricep ripples, a tiny grin playing at his lips.

Priya had an odd look on her face.

"Pri, you okay? You need some air?"

She shook her head, typing something on her phone.

Levi shot me a concerned look and I shrugged, rubbing the back of my neck, a rolling sensation in my stomach. Was inviting him here a bad idea? Should I have kept us on a professional footing? Was he uncomfortable right now?

Why did I care? I slammed back my Jack Daniels.

"Whatcha need, sweet cheeks?" Jodie said to Miles.

Arkady made Priya switch seats with him. "Shots." He answered before Miles could. "Lots and lots of shots."

"Kick in the Balls." Priya and I chorused loud enough to attract attention from other tables.

Levi slid down in his seat, one hand over his face and my heart kicked up. The drinks arrived and the world got a little rosier, a little more full of wonder, and a little more of a place where two people with a long and fraught past, could, for a moment, put down their weapons and be friends.

Chapter 26

Kenneth, our beer-bellied and bearded karaoke host with the most, stepped up on the small stage and announced sign-ups were open. Priya, Arkady, and I hustled to get the first slots.

Autumn elbowed me with no remorse whatsoever and ripped the pen out of my hand.

I rubbed my ribcage. "Nice Hippocratic oath, Dr. Kelly."

She readjusted the flowery scarf around her neck. "I convinced Emily to sing 'Enough is Enough.'" She waved at her wife, who was nervously drumming her fingers on the table. "If we're not first, she'll bail. You wouldn't want to deprive her of the joys of disco duets, would you?"

"Sure, play the guilt card." I stepped aside so she could sign up first.

When we got back, our shots were already on the table along with three platters of fries. Levi was eating off the one at my seat.

"You're failing your friend probation period," I said.

He dragged a fry through ketchup, doing this funny little tap at the edge of the plate with the potato. "Friends share."

I'd invited him thus I didn't stab him with a fork, but I did divvy up the fries, giving myself the lion's share.

Arkady pressed shots into all our hands. "To wanton women," he said, raising his glass in cheers.

"Here, here," Priya said.

"L'chaim," I said.

We clinked glasses and fired them back. I shivered at the delicious burn.

Priya pointed out various people in the bar to Arkady and Miles, giving them their life histories, though she kept checking her phone.

Autumn and Emily took the stage. Autumn, singing Babs' part in the song, had to carry more of the performance, but by the time they got to the first chorus, Emily had stopped looking like she was going to bolt and started having fun as Donna Summer. I whooped in encouragement.

Then I opened Levi's jean jacket wider to take in the full glory of the shirt. Was this appropriate friend behavior? If I really stretched the definition? Let's go with yes. My palms flattened against his hard pecs and my breath came a bit quicker. "Why the need to channel your inner metalhead? In public?"

"I live to surprise you."

I folded my hands primly in my lap so I didn't move on to stage two mauling. "Okay, but why did you keep those costumes from the camp talent show senior year in the first place?"

"These are costumes?" His eyes widened comically. "They were in Mom's basement. She was cleaning it out and called me to come get some boxes last week." He ate another fry. "What are you singing tonight?"

Kenneth called me up to the stage, raising his voice over the applause for the duet.

"It's a surprise."

I tapped my booted toe to the opening kick and bass of Def Leppard's "Pour Some Sugar on Me," both hands wrapped around the mic and my hips rocking. When I got to the chorus, I ran a hand down my body, grinding down to the floor.

The place erupted into catcalls, with my table the loudest of all. Except for Miles, who quietly head-banged. Levi watched me with a perplexed smile.

I finished the song with two heel raps and dropped the mic. Then I swaggered back to the table, high-fiving Arkady on his way to the stage.

Priya shoved a Kick in the Balls at me. "Catch up."

That first shot had made what I faced with Abraham tomorrow slightly easier to bear. Two shots might even dent my self-disgust. Three and… I ogled Levi shamelessly.

"That is not the woman I know who hates attention," Levi said, giving no sign of whether he'd noticed my appreciation of his fine form.

"Karaoke Ash is a separate personality," Priya said. "Karaoke Ash is an attention whore."

"True that." I shot back the Kick.

"She can also sing," Levi said. "Why didn't you ever do the talent shows at camp?"

I shrugged. "Didn't feel the venue."

He twirled a finger. "Whereas this fine establishment inspires you?"

"Yup."

Arkady did a kickass rendition of "Don't Stop Believin,'" followed by Priya's bootylicious rendition of "Push It." My bestie loved her 80s and 90s rap.

By that point, more fries and more drinks had been ordered and the night slid into a glossy haze, punctuated by much laughter, animated conversation, and Miles taking a perverse pleasure in riling Arkady up and making him flush.

Somehow my chair and Levi's had gotten shoved

together and his thigh was pressed against mine. Every time he moved, even the tiniest motion as he spoke, the scent of his scotch and chocolate magic infused a bit more of me. My eyes darted down to the hard line of muscle, wishing I could lick up the inside of his thigh and watch him do that cute little squirm that he did.

Priya handed me a glass of water. "Drink. Now."

Nodding, I gulped half of it back, and then pressed the glass against my forehead.

"You gonna sing, Mimi?" Arkady said.

Miles poured himself a glass of water. "I don't sing."

"You will. You've been riding my ass all night and not in my preferred way." Arkady ran a finger around the rim of his shot glass. "How about this? If I can make you blush like you've been so set on doing to me, then you sing a song of my choosing."

Priya's phone vibrated. She went poker-faced for a second, then placed it screen down before I could see.

"Good luck," Levi said. "Miles is hard to fluster."

Miles stretched out his legs, his mullet askew. "Go for it."

Kenneth called me up.

"Don't do anything without me as a witness," I said and ran to the stage to sing Joan Jett's "I Love Rock 'n' Roll."

Arkady took the stage after me with a wink. The Jonas Brothers' "Sucker" came on and Arkady hammed it up, singing directly to Miles. He was hammered past the point of having any filter, but this was Arkady who barely had one on a good day. There was much ass wiggling, finger pointing, and batting of lashes.

Levi hooted with laughter, his shoulder falling into mine. I didn't know if it was an accident or not, but he didn't move away. Neither did I, telling myself this was the best position to watch Priya from, because something was going on in that head of hers.

Miles sat there looking stoic and long-suffering. Levi leaned over and said something to him that I didn't catch, but Miles laughed and shook his head.

When Levi sat back, he'd shifted so no part of us touched. Good.

I did another shot.

Arkady returned to the table to high applause from the rest of the bar.

"You lost the bet, Arkady," Miles smirked. He deliberately mispronounced the name as "Ar-CADE-y" and not "Ar-KAH-dee," knowing how much Arkady loathed it.

Arkady braced his hands on Miles' shoulders and ever so slowly leaned in.

Even though Miles had about fifty pounds of muscle on Arkady, he didn't break free. When their lips were almost, but not quite touching, Miles said, "That isn't part of the song."

"Nothing gets by you." Arkady hadn't moved away yet. "Glad you noticed."

Miles ran his teeth over his bottom lip, his heated gaze fixed on Arkady. "I noticed. But you didn't make me blush."

Arkady raked an extremely languid and thorough gaze over Miles. "I will." He sat down smiling like the cat who swallowed the canary.

"I broke up with Kai," Priya blurted out. She burst into tears and ran off.

I made my excuses and ran after her, catching up with her at the sink in the women's bathroom where she was splashing water on her face. "I'm sorry."

"No, you're not. You constantly disparaged Kai."

"Yeah, I did, but he wasn't right for you."

"He was safe and dependable and it was all fine. Except neither of us was upset about the breakup, so maybe it wasn't. After I was kidnapped, I convinced myself that I'd get counselling and I'd be okay. Life could go on as usual. Then

I saw how Miles looked at Arkady, and I was so happy for them, but suddenly I couldn't breathe and I needed out." She twisted off the taps, her gaze dropping to the sink. "It's like this virus has gotten into my code, breaking me down into chaos."

I wiped the counter down with a tree's worth of paper towels before sitting on it. "Out of their wreckage, viruses open up new possibilities."

"Don't quote me to me." She dried her face. "I've been on pause since my engagement with Ravi blew up, haven't I?"

"Kind of."

"I hate myself for letting it happen and you're a shit best friend for not saying anything." She blew her nose loudly and then tossed the paper towel in the trash.

"Nicknaming your boyfriends after spreadable food products wasn't hint enough? Listen, if you want Miles to look at you that way, I'll totally take Arkady out for you. I hear groves are a good place for body disposal."

She gave a watery laugh. "I don't. I just want to stand on the edge of a dangerous cliff not certain if I'm going to go into free fall or plunge to a horrible end, but either way, I feel brilliantly alive and I'm ready to jump. Like you with Levi."

"The only way I'm going off a cliff for Levi is if I suddenly transform into a lemming. I want to shag him, baby," I drawled in an Austin Powers impression. "That's it." I shook my head. "No, that's not fair. I want to be friends, and everything else is over anyway because I'm working for him."

"Levi should sing."

"No way."

"Why?" She nudged me with her shoulder. "Don't you want to know your friend's musical tastes?"

Evil, evil wench. We'd spent far too many drunken

nights discussing the importance of karaoke song selection and my current conviction that the perfect guy would perform a cheeky version of "You Shook Me All Night Long" by AC/DC, that dirty and double-entendre filled rock classic.

"I'm not the romantic you are, Pri. Leave it."

She smoothed a hand over her dress. "I made a fool of myself in front of my boss."

"Levi won't care."

"Not Levi. Miles. I have to apologize."

I followed close on her heels, ready to tear a strip off him if he was his typical belligerent self.

Priya sat down, lightly touching Miles' shoulder. "I'm sorry for my behavior. I'm generally not a drama queen."

Miles jutted his chin at Arkady. "No, that's his schtick."

Arkady made an insulted noise then shrugged and reached for my tiara. I slapped his hand away.

"Besides, you're not on the clock and life happens." Miles smiled kindly at Priya. "Don't worry about it. I know I hired the best."

Look at him being all nice and shit to her. It wasn't flirtatious either. If Miles had harbored some attraction for Priya, it was gone now. He and I would likely never be friends, but Pri needed all the support she could get. I'd try and remember that the next time he made some asshole comment to me.

"Does he get to live another day?" Levi sounded highly amused as he whispered the question to me.

"I suppose."

"Since fun-killer here won't sing." Arkady nudged Miles' shoulder. "Who's going next?"

"You should," Priya said to Levi.

"No, he shouldn't. Let's focus on you," I hissed at her.

"I've had my epiphany. I'm good for tonight," she said.

"I can sing." Levi headed for the song selection book.

Arkady leaned over. "Am I missing something?"

"Yup," Priya said. "Carry on."

Levi flipped through the book.

"Fuck," I said and pushed my way to him, but by the time I got through the crowd, it was too late.

One of the newbies finished mangling Whitney Houston and Kenneth handed Levi the microphone. His selection wasn't written down.

Whatever the song was, it was not "You Shook Me."

I smirked at Priya, not recognizing the tune until Levi rapped the chorus. It was "Get Ur Freak On." I stood at the side of the stage, my smirk falling away, because he was nailing the rap. He was just drunk enough that his words were slightly slurred, but his voice was low and rich, rolling through me.

About three-quarters of the way into the song, Levi started twerking, one arm flung up like a drunk bride claiming her victory dance, and suddenly AC/DC wasn't much of a barometer of anything.

When he got off the stage to a standing ovation from our table, he came over. "Surprised?"

"Hot damn, son," I said, "you're my hero."

"Am I?" His deep blue eyes were unguarded and soft as a lazy summer sky and his lips curled wickedly doing kicky up things to my insides, and it was very hard to remember that we were friends now and not the kind with benefits.

I ran my tongue over my bottom lip, Levi tracking my movements.

"Come home with me," he said.

"What happened to the whole boss-employee paradigm?"

He ran his finger over my lip and I swallowed hard. "Technically, you haven't started yet. Are you going to report me to HR?"

"Are you going to give me an orgasm?"

"That's the plan."

"Then you're good," I said.

"Get your jacket. Now." He grabbed my hand and hauled me back to our table, where he tossed a credit card down. "Stay. Drink. We have to…" He looked to me to provide the lie, but I was caught off guard.

"We know what you have to do, thanks." Priya rolled her eyes.

I placed the tiara on her head and kissed her cheek, then waving at the guys, I let Levi lead me out the door.

Chapter 27

We jumped into a taxi, laughing at our terribly obvious escape. Levi gave the driver his address, and we spent the ride in silence, the only part of us in contact the sure curl of Levi's fingers around mine.

By the time we got to Levi's house, anticipation had made my nipples hard and I was dizzy with wanting him. He got us inside in record time, and pushed me up against his front door, his body pressed along mine.

"You were pretty fierce on stage," he said.

I slid my hands around to his ass and squeezed. "You weren't so bad yourself."

"Now I'm going to do something I've been wanting to all night." He brushed his mouth against mine and arousal licked through my veins.

I nipped his lower lip, returning the kiss more forcefully. Levi groaned and arched his hips against mine. The kiss was intense, hungry, flavored with alcohol and desire. I slid my hands under his shirt, over the ridges of his abs, his skin as hot as his mouth.

He gyrated against me, his hand curled possessively

around my waist. Stars exploded behind my eyelids and I hooked my fingers into his waistband for balance.

Levi pulled away, his breathing ragged.

I tipped my head up to his with a smile. "All night, huh?"

"Maybe a little longer." He trailed a finger across my jaw and down my neck, worming it under the scarf, until one end of the fabric floated free. Twining it around his fist like a boxer's wrap, he unwound it until it slid away, then he set his lips to the skin.

My head fell back against the door, my fingers playing with the silky strands at the nape of his neck. He kissed his way back up my sensitive throat and then bit down on my bottom lip, punishingly. I moaned.

"Strip," he said in a smoky voice.

"Just me?"

"Yes." He snapped the scarf taut between his hands.

My breathing sped up. This was going to go one of two ways: both involved being bound, but only one ended with my limp body accompanied by a shit-eating grin.

I curled my fingers into the hem of my shirt but didn't take it off. "Is this payback for barging into your office and making demands?"

Levi chuckled. "I'd need a lot more rope and a body disposal system. This?" He slid his hand along the bare skin on my side, his lips brushing against mine again. "Is because you banked your future on my help. Do you know what that did to me? This maddening, mouthy—"

"Monster?" Spare me the alliteration. I got the point.

"—magnificent, motherfucking woman, who antagonizes me at every turn and fights me more often than a feral cat, trusted me."

Oh. I bit my lip, turning my head away so he couldn't see the flush on my cheeks. It's not like I'd never had a man compliment me before, but somehow coming from Levi, who'd thought the worst of me for so long, it was especially sweet.

"Let's not get crazy." My voice was reedy because Levi was lazily kneading my left tit. "You had resources. I had resources. It was a business proposition."

"No, bella." My stomach flipped over at the purred endearment. "You trusted me and I don't take that lightly." He flicked a finger over my tight nipple and I hissed. "Now I'm going to fuck you boneless."

I squeaked and peeled off my shirt and bra so fast, I almost lost an ear. I tried to walk past him to collapse on a horizontal surface because I wasn't sure my legs would support me for much longer, but he caught my wrists and wrapped the scarf around them, tying it off with a bow.

I held my bound hands in front of me. "You're complicating the undressing process unnec—"

He captured my mouth, his tongue sliding inside and his hand exerting the tiniest pull on my hair. The mechanics of breathing were temporarily dashed from my brain, which was good because Levi kissed me for so long he'd moved on to some oxygen-optional plan. I lost the ability to stand, but he helpfully dug his fingers into my hips, pinning me in place.

He lifted my hands above my head. "Keep them there."

My clit pulsed at his growl, but I figured I should register a token protest. "You're very bossy."

Levi popped the button on my pants open and put his hand inside to cup me. "And you're soaking, so are you honestly objecting?"

"Yes. I do not get off on your presumptuous and arrogant ways." I rolled my hips mindlessly against his hand. "Should you tell anyone otherwise, I will rip your balls off and feed them back to you, and fucking hell, put your fingers inside me already."

"That would be presumptuous and arrogant."

"I hate you," I said.

"I can live with that because you truuuussssst me." Levi grinned and I rose up on tiptoe to kiss him because I was losing the taste of him and losing my damn mind. When I broke the kiss, he knelt down to help me take off my boots, then walked away. "Coming?" he tossed out over his shoulder.

"Not if you keep teasing me, you son-of-a-bitch."

Levi chuckled, padding down the hallway to his bedroom. "Strip along the way."

Muttering that this better be worth it, I wriggled out of the rest of my clothing, more hopping than walking. I entered his bedroom and sighed softly.

The curtains were thrown open to the inky sky and the waves gently lapping at the beach beyond. Levi stood naked in silhouette, all long lines and velvet skin over corded muscle, night-kissed.

"Get on the bed, bella."

I lay back on his decadent mattress, his ridiculous thread count sheet as soft as a baby's blanket.

Levi pinned my arms above my head and lazily claimed my mouth again, one of his legs between mine. I tried to buck up against him and kiss him more frantically, but he whispered, "You got some place better to be?" which made me laugh and slow down.

Behind my closed eyes, I lost all sense of time and perspective, anything that wasn't his mouth on mine of secondary importance. His hands mapped my body, charting each curve and swell with gentle awe.

My hands remained above my head on a pillow. He no longer held them, but I needed him to call the shots. I was touched where Levi chose to touch me, kissed at a pace he set. My brain shut down, my magic cravings drowned out by every precious dose of contact.

Achingly, tantalizingly slowly he worked his way down my body, melting me inch by sweet inch.

"I feel bad that there isn't a high level of audience participation here," I said huskily.

Levi hauled himself back up to cover my body, pressing his hard cock against me. "How bad?"

I kissed him again. "I mean, if you fuck me, I'll move."

He laughed. "Wow, what a high bar. I'm honored. Okay, prepare to do the bare minimum."

"Always." I licked my way across the perfect smattering of freckles on his collarbone and he groaned.

He opened the bedside table and I rolled onto my side, closer to him, working the scarf off my wrists. Once I was free, I took the condom from him and slid it on to his dick.

Levi sighed softly. His eyes were a blown-out deep indigo, his lips swollen, and his hair a mess. Something squeezed tight in my chest. He was woven from shadow and moonlight and I wanted the same feeling of utter abandon from him as when I was lost in a good song, even if he had to wring it out of me.

Especially if he had to wring it out of me.

Levi pushed inside me, his hands on the side of my face. I grasped one and kissed his palm, two people tangled up together in the darkness.

"Brace yourself," I said, and gave the feeblest roll of my hips imaginable.

Levi blew a lock of hair out of his eyes. "Mind blown."

I pushed him off me and straddled him, sinking slowly down and then up again. "Better?"

"Uh-huh," he said in a choked voice.

I sank down once more and that low simmer of desire we'd stoked exploded. Hands grasped and tongues tangled while I rode him in a frenzy, my hair falling forward to shield us from the world.

When I came, my entire body lit up, incandescent.

Levi orgasmed seconds after me and I rolled off him, my limbs all floaty. "You done good," I said.

He propped himself up on his elbow. "Can we skip a magic crisis or you running out and go with the part where you sleep over?"

"Are we friends?"

He scrunched up his face, his hand covering it for a second, before unfurling a slow, brilliant smile. "Yes, Ash."

"That's good." My words came out in a rush.

"But you're still leaving?" His voice was flat.

"Can friends be enough for now?" I rolled out of bed, missing the warmth of him already.

"I don't know. Can it?"

I kissed the top of his head. "I'm still leaving."

"Why?"

"Do you want the PowerPoint presentation? I have talking points."

He followed me back through his house, wrapping a sheet around his waist, while I retrieved my fallen clothing and got dressed. "We're in the reality where you trust me now, remember? Or was that just to butter me up and get what you wanted?"

I tugged on my shirt, stuffing my bra into my jeans' back pocket. "I have stuff to do in the morning and I have to mentally prepare. Please don't ask me what."

"This is about the vials, isn't it?" He grabbed me by the shoulders far more gently than I'd have expected, given his tone, and spun me around. His body was a taut line of muscle from the strain of holding himself in check. "What's she making you do for them?"

"Levi…"

He threw his hands up, already walking away. "Close the door on your way out."

"Hey!"

Startled, he stopped and turned around.

"Trust has to go both ways. My magic requires me to do ugly things. Coming out on the side of good requires me to do ugly things. It's"—I unclenched my fists—"hard enough reconciling them for myself. I don't want others seeing all of it. Not even you. I'm giving you everything I can right now."

"Ash." His expression was carefully arranged into a soft sympathy. "I know you have warts."

"That was one plantar wart one time, you jerk, and if you dumb boys had cleaned the changing rooms at the dock like you were supposed to, I wouldn't have even gotten that."

"Go be ugly."

"Phrasing." I shrugged into my jacket, and knelt down to put on my boots.

"If you want to talk, the monster support group is open 24/7."

I looked up from tying my laces. "Is there biscotti?"

He winked.

ABRAHAM DERSHOWITZ LIVED IN DUNBAR, an upscale residential neighborhood that bordered the University of British Columbia and was characterized by large tracts of forested land and stately Craftsman and Edwardian homes, most of which cost upwards of two million dollars.

I spent the drive over wanting to puke, unable to meet my eyes in the rearview mirror. There had to be another way to get the vials that wouldn't require a heinous act.

The Queen appeared as I was parking the car, resplendent in a double-breasted red pantsuit, and holding a metal case. "Don't look so glum, blanquita. Do your job and you can console yourself that you've taken these dangerous smudges off the streets for good." She tapped the case.

Her heels clacked on the flagstones and her knock on the front door was brisk.

The door opened to the soundtrack of a symphony recording played loud enough to simulate an orchestra in the next room and the sight of a hunched-over old man in sweats and a bright yellow visor from a cruise line, holding a long-barreled antiquated gun.

"Is that a musket?" I said.

Abraham jabbed it at us. "Fully loaded and in perfect condition. If you won't take no for an answer, you can take a bullet."

"Hear me out and then make your decision." Completely unruffled, the Queen pushed past him into the foyer and through an archway into a living room that was dominated by the largest vintage stereo system I'd ever seen.

The separate components were housed in an intricately carved wooden shelving unit, while two massive speakers sat directly on the floor, encased in their own carved housings and streaming crystal clear sound.

The Queen walked over to the middle component and flicked a switch, stopping the reel-to-reel tape and killing the music dead. She pointed to the sofa, set a few feet back from the speakers in front of a wall lined with brackets. All of them held muskets, except for the empty bracket dead center. "Sit."

Abraham's trigger finger twitched, I flinched, and the Queen merely raised an eyebrow.

He sat.

This woman was a stone-cold boss.

She motioned for me to proceed.

"You understand the gravity of the situation with Hedon?" I sat down beside Abraham, pushing the scary end of the barrel away from me.

He humphed. "Not my problem."

"It is," I said. "If you don't save it, I've been ordered to take Shannon's magic."

"That's impossible."

Manifesting a blood dagger, I made a small cut on the fleshy part of his thumb and sent my magic in, hooking into his and tugging. "I can pull it out of your body and destroy it. We can have Shannon here in minutes if you'd like a demonstration."

His face drained of all color. "You're evil," he whispered.

I took advantage of his total and utter shock, grabbed the gun, and yanked it away, tossing it into the corner.

The old dude was down but not out. He swung, clipping me across the jaw.

I grabbed his wrists. "Enough. You know that Shannon is staying in Hedon right now?"

His caterpillar eyebrows drew together. "So?"

"Hedon is falling apart." I released him. "What if that happens during the wedding? Are you willing to risk Shannon's life?"

He twisted his knobbly arthritic fingers together. "She'll be fine. Her Majesty"—the words weren't sneered but only just—"would have dragged me off if collapse was imminent."

The Queen made an impatient noise that curled into me like an ice pickaxe. "Ashira has no choice. If you refuse, Shannon's magic is forfeit."

I pressed my lips together. The Queen was making the same mistake with Abraham as I had with Nadija. Abraham had used his magic and his wife's death was the result. That kind of guilt would take time to unravel, and a strategy built around blackmail and intimidation would only cage him in more, not get him to open up.

It was always easier to see it from a less emotional standpoint, but still, I'd expected her to know better.

I pulled out my phone and pressed a button. "Hi, it's Ash. Yeah, I'll put him on speakerphone."

"Zaide?" Shannon's thin voice floated out into the loaded silence.

"I won't let her hurt you, lollipop!" Abraham rose half out of his seat, twisting my forearm, but I gently pushed him back against the cushions.

"Listen to her," I said.

"No one is going to hurt me," Shannon said. "Ash has done nothing but help me. There wouldn't be a wedding if she hadn't saved Omar's life. Please, Zaide, I know you're scared to use your magic, but I'm asking you to come watch me get married and do whatever it is Ash has asked of you. I love you and I believe in you." Her normally tremulous voice went steely with resolve.

"Thanks," I said and disconnected.

"You think playing the guilt card will work? It won't." His voice quivered.

"I'm not playing. If you don't do this, people will die. You're the only one who can save that world. Shannon believes in you, as do I. That's why I'm making it your choice."

"Interesting move." The Queen lightly ran a manicured finger along her neck.

I shivered and pressed on. "Abraham, you didn't kill Sarah. You honored her last wishes."

His head jerked up. "How do you know about that? I never told a soul."

"I found the nurse. I'm very good at what I do." As was Priya.

Abraham stroked his chin in short, nervous motions, while I tried to think positive and glue-like thoughts about my head staying on my neck. He cut his eyes sideways to the Queen. "Okay. I'll do it for Shannon."

Moran appeared, blade in hand, and Abraham and I jumped. Were he and the Queen psychic, because come on.

"It's my favorite fully-cocked swordsman." I saluted Moran. "Here to escort Abraham to Hedon?"

"You assume I'm here for him? Fascinating."

I whirled on the Queen, my neck hunched into my shoulders. "Abraham agreed. I did my part and—"

Moran laughed. "Gotcha."

"You're not funny."

He grinned at me.

Abraham looked between us in bewilderment.

"Come along and get dressed." Moran's sword disappeared and he held out a hand to help Abraham up. "You're going to love the wedding. There's a chocolate fountain."

"Fruit or graham crackers?" Abraham said.

"Both."

The old man brightened and hopped spryly up. "We'll have to get my tux out of mothballs."

They left the room.

The Queen had been scarily silent for a very long time now.

"He would never have agreed if I threatened him, and then I'd have to follow through and Hedon would still be in danger," I said.

"Gracias, Ashira, for explaining the difference between the carrot and stick."

I swallowed. "Sorry."

"I admit, you were correct. In this instance. But you only fulfilled half of the deal. There is still Abraham's magic to neutralize. I won't have his abilities out there to be used against me."

I placed my hands on my ribcage as if that could help me drag a breath into my lungs, and spoke the words that could be my death sentence. "I won't do it."

The Queen delicately massaged one temple. "I like you, chica, but I am a woman of my word. If you refuse, then you will end up in my garden."

Make your case like your life depends on it, Cohen, because it does.

"Abraham would have to be in Hedon to do any magic

damage and he's the only Architect powerful enough to affect its structure, right?" I said.

"Correct."

"You said he could fix Hedon. For good?" She nodded. "If the world is stabilized once and for all, and there are no other back doors into Hedon, *he's* the only back door to worry about. If he locks himself out, then Hedon is safe."

"Is that possible?"

"Yes. His wife Sarah had cancer and when it became terminal, she had him create a slice of reality, her own tiny world of a cottage by the river like the one they'd lived in when they were first married. She chose to end her life without him having to see it, so she made him design it so that her hospice nurse could go in with her but Abraham could not. When the nurse came out and broke the news of the wife's passing, Abraham carried out Sarah's last wish and imploded the reality."

"What's to keep him from doing the same to Hedon?"

"He built the detonation into the fabric of the world. You're connected to Hedon, so you would sense if that was the case. When Abraham destroyed the world, he felt like he killed her, even though the cancer had. More relevant to this discussion, he locked himself out before he destroyed it. If Abraham can't get into Hedon once he's fixed it and no one else can use him, then there's no reason to take his magic."

The Queen picked up the metal case with the vials and placed it on her lap. "No reason other than we had a deal that you've found a way to wriggle out of."

"You keep learning about who I am every time I go into Hedon, and yet that habit of mine continually surprises you." I held up my hands. "Look, I'm not being a dick." I winced. "Sorry, language. I mean, I'm not being malicious. I just have to be able to face myself in the mirror. What I did to Sharp was hard enough, even if there was an argument that he deserved it. I can't make that argument for Abraham, and I refuse to become a monster. I've presented you with a solution that keeps my humanity intact. Will you accept it?"

Still holding the case, the Queen rose and crossed to the window. She stared out at Pacific Spirit Park across the street, a forest that was larger than Golden Gate Park in San Francisco.

I alphabetized items in the room to stay calm: AM FM receiver, bookshelf, ceiling fan. I'd gotten all the way to "wires" and was currently stumped on "x" when the Queen shoved the case at me.

"Vete. Go, before I change my mind."

I scrambled to my feet, the case clutched to my chest. "Highness? I'm not your enemy, either."

"Not yet. Whether you stay that way remains to be seen."

I bowed my head and backed out the door, the case securely in hand. Hitting the sidewalk, I took stock of my situation. The vials would soon be destroyed and I'd thwarted Chariot on that front, but my fight with them was just beginning in earnest. On the one hand, I faced a group of unknown enemies, and, I flicked a glance back at the house, the Queen, a known potential one.

On the other, I had a team. It wasn't my heart's desire, but as futures went, it wasn't half-bad.

A dark cloud passed in front of the sun. I hurried to my car, taking it as a sign of impending rain.

I should have taken it as an omen.

THANK YOU FOR READING DEATH & DESIRE!

Brace yourself as things heat up in SHADOWS & SURRENDER (THE JEZEBEL FILES #3).

Ash wanted a career filled with challenging mysteries. She should have specified she didn't mean her family.

When a murder scene reveals a connection to Ash's father who abandoned her when she was thirteen, she's stunned. He may be the key to stopping Chariot from achieving immortality.

The catch? He could be hiding anywhere in the world.

To make matters worse, Levi, Ash's romantic entanglement and brand-new boss, has his first official case for her: helping his ex-girlfriend, a.k.a. Ash's childhood tormentor.

No one ever said adulting was easy.

As secrets multiply and alliances get deadlier, Ash's investigation takes her back into Hedon and into her own past. Cracking this case could reunite her family... or cost her everyone she holds dear.

Actual ghosts have nothing on the ghosts of her past.

Get it now!

Every time a reader leaves a review, an author gets ... a glass of wine. (You thought I was going to say "wings," didn't you? We're authors, not angels, but *you'll* get heavenly karma for your good deed.) Please leave yours on your favorite book site. It makes a huge difference in discoverability to rate and review, especially the first book in a series.

Turn the page for an excerpt from *Shadows & Surrender* ....

Excerpt from Shadows & Surrender

Lying to the cops wasn't generally something I advised, but as everything in my life was now being judged on a case-by-case basis, it had become more of a suggestion than a rule.

The man in the photo possessed that specific shade of forgettable light brown hair generic to many a white boy, and his facial features were unremarkable, but he was saved from obscurity by a purple birthmark shaped like a comet under one eye.

"I've never seen him before." I handed the photo back to Sergeant Margery Tremblay of the Mundane Police Force and the closest thing I had to a friend among cops. "Who is he?"

"Can you confirm your whereabouts two nights ago between the hours of midnight and 3AM?" Despite her flawless make-up and cute silver pixie cut, her eyes were steely and she asked the question with no trace of familiarity.

I leaned back in the plastic chair. "I was asleep."

"Alone?"

"Shocking, I know. My roommate was home."

"There's no one to confirm you didn't leave your place?" she said.

"No." I crossed my arms. "What's this about, Sergeant?"

She tapped the photo. "Yevgeny Petrov was shot dead."

My questions were legion, but I hurriedly crossed off the ones it would seem odd for me, a total stranger and a supposed Mundane, to ask. Questions such as: "Why are Mundane cops investigating this when Yevgeny is Nefesh?" Or, "How was he shot when he can turn his skin to rubber? A fact I knew because that's the form he'd been in when he attacked me, and I accidentally tried to rip his magic from his body. A girl never forgot her first time, dontcha know."

"My condolences," I said. "I'm sure his mother loved him. What does this have to do with me?"

Margery massaged her temples. "He's the one you allegedly attacked in that anonymous assault charge. When you were undercover as that old woman."

Yevgeny had never seen the real me, just the Lillian persona who I'd been illusioned to look like. However, when I went for his magic he'd recognized I was a Jezebel, enemy to the shadowy religious organization that he worked for called Chariot. Jezebels were a special breed.

"You think I found out and shot him? Bit of a leap, no? The assault complaint was bullshit. I don't have magic, so what's my motive in taking him out, Sergeant?" I said coldly.

Continuing my Mundane status on public record had its uses.

Margery made a sound of disgust. "All right. Quit it with the 'Sergeant.' I'm just doing due diligence. I don't think you're involved and you're not being charged with anything, but you might know something. You're sure his name doesn't ring any bells?"

I shook my head. "Where was he found?"

"One of our squads took down a dogfighting ring. They found his body and called in the Nefesh homicide unit."

Last time I'd seen him, Yevgeny was laying on the floor, a whimpering wreck believing that ants were swarming him, an illusion courtesy of my partner in crime that night. Guess Yevgeny'd gotten over the trauma enough to continue being a productive member of the criminal fringe.

"Yevgeny has magic?" I put the right amount of curiosity into my voice. "Is House Pacifica involved?"

"No. He's registered with House Ontario. He was just here visiting his sister. She's been notified already as next of kin."

What a load of crap. Even if the sibling part was true, my investigations had revealed that he'd been in Vancouver working for Chariot, kidnapping marginalized teens in order to sever their magic. It was then sold at an auction where he'd also provided security.

"Are we done?" I said.

As I didn't have anything more to add, Margery cut me loose with a sigh and instructions not to get in any more trouble until she went on vacation in the fall.

"You live for our encounters," I said and left.

I legged it back to my car, Moriarty, and logged into the House Pacifica database. Look at that, Yevgeny did have a sister. Tatiana Petrov, a level five Weaver. Yikes. There weren't a lot of people with level five magic in any specialty. What were the chances that she'd been the Weaver hired to set the security ward on House HQ, only to later null it and enable a German Chariot assassin to take out a person-of-interest?

There was one way to find out.

Become a Wilde One

If you enjoyed this book and want to be first in the know about bonus content, reveals, and exclusive giveaways, become a Wilde One by joining my newsletter: http://www. deborahwilde.com/subscribe

You'll immediately receive short stories set in my various worlds and available only to my newsletter subscribers. There are mild spoilers so they're best enjoyed in the recommended reading order.

If you just want to know about my new releases, please follow me on BookBub: https://www.bookbub.com/authors/deborah-wilde

Acknowledgments

I want to thank the women who keep me sane on a regular basis: Elissa and my Binderhaus friends. I don't know what I'd do without you all and let's hope I never find out.

My divine editor Alex Yuschik, you are the bomb. You make editing fun and I am so grateful to have you in my corner.

This book is dedicated to the memory of my impossibly cool and beautiful friend, S.D. I love you and miss you every day.

Go out and hug your loved ones. xo

About the Author

A global wanderer, former screenwriter, and total cynic with a broken edit button, Deborah (pronounced deb-O-rah) writes funny urban fantasy and paranormal women's fiction.

Her stories feature sassy women who kick butt, strong female friendships, and swoony, sexy romance. She's all about the happily ever after, with a huge dose of hilarity along the way.

Deborah lives in Vancouver with her husband, daughter, and asshole cat, Abra.

"Magic, sparks, and snark! Go Wilde."

www.deborahwilde.com

facebook.com/DeborahWildeAuthor